# EVE OF CHAOS

# Other Books by D.I. Telbat

*The COIL Series: Christian Suspense*

*The COIL Legacy Series: Christian Suspense*

*COIL Legacy Collection: 3 Books in 1 Volume*

*The ELM Series: America's Last Days*

*The RESOLUTION Series: America's Last Days*

*The STEADFAST Series: America's Last Days*

*STEADFAST Collection: 6 Novellas in 1 Volume*

*Last Dawn Series: America's Last Days*

*Leeward Set: Where Christians Dare*

*Never Lost Series: Trafficking Rescue Novels*

*Arabian Variable*

*Called To Gobi*

*God's Colonel*

*Soldier of Hope*

*Short Story Collections*

# EVE OF CHAOS
## America's Last Days

BOOK ONE OF THE ELM SERIES

# D.I. TELBAT

Every Life Matters

IN SEASON PUBLICATIONS
USA

*Printed in the United States of America*

EVE OF CHAOS: America's Last Days
/ D.I. Telbat -- 1st ed.

Categories: Futuristic Christian Fiction;
Christian Suspense

D.I. Telbat / In Season Publications
https://ditelbat.com
https://books2read.com/DITelbat

ISBN 978-1-7371777-5-3

Cover Design by Streetlight Graphics

This book is for those eager to run in these last days.
May they learn to walk first—and to listen
to those who have run before them.

# Map of San Diego, California

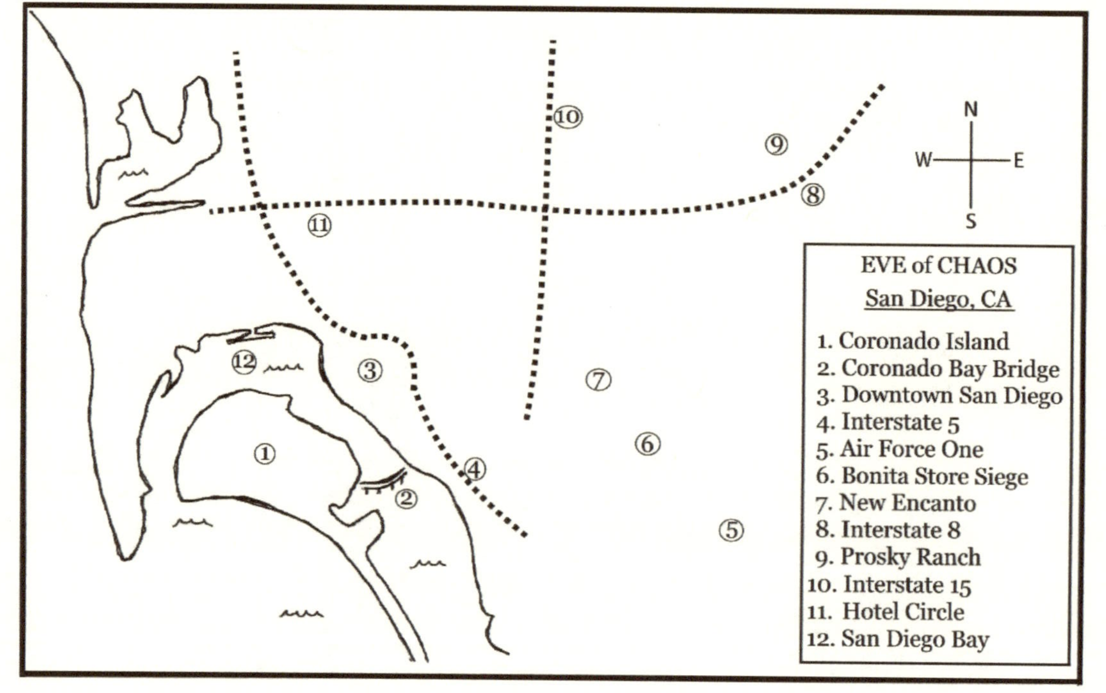

# A Note from the Author

Dear Reader,

Through the years, I've heard the pleas of readers who wanted to know what happened to the Caspertein family during the twenty years between *The COIL Legacy Series* and the *Last Dawn Series*. As I wrote the two *Never Lost Series* books, I anticipated returning to the Caspertein story to share with you more of Titus and Levi's dry humor and witticisms through many more adventures. I believe their challenges in *The ELM Series* will be especially relevant in our last days in America as we live as lights for Jesus in the midst of the darkness of this world.

In years past, while writing the *Last Dawn Series*, I intentionally accelerated Levi's age a few years to better facilitate the events regarding the Meridia Virus pandemic. Naturally, this has affected this new series, which occurs before *Dawn of Affliction*. I have presented Levi as nineteen here rather than fourteen, which is where I left him in *Distant Harm*. For readers paying very close attention to the timeline of COIL and Caspertein character ages, I have chosen to remain consistent with the *Last Dawn Series* where Levi is an older teenager at the beginning of the pandemic. While writing fiction affords an author some liberties, I have made an effort to hold true to the rest of the timeline that spans several generations across numerous book series.

This *ELM Series* of novels does not need to be read in conjunction with other COIL or Caspertein books, but the reader will have the added benefit of seeing many familiar characters in action before and after this series takes place, if you are able to explore the other series.

I pray you enjoy reading this novel and coming series as much as I have enjoyed writing them! —*David Telbat*

# *Prologue*

Oliver Gleason was starving, but he forced the fog from his mind to watch the littered street in front of his house. Most of the neighbors in the quiet Southern California community had left weeks earlier, but that didn't mean there weren't dangerous strangers who had occupied those vacant homes by now.

He crouched next to the shrubs at the edge of his front yard. The evening breeze made him shiver. Or maybe that was his fear . . . or his hunger. This was the first time he'd left the house in weeks.

"Oliver!" Milli whispered behind him. "What do you see?"

Taking his eyes off the street, he glanced back at the front door. Milli's face filled the small hole he'd cut in the door to crawl through. He resisted the urge to turn around and quickly return to the safety of their house. But they had no food left. They'd shared the last can of cranberry sauce two mornings earlier. Oliver had made sure that Milli and their six-year-old son Rory received the largest portions, but he'd later used his finger to wipe clean the inside of the can.

"I don't see anyone," Oliver said quietly, hoping his fear was hidden from his voice. He'd been with Milli since their junior year of high school. Protecting and impressing her continued to drive his very shaky courage. "I'm going out to the mailbox now."

"Don't go far." Milli's anxiety the last few weeks had led to uncontrollable bouts of sobbing that had overwhelmed entire days. Since Oliver didn't want Rory to see his mother that way, he'd had to entertain Rory in a separate room. *"Oliver!"*

"Okay," he answered patiently. "I won't go far."

After lowering himself to his belly, he wormed his way along the shrubs toward the street. He'd managed to exist inside the house with her and Rory only because his parents had helped him stock up on food months earlier. Now, without even a kernel of creamed corn to chew on, he wasn't sure how to survive. Somehow, he had to protect Milli and Rory, but since he didn't know how to find food or water, how would they even live another week?

The moon was high and the stars shone so brightly that Oliver felt exposed when he finally reached the mailbox. Trash and rotting refuse choked the curb, piled so high that Oliver had to raise up on his elbows to see the street over the garbage. Some of the trash was theirs, thrown out in the early days of the collapse of the country. But Oliver was pretty sure his neighbors had thrown their garbage against his curb when they'd probably suspected no one was living in his house any longer.

Oliver craned his neck to gaze up and down the street. There was a lot of paper trash and leaves on the pavement, but except for the single vehicle eighty yards away, the neighborhood street appeared quiet. There were no lights behind the windows of the nearby houses, and their garbage bags were piled just as high as his.

He lowered his head and closed his eyes, trying to steady his breathing. What was he supposed to do now? Outside of hoarding all the food in the house, his parents had never taught him how to hunt, build a fire, or cook raw meat. Were there plants to eat nearby that grew naturally or clean water he could draw from a well? Now twenty-five-years-old, Oliver felt willing to learn how to do all of those things, but who would teach him?

On shaky legs, thin from malnutrition and inactivity, he stood upright. For a moment, he held his breath, expecting someone to shoot at him or a wild animal to attack him. He and Milli had heard all of those things happening to others during the past weeks, but they'd never uncovered the windows to look outside.

However, no gunshot blasted in the night and no wild animals snarled. From his pocket, Oliver drew a folding knife, a tool his father had left him, which he'd used to open a hundred food cans in recent weeks. Now, he held the knife low and at his side, ready to thrust, though it'd be hard for anyone to surprise him in the open street since the night sky was so bright.

Slowly, he chose his steps to emerge from the trash heaps to reach the middle of the street. Still, nothing happened. Maybe his fear was for nothing. Everyone seemed to have left the nearby houses, or maybe they'd died inside from the virus. They hadn't heard distant yelling or even a gunshot for days now.

Eighty yards later, he arrived at the bumper of the only vehicle on the street. It was a minivan. The side door was still open. Oliver glanced around with concern, afraid that he was walking into a trap. It was too much to hope that he'd find food in the van, but just making it this far to explore was exhilarating!

He edged up the side of the van and peeked past the door. A shadowy man sat, seeming to be staring at him. In his lap lay a rifle of some sort. Oliver froze, not sure what to say or what to do. But the man didn't move, either. Was he asleep? In the dimness, Oliver couldn't quite see the man's eyes. No, the eyes of this man were black sockets. Sniffing at the night breeze, Oliver recognized the smell of decaying flesh. Evidently, the man had been dead for some time.

Since he felt unprotected standing beside the van, Oliver climbed inside and sat behind the deceased gunman. Gently, he nudged the rifle stock to see how securely the corpse was still gripping it. With a couple of controlled tugs, he pulled the weapon free and admired it in his own hands. Finding a rifle had to be just as good as finding food and water!

Oliver had never held a gun before. He jiggled the sliding bolt a little before it glided up and back, and a brass cartridge flipped over his shoulder. A bullet! A few seconds later, he found the cartridge on the floor, then he fumbled unsuccessfully to reinsert it into the rifle. Maybe with more light, he could figure it out. Or maybe someone could help him.

Seemingly out of nowhere, Oliver was overwhelmed with emotion. He covered his mouth to muffle his sobs. For weeks, he'd kept up a brave front for Milli and Rory. But out here, feeling the weight of lonely responsibility and expectation to care for his family—it was too much. If there was a God, why didn't He help him or send someone to teach him how to survive? Why all the suffering? How could this be the end of his life—so alone, so helpless, such a failure?

He wiped his eyes and nose on his flannel sleeve and climbed out of the van. The rifle felt awkward in his hands, but he knew he'd need to learn how to use it. Maybe there were still some animals around to shoot and eat. Milli might know how to cut up wild meat if he brought some home.

But tonight, he'd return without food. The walk back to the house was a long walk, a walk of shame. His family would sleep on empty stomachs again—because of him. If no one helped him find food and water, then he had to find it himself. Alone.

# *Chapter One*

It was evening. The city was strangely quiet. Nineteen-year-old Levi Caspertein gazed through his high-powered telescope at the remnants of buildings and the skeletons of cars far below. Even the fires had burned themselves out. For weeks, black smoke had choked the San Diego shoreline, but the fires weren't the worst part. The screams had been worse. Hiding on the fortieth floor high above hadn't made him deaf to the screams. They were usually mixed with gunfire as the city had been pillaged, neighbor against neighbor.

He adjusted his scope to peer west across the bay at Coronado Island. It was evident that the shops and buildings had been transformed and inhabited as housing units for military personnel and their families. The area, as well as the nearby Naval Air Station, remained without power, but they still had fuel for their vehicles. The military had barricaded themselves on the island behind the fortified Coronado Bay Bridge, but they still ventured out three times a day to cruise slowly through the streets and beyond. Levi had learned the patrol routes of their heavily armed Humvee convoys. They never stopped to aid civilians, bury the dead, or rebuild infrastructure. It seemed they were waiting for something—maybe for everyone to die. They were such a menacing presence that Levi wondered how God might use his family to confront them.

The rest of the country may have been ravaged by the Meridia Virus and the subsequent panic of an unhinged and starving populace, but Coronado Island had maintained itself without incident—not even a fire.

As Levi watched, three Humvees drove slowly from the fortification on the west end of the Bay Bridge. It was another patrol setting out to monitor the nightmare on the mainland—or maybe to inventory resources. As the sun set on the early summer night, Levi tracked the vehicles by their blue-white headlights. They were coming.

Where he lay prone, Levi moved the telescope and tripod aside and rested his head on his forearm.

"Lord," he prayed, "don't let me fail . . ."

He tried to be brave—like his father and stepmother in the adjacent apartment. At only nineteen, he found himself praying to God for courage and strength more than he guessed he would have if he weren't in the middle of a collapsed society and ravaged city. His birthday was in three weeks, but he wasn't saying anything to anyone. He didn't want a party or a cake. Birthday parties were for kids, and he wanted to be like his father and those stoic soldiers who were gathered around him. Sheltered inside the tall building, he felt relatively safe, but during dinner the night before, his father had made the announcement that Levi knew would test his resolve in becoming a man.

"It's been ninety days," Titus had said. "Tomorrow night, we put boots on the streets. God will direct us."

Levi knew what that meant. It meant applying all of the training he'd taken before the pandemic. It meant fitting on his ammo vest and strapping on his sidearm. It meant clipping on his battle rifle and standing firm when his nerves told him to run away. He had to think of others more than he thought of his own safety. His father had shown him that, but Levi had also learned it from reading his Bible. God wanted him to be courageous. Without courage through fear, he couldn't care for the weak. Every day, he'd imagined himself grown up, using the wisdom his father had passed on to him. Now, it was time.

"Hey, Levi?" his father called from inside.

"I'm out here." Levi rolled away from the telescope then crawled through the doorway. He pushed the black-painted sliding glass door closed with his foot. Out of sight from potential observers, he stood and acknowledged his father in full battle dress. "I didn't hear you come in."

Titus stood inches over six feet. A black baseball cap turned backwards covered his blond hair, which was now turning white on the sides. His boots were scuffed from hard labor and his trousers were worn at the knees. Levi hadn't seen much of his father the last couple of weeks since the man had spent most daytime hours on the HAM radio networking with radio operators near and far. Many frequencies were being mysteriously jammed, but he was driven to make contacts.

"It's time." Titus lifted his chin. "You ready?"

"Who's going to stay back and protect Mom?"

"Your mother's tougher than both of us combined." Titus chuckled. "She has her own battle rifle. She and Aunt Wynter will hold down the fort here until we get back."

"There's a patrol heading out from Coronado." Levi moved to the cabinet next to the fridge where he kept his gear and donned his ammo vest. "What if they see us?"

"We've got to meet our Coronado neighbors sooner or later." Titus smiled. "But hopefully, later."

Levi fumbled with his shoulder holster strap. His hands trembled with excitement, or fear, or both.

Annette wasn't really his mother, but she'd lovingly adopted him after he'd driven cross-country to find his father a few years earlier, so he didn't mind calling her his mom now.

He fit the battle rifle sling over his head and clipped it to his vest. Titus stepped close to tug and jostle his son's gear. Levi was as tall as his father, but much lighter in frame. Satisfied, Titus stepped back and nodded.

"Gel-tranqs? Check your mags."

Levi unclipped the magazine from his rifle. The magazine was marked with green tape for gelatin tranquilizer .308 non-lethal bullet rounds. He had one magazine in his vest marked with red tape—lethal rounds for deer, dogs, and other animals if they saw any.

"I'm green here." Levi slammed the magazine back into place. "Where are the guys?"

"They're waiting downstairs. Don't chamber a round until we get to street level. Stay behind my left shoulder about seven feet and stay alert. If we face opposition, pick your target and move with me. Got it?"

"Got it," Levi said with a gasp.

"It's okay to be nervous. Don't hold your breath. Stay loose. Remember who we're doing this for."

"For God." Levi took a deep breath and exhaled. "And for the needy."

"We've got neighbors to look after." Titus slapped his son on the shoulder. "Course, some of our neighbors don't want to be looked after, but that's why we have gel-tranqs, right?"

"Right."

Levi followed his father out of the apartment. Annette was waiting at the elevator, a half-eaten energy bar in her gloved hand. She was also in complete battle dress and Levi was amazed that she seemed perfectly comfortable with the fact that they could be marching to their deaths. She'd been a fashion model and a UN representative in her younger years, and Levi noticed she still seemed fashionable in everything she wore, like the blue silk scarf tied around her neck now.

Titus led the two into the third of four elevator shafts. Just one of their many projects in the building during previous weeks had been to lower the original elevator cars to the bottom of the shafts and rig up a counterweight and dolly system in their place. The dolly floor was made of wood. It had no walls, only a thin cable with an eight-hundred-pound limit.

The pulley system groaned as Levi stood close to the central cable. Annette gripped his arm to steady herself.

Titus released the brake and used his gloved hands to lower the dolly one arm-length at a time.

At floor twenty-eight, they disembarked, descended to floor twenty-six by staircase, and climbed into elevator shaft two for the second dolly stage. This one took them to floor sixteen. From floor fourteen, they used elevator shaft one to descend to the fourth floor. Any stranger who ventured into the building would be limited to the stairwells since the dolly system had been designed as a maze known only to the building's few residents.

From the fourth floor, they used the stairs to reach the second floor where they came first upon Avery "Chevy" Hewitt. He was a slender man in his forties with salt and pepper hair, the last survivor of the Kindred of Nails operatives sent to North Korea in times past. Since learning machinery and engines during a lengthy prison sentence, Chevy had been a useful member of the team under Titus' leadership. Sometime earlier, Levi had seen the quiet man without a shirt on. He had a giant Chevrolet tattoo on his chest.

"Headsets." Chevy gave one comm to each of the three. As usual, unless Chevy was preaching or praying, he was a man of few words. "Four-hour battery."

Levi fit the earpiece around and in his left ear, then clipped the small transmitter to his ammo vest.

The four moved together to the floor's observation deck thirty feet off the ground level and lobby of the apartment building. The window glass facing the balcony was broken out and gone. Levi had swept it up over two months earlier. On the balcony, they came upon one-eyed Wes Trimble and Wynter, his wife of only a few months.

"Tighten your sling, Levi." Wynter fingered the slack in his strap. "And keep your finger outside the trigger guard unless you know what you're shooting at."

Aunt Wynter was Titus' younger sister, but Levi had experienced her only as a fussy mother figure. He'd asked his dad about her attitude since she fussed over Titus just as much. In response, he'd said only one word, with a broad smile, "Tolerance."

Levi had understood that Aunt Wynter was family and she meant well.

The blond woman, nearly forty now, had once been an underwater archaeologist, uncovering artifacts the world over—until the accidental death of a guide in Azerbaijan. CIA Agent Wes Trimble had been instrumental in her escaping jihadi wrath, and the two had married during the preparation time for the pandemic.

Though Wes Trimble had only one eye, he had a different color eyepatch for each day of the week. Consistent with the man's easy-going personality, he also had a different tale for every day of the week about how he'd lost his eye. When Levi had asked his aunt how he'd really lost his eye, Wynter had said, "He'll tell you when he trusts you. The true story is much less exciting than his fiction."

Wes and Wynter lived in an apartment on the fifteenth floor on the south side of the building since Wynter wanted sunlight all day.

"Where's Oleg?" Titus asked Wes softly as they all looked over the balcony railing at the street full of wreckage below.

"There." Wes pointed northwest at the shadow of a building. "He has all three zip line spools. He rappelled down using them."

Annette and Wynter moved aside as the men gathered in a circle, side by side. Levi wasn't as broad in the shoulder as Wes or his father, but he was amongst them. He knew their acceptance also meant that they were relying on him to remember his training—and to watch their backs if necessary, during conflict. It was time for courage in the presence of veteran operators. If given the opportunity, he'd show them all that their instruction hadn't been in vain. Soon, he would no longer be a teenager.

"It'll be a full recon night," Titus briefed the four. "Hopefully, it'll be uneventful. Let's anchor those zip lines at the train station, then get to Gustavo's place to bring him in. Watch for others who need help. Take note of the dead that need burial later. Levi says there's a patrol from Coronado out there, too, so stay close to cover. Oleg has point. Levi and I will stagger second. Wes and Chevy, you two bring up the rear. Chevy, how about a little heavenly support? It ain't easy walking into an active war zone."

Levi had labored with and prayed beside these men many times. They'd built indoor fortification walls in the underground garage and engineered the dolly system together. They'd built the solar panel racks on the roof beside the reverse humidification tanks and planted gardens on the apartment balconies. They'd even enjoyed Sunday services with open Bibles. He'd listened to how they spoke and articulated the Scriptures and learned from their open lives to be genuine before God and men. But never before had Levi been more proud than at that moment—to bow his head and honor their Lord before venturing into the dangerous unknown. Their lives weren't their own in this strange new world, and these mighty men lived like they talked.

When Chevy finished praying, Titus nudged Levi's shoulder as he headed toward the stairs. Levi fell in behind his dad. He looked back to see Chevy following, but one-eyed Wes stole another moment to embrace Wynter. Romance hadn't been on Levi's mind much as a teen, but he wondered if God had a wife for him to love like that someday.

Reaching ground level, Titus chambered a round in his battle rifle, and Levi took that cue to do the same. They moved to a sheet metal wall that enclosed the entire old lobby and ground floor. The metal had replaced the glass windows. They'd been welded in place within forty-eight hours after the riots had started three months earlier. None of them had left or entered the building since.

One doorway had been fashioned almost seamlessly into the north wall. Titus turned the wheel lock, already greased to spin with just a whisper. Levi understood that Oleg had used the zip line cables to rappel from the second floor down the outside of the wall. He was waiting outside covering their street entrance.

"Here we go." Titus opened the wide door with a foot-high threshold meant to help limit flooding. "Eyes open."

Titus moved stealthily down the dark street and settled near a lifeless streetlight. There hadn't been any power in the city for months. Levi darted after his father, then took a knee on the littered sidewalk a few feet off his father's left shoulder. The stench of death was stronger here and Levi fought the urge to gag. No one had buried the rotting corpses in the city, so they'd decayed where they lay. Wild animals had eaten some of them. Others had been forgotten. But Levi knew where many of them lay. Using his telescope on his balcony, he'd identified over forty dead who'd fallen the last three months—a few in the last couple of weeks. Bandits and killers still occasionally roamed the streets.

Chevy crouched and ran across the street, his boots silent like the stealth operator he'd become. Wes closed the building door with a dull clang, then followed Chevy across the street. The weathered, one-eyed operator moved with less agility, but Levi guessed his experience made up for his diminished physical mobility.

Watching his father's head shift, Levi knew he was orienting himself with the streets he hadn't observed for months. While Levi had been scoping the city from forty stories up, Titus had been gathering intel from the radio.

Without warning, Titus took off at a run to the northwest. Levi hustled to keep pace, focusing his eyes on the dark street ahead, watching for movement. The moon was out and the stars were bright. He didn't remember it raining, but the pavement was wet, adding an odor of mildew to that of decaying bodies.

They reached an archway and sheltered within its cover. The adobe-style Santa Fe Train Depot had been looted and torched, but not this building. And someone else was under the archway with them—Oleg Saratov.

"These cables are too heavy for one man," Oleg whispered, his Russian accent barely distinguishable. "We each need to take one."

Levi let his rifle hang off his vest the instant a heavy spool of ultra-fine cable was thrust into his hands. It must've weighed forty pounds. Somehow, Oleg had carried all three this far. Each spool was attached to a cable that stretched diagonally up to their building. Though Levi couldn't see the cables themselves against the night sky, he could feel the draw of his spool back toward the building.

Oleg Saratov was an ex-Interpol agent who'd once hunted Titus Caspertein as a fugitive. Now, the short, thick-necked Russian was a believer working alongside Titus, the two having endured trials together all over the world. Levi wasn't surprised that Oleg was already outside with the spools since Titus had told him that Oleg had often placed himself in harm's way first so others didn't have to.

"Follow me." Oleg left the archway and moved north where Levi knew the railroad tracks paralleled the bay two blocks away.

Titus followed Oleg, laboring against the tug of his spool, yet allowing the cable to unwind the farther he ventured from their building. Levi fought his own cable's pull by leaning away with all his body weight, hoping no enemy approached them since their hands were too busy to clutch a rifle.

Since each of the three cables were anchored to three different floors of their apartment building, they hoped, in an emergency, to be able to escape their building by way of one of the zip lines. One was attached to floor twenty-seven where Oleg and Chevy lived in apartment one. And one was attached to floor fifteen where Wes and Wynter lived in apartment three.

By the weight of his spool and the extreme upward direction pulling at the cable, Levi deduced that his cable reached to the fortieth floor. He had the heaviest cable to wrestle against, but losing that fight by giving up could cost them all valuable time that night.

Stumbling over railroad tracks, Levi sniffed the air. The smell of the sea was stronger now. If he weren't straining so hard, he guessed he could've made out the shape of the sunken Midway Aircraft Carrier that had listed and taken on water a couple months earlier alongside the other harbor museum attractions. No tourists would be coming to San Diego Harbor to see the sights for a very long time, if ever.

Oleg and Titus had stopped. By the light of the moon, Levi was relieved to see both men struggling with their cables as much as he was with his. Between the tracks, Oleg circled his cable around a thick signal pole, about twenty feet tall. Titus did the same, then Levi followed suit. Once wound around the pole, their cables weren't pulling against them as much.

"It ain't easy losing at tug-of-war against a building, huh?" Titus laughed breathlessly.

"We need to anchor them as high off the ground as possible," Oleg said. "Levi, you're the lightest. Up you go."

Squinting, Levi peered up at the dark pole. How was he supposed to—?

"Give your cable to Oleg," Titus instructed, "and climb onto my shoulders."

Levi was glad to rid himself of his spool. Holding his ground with his cable, Titus crouched enough for Levi to use his father's thigh as a step to reach his shoulders. Titus stood up straight and Levi steadied himself against the pole next to him.

"The lever-hoist, Levi." Oleg handed Levi a heavy lever and chain-puller apparatus. The Russian had been carrying this along with his own spool! They'd used the same hoist for the dolly system installation, so Levi knew its function. "One at a time, tighten each cable so they don't droop so much. Take your time. Titus has all night."

Chuckling, Levi heard his father grunting below. No doubt his boots were grinding into his father's shoulders, but Titus wasn't one to complain. He would crack a joke long before he ever expressed any sense of discomfort.

Oleg passed Levi a clamping tool to bind a separate thick cable loop to the pole. Then Oleg shifted the first cable up to Levi with Titus' help. Levi attached the cable to the hoist and anchor loop, then winched the cable tight. He couldn't see the cable span the two city blocks back to their building's heights, but he imagined it was taut enough to zip down and natural-looking enough to avoid much curiosity. Since the cable was so thin, from a distance, the lines would be undetected. Perhaps under extreme conditions, he could even climb up the cable to the building, but a bell alert had been attached to the other end to give notice if strangers attempted such an invasion.

Fifteen minutes later, he had the other two cables anchored to the same loop. He hopped down and his father collapsed to his knees.

"Next time, you stand on Oleg's shoulders, son. God gave him broader shoulders for jobs like this."

Oleg offered his hand to his companion and pulled him to his feet.

"Be honest, Titus." Oleg clapped him on the back. "I know you. You're really just thinking about test-driving that zip line."

The three gazed up, but saw nothing in the darkness.

"It's about fifteen feet up the pole," Levi said. "Nobody'll mess with it, right?"

"Hopefully." Titus gathered the discarded spools. "As long as no one sees us monkeying around this pole in the daylight. But yeah, I'd love to give it a test ride!"

"And hope the brakes work?" Oleg scoffed. "You two are welcome to your cable ride. I'll pack a chute and base-jump off Levi's balcony before I fly down that spider's line."

"Okay," Titus said, ending their revelry. "Let's get to Gustavo's. He'll be waiting."

They started east. Shadowy movement ahead alerted Levi, but he quickly realized it was only Chevy and Wes moving from where they'd been covering the zip line installation.

Levi knew of Gustavo Hernandez as a radio operator and a believing Christian that Titus had made contact with weeks earlier. The aging man lived alone up on Fifth Avenue, only nine blocks away according to the map Titus had shown them.

Oleg took point, moving up Ash Street on the left side. Titus and Levi walked on the sidewalk on the right side, silently acknowledging looted stores and burned-out shops. Wrecked and parked cars littered the street. Civilians had darted from them suddenly weeks earlier when violence had claimed the city. Some streets had been cleared for the Coronado military to make their patrols, but most streets were impassable to vehicles.

"We've got company," Oleg announced near First Avenue.

Titus hustled into the street and rested his rifle on the hood of a car with its four doors open. Levi knelt and leveled his weapon over the hood as well. They'd removed their scopes for the night and now relied on quick sights to aim in the darkness. Though Levi couldn't make out Oleg, he did see a party of three or four people cross the street pushing a rattling grocery cart. They carried one flashlight to light their way. The strangers didn't speak or stop, so Levi guessed they never knew that five men armed with tranquilizer rifles let them pass in peace. Whatever provisions the scavengers had in the cart were their own. The Casperteins had more than their share inside the parking garage of their building.

"Clear," Oleg notified.

Exhaling, Levi realized he'd been holding his breath. He could barely contain his excitement to be prowling around like this with experienced soldiers!

On the move again, they paused only once more to listen to a nearby engine before reaching Gustavo's house.

"That's over on the highway," Titus said to Levi off-comm. "What's their nearest route through downtown if they turn through here?"

"B Street," Levi said from memory. "Two streets over. It's cleared to Third Avenue. But sometimes they drive past our building."

"Let's pray they don't come through on our way back," Titus said, "but we'll be ready if they do."

"We haven't talked about that. So, we'll actually fight the military?"

Titus didn't answer. In fact, as Levi hurried after him, he realized his father hadn't revealed any of his plans or contingencies—only that he hoped they would find ways to aid the community and residents living west of Interstate 5.

Gustavo's house was two stories tall. Clouds obscured the stars and a light drizzle wetted Levi's bare head, so he was happy to climb onto the covered porch with his father to meet Gustavo face to face. He was a tall Hispanic man with a ready smile and a firm handshake.

"It's been lonely hunkered down here," Gus said as he held Titus at arm's length, maybe to ensure his visitors weren't apparitions. "Our daily radio talks have kept me sane. Thank you so much for coming!"

"You're ready?" Titus asked. "We're on foot. We didn't bring a cart, but we have strong backs if you need a hand."

Levi smiled at his father's words—probably volunteering his son's back to bear another load. But there was nothing Levi wouldn't bear to prove to these men he wasn't the youngster he once was.

"I have just one bag." The man hefted a duffel bag to hug it with both arms. "And the billies. They're out back."

*"Billies?"* Titus glanced at the tall wooden fence beside the house. "Please tell me that's slang for candles or something."

"Please understand, I couldn't say anything on the wire," Gus apologized. "We can't leave without them. Otherwise, somebody'll kill them."

"Show us." Titus stepped off the porch as Gus went to the fence and used a key to unlock a padlock. "Levi, tell me what we're dealing with here. Careful what you say on the radio if it's something valuable."

Titus faced the street and remained outside the gate as Levi followed Gus into a huge backyard consisting of soft dirt. *No grass?* Gustavo led him to a lean-to and Levi bent low under the awning to see what his nose already suspected.

Gus turned on a flashlight and shined the light across the animals—nine goats, four of them mere kids. Two does with full udders were chewing their cud, and the rest were bucks. They blinked lazily in the beam of the flashlight until Gus turned it off.

"You see why I couldn't say anything on the radio. Their milk is invaluable nowadays—two gallons a day between the two does. People are starving. They'd slaughter them for meat without thinking."

"What do you feed them?" Levi squinted through the drizzling rain at the yard's expanse. "They've eaten everything in sight."

"I take them out at night on neck leashes to graze out back. There's a lot of brush between here and Cabrillo Bridge. They like twigs, pine needles, and bark more than grass, but they'll eat grass down to the roots if they have nothing else."

"Okay, um." Levi tried to think like his father. "Get them all on their neck ropes. We have about nine blocks to walk, so we'll need to keep them together. Hopefully, no one sees us. Animals like this could start a war!"

Gus reached for lead ropes on a high shelf, and Levi returned to the gate.

"Nine goats, Dad."

"I was afraid of that when he called them billies."

"Five adults and four kids. He's roping them together so we can get them through the city in one piece."

"We can't leave them here? The city's no place for farm animals."

"They'll starve unless they're fed. And he can't turn them loose because someone'll kill them. Two of the adults are wet does. He says he gets two gallons of milk a day. *Two gallons, Dad!*"

"Wow. Good call. It's worth it to get them back." Titus touched his comm. "Oleg, we're close to moving out. Gustavo and nine in tow."

"Nine *what?*" Oleg queried.

"It ain't easy escorting half of Noah's ark up the street."

Laughing, Levi jumped aside as a kid goat butted his knee. The rest of the goats followed on a length of nylon with collars around each neck.

Gus led his animals out to the street and toward the shoreline. Wes walked up and scratched his head.

"I'm getting rained on for a bunch of goats?"

"No." Titus didn't stop. "You're getting rained on for Gustavo to join us with a source of fresh milk for your morning corn flakes."

"I don't mind." Chevy followed the last goat. "Powdered milk was losing its appeal."

Levi figured there wouldn't be nine goats for long. The females and a buck would be kept for milking and breeding, but the rest would probably be used for meat.

Oleg led the party. Even on their leashes, the goats weren't easy to escort. Gus, Titus, and Levi did their best to keep the group moving, but the four kids were excited and curious. Their leashes were too long for an escort and better meant for grazing. Every fifty yards, Levi had to untangle one of the animals from the nylon—and twice from around his own legs.

Their apartment building came into sight. It was among a group of six condominiums of the same height and floor plan. The Caspertein building stood nearest the shore on the north. Levi couldn't wait to see the zip lines in the daylight. But there would be other work as well, now that his father had agreed it was time to emerge from their secured building.

"Vehicles," said Chevy so calmly that it took a few seconds for Levi to realize the warning. "I said, *vehicles!*"

"Annette, open the door." Titus ran ahead. "We're not alone."

"The door's open," she assured on comm.

Levi picked up the nearest kid on the leash and hurried the goats to the metal plating around the Caspertein building. Wes and Chevy jogged up from behind as Levi heard the engines himself. Then he saw their headlights. Sure enough, three Humvees. He did the math—probably four soldiers in each vehicle.

Titus manually transferred the last few goats over the door threshold and into the lobby. He grabbed his son's collar.

"Levi, take up position on the second-floor balcony. Let them see you. Cover me."

"Okay." Levi bounded through the door, hurdled a pair of goats, and vaulted for the stairs. He glanced back to see his father speaking firmly to one-eyed Wes.

Chevy closed and locked the metal door, leaving Titus and Wes outside.

Brakes squealed and soldiers hollered.

Levi reached the top of the stairs and charged toward the balcony where Wynter knelt on the ledge, her battle rifle aimed downward at a sharp angle. Oleg was already there as well, spaced ten feet from Wynter. Annette was standing upright, her cheek against the compact stock. She didn't seem to be trembling or panicked. The stories of her experience under pressure were confirmed.

Oleg, Chevy, and Levi joined the others on the balcony, evenly spaced, looking down their barrels at the three Humvees that had parked in a semi-circle against the building, trapping Titus and Wes directly below.

The soldiers yelled all at once for Titus and Wes to lay down their rifles and to raise their hands. Titus and Wes calmly aimed their rifles back at the men who'd emerged from their vehicles. Three pairs of headlights shone on Titus and Wes, but Levi didn't see either man shield his face.

The soldiers, caught in the headlights as well, weren't wearing traditional uniforms but crimson jackets, like the Coast Guard might wear. Their trousers appeared to be mostly jeans and their boots were Army surplus. Their hair was military cut with no beards, and they wore no helmets. Their assault rifles were standard issue .223 long guns.

One by one, the soldiers silenced themselves—as they noticed the elevated perch of gunners they faced. Their overwhelming number of eleven soldiers suddenly hushed as they looked into the barrels of the .308 battle rifles above. Levi watched trained soldiers take a step back and glance at their comrades since they'd found themselves suddenly outgunned.

The passenger door of the middle Humvee opened and a stern-faced soldier stepped up to the front bumper. He had no rifle, only a shoulder holster over his crimson jacket. There was no fear on his face, and as he signaled to his men to stand down, Levi studied the man's frame: discipline and poise had shaped this leader.

"Please," he called to Titus and Wes, "no bloodshed tonight."

Titus and Wes lowered their rifles, but kept them in hand. Levi noticed no one on the balcony moved, so he continued to hold his bead on a young soldier behind the leader. This soldier didn't appear any older than Levi, and besides a rifle, he carried a hatchet on his belt.

"I am General Galt Brogdon," the leader said and attempted a smile, but it only came out as a snarl. "We didn't know we had such an organized force of survivors so close to Coronado Island."

"We've tried to keep a low profile," Titus said. "We believe there's value in minding our own business and looking out for our neighbors. If you're friendly, General, then we'll have no problems with one another."

"Well, those are some serious rifles you've got there. They look like they came from an armory of some sort. I've never seen next-gen weapons like that before."

"They're custom. We're what's left of COIL on the West Coast—the Commission of International Laborers. I'm Titus Caspertein and this is my family."

"Big family." Galt Brogdon winced as he again took in the shooters on the balcony. "I won't lie to you. Sure, I've heard of you, Mr. Caspertein. I believe they used to call you the Serval. Rumor was that you left a life of arms dealing and joined our side."

"I came to the foot of the cross of Jesus," Titus said, "if that's what you mean. I trusted in my Savior and joined others who care for souls on behalf of God Almighty."

"Well, I think we'll get along just fine, Mr. Caspertein." Brogdon hooked his thumbs into his belt. "We're putting the word out: government elections are this weekend. Senator Arthur Criswell is with us at Hotel Del Coronado. That'll be the new capitol building for the

Pacific States. Criswell will be elected president in a few days.”

“Who’s running against him?” Titus asked.

“No one,” said the general. “No one needs to. He’s the right man for the job. Resources need to be consolidated and law needs to be established.”

“And you’re the law?” asked Titus. “You’re the new police force?”

“I am. We are.” Brogdon extended his hand to the youth behind him. “This is my son, Kip. And this here is Sergeant Dom Lesage. He’ll be my right hand in keeping the peace far and wide.”

Levi shifted his rifle from the youth to Dom Lesage. The sergeant was bald and wore a black armband on his left arm. None of the others had an armband. He also carried a sawed-off shotgun on a sling on his back, its pistol grip prominent over his shoulder. A Bowie knife was strapped across his chest in a black leather scabbard. This man was some sort of elite warrior in the company of standard soldiers.

“We have three laws we’re telling all citizens of the Pacific States,” Brogdon said. “Staying informed will keep us working together. Don’t you agree, Mr. Caspertein?”

“Depends on the laws, General,” said Titus. “What are they?”

“Law One, your guns are allowed, but they need to be registered. Bring your firearms to Hotel Del Coronado and you’ll be given a permit to carry as a citizen reservist for the Pacific States Defense Forces.”

Levi almost laughed aloud, aware that any military would love to get their hands on the COIL battle rifle armory. He doubted they’d return with their rifles if they took them to be registered on the island.

“What’s Law Two?” Titus asked.

“No vehicles are to be driven except by the PSDF. Fuel and operable vehicles are to be delivered to Coronado Bay Bridge for government use only. We have a lot of territory to bring into compliance. Your cooperation would be appreciated."

"And Law Three?"

"Rebellion against the Pacific States will be met with swift justice. The penalty is death. If you're not working with us, then you must be an enemy. That's the way it is."

"I see." Titus lifted his head and smiled up at the balcony of support shooters. *He actually smiled!* "It ain't easy responding to your line in the sand, General, but I feel you should hear our terms since you've shared yours."

"I'm listening." Brogdon's eyes darted about—the first sign of uncertainty Levi had seen in this stoic commander. "Speak."

"The few people you see here in my company are Christians. We're followers of Jesus Christ, General Brogdon, and we'll die before we deny Him by vowing loyalty to anyone else. Because we're His people, we believe in peacekeeping. Your three laws are fine by us. We submit. You'll find us to be hospitable to you and your people. And more than that, we have planned to take care of the remaining residents of this city—from Chicano Park to Interstate 5. We'll bury the dead, clear the streets, and build up a nice community here for you as if we were doing it for God Almighty Himself."

Levi smiled as the soldiers and Brogdon glanced at one another speechlessly. Oh, to be like his father and leave mighty men speechless!

"You'll register your weapons?" Brogdon pointed at the balcony. "Those weapons? That's Law One."

"Absolutely, General." Titus lowered his rifle even more and gestured to his shooters. "I think you'll appreciate this. You see our two rifles here and five more on the balcony. That's seven .308 bullpup battle rifles in the hands of experienced sharpshooters who can each hit their mark at four hundred yards or greater. I'm appointing you, General Brogdon, to be our single representative to register these seven rifles with the Pacific States government."

"You're . . . appointing me?" Brogdon scoffed. "No, you need to go to the island to register them yourselves."

"Oh, that just won't work, General. We couldn't possibly leave our important work around the city streets here. We trust you to mark us down for seven rifles. And handguns? We have at least that many. I know you wouldn't want your most valuable civilian asset on the mainland to be unarmed against the raiders."

"Raiders? What raiders?"

"I've heard reports that there are bands of raiders up in the hills coming down and stealing from communities. You certainly don't want to busy yourself with that nuisance, not when you have other armies like Riverside Guard and others as far away as Seattle willing to challenge your new authority."

"You . . . appear to be well-informed."

"And you may count on us to remain so, General," Titus assured. "As for Law Two, we have no vehicles. Any unclaimed fuel stashes we come across, we'll collect them for you or notify you of their location."

"Uh, good. That'll work fine."

"And Law Three, rebellion against the Pacific States will be met with swift justice? I suppose you could define rebellion as anything you don't like, General, so let me be more specific about where we here stand: no stealing and no killing. You can count on us to uphold that much civility around here. And that's an expectation I extend to your troops as well when they come out here on patrol."

Sergeant Dom Lesage scowled at Titus. Levi licked his lips, ready to tranquilize the soldier if he raised one of his weapons.

"You don't dictate what my troops do and don't do, Mr. Caspertein," Brogdon said. "They don't answer to you."

"Oh, they can do what they want to do, General," Titus said. A single finger from his right hand tapped a few times on his rifle. "But actions have consequences. I know you want us to keep the peace here on your shores. I know you and your troops will make an effort to oblige. And sir, I'm staying out of all your government affairs, but I sure do look forward to sitting down and visiting over coffee sometime."

Titus extended his hand and stepped forward. The soldiers had followed the dialogue closely, so no one raised his rifle to intercept. Brogdon was inches shorter than Titus, a fact which seemed magnified when he stepped up to the military man—close enough to shake his hand with his right and pat his shoulder with his left.

Levi wanted to cheer. His father had orchestrated something unimaginable—peace with a military force clearly set to conquer all in its path.

"Wait." It was one-eyed Wes. He moved up beside Titus. "I'm a military man, General. Agent Wes Trimble, formerly Agency intelligence, PRS Division. I know Titus here means well, but I'm of the more aggressive type. If you have room for an intelligence officer, especially with war coming, I'd prefer an island fortress over an exposed condominium. No offense, Titus."

Levi's mouth opened to object. *Not Wes!* What was happening? He looked to Wynter. But his wife just stood there!

"Wes," Titus said, "please, don't do this. We need you here. We have work to do!"

"Wes!" Annette cried from the balcony. "What are you doing? Titus, do something!"

Wes ignored Annette's plea and turned to face Titus directly. The one-eyed man shed his comm device and handed Titus his battle rifle.

"Titus, you and I have disagreed on about everything for months. You should be glad I'm finally out of the way. We have completely different ambitions in the world now.

General? If you'll have me, sir, I can send for my belongings here later. I don't have much of value except a fighting heart."

"Sorry, Mr. Caspertein," Brogdon said triumphantly. "Looks like you're not as in control of your peacekeepers as you thought you were. Welcome aboard, Mr. Trimble. We have much to talk about."

Wes shook the general's hand, then he moved behind the general toward a vehicle. Levi waited for him to look back, to look up, to say goodbye to his wife, or maybe to call for Wynter to leave with him. But then Levi cocked his head. No, this wasn't Wes at all. He and Titus had never disagreed or shared a harsh word. This was so wrong and backwards that it couldn't possibly be real! But Annette and Chevy's faces showed that they understood the betrayal no more than Levi did.

"Uphold your end, Mr. Caspertein," Brogdon said backing away, "and we'll have no problems here. Cross me and I swear you'll find out what a wolverine on a lamb looks like. I know you Christians are partial to sheep. Be one—and leave the military business to the fighting men."

Titus only nodded submissively as the soldiers loaded up, including Wes, and drove away. Levi watched their taillights disappear, then he darted from the balcony and bounded down the stairs to the ground floor. Almost tripping, he waded through the goat leashes and brushed past Gustavo to reach the metal door. He spun the wheel to slide back the bar and yanked the door open to see his father. It was too dark with the vehicle headlights gone to see Titus' face. Entering through the door, Titus set a hand on Levi's shoulder and Levi sensed his father's heavy heart. *He'd just lost Wes Trimble!*

"Dad, how could Wes—?"

"Not yet, Levi. Let's wait for everyone." Titus walked toward the stairs where Annette was waiting. "Everyone, back up to the balcony. Gustavo, you and the goats okay down here for an hour or so? Turn those creatures loose and let them explore. There's no way out that I know of."

Up on the second-floor balcony, Titus set a lantern on the floor and sat cross-legged in front of it. The rain pattered nearby. Levi sat across from him, eager for answers. The others shifted their rifles aside to sit around the lantern.

Titus licked his lips and gazed at their faces one at a time. Now in the light, Levi identified a glimmer in his father's eyes. Levi watched their faces. He wondered who knew what.

"Yes," he said softly, "it was inevitable that we would cross the Coronado military, so there was a plan. Wynter?"

"It was Wes's plan." She smiled, but there was sorrow there as well. Her hand went to her heart like what she said pained her. "He said he wouldn't do it unless I allowed it, especially as newlyweds. He's a spy and spies do spy work. I know that. That's how we met. He needed it to look real for his own safety. That's why no one else could know."

"But you knew, Titus?" Annette asked.

"Wes approached me about a month ago," Titus said. "He disclosed his concern about the military build-up across the bay. He said we'd need first-hand intel. That's all."

Levi was thrilled that a group as small and intimate as theirs had kept such a huge secret so quiet. It was genius!

"What's the end game?" Oleg asked. "How will he get out safely after he's seen what he needs to see over there? His wife is here."

"When Wes feels it's time," Titus said, "he'll fake his death or capture or something. Meanwhile, they'll be asking Wes all about us. By this method, he can control the information and misinformation they get about us.

You could say Wes is on loan to them for our long-term goals."

"I'm going to move up to the fortieth floor," Wynter said mainly to Annette. "You guys have two more apartments up there. I don't want to be alone without Wes."

"My heart about broke for you when Wes pulled that stunt!" Annette took Wynter's hand in hers. "I'm relieved it was staged, but it was still horrible to witness."

"I knew it." Levi grinned. "I knew it was all wrong!"

"Giving you back the rifle might've been a bit much," Chevy said. "That's when I knew something else was going on."

"If anything happens to him," Titus said, "he didn't want even one of our powerful weapons to fall into the wrong hands. It's not difficult for a tool of peace to become a weapon for killing in the hands of wicked men. Wes left on his own terms. He'll return when he's ready. Besides, he'll stay in touch."

"I would've thought the collapse of America would stop you boys from playing your war games." Annette shook her head. "Well? How's Wes staying in touch?"

"Coronado Island has a radio. I've listened to their frequencies when they're not jammed, and Wes knows a frequency that I monitor. Besides a radio, he'll find a way to make excursions to the mainland, maybe even with the patrols. He'll have drop sites for messages." Titus opened his breast pocket and drew out a folded map. "Levi will recognize these locations. No one knows the city better than you, Levi. Hopefully, Wes will return before we need all this, but just in case . . ."

Levi unfolded the map, hand-sketched by Wes. Several sites were labeled north, east, south, and along the shore of the city.

"I know these places." Levi pocketed the map. "I mean, I've scoped them before. We can leave the building now more often?"

"When we leave, I recommend we leave in pairs," Titus said. "That would be wise—and only during the day for now. And always armed. We'll begin to be a presence for those who still live all over this city, hiding in buildings, drinking rain water, and living off whatever they've hoarded ahead of time. We can help them emerge and safely move about the city. A barter system will naturally develop. The goats will need to be fed, but they'll have to be milked every twelve hours. Folks can bring us whatever those animals eat, and we can pay them from our gardens."

"They eat twigs and bark," Levi said. "Gustavo told me."

"Twigs and bark it is." Titus sighed. "This is a new chapter for us. It can be about us or it can be about Christ. I think we'd all like our last days alive to emphasize the Savior who bought us. In keeping with that, I've thought of a motto for us, something to get the word out about what we stand for here. Think about this: *every life matters. E-L-M.*"

"You mean like an elm tree?" Wynter asked. "As boys, you and Rudy loved to climb those elms back in Arkansas."

"Elm trees carry all kinds of spiritual parallels," Titus continued. "This building becomes ELM headquarters. People will learn that because of Jesus in us, their lives matter to us. That goes for the soldiers on the island as well as the hungry in this city. Every life matters. How's that sound?"

"I like it," Levi said. "I can spread that around the streets."

"Our symbol can be a big elm tree," Titus said, "where people can come and find rest in the shade. Oleg, what do you think?"

"ELM," Oleg repeated. "I like it. And it's short enough that even you can spell it."

Titus smiled as everyone laughed.

"It's not my spelling I'm worried about," he said. "It's my trying to draw an elm tree that doesn't look like a cactus. Actually, Levi will be moving around the city more than most of us, I expect. Levi, I'm glad you know it'll be up to you to get the word out. ELM is here. We have God's love and God's Word to offer people. We didn't store all those Bibles in the garage for nothing."

"It ain't easy being the people everyone will rely on," Levi said.

"Oh, no!" Wynter wrung her hands. "Like father, like son. There's *two* of them!"

"I couldn't have said it better myself, Levi." Titus chuckled. "The Lord's with us, my friends. And the Lord is with Wes."

Alone in his apartment that night, Levi couldn't sleep. All he thought about was proving himself for God and family across the ruined city of San Diego. He felt ready for anything. ELM would be his new life motto!

He sat up suddenly in bed, still adjusting to the solitude of his own apartment and the responsibility that came with looking after himself. But he wasn't responsible only for himself now. The others in the building needed to know he would protect them, even sacrifice himself for them.

In the darkness, he quickly pulled on his trousers and ammo vest over his bare chest. Leaving his rifle behind, he walked out onto his balcony with only his sidearm in the shoulder holster. The military headquarters across the bay was as quiet as the city. Nothing seemed to move. This was the perfect moment!

On the right side of the balcony, he felt in the starlit dimness for the zip line cable anchored to a steel beam. The cable was as taut as he'd tightened it that evening. Leaning over the balcony railing, he reached down the cable to gauge its angle to the train depot two blocks away.

The muscles of his stomach trembled. *Did he dare?* His father and Oleg had joked about testing the escape route, but it seemed to Levi in that moment that someone really should ensure it was functional.

Licking his lips, he picked up one of several pulley assemblies Chevy had engineered. The thing weighed nearly thirty pounds, complete with two steel wheels, a harness for one person, and a bicycle brake handle.

With a grunt, he positioned the wheels on top of the cable. There was no guide to keep the wheels on the cable except the weight of the assembly against the grooves of the wheels. He ensured the brake was locked, then he climbed over the balcony railing.

In the darkness, his foot slipped off the outer ledge. A loud cry escaped his lips, but he quickly shut his mouth as he dangled off the balcony, one hand on the rail, the other on the harness strap, and his feet hanging forty stories over nothingness.

Using only his arm strength, he slowly pulled his weight up until his booted toes found solid purchase on the ledge again. For a moment, he listened to the building and the street far below. Had anyone heard him? How embarrassing to scream out like that! But it seemed there were no witnesses.

With renewed caution, he used one arm to fit the harness over his head and down his torso. A clip allowed him to tighten the harness single-handedly. Steeling his nerves, he let go of the balcony, then allowed his boots to slide from the ledge. Again, he dangled in midair, this time by the single harness strap around his body. His frame swayed slightly. *What a thrill!*

His left hand held onto the strap of the harness where it became a thick handle under the pulley. His right hand felt above for the brake handle.

"This is for my family," he whispered, knowing full well he simply couldn't resist the excitement of testing the contraption.

With a flick of his fingers, he released the brake, though keeping his hand on the handle. The wheels hummed against the cable, even as it moved very slowly at first. But the cable angle was steep, and in a matter of ten yards from the building, Levi was descending at full speed!

His legs peddled in the air as he dropped, trying unsuccessfully to turn his body to face forward. He gave up and clenched hard on the brake. The brake pads seemed to grind louder over the noise of the humming wheels. But seconds later, he came to a stop.

While holding the brake, he gasped and collected his wits. Only seconds had passed, yet he was already halfway down the cable length!

It took him several attempts to twist his body around to finally face forward. The train depot was directly ahead and below, the few island lights were far to the left, and the silent, dark mainland spanned to the right.

He released the brake. The wind ruffled his blond hair and he couldn't help but smile from the excitement of flying.

Yet, even in the starlit darkness, he saw the land and buildings rushing up. The moon's reflection flashed off railroad tracks where he'd helped Oleg and his father attach the three zip lines hours earlier.

When he clamped down on the brake this time, he knew what to expect. Controlling his decent, he extended his left foot to meet the signal post with a gentle nudge.

He immediately wanted to do it all again.

With stifled laughter, he craned his neck to look below. He was fifteen or more feet off the ground. His dismount could still be perilous if he weren't careful. Then, he'd need to detach the pulley and carry it back to the building two blocks away.

*The building!* Levi's mouth went dry. How was he supposed to get back inside? The only ground floor door to the condominium was locked from the inside and armored against tampering.

His mistake in planning made him groan. So much for testing the zip line in secret. Now he'd need to hide outside the building until someone came outside, or someone noticed he was missing. His recklessness would be known to everyone in ELM. They'd see his immaturity, his lack of foresight, his endangering of the building's security because he couldn't resist a short joyride . . . It hadn't been worth it, not at the expense of receiving everyone's disapproval.

There was only one alternative—return up the cable!

As soon as he thought of it, he knew he had to try. The grueling process of climbing the cable would be infinitely better than disappointing his family and friends.

But the cable was thin and potentially damaging to human skin. He hadn't brought any gloves. Under his ammo vest, he hadn't even worn a shirt that he could rip off to wrap around his hands.

Lifting one foot at a time, he stretched awkwardly in the harness, untied his boots, and tugged off his well-used footwear. His socks slid off easily, but while wiggling his bare feet in the night breeze, he lost hold of the second boot. It thumped lightly on the gravel below.

"Smooth, Caspertein," he chastised himself. "Real smooth!"

There was no way he was climbing down for just one boot. He had lots of boots in his apartment closet. Besides, he didn't need his boots to climb the cable.

Now, he thrust his hands into the socks and reached overhead, above the brake handle, to grip the cable. The socks seemed inadequate to protect his palms, but if he went slowly, he just might make it without injury—and only minus one boot.

With no more forethought, he released the brake. Hand over hand, he drew himself up the angle of the cable, dragging the pulley along by the length of the harness. The wheels hummed lightly and rolled smoothly with every effort, but only a minute later, he needed to rest. He locked the brake and cringed as he flexed his hands. It was torture gripping and regripping such a thin cable, but there was no other method.

He continued up, agonizingly slow, and resting more often. At the halfway point, he strongly considered descending and not continuing up. Just take the disappointment and shame, he told himself. Reaching the top seemed impossible. His arms felt like lead and the socks were torn to shreds already—so much so that he had to tie them on each hand to continue.

But he continued stubbornly. Two hours had passed since he'd left the balcony, but he finally reached overhead to touch the ledge—to ensure it was real and not farther away.

Instead, a strong hand gripped his wrist! From the amazing force from someone above, Levi was drawn the last yard up the cable until the pulley wheels bumped into the clamp against the wall.

He stared breathlessly into his father's face a few seconds before he realized he was indeed discovered. His scream earlier must've been heard after all, and his dad had been waiting the whole time.

Titus pulled Levi's body over the balcony rail and released the clip on the harness. Levi fell against his father, wishing he could've helped his dismount more, but he was too exhausted. Unable even to stand with his bare foot and single boot, he collapsed onto the balcony floor.

As Levi panted, Titus removed the pulley from the cable and stowed it in the row of others just inside the sliding door. A few seconds passed before Levi noticed his father was standing over him, his hands on his hips.

Using the railing, Levi wrestled his weight upright to stand unsteady before his dad. The night was too dark to see his father's eyes, but imagining their rebuke, Levi was glad he couldn't see them—or that his father could see his son's desperate state of defeat. However, if he wanted to be a man, Levi knew he needed to stand there and accept correction like a man, just like the Bible taught. He prayed and waited for his dad to speak.

"I guess that's all I'm going to say about this stunt," Titus said after several minutes, and he returned to the apartment.

A moment later, Levi's apartment door closed softly and he was alone again.

On shaky legs, he entered the sliding door and fell face-first onto his bed. He had read volumes from his father's silence and then from his single statement. If Levi were to be trusted in ELM, he couldn't be taking such immature, foolhardy risks. And for what? *For a thrill?*

As Levi drifted to sleep where he lay, a grin slowly crept onto his face. Fool or not, he'd tested that zip line and survived. But he hoped he never had to climb that cable ever again!

✝

Carla Criswell was afraid to die. While seated atop the wrecked fuselage of Air Force One, she stared at the empty horizon. They weren't coming back. They'd lied to her. And now her water was low—maybe less than a week left. Then she would die.

The wind gusted through what was left of her straight platinum hair. The burn scars that covered half her scalp no longer grew hair. Two weeks earlier, she'd looked in the bathroom mirror and noted with horror how her skin had melted from the top of her head to her jawline on the left side of her face. Even her left ear was indiscernible flesh, but at least she could still hear through it.

The sun felt good on her head, so she wore no hat or covering, not since the bandages had been removed. And there was no one left from whom to hide her ugliness. Not anymore.

She lowered her eyes to the two mounds of earth she'd dug a week earlier. They'd known there was no hope so they'd committed suicide together. But Carla had been too afraid to die with them.

For two years, she'd traveled on Air Force One, a Boeing 747-200B, as part of the press corp. Everything that happened on the Hill was relevant news, but she'd been responsible for writing about the president himself. All of the stories that were dear to her heart, she wrote with flourish and creativity, spin and intention. Commentators had discussed her articles. Americans said she was making a difference, advancing the cause toward a new world. She was a good and valuable citizen.

But they'd still left her for dead. When they'd had their chance to prove her worth, they'd walked away from the plane and crossed the wilderness to the west. Their footprints were long filled with sand. Six of them—three from the crew lounge upstairs and three support crew engineers and techs—had left the plane to search for help.

Carla hadn't been able to walk a month and a half earlier, so they'd left her behind with two other press personnel, a man and a woman, her colleagues. They'd loosely looked after her when they weren't hiding in the back of the plane, afraid that strangers they'd seen far away would come and harm them.

The president and his staff hadn't been on the plane the day it had gone down. It had been en route to pick him up in Atlanta after departing Orange County. All nine on board had survived the crash, but Carla had been burned by a fire that had ignited over the starboard wing section. That had been six weeks earlier. The six plane crew members had left on foot a week later, carrying all the water and food they could collect from the galley and lower-level lockers.

Turning to face the northwest, Carla stared into the wind, not minding the bits of sand that brushed against her skin. The plane had buried itself halfway upon impact, and the wind had blown a drift on that side so she could climb on top of the fuselage. This was her favorite spot, just in front of the sloping tail section. It seemed she could see for miles, but she wasn't sure. The wilderness seemed to play tricks on her eyes. One thing was for sure: she was alone.

She slid off the fuselage to the drift and walked around the tail. At least she could walk again. Part of her leg from knee to ankle had been burned as well, so that wearing even a sock had been impossible for weeks.

Past the port side wing and two jet engines, she reached the president's entrance toward the front of the plane. Here, one of the others had placed an empty milk crate from the galley as a step up to the door, which had been jammed open. With a hop, she got one knee over the edge and climbed aboard. If someone found the plane out here, they could hop aboard just as easily. Carla imagined that the world consisted only of killers and rapists now, but she hadn't seen anyone in the distance for days. If just one local happened to come near, she could have asked them in which direction she might walk to reach civilization—whatever might be left of it.

Carla had moved herself into the flight crew lounge next to the upstairs flight deck. Two bunks with sheets and blankets afforded her an otherwise comfortable sleep at night when the wilderness chill pierced the thick hull of the plane. The crew lounge also offered the most secure door, much better than the press section where seat cushions on the floor had been her bed while others had cared for her. It was hard to miss them. Every few days, they'd neglected to feed her or bring her water or help her to the head. Somehow, she'd survived, but no mindful thanks to them. She counted them lucky she'd even dragged them out and buried them.

In the crew lounge, she closed and latched the secure door and sat at the lounge table. She'd brought armfuls of food up from the storage below deck. There were two food preparation galleys on board capable of feeding one hundred people at once. The perishable food was long gone and the rest would last weeks since she was now alone. But water was her real concern.

Idly, she ate a bologna sandwich from a vacuum-sealed package. Another day of indecision. If she had more water, maybe she'd stay here. Anything was better than what she dreaded to find wherever civilization still remained. Things had been bad—really bad—six weeks earlier when she'd flown out of Orange County. The virus had spread everywhere. Nobody was shaking hands and everyone wore masks since there was uncertainty as to how the Meridia Virus was transmitted. Reports of riots and pillaging had flooded into the communications center of the press section. Power in every city was out and Carla had wondered how her articles would be read if no one could access her network news site any longer.

While eating her sandwich, she drank only a few ounces of water. She had to think seriously about leaving—and carrying the remainder of water with her. Hiking west seemed foolish since the six crew members had gone in that direction and not returned. Carla didn't doubt they'd found something or someone, but whether they'd been killed in the upheaval or merely washed their hands of her—she didn't want anything to do with them. At this juncture, traveling north, east, or south seemed just as hopeful.

With the trek before her in mind, Carla crossed to her bunk and picked up the only weapon the crew had unlocked from the armory for the three who'd remained at the plane. Since she was unfamiliar with firearms and had never fired a gun, they'd given the journalists a single shotgun. Thankfully, it'd come with a laminated instruction card. It was a tactical shotgun with a short eighteen-inch barrel for close contact. The sights offered a wide-view red dot optic, which Carla thought seemed practical, but she still hadn't fired it. So far, she'd loaded and unloaded it several times a day, figuring it was best to be familiar with the thing since shooting the monster seemed fairly elementary.

She hefted the heavy weapon in her hands and held it against her shoulder. There was some irony that she even held a gun since she'd been such an advocate for disarming Americans in years past. Universal disarmament had been her battle cry, always supporting her father's stance as a California senator who'd pushed for tighter gun control laws. Now, she was pretty sure the whole country lived and died by the gun, and the last she'd heard, her father was flying to San Diego's Coronado Island where the virus and rioting wouldn't reach as easily due to the natural barrier of water.

After her parents' divorce, she'd been closer to her father than her mother. But after her father's corruption scandal and misappropriation of funds investigation, she'd distanced herself socially even from him. Nevertheless, she'd stood with him ethically throughout her journalistic career, pushing for progressive rights for all Americans. Carla herself had spoken to classrooms full of children, urging them to adopt the world's transformational viewpoints on gender fluidity, prison reform, and population control. For all these topics, she'd found the environment as the common link that urged her to preach with desperation to ignorant audiences. The Earth itself demanded a change to the social structure she believed was traditional and outdated.

Now, so many of her views seemed to conflict with her will to survive. All of her declarations for population control had never actually reached her mind that she could possibly be one of the people who would be removed from the Earth so nature could continue to exist. And here she was holding a deadly shotgun, afraid of being raped by brutes who didn't care what pronouns she preferred. Even her zealous push to ruin the oil industry through her writing seemed counterproductive since electric cars were now inoperable—and California had banned nearly all gasoline vehicles, which could've been used to drive through the wilderness to rescue her that very hour!

Carla set the shotgun back on the bed and wandered into the comm-center behind the lounge. Only a week earlier, she'd found one radio still functional, its battery not yet dead. She now sat down at one of the consoles and donned the headphones. When she flipped the power switch, she heard what she usually heard: static. After spinning the dial all the way to the left, she started a ritual she'd begun the day she'd found the radio still had a little power.

"Mayday, mayday. This is downed aircraft Sacred Cow asking for assistance."

She repeated the message twice more, then watched the second hand on her watch. After thirty seconds of silence, she turned the dial one mark to the next frequency.

"Mayday, mayday. This is downed aircraft Sacred Cow asking for assistance."

Anyone connected to the government she hoped would hear and understand her reference of Sacred Cow. But no one was listening. Perhaps everyone was dead. There had been rumors that North Korea may have been responsible for the Meridia Virus. Maybe they were also responsible for disrupting communications. A single nuclear weapon detonated on the edge of space could send out an electromagnetic pulse and knock out countless space satellites or local electrical components. The president's plane had a hardened body to withstand an EMP, but the plane relied on other ground-based signals that may have disrupted navigation enough to bring her down.

"Mayday, mayday. This is downed aircraft Sacred Cow asking for assistance."

Carla was about to change the frequency when she heard a change in the pitch of static. She adjusted a squelch knob and listened. There!

"We hear you, Sacred Cow. This is ELM777. Do you copy? Over."

"Yes!" Carla screamed. "Yes, I hear you! Oh, please tell me you can hear me!"

"Yes, Sacred Cow, you're coming in very clear now. We heard you yesterday around this time, so I knew to scan for your signal again. What assistance do you need? Over."

"Um." Carla wiped her eyes. Forty-two years old and crying like a baby! The man on the other end sounded friendly. His voice rang with authority. "Um. This is Sacred Cow. We went down in the wilderness six weeks ago. The crew of six went for help five weeks ago. Two more killed themselves. There's one survivor. Do you understand? Over."

Seconds passed. Agonizing silence. The frequency buzzed, perhaps distance or other interference was impeding the transmission.

"Yes, Sacred Cow. We understand. One survivor. Are you injured? Over."

Touching her face, Carla figured even her own father wouldn't recognize her now through the scars, at least on her left side. She was a creature from a horror movie!

"ELM777, negative. My injuries have healed. My water supply is low. I need somewhere safe to go. I see only wilderness all around Sacred Cow. I . . . don't know where I am. Over."

"Sacred Cow, your signal is strong here in San Diego. A second radio operator is in Tijuana who's helping me to triangulate your location. Give us a minute. Over."

But Carla couldn't wait a minute.

"You mean I'm still in California? Am I in California? Over."

"Sacred Cow, we have a good fix on your position. If you are alone, I recommend you stay where you are. We can send a rescue team for you first thing in the morning.

It'll take them all day to reach you. Can you hold out until then? Over."

"Oh, yes!" Carla wept openly. "Yes, I can wait. I have about a week of water left. Lots of food. Can we keep talking? Please? I've been alone for so long. Over."

"Of course, Sacred Cow. I'm not going anywhere. Check the time. It's coming up on noon right now. If we lose the signal, check here again each day. Memorize this frequency. I'll be here until you're brought out. Over."

"Thank you so much. So, San Diego isn't far away? Over."

"Sacred Cow, you're probably just a couple hills and valleys east of the suburbs. You're close. But the city and suburbs are a mess. Troublemakers are everywhere. The rescue team I'll send will be heavily armed. They'll see you safely back here, downtown. Over."

"But if it's so dangerous, ELM777, they'll be putting their lives in danger for me. I'm just one person. My own people abandoned me. I don't want anyone to get hurt for me. Over."

"Sacred Cow, every life matters to God, so every life matters to us. We're coming for you. You can count on that. My own son will probably insist on being one of your rescuers. He's restless to get out and prove his courage and test himself against this new world. He would consider it an honor to risk his life for someone else. And if he perishes in the act of showing mercy, well, he's a follower of Jesus Christ and he knows death is a possibility for anyone. His faith is strong. And we know death isn't the end. Over."

Carla didn't know how to respond. She needed to be rescued, but these people were nuts! Followers of Jesus Christ? She'd written articles over the years mocking such radical and conservative extremists who promoted their bigotry and morality in the name of their God. She'd even proposed that they be rounded up and placed in reeducation camps to be deprogrammed. They often stood in the way of scientific advancements, environmental action, and global unity. But dying of thirst in the wilderness or slaughtered alone while trying to reach safety sounded like a much worse fate than the company of some conservative Christian wackos. After all, she was terrified of dying. The great unknown had to be avoided at all costs.

"ELM777, I'm thankful you're willing to come for me. I know people in California, even in San Diego. Maybe you can help me get to them? Over."

"Whatever you need, Sacred Cow. Every life matters. How about tomorrow at noon we connect again? That rescue team should be well on their way by then. Over."

"Okay, thank you again. I'll talk to you tomorrow. Over."

"ELM777 signing off. Out."

Turning off the power, Carla doubted she'd find anyone else on any frequency willing to come for her, not with bandits roaming the streets. And the virus keeping everyone isolated and suspicious of their neighbors.

She thought suddenly of her face. Strangers were about to see her ugliness, her scars and missing hair! Oh, it was depressing even to think of enduring their attention as people pointed out her melted skin.

Maybe just as importantly, she needed to keep her identity to herself. As a famous reporter alongside the president, she could have enemies out there. She could probably go by any name she chose and no one would know better. Certainly no one would recognize her, not now that she was so disfigured. At least she'd be safer soon. A rescue team from ELM777 was coming.

# *Chapter Two*

General Galt Brogdon would normally do anything for his son, Kip, but he couldn't do this.

"Kill her," he told his most trusted military officer, Sergeant Dom Lesage. "Make sure this never gets back to me."

"Yes, sir." The thirty-five-year-old had been on loan to Coronado from the Canada Special Forces branch when the pandemic had struck. The intimidating muscled man kept his head shaved bald. Rumors on the island were that he used the Bowie knife in his black scabbard to shave. "What about Kip?"

For now, no officer on the island had the rank above sergeant to separate Galt from all other personnel, which better secured his close position with President Criswell. If anyone deserved a higher rank, Galt thought, Lesage did, but all in due time.

"Tell Kip nothing. I'll deal with him. He's like a buck in rut. There are women on the island for this. He doesn't need to kidnap anyone. Make sure this doesn't happen again."

"Yes, sir." Lesage nodded rather than saluted, then left the hotel room on the top floor of Hotel Del Coronado.

Galt was alone again in the room he'd turned into his own command center. Next door, the newly elected President Arthur Criswell had claimed two of the rooms for his executive offices—living quarters and office suite. The view wasn't bad out the west or east windows. To the west, where Criswell lived, he overlooked the beach and a view of the ocean all the way to Point Loma. To the east, where Galt lived, he had a view of both the Naval Air

Station runways and the residences. He could even see across the bay and the cityscape farther off.

"Ah, Kip." He watched the airport for a moment as a two-seater reconnaissance plane taxied for takeoff. "Why can't you grow up?"

True, Kip was only fifteen, but he had the wits of a young man with no self-restraint. He wanted to ride with the elite soldiers like Lesage on their patrols abroad, but then he did things like this! Galt had appointed himself as general over the island, but his authority over the military personnel could deteriorate by way of his son's scandals.

Kip had thought his father's power extended to him, and during a recent patrol, he'd seen a girl he wanted. The girl's only living parent, according to Lesage, had resisted Kip's taking her. Another soldier had overreacted and killed the father. His son had come home with his prize, but Galt wasn't allowing her to stay on the premises. It'd only been three months since he'd taken command. He needed to uphold some semblance of law and order, even in regard to his son, who apparently couldn't understand such social conventions needed to be maintained.

Lesage would make sure the girl disappeared. No trace of her would remain to sully the reputation Galt wanted to project to his growing territory. Kip would just have to find comfort in the arms of the ladies who lived on the island. Maybe when he was older, he'd find a woman who could love him back—and she'd bear Galt some grandkids, but that time wasn't yet and it couldn't be done like this.

He watched the plane take off and ascend rapidly heading north. War was coming. Riverside Guard contingents had amassed and consolidated resources. Intel showed there were militias north of Interstate 8, even east around Cuyamaca Rancho State Park, who were loyal to the northern armies. Galt had exerted his power early and harshly in those hills, and now he was paying the price. Kip's act of abducting the young woman showed he didn't understand that they were trying to win and rule the people, not push them away.

The northern army's radio frequency jammers most often affected long-range communications, limiting Galt to line-of-sight comms and walkie-talkies. Limited comms or not, his patrols had seen evidence that his island was soon to be attacked.

Galt turned from the window and sat at his desk where his notes lay scattered. Titus Caspertein was a man who knew how to win the people. Now *there* was a military mind! Having Wes Trimble on board was the next best thing. By working with Trimble, Galt hoped to find a weakness in Titus and perhaps win him over. Owning the Casperteins would definitely be a step toward winning the people.

Trimble had told him much about the Casperteins, but Galt was suspicious of the one-eyed man. He was too experienced, too intelligent. The man was old-school— loyal and moral. Galt wasn't convinced the ex-CIA agent was fully committed to PSDF interests, but Trimble had already offered valuable insights in regard to the coming conflicts with northern forces.

And Galt hadn't hesitated to offer Trimble the intel they'd collected on the approaching armies. Trimble had a strategic mind, and to be an asset, even for a short time, he needed to know the score. Coronado had as many as five thousand fighters. The northern armies had half that.

"You can dissolve the threat they are," Wes had told him while standing before a wall map, "simply by waiting."

"Waiting?" Galt had asked. "You've only looked at our reports for ten minutes, and you're telling me already how to defeat them?"

"They have no resupply system like you do. They're ill-equipped. Hungry soldiers don't fight well; they run. If you can put off all-out war this year, they'll dissolve away. You can probably absorb their fiercest fighters and take their equipment after that. You'll need it all for what seems to be building up in Seattle. If I were you, I'd get ready for that, not this Riverside rabble."

Galt hadn't expected to be directed by such clear-minded thinking. Indeed, Los Angeles was still reeling from at least one barrage of earthquakes, and fires had wiped out whole suburbs. The riots and aftermath were rumored to have killed a million people.

He could win by waiting. If Riverside Guard would just hold off a few months, they wouldn't even be a threat. But that was a big *if*. Riverside needed Coronado's stockpiles, and Lesage wouldn't be easy to hold back. He was spoiling for a fight, evidenced by reports of his brutality in confiscating excess materials from locals around the city. And the Casperteins obviously had resources and supplies, so it was just a matter of time before Lesage tested Titus' resolve as well.

"Come in," Galt granted when someone knocked on his door.

President Criswell's aid, a young man of twenty with tape on his glasses, entered. He wore a crisp business suit, which had drawn ridicule from soldiers in the dining hall, so the young man no longer ate in the mess hall.

"General, President Criswell is asking for you."

Galt followed the aid into the office next door. Criswell removed his glasses and stood from an ornate dining table they'd confiscated from a downtown hotel. The president was a slender and tall man, his hair and beard white. His ready smile and willingness to listen made him welcome anywhere on the island.

"I have more executive orders for you, Galt."

"Very good, Mr. President."

The furniture in the room was situated much like the Oval Office in Washington, D.C. Galt sat on a sofa facing Criswell.

"We need to rebuild confidence with the people that their best interests are our priority."

"Of course, sir." Galt leaned forward. "Let me see what you have here."

"Inclusion and diversity policies." Criswell gave the file to Galt. "No one will be able to say that the Pacific States doesn't involve everyone and anyone in this new administration. I want this followed, Galt. Get all sexes, religions, and races inside the walls of this capitol building, anyone who may be a symbol of their culture or heritage."

"Of course, sir." Galt browsed the first few pages of proposals. "I'll get on this right away."

He closed the file as the president droned on about his sensational goals of the past—and how he was now fulfilling them by codifying them into laws within the Pacific States.

But Galt wasn't listening. Not really. It was more weak policy that fractured the populace to look at the sexes, religions, and skin color instead of what each individual had to offer. People were starving across the city, and Criswell was talking about his image. There was an enemy army testing his resolve up in the hills. Bandits still roamed the land at night and several of the zoo's wild animals had been seen in the headlights of their patrol vehicles. And Criswell wanted to welcome people based on inclusion policies of the past instead of loyalty to the fighting cause?

No, Galt wouldn't implement these policies, laws or not. Arthur Criswell was a necessary nuisance, a buffer that Galt needed to keep under control, to pacify the people by force and compliance. Criswell's job was to offer the people a friendly face—and to take the blame when things went south. In which case, Galt would simply institute another "elected" president.

"And another thing," Criswell said, "why hasn't there been any news about my daughter?"

"Sir, we don't have any contact with the East Coast. I'm sure they're in just as much upheaval as we are."

"She would've been a great public relations manager, Galt. Imagine winning over the people using the speeches of a master writer like Carla. We need her here. We could unite this whole country again with her help. We'd promise the people freedom and you could secure it. The ways of the past are long gone. Carla is a visionary. I want her at my side as soon as possible, Galt."

"We'll continue to try to make contact," Galt assured, but meant no word of his promises.

Due to frequency interference, their radio barely reached halfway across the city on a good day. Galt had seen the antenna erected on the ELM building. Trimble had said he wasn't sure of Caspertein's range, but Galt knew it had to be at least twice what Coronado was getting.

Galt left the president. The aging man seemed completely delusional about the true state of the country if he expected his daughter to be contacted somewhere on the East Coast. There was no way Galt was wasting resources looking into her whereabouts. It was ridiculous!

He returned to his office and found a message in his inbox. Another patrol had been fired on in the northeast near I-8. His troops could fight in the forested hills and ravines, but morale would suffer by a drawn-out conflict. He needed to win over the solitary militias before they broke the nerve of his people. Defeating Riverside, if they invaded, would be that much more difficult if his forces were already discouraged by border skirmishes. Riverside would know that, so he suspected they were convincing the hill people to encroach on Pacific States territory—though even Galt himself didn't know where those lines were drawn exactly.

"Dad!" It was Kip coming up the hallway. "Dad, are you in there? Get out of my way! I'm here to see my dad!"

Kip threw open the suite door but Galt was ready. He spun and punched the youth in the gut, then stood over him as he wretched.

"You're supposed to be a soldier." Galt closed the door and spoke softly so no one in the hallway could hear. "You disgraced me by kidnapping some tramp across town? I know that's why you're here. Yes, I ordered Sergeant Lesage to get rid of her. Don't you realize we have a reputation to uphold as military men? You take what I tell you to take and nothing else—until you learn the discipline of what it means to be a soldier. Do you see Lesage running after skirts in the city? No! We're fighting for our lives here, Kip. Stand up. *Stand up!*"

Kip slowly rose to his feet, bile drooling from his lips. He held his stomach as his tears ran.

Then Galt embraced him. It was a forced embrace, which Kip resisted initially, but Galt held it long enough for Kip to hug him in return. Then Kip wept. This was healing, Galt thought. He'd continue to use a firm hand on the people of San Diego to bring them into submission as well.

After all, he was protecting them from invaders who would certainly do worse.

"I love you, Kip. We're gonna do this together. This is your empire, too. You'll become the leader I want you to become."

Avery "Chevy" Hewitt remained in the shadow of an elm tree, his back to the thick bark as Levi used a pick and shovel to dig. Grave duty hadn't been on Chevy's list of things to do before he died, but he was pleased that Titus had asked him to attend to the city's dead with his son.

It was Levi who'd insisted in doing the backbreaking work of digging. At only nineteen, the teen was no longer a boy. He was his father's son—lean, fit, and witty. Above all, Levi was teachable, evidenced by his willingness to listen rather than speak.

After ten minutes, Levi was still shoveling the soil out of the growing hole at a pace that equaled two men. It had been Levi's idea that Chevy stand watch while Levi did the hard labor. Chevy wondered if that was the young man's polite way of requesting that the older man stay out of the way, which Chevy didn't mind. He wasn't a strong man and he wasn't a soldier like the Casperteins, Oleg, or the spy, Wes Trimble. Soldiering had only come to Chevy when COIL had needed expendable people to send to North Korea, and he had gladly volunteered.

Levi and Chevy had gathered two dead from Seaport Village, a man and a woman. Chevy had searched their torn clothing and found identifications. They were husband and wife. He'd already written their names on an empty page of his Bible. Titus had sent them to clean up the city and begin to influence the living, but Chevy understood he was there to record the dead as well in case their loved ones came searching.

The husband and wife would be buried in the same grave, as they had died together on Harbor Drive. Their boots and possessions had been taken by scavengers. Levi had admitted to finding them on the street in his telescope a month earlier. One morning, they were just there. The cause of death was unknown to anyone but the killers. Their identifications indicated they'd lived in the Gaslamp Quarter a few blocks from the shore. Maybe they'd been trying to flee the ravaged city, and night prowlers had surrounded them.

The thought reminded Chevy to check his own lightly forested surroundings right then. The elm trees were thick so they cut off direct sunlight. It wasn't the normal environment to find a new cemetery, but it was the only ground with any cover where the grave diggers could dig in relative safety.

Chevy carried the weight of his own losses. The other four in his Kindred of Nails team sent to North Korea had all perished, sacrificing themselves for others, even for himself. Titus' new directive for ELM rang true in Chevy's heart. Every life *did* matter. That's why he looked forward to seeing his KON teammates again someday in glory. And that's why he wrote down the names of the deceased in the back of his Bible. The dead couldn't be helped, but the living could learn from their losses. All loss was instructive.

"You think that's deep enough?" Levi climbed out of the grave and clapped his gloves free of dirt. He stood at the foot of the hole, the mound on one side, and the fragile remains of the bodies wrapped in two sheets on the other. "I wonder who they were."

Moving from his tree, Chevy stood at the head of the hole. It pleased him that Levi cared to reflect on such things. The young man had grown rapidly in the faith and character of Christ in the last few months. Titus and Oleg hadn't been believers for more than a few years, but Chevy and Wes had been followers for most of their lives. Before Chevy had left prison, he'd discipled dozens to remain independent students of God's Word and to follow in the Savior's footsteps.

During Levi's downtime between projects, it was Chevy that the young man had often searched out to accompany since Chevy was always working on some electrical or mechanical puzzle. It was much more than mere companionship, Chevy understood now. Levi had been hungry. His soul had been wide open. His questions about the faith ranged from the doctrine of angels to how to counsel the burdened and depressed. The youth's teachability had made it an honor for Chevy to accommodate. Quite naturally, he'd become the teen's mentor, and he'd even developed an idea from the Scriptures for Levi to incorporate into his life—bondage breaking grace—the BBG of God.

Titus' ELM concept complimented Levi's spiritual training on the BBG. If Chevy did nothing else with the remainder of his life, he was happy to instill tools into Levi's heart and mind that would make him an effective evangelist and soldier for Jesus Christ. Already, Levi had adopted a way of speaking that reflected a much more mature man's vocabulary and wisdom, though he still lacked life experience. Levi was rapidly moving in his father's footsteps as a leader. And now he'd have the Gospel power to influence souls by way of bondage breaking grace.

The two gently lowered the husband and wife into the grave. Then Levi took up the shovel to fill the hole. Chevy returned to his elm tree and thought of Wes Trimble, alone in enemy territory, yet certainly in his tradecraft element. The Lord was with the one-eyed man who loved his friends enough to offer his life if necessary to search out threats. Titus was assertive and always taking the initiative, but Chevy was drawn more to the quieter disposition of Wes, though the aging agent had no less a sense of humor than Titus. Chevy still wasn't sure how the man had really lost his eye after all the tall tales he'd told.

Chevy was alerted to a form moving in the trees. He didn't yet level his rifle, but there was definitely someone out there now hiding behind another elm tree, perhaps three trees away. Levi panted as he spread the dirt and packed it into place. The young man's pack and rifle lay at the foot of another tree nearby.

"Should we say something?" Levi stood and folded his hands at the foot of the small mound of earth. "Seems we should."

"Go ahead." Chevy didn't join him since potential danger was lurking. "I'm listening."

"Okay. Um . . ." Levi lifted his head. "It's a sad day that we bury these two. We learned their names, but not much more. Their deaths remind me of what Jesus said about the days of Noah. It sure seems like we're living in them—when everyone is thinking about violence, ready to kill because they're afraid they'll be killed. Maybe like Dad said, we can make a difference about that around here. Show some grace. Break some bondage. Make some disciples of Jesus. Amen."

"Well said. Hold one, Levi."

Levi didn't move. Chevy knew he'd understand the command to hold fast for a moment, that a situation was developing that required more observation before reaction. They'd both gone through Bible Boot Camp together out in the desert and received the training to die well for Jesus, if necessary, but also how to preserve life as skilled operators through non-lethal means.

A few seconds passed. Then the form behind the tree not far away moved into sight. It was an old woman, no taller than four-and-a-half feet. She wore a dirty smock over filthy trousers. Her gray-white hair hung straight at the sides of her blank Hispanic face. She clasped a bouquet of wild flowers in one of her hands.

Chevy offered a casual wave, figuring she was certain to be wary of a man with a weapon. She turned her head and slowly searched in all directions. Concerned that she might not be alone, Chevy did the same.

Then she walked slowly toward them. Stopping a few feet from the grave, she set down her flowers. Levi stared at her as she looked between both men and the mound of dirt. There was something wild about her, something primitive.

Slowly stepping away from the tree, Chevy approached her. He took a knee directly in front of her and held out his open, upturned gloved hands. She didn't appear to have any Meridia symptoms, but the gloves were a safety measure.

"Do you speak English, my sister?" he asked.

She placed her small wrinkled hand in his and he held it gently with both hands.

"Yes." She didn't frown or smile, only looked down at him. "Who'd you bury?"

"A man and a woman. We didn't know them." Chevy offered a sad smile. "But now they rest together. We'll be burying more from the city streets. Do you think this is a good place?"

"There's no sun." She glanced about. "I like the sunshine. But there's birds and squirrels here."

"Yes, it has its pleasant features, I think. My friends call me Chevy, like the truck brand. And this is Levi Caspertein, a loyal friend to have at your side. May I ask your name?"

"I . . . don't remember."

"That's okay." Chevy nodded. His eyes fell to her feet. She wore only dirty house slippers. "Where do you live?"

"Back there." She pointed northward. "There's a house and a garden. There are dead people in the street. They need to be buried, too."

"Okay. Levi and I will see to them in a few days. Have you been living alone?"

She nodded.

"Do you know the house number of where you live back there?"

"No. I don't think it's my house. I just live there. Fruit grows on the trees."

"I see. I'm a little concerned that you're alone out here. Would you like to—"

"I'm always alone."

"What should I call you?"

"I . . . don't know. I don't remember."

"Levi, we need a name for her."

"She noticed there was no sunshine a minute ago," Levi said. "Maybe she'd like the name Sunshine."

"Sunshine." Chevy smiled. "May we call you Sunshine for now? Would that be okay?"

Nodding, she slipped her hand away from his, and turned. Before Chevy could ask anything else, she jogged to the north and was gone through the trees.

Chevy rose to his feet and found Levi standing beside him.

"I think we'll find more like her out here," Chevy said. "Pan-Day was such a shock to some people that something broke in their minds. Change from what they knew and loved disturbed them beyond their capability of processing those changes."

"Pan-Day?" Levi asked. "What's that?"

"It's a term I've been thinking about. I shared it with your dad. It describes what happened—the pandemic and all the panic that followed. It seems like it needs a name instead of just an abstract event in the past. The world changed on Pan-Day. Cities were quarantined. The electrical grid collapsed. Then people panicked as they starved and we have what you see today.

"Pandemonium."

"That's another good word for it." Chevy turned and picked up the shovel and pick and put them in the pushcart they'd used to bring the bodies. "Maybe we'll see more of Sunshine, huh? Might be someone we can care for."

"ELM?" Levi started pushing the cart toward the nearest city street to the south. "Wow, I've learned so much from you the last few months, Chevy. If I hold it in any longer, I feel like I'll go crazy. I've got to get out here more and more."

"God's grace was never meant to be held in." Chevy chuckled. "God will guide you. There'll be bondage He'll use you to break. You have what you need, Levi. Trust the Lord to give you the right words for how and when desperate souls need them most."

"Go home for some lunch?" Levi offered. "That digging made me hungry!"

"That's strange." Chevy patted his stomach. "All that digging didn't affect my appetite at all."

"Very funny!" Levi laughed and shoved Chevy on the shoulder as they emerged from the elms.

✝

Titus Caspertein used binoculars to search to the northwest for his son. Chevy and Levi had gone out on their first grave detail, and Titus was nervous about how the city might respond. The best-case scenario was that civilians would see the two gunmen carting away the dead and welcome them as servants in the community. The worst-case scenario was that hungry civilians would see the two gunmen as threats or a resource to attack and steal from.

"I thought I'd find you out here." Annette joined him on the balcony of unoccupied apartment one on the fortieth floor. She took the binoculars from him and gazed in the general direction he'd been looking. Her auburn hair was up and she wore a khaki shirt and trousers. "How's our boy doing? Where am I supposed to look?"

"See the Air and Space Museum? Look in the trees to the left." Titus rested his callused hands on the balcony rail. "They loaded up the pushcart with two bodies. Chevy escorted while Levi pushed the cart. You can't see them now, but I was watching for anyone else who might be moving near them."

"If you saw someone, what would you do? Your rifle won't reach that far."

"No, but my radio would. I know their comm frequency. Their transmitter couldn't reach us, but mine is strong enough to warn them if an enemy were about. Two men are easy pickin's for people. Maybe I should've gone with them."

"Seriously?" She handed back the binoculars. "You're talking about Chevy, who blasted his way out of North Korea. And last time I saw Levi shoot, his marks were closer than anyone else's."

"I know, but he's still young." Titus spotted a scavenger team of five people on the off-ramp of the interstate. They didn't appear to have rifles, but they could have handguns under their faded jackets. "His confidence won't grow unless he starts facing these challenges alone, but I also want to protect him."

"That just means you love him." Annette kissed his cheek. "It's actually a good thing that Levi doesn't know he's so skilled, isn't it? He might get cocky. As long as he keeps trying to prove himself, it means he doesn't see himself as having reached the top."

"Well, he's about to be tested in a real way. I spoke to someone on the radio this morning. They are in our sphere of influence."

"Somebody you haven't talked to before out there?"

"Right, someone new. She needs help. You ever heard of the call sign Sacred Cow?"

"Sacred Cow?" Annette grunted. "Sounds like a burger joint in India."

"It ain't easy craving a side of beef, huh?" He chuckled. "No, Sacred Cow is sometimes the call sign for Air Force One. Truman and Roosevelt called it that, at least."

"Air Force One? The president is out here?"

"No, I think rumors of his Meridia Virus death are true. But I think one of his 747s crashed out in the wilderness a few weeks ago before a new president could be implemented. There were survivors. One was left with the plane. Her water is low. She sounded pretty scared."

"And you want to send Levi?" Annette nodded. "With who? Chevy?"

"No, someone with more urban warfare experience. Maybe Oleg. He already needs a break from milking goats after only one morning."

"Hey, he volunteered!"

They laughed, knowing the tough Russian probably preferred something other than escorting Gustavo up the street to gather edibles for the goats now living on the first floor in the lobby. The animals could climb on the old marble where the fountain once ran, and play in the empty fish pool. Gustavo had set up a couple milking stations for the does, and the four kids had been moved into a separate pen to be fed by bottle so they didn't butt and bruise the udders of the does.

"Oleg will be good for Levi," Titus said. "They haven't been alone together before. Levi needs to learn the value of people who don't talk much, but have lots to offer."

"Yeah, but can Oleg tolerate a youngster who's still figuring out who he wants to be?"

"Hey, Oleg tolerated me for years." Titus grinned. "He'll keep Levi out of trouble. And I'm curious about what news this female survivor may bring us, if any."

"Always intel gathering, aren't you?" Annette sighed. "Well, at least you're not rushing into danger yourself like you used to."

"I'd rush into danger for any of you." He shrugged. "I'm just not rushing into danger for no reason."

"People depend on you now." She hooked her arm in his. "We all do."

"Actually, I was thinking Gustavo might make a play to court you if I weren't around anymore."

"*Gus, the goat man?*" She shoved him. "Please! Maybe I'll send you out there with Levi just for you to interact with some people so you can work on your sense of humor!"

"Oh, wait." Titus steadied the binoculars. "Chevy and Levi just came out of those elm trees. There are five civilians to their left. They all stopped. They're about thirty yards apart. Levi is waving and talking to them."

"What's Chevy doing?"

"He moved to the side. It looks like his guard is up, but he's not raising his rifle."

"Are the five armed?"

"No rifles, but maybe handguns. Levi is walking toward them."

"They could have the virus!" Annette fretted.

"Levi must've had food in his day pack because he's offering them something. No, they're backing away. Now they stopped. One of them is coming forward. Levi is holding out . . . I think he drew his knife from his belt?

Yeah, he's giving them his knife. And the food. I think it's a woman. He's talking to her."

"Why would he give her his knife?"

"Maybe as a sign of peace? I don't know."

"What's she doing?"

"Just talking. She's older. Now she's pointing south, maybe telling Levi where they live. She's giving Levi something. It's wrapped up."

"So, they're exchanging gifts?" Annette's hand went to her lips. "What about the virus, Titus?"

"They aren't shaking hands. Levi must've bared his face to show he has no symptoms. He's a regular ambassador at nineteen years old, huh?"

"Nearly twenty in a few weeks."

"I know. You marked it on the calendar."

"Has he brought it up? We could throw him a surprise party."

"No. Honestly, I don't think he wants the attention. He's said several times this year that he's not a kid anymore, and he's said birthday parties are for kids."

"That's not true. People of all ages celebrate their birthdays."

"I know, but that's the way he sees it. He just doesn't want to be treated like a kid anymore."

"What are they doing now?"

"Okay, now he's shaking her hand, but he has his gloves on. Chevy waved at them. He's still at a distance. And now they're going their separate ways." Titus eyed Annette. "You okay?"

Annette lowered her folded hands.

"That was our first real contact with locals." She exhaled slowly. "It went okay—this time."

"There'll be many more times if our plans work out. Chevy and Levi are on their way back. I'm gonna go down and meet them. You want to come?"

"No, you guys do your thing." She turned toward the sliding door. "I haven't cleaned off the solar panels for a few days, and I think weeds in the garden need pulling. Wynter's already up there."

They walked through the apartment together. Titus picked up his rifle, ammo vest, and pack. Annette slowly climbed the stairs to the roof and Titus entered the dolly to descend.

At ground level, he admired the fencing Oleg and Gustavo had erected to keep the goats in their respective pens, especially for the sake of humans walking to and from the stairs without tripping over kids or stepping on goat droppings.

"I think I'm trading you in for this billy," Oleg said to Titus, a nibbling kid in his arms and another trying to climb his leg.

"Be honest!" Titus laughed. "You just found a new friend who looks like you."

"Hey, at least this little guy has less ear hair than you do!" Oleg fired back. "Gus has some shears around here somewhere if you want to borrow them."

Titus unlocked the door and readied his rifle. He opened the door a little at first, checking the street and the intersection beyond. Everything appeared so different now in the daylight. Oleg may have been wrestling with the goats at that moment, but his battle rifle and gear were there by the door. Vigilance was still their life, even while chores split their attention.

Levi walked into sight, his face beaming proudly as he pushed the four-wheeled cart up the middle of the street. Chevy walked along the shoulder, his rifle leveled and his eyes alert.

"We talked to people!" Levi said as Titus lifted the cart over the threshold. "They live down near Petco Park. More people are there, too. I told them we'd come visit sometime, and that we'd come to an agreement with the military patrols. There'll be peace in the city. The lady said if that were true, more people would move back here because the suburbs are really violent and fractured still. Her name was Kathy. Chevy, what was her last name?"

"McShane." Chevy closed and locked the door. "Kathy McShane."

"She gave us some pumpkin seeds she dried herself. They looked pretty poor, Dad. I told her if she has any problems with anyone, she just has to come to the high-rise by the depot that has a giant elm tree painted on the north side."

"An elm tree?" Titus rested his hands on his hips. "So, you told her about ELM?"

"That's what you said, right? People need to know about us. Every life matters."

"That's it. That's our job." Titus scratched his chin. "But Levi, we don't have a giant elm tree painted on the side of the building."

"I figured the north side, here would be a good place since the sun won't break down the paint so much. We'll put it above the door. It'll last forever. Everyone in the city will become familiar with the symbol. It's not like we're looking for attention. We're just letting people know where they're safe."

"You know what I think?" Oleg called from the goat pen. "I think you're going to be painting a giant elm tree on the building, Titus."

"No, I'll do it," Levi said. "Chevy and I came back for lunch, then we'll go back out for another burial. I'll paint the tree on the wall tonight."

"That's ambitious of you, Levi," Titus said, "but the dead will have to wait a few more days. We got an SOS from a woman out in the hills. Her plane went down and her water supply is low. She's alone and she shouldn't be running around without protection. I was thinking you and Oleg might want to go get her."

"How far out in the hills?" Levi's eyes widened. "Past the suburbs?"

"Yep. Way past. It's about seven miles from here, but it'll take you all day to get there tomorrow with full packs and armed for conflict. Stay overnight at the plane, then you three can return here the following day. Oleg?"

"Actually," the Russian said, "I was making plans to watch you try to milk a goat tomorrow. My money's on the goat."

Titus chuckled, knowing his old friend would love to see the countryside, and probably some action along the way.

"You two get cleaned up and come upstairs for mission prep." Titus started toward the stairs. "We've got some maps to review. Chevy, looks like you and I are painting that elm tree above the door tomorrow."

"I've seen you paint, Titus." Oleg moved through the goat pen gate and latched it closed. "Why don't you hold the ladder and let Chevy do the painting or we're liable to end up with a giant ostrich on the side of our building."

"Hey, what's wrong with an ostrich?" Titus asked as they all laughed.

Upstairs, Titus gathered the right maps, then went to Levi's apartment where his door was unlocked as usual. Though the teen had asked early on for his own apartment, Titus wondered if he left the door unlocked because he was hoping for company. Levi was lacing his boots when Titus walked in. Thanks to the solar panel array and battery bank on the roof, Levi had enjoyed a hot shower. His hair was still wet and uncombed. He reminded Titus of his brother, Rudy, a seismologist who'd determined to ride out America's last days in Meeker, Colorado. Rudy had chosen a life spent in the wild, often surveying rugged land where few others dared to venture.

"Before the others arrive," Titus said, "I want to talk to you alone."

Levi stood and nodded. The youth swallowed nervously.

"I'm listening. What is it? Is this about last night? I know now it was stupid, Dad."

"This isn't about the zip line. This is about security. Wes Trimble is risking his life for valuable intel we may need to defend ourselves, but Wes is a spy. Spies don't only gather intel. They also offer intel. In most cases, spies offer misinformation to misdirect enemies."

"But we're at peace with the Pacific States, aren't we?"

"We are." Titus nodded. "Until General Brogdon and their new President Criswell find a way to use us. Or if they see something they want."

"Like our rifles," Levi said with understanding.

"Exactly. Only two people know where that COIL armory is hidden, and those two people are in this very room. We can never put those weapons in the hands of men who are given to killing and not healing, Levi. The battle rifle is too superior to let even one go to an enemy. We've submitted to President Criswell since the Pacific States is the acting government—but we won't submit in matters that compromise what we know is right before our Lord and Savior."

"I understand. I'll die before I tell anyone where all the guns and gear are kept."

"I'd rather you live, Levi, using your wits and predisposition towards mercy."

"Like you did with the general? Chevy said that's not the first time you dictated what would happen to a military man without firing a shot."

"If your heart is prepared, you can offer peace to a foe by setting aside your own ego. I overcame Brogdon because I'm not trying to take control. Our influence for Christ in this city is more important than our sense of superiority. No, we can let Brogdon have his military. We have a higher calling."

"You could remove him from power, couldn't you?" Levi smiled proudly.

"Levi, with the men in this building and Wes already implanted?" Titus scoffed and shook his head. "Together or alone, we've toppled and erected governments. Wes did it for the CIA. You know what Chevy did in North Korea. Oleg has single-handedly taken down international monsters for Interpol. And for my own selfish desires, I ruined or replaced regimes or princes across Africa and the Middle East."

"And now Wes is doing it again."

"No, he's not. We're not. But we *could* do it. What I'm saying is that just because you can lead in the world doesn't mean you should—not when you can serve in the kingdom of God. Serving in the kingdom is greater than ruling in the world. Wes is only on Coronado Island to ensure that our service as ELM proceeds unhindered."

"What misinformation is he giving them?" Levi asked. "Is it about us?"

"Yeah, it is. He's painting a picture for Brogdon that makes us seem both inconsequential and mysterious. Both of those traits will keep the PSDF off our doorstep. And there's something else—a name you need to remember. Wes is sharing a name with them. As long as this name is out there, we're safe. You've got to protect this name and keep it alive. This name is our security buffer."

"What's the name?"

"Maddix Striber. Say it."

"Maddix Striber. Who is he?"

"He's our benefactor, our hidden leader, our secret muscle who offers weapons and resources and designs that are unimaginable."

"*What?*" Levi's face showed his disappointment. "I thought it was just us. You've never talked about Maddix Striber. So, you know him from the radio? I've never even heard his name."

"No, Levi, listen. Maddix Striber is Wes's misinformation. As long as Maddix Striber is out there, hidden and powerfully backing us, Brogdon won't move against us. You can't target the unknown or the unseen."

"Because he doesn't exist!" Levi's hands went to his head. "Dad, that's *ingenious!*"

"The Lord gave us good men, son. Maddix Striber was Wes's idea. And there's more. Maddix Striber is known by his people as the Chronicle."

"The Chronicle?"

"Exactly. A fake agent may as well have a fake codename, too. General Brogdon will be looking for this guy. He's completely fabricated, but you need to drop his name occasionally during your travels to keep him alive. Maddix Striber can be our fall guy, our excuse—anything we need him to be. But only you know about him. Fake secrets are best protected and fostered only if they're treated like real secrets."

"He's a decoy. The Chronicle is totally artificial. Dad, this is brilliant."

"It's just tradecraft, Levi, and it's time you understood how a Christian can use it. Jesus said to be wise as serpents and harmless as doves. We hurt no one by creating a fictional character for our enemies to chase— and we protect everyone. Don't overuse it and you'll never expose him. Maybe when the time is right, Maddix Striber will fall ill, like when Brogdon's investigations start closing in. Then we'll erect a new decoy. Maybe an organization or even a fictional settlement out there beyond the city limits. It's all subterfuge."

"Meanwhile, we stay secure in the city," Levi said, nodding.

"Yep, while doing God's work. Evil, proud hearts will always chase after what is just out of sight, unknown, or a threat. A dog that's chasing its tail can't bite anyone. That's all Wes is setting up—then he'll return to us. Somehow. He's the real spy."

"I feel like a whole new world has opened to me. You guys are playing chess twenty moves ahead of Brogdon."

"Don't underestimate the PSDF. But yes, thinking ahead usually bears favorable results." Titus was silent for a moment. "One last thing. I want you to take risks for people's souls, Levi."

"Take risks?"

"Yes. I want you to trust God so intimately that you're guided to show mercy toward someone who seems utterly hopeless in anyone else's eyes. You know my past. And you know how Corban Dowler won over Luigi Putelli. Who does Levi Caspertein win for Jesus? Who will you take a risk with? That's the reason I'm sending my son out into this dangerous world."

For the rest of the afternoon, Titus worked out a route to reach the Sacred Cow caller. Chevy wasn't going, but he offered meaningful counsel for Oleg and Levi as they huddled over old maps. Titus watched Levi's face, the way he gloried in the responsibility given to him, even after his zip line lesson. Sending the nineteen-year-old out alone with Oleg wasn't easy, but it was necessary. Levi would need to learn how to rely on God and his own wits eventually. Now seemed as good a time as any.

The two were to leave before dawn.

✝

As evening settled over the wilderness, Carla Criswell walked slowly around the huge plane half-buried in sand drifts. She guessed that in a year the whole plane would be buried except maybe the tall tail section. It was a sad thought—abandoning her refuge after six weeks. Of course, the first weeks had been spent in delirious pain, but her burns had left her numb in more ways than one. The side of her face was as numb as her heart was indifferent about seeing people again. The world wasn't the same. What she'd built for herself couldn't be used in this new society. What good was a news reporter who had no platform from which to speak or write? Her purpose in life had been destroyed by anarchy.

She climbed onto the fuselage and sat staring south as the stars blinked above. All that day, she'd warmed to the idea of the ELM777 people coming to rescue her. Like a survivor on an island, she couldn't choose who the other survivors were to be. The very people she'd sought to ruin in the past were the same people who would now risk their lives to save her. Since they hadn't asked who she was, she'd offered no information. They were coming because she'd asked for help. None of her old friends had such unconditional compassion. Those friends had actually lived to cancel anyone who didn't comply with the progressive agenda that the so-called enlightened world was adapting to as a human species.

How awkward it was to admit her "enlightened" worldview hadn't rescued her from the realities of a society swimming in chaos.

Carla heard them before she saw them—four or five men's voices. Even one was too many. This couldn't already be the ELM777 rescue team!

Turning, she slid off the far side of the fuselage and knelt in the sand against the starboard wing. At least two had flashlights. They must've seen the plane from afar and come to investigate. Or some of the crew may have finally reached someone who was returning to help her, but that was unlikely. Five weeks had passed since they'd left. These people were here for the plane. Hopefully, they hadn't seen her. And with any luck, they would trample her footprints in the dark before they realized her tracks were fresh.

But outside the plane, she had no water, no food, and no weapon. She admitted to herself that she wasn't a very good survivalist. If she abandoned the plane for the wilderness right then, she'd be dead in a day. This area was very cold at night. Without the shelter of the crew cabin and the stores of food in the plane, she had no hope. It seemed her ELM777 rescuers were one day too late.

"Can you believe this?" said one man on the portside. "How long has Air Force One been parked in our backyard?"

The men laughed. Definitely five. Carla eased up to the nose of the jet. If she'd thought ahead, she could've had a rope dangling from the cockpit window to climb up.

"This thing is huge!" exclaimed a second man. "Here, boost me up. They left the front door open. Shine that light over here, Dusty."

"There's a step," a third voice said. "Just climb up. Have your gun ready. Someone might still be here."

"Shut up and get up there," another said, "or get outta the way. I didn't tell you guys about this to talk all night out here."

The men continued to argue and joke about what might be inside. Carla peered around the nose section in time to see the last of the five men climb inside. She eased up to the doorway. It was dark now. Her own flashlight was inside the crew lounge. The stars and moon were bright outside, but they'd all need a flashlight inside the dark plane.

Carla hopped into the opening and climbed up. She could hear their voices to the right as they explored down the length of the main deck. The stairway to the crew lounge was next to the main galley, a quarter of the way down the plane's length. In the darkness, she wondered if she could slip past them, dash upstairs, and lock herself inside. It was a lot to hope for, but she saw no alternative. Revealing her presence to five strange men was out of the question. After traveling the world, she'd seen how people acted where no law and order existed.

From the door, she could see the president's office was empty, so she crossed the aisle and crouched behind the wall. The sound of men's laughter came from far back in the plane, maybe as far as the office staff section. Carla and the two others had lived back there for weeks, so she knew it was a smelly mess. Even the lavatories in the rear had backed up so she had avoided that whole section of the plane.

She eased into the corridor. The stairs were two doorways away, but she heard noise in the medical office. It still had some supplies in there, so that might keep someone busy and distracted.

Sure enough, she slipped past the medical office doorway without notice. The light and voices were coming from the aft section. Silently, she continued to the stairs, ignored the galley, and dashed up two steps at a time. In the darkness, moving by feel, she plowed headfirst into a body coming out of the crew lounge. She froze in the beam of his flashlight.

"What the—?" He cursed and grimaced, then reached for her. "Come here, you!"

He grabbed for her but missed as she backed down the stairs. But she couldn't go anywhere now. Others were nearby!

"What happened to you?" He shined the light in her face. "Anyone else here or were you just waiting for me? Where you going, honey?"

Carla darted into the galley. In the dark, she clawed across the counter and cutlery scattered from where she'd used kitchen knives to open food packages.

The flashlight beam reached her. *There was a fillet knife!*

"Hey, guys!" her adversary called to his friends. His body odor smelled bad. Maybe hers did, too, but at least she'd had wet-wipes to clean up a little each day. This man smelled like he hadn't bathed in weeks. "We've got a live one here! Come on! Some crazy lady's been living in this dump!"

Charging the flashlight, Carla aimed her knife at his face. She'd never been aggressive toward anyone, not physically. Her aggressiveness had always portrayed itself in her writing.

The man slapped the back of her hand aside and clubbed his flashlight over her shoulder. The knife clattered aside. Her whole right arm went numb and she stumbled backwards in an effort to stay on her feet. *Such pain!* She held her right dead arm with her left. In her fog, she saw him bend over to pick up the knife. That's when she stepped forward, brought up her knee sharply, and connected with his head.

She didn't wait to see if she'd knocked him out. His flashlight wasn't even a priority. The others were coming! Stepping past him, she gasped from her shoulder pain. Every move hurt.

Somehow, she clawed her way up the stairs to the crew lounge. From the dark recess above, she glanced back. Men ran past the stairs to enter the galley to see to their friend.

Carla quietly closed the door and locked it. It had one manual lock, but the one lever slid several dead bolts into place. It was a door designed to repel a variety of assailants or hijackers. That was the only way in—unless they tried to fling a hook and rope through the cockpit windows, but that glass was shatterproof.

She moved past the seats of the crew lounge to reach her bunk and fell onto its unmade mattress. Her head hit the shotgun, but she didn't care. Now blood from her head wound soaked the pillow under her as she curled up on the mattress, favoring her shoulder and numb arm. The pain was too great. And help was too far away. It was unthinkable that she'd last another day with five threatening men on the other side of the door. They were certainly armed. Her ELM777 rescue party was walking into danger and there was nothing she could do to warn them.

Sleep came seconds later amidst thoughts of a disappointing life and anger at her fate. It all seemed so pointless. Her two companions who'd committed suicide rather than continue in this ruined world now made sense. If only she weren't so afraid to die . . .

✝

Once Levi passed under Interstate 5, he no longer recognized the city. He placed his back against a parked city bus frozen in traffic and waited for Oleg to catch up. His father's Russian friend was a legend. All the old COIL personnel like Corban Dowler and Nathan Isaacson had said so. Levi couldn't believe the operative with biceps the size of bowling balls had no qualms about going on a mission with him!

Oleg wasn't a fast walker. His legs were short and he seemed intent on checking every vehicle they passed and scoping every street they crossed. Levi had a location on the map in his mind, and the faster they reached that point, the sooner the Sacred Cow survivor could feel safe. But Levi said nothing to Oleg as the older man finally caught up to him. He took a swig of water and eyed Levi critically.

"You've got your father's stamina. We haven't left the building for three months and you march along like you've been training for a triathlon."

"I've been climbing the stairs more than using the dollies," Levi said. Then he thought he might have sounded arrogant, so he continued. "I should probably slow down and be more cautious like you."

"Yeah. That's why I'm going so slow." Oleg thrust his water bottle back into his belt pouch. "I'm just cautious. But I've seen you checking the streets and alleys same as me. You're not missing anything—just like a good point man should do."

"Did you want to take point?" Levi offered. "We could take turns."

"No, it's better this way. Your father usually took point in the field. He said someone moving faster than me was the only way to get me to where I'm going."

"But he said you were always the one who put yourself at risk first."

"Well, I figured it was only fair. Titus puts his life on the line for everyone else. It seemed right for someone to do it for him once in a while."

Levi watched the dark windows of a flower shop and the art gallery next door. Twice since leaving ELM headquarters they'd seen strangers ahead, but people were skittish. Too much had gone badly for so many that neighbors wouldn't trust two gunmen walking on their ghostly streets.

"Go ahead and move us on out, Levi," Oleg said. "If you let me rest too often, people are liable to think we're weak enough to pick off."

With his rifle aiming in the direction he was facing as he was taught, Levi marched away. There were potential ambush spots on every street, so he zigzagged from vehicle to vehicle for cover along the way. He kept an eye on Oleg's pace and tried to accommodate. Even though they carried comms, the reason there were two of them was to provide cover if the other came under fire. As long as Levi stayed within six hundred yards of Oleg, he knew they could cover each other—like few others could with rifles of more limited range.

East of downtown, they worked their way through South Park, steadily moving east, avoiding main highways and sticking to the quieter avenues whenever possible.

The farther they walked from the city center, the more signs of life Levi noticed. There were little signs, like footprints in the dust that coated the pavement, or fresh drag marks of scavengers, or even curtained windows that shifted as he trekked down quiet neighborhood streets.

Near noon, Levi spread a map on a picnic table in a park where even the chains to the swing set had been stolen for someone's use. His map was his own, copied the night before from his father's maps. It was traced on thin wax paper. He didn't really need the visual aid since he'd memorized its details as he'd traced it. But he thought Oleg might need to see how far they'd come in six hours.

"That's a good distance." Oleg set his pack beside him on the bench and pulled out a sandwich with his bulky hand. The bread was freshly made by Annette. "Would you say we're halfway?"

"Yeah, but I think the last half will be faster." Levi pointed to the brown hills to the east. He'd already eaten his sandwich while he'd walked. "Once we get out there in the hills, there won't be much to distract us."

"Sounds good. It feels like we're too exposed on these streets. The open wilderness allows you to see your enemy coming."

Levi drew a can of white spray paint from his pack. After shaking it, he walked to a small structure—the park bathroom. Reaching up, he spray-painted an elm tree—trunk and canopy foliage—on its east wall.

"Dad's told me some stories of your days in the Syrian desert," he said as he returned. "And in Africa, too."

"Your father was called the Serval for good reason. He was at home in the desert like the desert cat. But your father's comfortable anywhere. It's in your blood, too. Even now, you're probably having the time of your life while others are hiding in their houses."

"But you like this, too, right?" Levi frowned.

"Like this?" He grunted. "Honestly, Levi, at my age, I'd rather be milking the goats. But some work—like this—needs to be done by someone equipped for it. Your father's like a general right now, so he sends the soldiers out here. I think he wanted to come, but he wants you to grow on your own."

"Why'd he send you with me?"

"Probably to slow you down." Oleg chuckled. "Chevy doesn't have much experience at urban warfare, and he wanted someone with you who does.

"Chevy survived North Korea."

"And that was no small feat. Chevy's a good man. He has his valuable skills. But his calling is a little different. Of course, if you and I get into trouble, Chevy will be the first person your father grabs to come to our aid. He didn't say it last night, but that's why he wanted to be with us to plan our route to Sacred Cow. If necessary, he could retrace our steps, even in the dark. No one reads sign like the Serval."

"What was that?" Levi lifted his head at the echo of a gunshot. "It came from over there!"

"That was a rifle." Oleg tucked the remainder of his sandwich in a pocket. "It sounded close. You've got younger ears, but . . . you sure it was from that direction?"

"Yeah, that way!" Levi nodded north, grabbed up his pack, and dashed off across the park.

"I didn't mean run towards it!" Oleg yelled after him.

But Levi couldn't resist. His time with his father had instilled in him the hero's motto: if someone was in trouble, he had to respond, risk or not. Every life mattered.

He hurdled a fence and stomped through the unattended backyard of what looked like a residential three-bedroom house. When he reached the front yard, he skidded to a stop behind a child's plastic slide and took a knee. A slender man crouched over the carcass of an animal in the middle of the street. The man's back was to Levi and the animal appeared to be a German shepherd. Levi had seen his share of wild dogs around the city, let loose by owners who didn't realize they were loosing a predator back to the wild.

The shooter's hunting rifle lay on the pavement next to him as the man used a pocketknife to gut the animal. The hunter's hair was a little shaggy but his clothing was in good condition. The man turned his head to check left and right—probably worried someone would be drawn to the rifle shot to steal his kill.

Levi approached slowly, walking through the front yard's open gate, and stood idly behind an overflowing garbage bin. It was the first time Levi noticed there was a worse smell than the dead animal, though anything could've been buried in that trash heap.

For a moment, Levi was disappointed that there was no one for him to help, only a nervous man gutting his kill. But then he noticed three people up the street to the east. All three had hunting rifles.

The hunter with the dog also saw them, and he swore as he hurried with his butchering. Even Levi knew better than to butcher a kill in plain sight. He should've dragged the animal away to tend to it elsewhere.

Looking back, Levi saw Oleg crouch on the side of the house. Oleg shook his head and Levi understood that he didn't want them to interfere. But Levi saw an opportunity, not an obstacle. He signaled to Oleg to watch the three targets to the east. Frowning, Oleg followed Levi's pointing, then noticed the three. Finally, Oleg nodded.

"Go for it," Oleg said quietly on his comm. "If you have to."

Licking his lips, Levi smiled. The approaching three were a half-block away. One was a woman, one was another man, and the last was a young man. Maybe a family. Their mere hunting rifles suggested that these were simply hungry locals doing their best to survive in a frightful world.

Levi walked carefully around the trash bags and snuck up on the butcher while he was distracted by the dog and the three approaching people. Without a word of warning, Levi knelt on the pavement at the shoulder of the man—his knee separating the hunter from his own rifle.

"Finish what you're doing," Levi said quietly. "I'll cover you."

The man leaped aside so frantically that he abandoned his knife and the dog altogether. From two paces away, he stood, his bearded jaw agape, his face otherwise pale. He wore a thermal long-sleeve over a t-shirt, and his jeans were faded but not torn.

"Go ahead and finish." Levi gestured at the dog. "You know those three up there? You looked like you were trying to finish before they got here."

"Yeah, I know them." The man's eyes narrowed. "You're not with them?"

"No, I'm with you." Levi rose from his kneeling position. "This isn't their dog you killed, is it?"

"No, it's just a stray." He was younger than Levi first thought. Maybe around twenty-five. "My girlfriend and our boy are starving. I've seen those three hunting around here before. There's been others, too, but I've never met them."

Levi eyed the three who had stopped and were discussing their next move. Clearly, Levi's presence concerned them.

"Oleg," Levi said on his comm, "this one's friendly. I'm going to attempt contact with those three."

"Copy."

"Here's what I need you to do," Levi said to the young father. "Can you cut off a quarter of the dog?"

"How do I do that?" The young man appeared close to tears. "I don't even know what I'm doing. I'm just trying to gut it and get some meat."

Sure enough, when Levi checked his progress with the dog, there was little sign to suggest he knew what he was doing. Levi had never gutted a dog, but his father had explained the process in detail to him. Gutting any mammal was fairly rudimentary, end to end.

"Okay, don't touch it anymore. Clean off your knife and step back for a minute."

"You're taking my meat?" The man's eyes spilled over. "I can't return with nothing. Not again. We're starving."

"No, no." Levi reached out to console him, but the poor man flinched away. Virus fears. "I'm not taking your meat. Just hold right here for a minute while I talk to these people. I'll make sure you have food to go home with if I have to give it to you myself."

"Who are you?" The man seemed to take in Levi's outfit for the first time—ammo vest, comm device, and assault rifle. "And who's with you?"

"Just know we're friends, okay?" Levi sighed. "I know you've been through a lot. I'm a friend. My name is Levi Caspertein. I live downtown. That's all you need to know. Now, stay here. Don't move. I'll be right back."

Levi started walking slowly toward the three in the street who stood their ground. One loudly chambered a round in his bolt action hunting rifle. In response, Levi raised his left hand, but gripped his rifle across his chest with his right. If need be, he could turn slightly and fire with only his right hand—not always accurately, but effective enough in an emergency. But with Oleg on overwatch, he knew he had little to fear. He'd seen Oleg shoot before.

"That's far enough," said the older man when Levi was still a short distance away. "We don't know where you've been and you don't know where we've been."

"True enough," Levi said. "My friend back there shot a dog. He's not sure how to butcher or quarter the thing, but he's starving. Being that you're good neighbors, I figured you'd help him halve his kill and you all part ways the better for his hunting."

The three glanced at one another, clearly puzzled.

"You're not from around here, are you?" asked the one who Levi figured was the father.

"I didn't know being from around here was necessary to introduce neighbors to one another." Levi gave them his toughest gaze, like he imagined his father might offer with a scolding. "Of course, if you're against sharing, we can just let this gentleman leave with the whole dog. I'll butcher it myself since he's never done it right before.

What do you say? Help him out or do we shoot each other over dog meat that I don't even have an appetite to eat?"

The woman said something too quietly for Levi to hear.

"What's that, ma'am?" Levi called.

"She said, half a dog is better than no dog." The father shifted his rifle on the sling over his shoulder. "I don't know where you were the other day when those army guys came through here stealing all our food. That's the real reason we're out hunting again."

The three approached Levi.

"Was it a three-Humvee convoy on patrol?" Levi asked.

"Wasn't no patrol," said the woman. Her cheeks were ruddy. "That was a hunting party. They hunted down what others had. They killed two horses over near City Heights."

"She's right," said the father. "Weren't their horses to kill or their meat to eat. You seen 'em, too?"

"Yeah, I've seen 'em." Levi fell in beside the father but a few feet away since they were nervous about the virus. "I don't like their style, but they're here to stay. They have five thousand in the barracks out on Coronado Island. We told them no stealing and no killing downtown, but there's no telling what they'll do out here."

"You *told* them?" The father frowned at Levi. "You're just a boy. A tall boy, but still a boy—I'm guessing no older than my own here. You trying to tell me those military men listened to you?"

They reached the dog.

"I'm Levi Caspertein. My father is Titus Caspertein. He's gathered some Special Forces Christians around him to keep the peace downtown. In time, we'll try to extend that influence out here, but one step at a time."

"Special Forces Christians, huh?" The father wrinkled his face. "Jesus and God and all that stuff?"

"Yes, sir. Jesus died for our sins. The least we can do is help neighbors enjoy that same peace. You all think you can work out a neighborhood watch or something? This guy here says he's got a young family to look after and feed. He shot himself a dog, so I figure he's an asset for what you've got going on out there."

The father eyed the young hunter suspiciously.

"You don't have any dry skin patches in your household?" the older man asked the younger.

"No. No virus with us. We've been careful. No contact with anyone."

"Well, you keep being careful and maybe we can work something out. Son, finish that dog." The father's boy knelt to dress the dog, then the men turned to Levi. "I don't know you or your father, but I do know one thing: you're about three months too late to be preaching your religion in this country. Nobody'll listen. We're all on the edge of death. It's over now."

"And that's why you've got to listen," Levi said. "Death isn't the end. Judgement is coming. You better find a Bible and get some answers for your conscience. If you're ever downtown, look for the ELM building by Seaport Village. I'll be there."

"ELM building? I had an office downtown. But I never heard of the ELM building."

"It's new. Or it's an old building with a new name. ELM. Every life matters." Levi backed away and smiled, not too bothered that they looked at him like he was crazy. "Remember that: *every life matters!*"

Levi took a different route back to the park and met Oleg at the picnic table. He briefed the Russian on his interaction with the strangers.

"Doesn't that anger you just a little?" Levi asked as they continued eastward. "Those aren't all patrols General Brogdon has been sending out. They're killing people's livestock and probably confiscating whatever they want. Maybe even killing people."

"Yeah, that angers me." Then Oleg smiled. "But you're doing what Titus always did. You take the evil that people do and you find a way to tell others about Jesus because of it."

"It felt pretty natural." Levi shrugged. "Maybe it was a little preachy, but all I've done is listen to Chevy's Bible teaching, so who can blame me if I sound like him?"

"I'll cover you anytime you want to get preachy, Levi. Anytime you want."

Nodding at his partner, Levi jogged to retake point by a hundred yards. He felt a tremendous sense of victory in reconciling the neighbors, but he immediately felt like a dunce a moment later for not learning their names, especially the young father. For an instant, he was compelled to run back and ask them their names, but their central mission tugged him east.

Suddenly, his comm crackled. Levi stopped and looked back at Oleg. Was he trying to talk to him? Or was there some sort of interference on their frequency?

Oleg walked closer, but he wasn't trying to communicate with him.

"ELM Duo," Levi's comm said in his ear. It was his fathers' voice, but very distant. "ELM Duo, this is ELM777. Listen up. I need your attention. Don't try to respond. There's too much interference where you are. Just listen. Sacred Cow made new contact. Five hostiles showed up. Subject is safe in cockpit. Double-time to remedy the situation. Respond to me with one column of black smoke. I repeat. Sacred Cow . . ." Titus repeated his message verbatim.

"Black smoke?" Levi gazed west. "We're not that far away. You think he'll see it okay?"

"The sun is past its zenith." Oleg studied the street, the countless vehicles, and the quiet residences on either side. "The wind is light. Shouldn't be a problem. We don't have time to roast marshmallows if that girl is cornered inside the plane. Gather some fuel and I'll grab something that will smoke black. Titus will see it and we'll be long gone before anyone else comes to investigate our smoke."

For fuel, Levi tore off the wooden doors of three decrepit sheds and even found some wooden lawn chairs. To start the fire, he used paper trash available everywhere the wind had blown it. As soon as the flames licked skyward, Oleg dropped a single spare car tire onto the fire.

"That's it?" Levi raised his eyebrows. "One tire?"

"That's how we saw them do it in Mogadishu. Your father would've remembered that signal and probably hoped I did, too."

Levi took point and led the way south and east. Restaurants were burned down and used car lots were abandoned. Smart phones littered the sidewalks here and there as if people had grown weary of waiting for the internet or power to be restored. The dead didn't lay stinking in the suburbs as they did in the city. People here had stepped up to bury the deceased. It was probably the same people who Levi saw occasionally out scavenging in the gutters and alleys. Whenever they noticed him, they ceased their work to watch him pass. After waving respectfully, Levi would continue with only a word of warning to Oleg. Most of the civilians they came across didn't appear to be armed.

One street Levi entered had been cleared of broken-down vehicles, store window glass, and even wind-blown trash. The pavement was dusty and bore plenty of boot prints, but Levi was pleased to find a tidy street for a change. However, its cleanliness became a harbinger for danger when he realized all potential cover had been removed from the street. Store windows on the left had been broken out, and he glimpsed a head duck below a sill. There was whispered movement on the right as well— from inside a school bus parked against the curb. Instead of the bus windows being smashed out, it seemed they'd been carefully removed from the frames.

"Oleg," Levi said on his comm, "hang back for a minute. It's awfully lonely here for such a clean street. Over."

"Strange place to park a school bus," Oleg responded. "Get out of there, Levi. Run back to me or run ahead, but get out of there! Over."

"No." Levi slowed his pace to give himself time to think. He resisted the urge to look directly at indications of people in hiding. They were all around him. "They're waiting in ambush to catch both of us. Over."

"I'm not following you in there. Get yourself out. I'll meet you on the far side or at the Sacred Cow if we lose contact. God help you, Levi. I'll cover you the best I can. Over."

Levi lowered his head and let his eyes wander to the right. The school bus probably housed a few ambushers. They had an elevated firing position, and combined with those in the shop windows on his left, running forward or backward wouldn't deliver him. The kill-box had been planned carefully, but not perfectly.

When he was abreast of the school bus, he suddenly darted to the right and dove beneath its chassis. He skidded and rolled behind the front tires when the first gunshots cracked and bullets bit dust near his legs. Men and women alike shouted orders so frantically that Levi guessed his response wasn't the response they normally received from ambushed travelers.

The front tires of the bus shielded him partially from the storefront shooters, but not entirely. Bullets smacked the front of the bus and ricocheted off the pavement. If they had any marksmen among them, he would've been dead already. They were panic shooting.

Before the ambushers on the bus could organize themselves to emerge, Levi lunged to his feet and charged over the sidewalk and up a steep stairway between shops. One flight up, a flimsy door barred his way, but a desperate heel kick smashed the door inward.

He found himself on the landing of a duplex apartment level. Left or right were unknowns. A gunshot fired at him from below. Choosing left, he barged through a deadlocked door. A woman screamed, *"He's up here!"* so he knew he wasn't yet among friendlies. After bounding over a kitchen counter, he crashed through a screen door onto a balcony with potted plants. It was too late to check his momentum. The balcony railing broke against his weight and he fell.

As he fell, he glimpsed his landing on a flat roof ten feet below. Guns still boomed behind him and shouted orders filled the afternoon air, but they seemed to be farther away.

When he hit the roof, he rolled with the collision, bruising his head and shoulder, but he found his feet and came up sprinting. His left pack strap was broken so it jostled against his right side, but there was no time to fix it.

At the edge of the roof, he paused only a second to judge his controlled descent. He leaped for a parked car roof in an alley. The windows blew out as his weight crushed the top of the car. From the roof to the hood to the pavement, he then ran east.

The first street he came to, he turned right and put his back to the cinderblock wall. Gunfire sporadically blasted too far away to be targeting him. *They were on Oleg!*

Shrugging out of his right pack strap, Levi examined the left one. A round had torn through the heavy nylon stitching. He drew a carabiner from a pouch and fastened it to the pack and strap, connecting the two. It was fixed for the moment.

Donning the pack again, he let his rifle hang as he drew his silenced .22 pistol from his shoulder holster. Now was the time to deescalate, not escalate. Working to steady his breathing, he tried to remember his training. Someone shouted nearby and Levi aimed at the edge of the cinderblock, but no one rounded the corner.

The gunfire to the west abated and stopped.

"Oleg?" Levi whispered into the comm. "Are you there?"

"Stay back, Levi." Oleg's words came in great gasps. "They've got me pinned. And I'm hit in the side. I think it's my hip."

Licking his lips, Levi took inventory. He had four thirty-round magazines besides the mag in his rifle. Since he hadn't fired a shot, he had one hundred and fifty rounds of .308 and two mags for his pistol.

"Hold on, Oleg. I'm coming for you."

"*No!*" Oleg panted. "Listen to me, Levi. I'm stashing the rifle. There's some piping here. It's under construction. It looks abandoned. They're probably just hijacking travelers for food. They want our packs. I'll give them mine. Maybe it'll buy me some medical attention. I gotta get this bullet outta me or I'm done. Running away with you won't help."

Levi fought the urge to charge back toward the bus with guns blazing. He didn't want to lose. His father was counting on him. Oleg was counting on him!

"What do you want me to do?"

"I'm not going anywhere, Young Caspertein. Now's the time for wisdom. Sacred Cow needs you more than I do. Get there and sort out her situation. I'll bring a handsome ransom fee. That's about all I'm good for now. Over."

Working out the timeline, Levi figured he could reach the downed plane before nightfall. Sacred Cow had a radio that could reach ELM. His father would know what to do.

"Okay, Oleg, give them your comm. Let me talk to them."

"Easier said than done. Otherwise, I'll see you on your way back—or in the clouds at the last trumpet. Remember who we are. Out."

The comm went quiet. Levi waited anxiously for a moment, thankful he heard no more gunfire. God was with Oleg, even if he was now among adversaries.

"Hello?" The comm clicked with a man's voice. "Is this thing on? Is someone there?"

"This is Levi Caspertein," he said in his firmest tone, as if he were twenty years older. "You have my man there. I'm assuming you're reasonable and want to work something out. Over."

"We don't want to hurt him, but we will." The voice was anything but confident. These weren't professional criminals, probably only townspeople pushed to the brink. "Wherever you're from or wherever you're going, bring us . . . a truck full of food. And we'll let your friend go."

"I understand." Levi sighed and prayed for God's words. "Thank you for keeping this civil. So, I understand we're just arranging a barter. Is that correct? All that gunfire was an accident? Over."

"That's right. Usually we just, um, wait and people surrender. We didn't mean for it to go all crazy like that."

"Okay, I understand your position." Levi checked the street and around the corner. No one seemed to be sneaking up on him. He doubted these people even knew where he'd fled. They'd panicked and opened fire until they'd probably exhausted at least some of their valuable ammunition. "My man there is wounded. You have a doctor or a nurse to keep him alive? Over."

"He says he can guide us to remove the bullet. We'll keep him alive."

"That's good. Thank you. Since you and I are going to work out a business deal together, what should I call you? Over."

"This is Reiser. I'm on the city council."

"And what city is this? Over."

"Well, we came up with a new name two months ago. We're New Encanto."

*A new name?* It wouldn't be on any map, but Levi had a good idea of where he was.

"Okay, Reiser, you hold tight for a day or two. Keep my man comfortable. We'll work this out the right way. I'm gonna find you and your people some food somehow. Try not to shoot anymore travelers, huh? Over."

"Okay, um, Levi Caspertein. No funny business! Or we'll hurt your friend here."

"I understand, Reiser. Now turn off the radio you're using. Save the battery. I'll be out of range anyway for a day or two until I return. Do you understand? Over."

"Yeah, but don't take too long. We have lots of mouths to feed—and now your friend, too."

"Sure, I understand. You'll be hearing from me. Every life matters, Reiser. Can you say that for me? Every life matters. Over."

"Every life matters."

"Good. See? Now we're starting to agree on what's important. I'm leaving now. Take care of my man, Reiser. Out."

Levi slid down the cinderblock wall to sit and bow his head. God hadn't abandoned him. Reiser wasn't a cold-hearted killer, but he was approaching his survival in the least neighborly way. There was a lesson to be taught to this New Encanto, but not yet. Sacred Cow came first.

# *Chapter Three*

Carla Criswell flinched behind the door as a gunshot cracked on the other side of the secure door to the crew lounge.

"Quit wasting our ammo!" shouted a man. "You're not getting through that door. It's built for this. Now get downstairs and help with the food. There's enough for us for a month down there."

"Dusty, you're not giving us orders! I just want to see her, maybe have some fun."

"Well, she's not coming out to play, now go on!"

Squeezing her eyes closed, Carla wished she could return to the silence of the plane when no sound could be heard but the wind blowing sand against the fuselage.

There was a light tapping on the door.

"Hey, lady, I know you're in there. I'm not with those other guys. Come on out now and talk to me. You can't have much food and water in there. We have plenty out here. Open up and let me take care of you. A woman shouldn't be alone in this kind of world. Don't make me force it on you. I'm not leaving until you open up. You can die in there or come into town with me. It won't be that bad. Everyone needs to be with someone these days."

Carla remembered his body odor. They'd called him Dusty. And he'd broken her collar bone. She might never be able to use her right arm again. The pain was still throbbing and constant. To keep the arm stationary, she kept it under her jacket. It was suede material, now ruined in appearance, but it was still warm.

Dusty continued to plead with her, but she was silent and tried to ignore his sick promises of fidelity. Three hours earlier, she'd connected with ELM777 again. At least there were friendly people still in the world, even if they were many miles away. She'd told him the bad news—that five men had trapped her in the upstairs crew lounge. Though she had her food, remaining water, and the shotgun, she couldn't hold out indefinitely.

The kind and confident voice behind ELM777 had assured her a heavily armed rescue team was incoming. He'd even given her the frequency for their comm devices to talk to them as soon as they were within range.

She turned on the radio to try the rescue team's frequency. Dusty was quiet for the moment, or perhaps he'd gone downstairs to join the others in stealing the rest of the provisions.

"ELM333, are you there? This is Sacred Cow. Your people at ELM777 said you were coming. Over."

Carla closed her eyes through another wave of pain from her shoulder. When younger, during her college days, she'd played volleyball and injured her ankle. Now older, the pain seemed more debilitating. It was depressing to think she was being rescued—only to be a continual burden to her rescuers. She wasn't even sure she could walk any distance with this much pain!

"Sacred Cow? I think you're calling me. This is ELM333. Over."

"Hello? Yes! You're there!" She let her tears fall free. He sounded so young! But a lot of Special Forces men were young. She'd interviewed Navy SEALS and Army Rangers before. "How far away are you? Over."

"Close enough to get your signal five-by-five. You still trapped in the Sacred Cow? Over."

"Yes. I'm up in the crew lounge. This is where the cockpit is with the flight-deck lounge and the communications room. I was living up here already. The door is holding, but they keep trying to get through. Over."

"How many? I was told it was five. Over."

"Yes, five. They have guns. They're downstairs bringing up all the food from the storage deck and stacking it near the door. There's a lot down there. They've been stacking it all day—when they're not eating it. Over."

"Oh! Sacred Cow, I see you!"

"You do?" Carla looked toward the cockpit. "What're you gonna do? Over."

"I don't see anyone outside. Can you climb out that cockpit window and drop to the sand? It's only about ten feet. I'll cover you. Over."

"I can't. I'm sorry. One of them hit me with his flashlight. I think my collarbone is broken. I can barely move my arm. Over."

"Okay, then drop me a line or something to climb up. I'll come up to you and we can figure this out together. Over."

"What about your other men?" Carla frowned at the radio. "Can't you just . . . shoot Dusty and the others? ELM777 said you're heavily armed. Over."

"Yeah, I am." The young man was silent for a moment. "I can assess the situation out here in the hot sun for a couple days, or I can join you and get Dusty from the inside. He won't be expecting that. Over."

"All right." Carla's confidence in the ELM people was waning. This wasn't what she'd been hoping for. "Give me a minute to find something to tie together. Over."

She left the radio and returned to the lounge to survey the tables and seats littered with food wrappers. There was no rope, but the bunks had sheets she guessed would work—if she could tie them together with her crippled arm.

From the spare bunk, she stripped off two sheets, twisted them, and laid them end to end on the floor. Not long enough. The spare sheets in the overhead compartment had all been taken in weeks past. The only other sheets were on the bunk she'd been using. She took one off and hoped the three together would reach.

Since there was no way to tie the sheets together with only one hand, she opened her suede jacket and allowed her right hand to hang down to help tie. That simple activity brought tears to her eyes, but she tried to limit her movement to just her fingers. The knots weren't too tight, but the sheets had a high thread count and seemed strong enough to support a grown man.

Finally, she took the sheets into the cockpit and tied one end to the left steering console. Then she slid open the port side window and fed out the remainder of the sheet length. It wasn't much.

Gazing out the window, she watched the landscape for movement. Where was the rescue team and the young man from the radio?

Suddenly, the sheet went taut. He was already at the plane outside—unless Dusty had emerged and seen her sheet-rope!

Carla tugged on the sheet. Someone heavy was definitely on the other end. She hurried back to the lounge, found the shotgun, and lifted it with her left hand. By bracing herself against the cockpit door, she leveled the weapon at the window. If it was Dusty or one of the others, she would kill him. Fear at the prospect of dying herself stole her breath.

A gloved hand grabbed the window sill. She didn't think Dusty or the others had worn gloves.

"Here!" gasped the stranger on the sheet rope. "Take my pack!"

It was him! Carla set aside the shotgun and yanked the man's bulky pack through the window.

"My rifle, too."

She accepted the short weapon no longer than her own arm.

Her guest squeezed his broad shoulders through the window frame, then grunted as he climbed across the pilot's console to drag his hips and legs through. He tumbled to the ground and rolled over, bumped into the co-pilot's chair, and pushed off the console. Carla stood back as he righted himself and stood. He was huge, clothed in a dark green ammo vest and khaki trousers with multiple pockets she'd seen other Special Forces soldiers wear. His hair was blond, his eyes were bright ocean-blue, and his smile was broad. Finally, a truly friendly face!

"Not the most graceful entrance." He chuckled and reeled in the sheet, then closed the window. "Levi Caspertein. Got here as fast as I could."

Carla acknowledged his offered hand, but instead of shaking it, she returned his rifle. He didn't seem bothered by her missing hair or melted face.

"My right arm is pretty useless. Sorry. I'm Carla."

He awkwardly accepted her left hand and shook it gently, but his smile didn't fade.

"No problem. My arms are in good shape." He lifted his pack from the floor and set it on the pilot's seat. "So, this is Sacred Cow, huh?"

She couldn't stop staring. This youth had presence, besides being handsome and tall. But so young!

"The rest of the rescue team is waiting out there?" She glanced at the window. "They'll help us, like, when we leave?"

"No, I'm it." He cringed. "Sorry. You were hoping for more people?"

"Well, I'm . . . glad you came, but there are adult men on the other side of that door. And they have guns."

"Guns, huh?" Levi clipped his rifle to his vest. He didn't appear worried at all. "Okay, that's pretty serious. Do you know what they're doing right now? I don't hear them."

"I think they're still bringing up food stores from the storage deck. There are three aisles of food below. There's a lot since it was fully stocked for the president and his staff when we went down. We were going to pick them up out East. Are you sure we shouldn't call in more of your friends to help?"

"You said there's just five of them, right?"

"Yeah, five. I know one guy's name is Dusty. He seems to be in charge, even though they don't seem to get along too well. He's the one who broke my collarbone."

"After I meet Dusty and his pals, I can make a sling for you. Is that okay? Through here?"

He went first into the lounge to find the sturdy door next to the comm office. His head brushed the ceiling. Her garbage littered the table and booths. She suddenly wished she'd tidied up the place a bit. What a mess!

"It sounds quiet," he whispered, his hand on the locking mechanism. "Close and lock this as soon as I leave. You'll know it's me when I return and knock twice, then twice more."

"What're you gonna do?" Carla felt her panic rising. "You just got here. If something happens to you, I'm in serious trouble. Maybe we can just sneak out during the night and escape into the wilderness."

"No offense, Carla, but I can tell you can't move too well. I'll need to help you out of the plane door, right? I can't help you and defend you at the same time. I'm going to remove the threat. Then we can figure out our exit on our own terms. Either way, we're not leaving tonight. I've just hiked all day. I've been chased and shot at, and I fell off at least one building that I can remember. I know you're scared, but I was born for this. Besides, God has my back. I'm not concerned and you shouldn't be, either."

Carla swore.

"*God?* Are you serious right now?" She covered her mouth with her hand. "I'm sorry, but this is a mistake. I asked for help and they send me a kid with God delusions?"

"God delusions?" Levi's smile returned. "Lady, you're the one who's delusional if you think my being here is just good luck. Close the door, lock it, and wait for me. I'd tell you to pray for me, but you clearly lost track of your Creator a long time ago."

Before Carla could snap a response, he thrust the lever to the side. The bolts slid free of the frame. He released his rifle to hang off his vest and drew a small caliber handgun from under his arm. She hadn't even noticed he had that one. Using one hand, he pushed the door open while aiming his gun with his other.

"There are stairs right there," Carla coached quietly. "They could be anywhere downstairs. There are rooms everywhere!"

He lifted his free hand to silence her, then he passed through. Regardless of his clumsy entrance through the cockpit window, he moved smoothly down the stairs, knees slightly bent, hands steady.

She softly closed the door and pushed the handle to a locked position. *Pray for him? Lost track of her Creator?* The nerve of this kid! He couldn't have been older than twenty-five, and he was lecturing her about God? She was probably twice his age. What did he know about life?

But he was all she had. No one else was coming. No one else on the radio had even responded to her maydays. No one else cared. They were too busy surviving— hoarding, stealing, killing, hiding.

Minutes passed. Carla waited by the door, too afraid to move, dreading that her only rescuer was about to be shot dead by bad men probably more experienced at looting and robbing than he was at shooting and killing.

Suddenly, there were two knocks on the door! Then two more. She was hesitant. He was back already? Something must have gone wrong. Maybe he was realizing he was way out of his league. Or he'd gotten lost in the giant plane.

"Carla, open the door," he said at normal volume.

She unlocked and opened the door.

"What happened? Were they already gone?"

"No." He gently moved past her. His pistol was holstered. "I'm gonna need those sheets."

Following him into the cockpit, she then glanced back. *The door!* Frantically, she returned to close and lock it. Barely had she secured the door when Levi loomed beside her again. He used his teeth on one of the sheet knots.

"Don't come downstairs yet," he said. "I don't want you talking to them."

"They're still here?" She clutched the front of her jacket. "What happened?"

"I took them out. They're unconscious." He eyed the length of one sheet. "This should do. I'll cut it into strips downstairs. You good?"

"What happened?" she demanded. "Just tell me, Levi! What do you mean they're unconscious?"

He sighed and set a patient hand on her good shoulder. She couldn't believe he looked so young yet behaved so maturely.

"You need to relax. Sit down. Eat something. Go through my pack. I brought some energy drink mix. I came to do a job and I'm doing it. Can I go now?"

"Yeah." She looked away and stepped back. "Sorry, I'm just . . ."

"It's okay." He chuckled as he opened the door and left it open to descend the stairs. "I regularly read a book about people who underestimate Christians. I'm not offended."

Carla watched him go then disappear onto the main deck. His pack! Maybe she could figure this kid out by going through his pack.

In the cockpit, she loosened the laces on the canvas and pulled out a dark green parka and another pair of trousers. A watertight pack of food caught her eye. There was energy drink mix, energy bars, and water purification tablets.

Unzipping the outer pocket, she found a toothbrush and a small book. Was it the book he said he'd read? No, it was a Bible. With really tiny print. It appeared well used, even marked up. Carla felt sick just thumbing through its pages. She was in the company of a crazy person. God wasn't even real. Humans had been on their own since, well, whenever humanity had evolved from, well, whatever they had evolved from.

He had nothing she wanted. She returned the Bible to the pouch. The Bible only depressed her. More of his kind probably awaited them wherever he was planning to take her. What did a kid know about this wild world anyway? They'd probably never get back to civilization. This was such a mistake to place her life in the hands of weirdos she'd met on the radio! But all the sane people seemed to be ignoring her or they were already dead.

"Okay, show me your radio. I need to call my dad."

She jumped at Levi's sudden return. He gestured toward the comm office.

"Of course." She left the cockpit and showed him the radio console. "This is his frequency written here, and this is yours. He's your dad, huh?"

"Yeah, back in Seaport Village. That's where ELM is. We run the whole building." He sat down and put on the headset. "The military has been stealing from civilians and ignoring the needs of people all over this area, so we're trying to step up, keep everyone friendly, you know?"

"Right. Friendly." She sat beside him and plugged in her own headset to listen in. "There. It's on. The power indicator says you have plenty of juice. You sure he's listening?"

"We'll find out." Levi pressed the transmit button. "ELM777, this is ELM333 with Sacred Cow. Come in. Over."

"Thank God! All good there, ELM333? Over."

"We've had our share of challenges, but I'm sorting them out. The Lord is providing. Sacred Cow is in good health besides a broken collarbone. We'll spend the night here and start back in the morning. Over."

"How's Oleg taking the march?" He laughed lightly. "He hasn't hiked much for months. He's holding up? Over."

"Oleg was wounded back off the 805 around noon. I'll be arranging transportation back to ELM once I get back to him. He's in the hands of some locals right now. At last contact, he seemed okay. Over."

"Wounded? How? He was shot? Over."

"Some locals panicked. I'm working it out with them in exchange for some food. Over."

"They're holding him hostage for food? Where are you going to get food? Over."

"Sacred Cow has crates of it. Like I said, the Lord is providing. Over."

"Glad to hear, ELM333. If you need assistance, three columns will send the message to me. Your mother and I will be watching the horizon in shifts. Over."

"Copy that. Out."

Levi sat back in the chair and rubbed his face with his hands.

"So," Carla said, "you had trouble reaching me today? Sorry about your man. His name is Oleg?"

"Yeah. He's a tough old Russian guy. Used to be with Interpol before he joined my dad's organization."

"The Christian Special Forces?" Carla tried to hide the disdain in her voice, but by the perturbed look on Levi's face, she hadn't succeeded.

"I should make a sling for your arm, but I need to know where the break is. There are two common kinds of fractured clavicles. The type of sling depends on the kind of fracture."

"You know about this kind of stuff?" She found it hard to despise him when all he did was offer his help. "You're so young. Where did you learn about this?"

"My mother, but Dad knows all kinds of field medicine, too. So does Oleg and Wes Trimble. Wes was CIA up until a few months ago. You'll meet all those people. They've taught me so much. Let's go in here where the lighting is better."

He walked into the lounge and sat on her bunk next to the port windows.

"You talk about your friends and family and their Christianity like it's the most normal thing in the world." She sat facing him and opened her suede jacket. "It's not normal. Your religious fanaticism isn't necessary anymore. Science and technology make God irrelevant. We've evolved."

"Science and technology, huh?"

"Yeah."

He leaned close to her, close enough that she expected to smell him like she'd smelled Dusty when he was close. But Levi didn't stink and his skin was clean.

"Last time I checked," he said, "my smart phone was dead. That's technology for you. It's not dependable. But I can talk to God easier than I can talk to you. Show me where it hurts most. Go ahead. I'm not going to hurt you. Show me with your own fingers."

"All this hurts." She ran her fingers over the skin of her collarbone. "But this most of all, right here."

"In the middle?"

"Yeah."

"Okay. I need to build a brace and not just a sling. It'll help align the clavicle as it heals. The brace will pull your shoulders back, so it might be uncomfortable at first. And you'll need to wear it at night, too."

"For how long?"

"Hmm. I don't know. You can ask Mom when we get seaside. But I'm guessing it'll be for weeks. The brace will help you walk easier without pain, too, and we definitely have some walking to do."

"What about Dusty and those guys?"

"I put them in the rear airlock behind the food storage. They're tied up. They'll get loose, but they can't get out. There's a containment manual override lever on that door. It was probably designed to detain trouble-makers midflight. They have a little food and juice pouches, so they'll survive."

"Well, I don't understand why you didn't just kill them."

"Oh, no. We don't do that. Christians save souls, we don't condemn them. Even bad guys need grace. I'll talk to them about it tomorrow. Tonight, they'll think about what kind of men they are and what kind of death they might be facing if they're left down there. We'll need to take them with us, though, so prepare yourself for that."

"Take them with us?" She scoffed. "Why, so you can try to save their souls?"

"Sure, there's that. But I need them to carry as much food as they can a couple miles west to pay the ransom for Oleg."

"The Lord provided the food?" She shook her head. "Is that what you're going to tell me?"

"Well, I could point out that the food did fall out of the sky." He grinned.

"In a plane!" She cursed. "Your God does nothing. He doesn't exist! It's all in your imagination. Religion is for weak minds. It's holding you back, not helping you."

"This, coming from the disfigured woman who can barely move without pain who was trapped in a crashed plane by men who hurt her?" Levi measured one of the sheet lengths for a brace. "Yeah, you clearly have yourself all together with your own beliefs, Lady."

"You're not being nice."

"Nice? How'd those people die out there in the sand? Two graves. Did you bury them?"

"Yes, I did."

"How'd they die?

"Suicide. They killed themselves."

"Exactly. That's all you have to look forward to—death." He shook his head at her, making her feel like a much smaller person. "At some point, circumstances will end your life. Science and technology won't change that. You say God doesn't exist, but I know Him personally. I'm not even twenty years old and I know God's deliverance from sin and His promises for eternal life. Wishful thinking by weak-minded fanatics can't possibly create the magnitude of joy and confidence I experience with Him. He's the reason I'm here, Lady."

"Stop calling me *Lady!*"

"If I had no compassion and no conscience, I wouldn't be here at all. When you say Jesus Christ doesn't exist, you make yourself sound pretty foolish because He's the reason you exist and the reason I'm going to get you out of here safely. Now stand up. I need to measure you."

She clenched her jaw and stood, offering her back to him to measure for the brace.

"Calling me Lady makes me feel like an old maid. It's disrespectful."

"I'm sorry. I won't call you that anymore. I'll call you by your name, Carla."

"And I'll stop saying your God doesn't exist."

"That's between you and Him." Levi drew a knife from a sheath and cut the cloth. "What people say against Him doesn't change the facts about Him. I'm just setting the record straight so you know what He offers. If you trust in Him for your forgiveness—that's your decision. Hold this."

He gave her the knife to hold. From a thigh pocket, he drew a sewing kit and threaded a needle. The thread was sturdy and she didn't need to tell him the brace seams needed to be double stitched to support the weight of her arm. This was not an unprepared youth.

"Am I really that disfigured?" she asked softly. "I mean, you brought it up."

"I was just stating a fact. Not talking about things doesn't make them disappear. You were badly burned. That's obvious. But scars don't have to be ugly."

"Like, I could use makeup and a wig?"

"What? No. I mean, scars can become symbols. You can use them to tell your story, what God brought you through and what you learned along the way. Scars are only as ugly as the person's heart who carries them."

"You don't talk like a nineteen-year-old."

"All the adults I know have scars. They don't carry them with shame. I mean, if your whole identity is wrapped up in your appearance, then I guess your scars would be pretty embarrassing."

"You think I'm that shallow?"

"I don't even know you, but since you haven't welcomed God into your life for stability, what's left for you to rely on? Your physical appearance? People close to you? Your possessions? I don't know if you're shallow or not. But I do know appearances, relationships, and possessions come and go. Lift your arm across your front. Lower your wrist. I'll tie it here in front so you can remove it yourself when you need to, but I'll help you retie it whenever you want."

"Okay." Carla submitted to his touch as he bound her forearm to her front, then wrapped two straps over her shoulders and connected them to hold her shoulders back. "Hey, I might come out of this with better posture than I had before, huh?"

"See? You're already seeing something precious in what seems worthless."

"Is that like saying I should find the good in a bad situation?"

"Yeah. Finding what's precious in what seems worthless is from the Bible. How's that feel? Try walking around. Lift your good arm. Twist and turn. Breathe with your gut. I know it's tight around your ribs, but you'll get used to it."

"It's good." Carla moved about. "Yeah, this is much better. I can travel with this. Good job. Thanks, Levi."

They stood facing one another for an awkward moment. Carla had her strong critical opinions about what the youth believed in, but she regretted some of what she'd said to him about his God. He was caring for her and he hadn't disappointed her in that regard. In an hour, he'd brought safety and mobility, which she hadn't previously known.

"I should go check on Dusty." He picked up his rifle. "They'll be waking up soon and wanting to know what to expect."

"What're you gonna tell them? Can I come?"

"That's not a good idea. I'm trying to get through to them, to win them. You can't be pushing them away with any animosity you may still carry."

"One of them attacked me."

"They don't even know you."

"So?"

"So, they weren't thinking about you. They were thinking about themselves. You're too close to this to help me help them."

"*Help them?*" Carla swore. "Of course, you want to help them. Fine. I won't say anything. Besides, I don't want to be left alone up here."

He stepped close and held up his index finger.

"Don't make my job more difficult. They're doomed if they don't listen to me, and we need their help to carry everything tomorrow. They're my porters."

"Okay, I won't say a word." She held up her hand as if swearing allegiance, but was unable to hide her smile at his attempted firmness. "But I'm not buying the tough-guy talk. You've told me too much about yourself to scare me."

"I'm not trying to scare you." He walked to the open door above the stairs. "If you and I are friends, I would hope you wouldn't want to disappoint me. I've expressed my plans. The rest is up to you."

She followed him down the stairs.

"What happens if I disappoint you?" She tried not to sound like she was teasing him, but this kid was no fool. "Tell me that."

"You're in a wilderness with violent people all around you. Do you want to grow closer or further away from your only friend?"

"Message received. I was just curious."

They squeezed past stacked pallets of provisions in the corridor all the way back to the conference and dining rooms. Dusty had been busy. His men would need a semi-trailer to haul away that much food.

Next to the security section, they descended to the lowest deck and approached an airtight door with a round port window. Carla peeked through the bottom of the window as Levi looked in over her head. The five men were awake.

"Which one is Dusty?" she asked Levi. "I never really saw them in the light."

"I didn't get their names, either."

"How'd you get them all back here?"

"My weapons fire tranquilizers. Here. Stand back." He knocked on the door, filling the window with his face. "Who's Dusty? Which one of you is named Dusty?"

The most slender and clean-shaven one of the five stepped up to the door. He shoved aside one of his buddies.

"I'm Dusty!" he yelled. He had a welt above his right brow that Carla guessed was from her knee. "Open this door, pal. Open this door or I swear I'll—"

The man swore several threats, but Carla wasn't surprised that Levi seemed indifferent.

"Here are the facts," Levi stated. "You five are my prisoners. Whether I leave you in there to die or let you out on one condition is my decision alone."

"What condition?"

"I want you each to carry a few food pallets for me to reach a nearby town."

"What town?"

"That's not important."

"I'm not carrying anything for anyone. Look at my eye! And what'd you shoot us with? I've got a big ol' bruise on my—"

"Does Dusty speak for all of you? You want to be left in here?" They nodded stubbornly, especially after Dusty glared at them. "Okay, then here's what'll happen. I'm leaving and not coming back. When I get to a town, I'm going to tell the townspeople exactly where to find the plane with all its provisions. And I'm going to tell them about you guys. You really think you'll be better off in the hands of those townspeople? It's a choice between coming with me or being left for a bunch of scared, paranoid, hungry civilians."

"We just have to carry some pallets for you?" Dusty asked. "What if we get out there and decide to carry the pallets for ourselves?"

"Oh, I'll compel you." Levi smiled. "I was hoping you'd accept your lashes as gentlemen, but clearly, I'll be treating you as hostiles along the way."

"What'd he say?" asked a bearded man from inside. "We're getting lashes?"

"Get a good night sleep," Levi said. "I'll get you up early to hit the road. Anything else you want to say, Dusty?"

Dusty stared defiantly. Carla followed Levi away from the detainment door. She didn't know how he was going to do it, but Levi would have his hands full with those five on the road!

✝

One-eyed Wes Trimble sat on the balcony railing of the Hotel Del Coronado gazebo and stared east. If he looked carefully—across the island and beyond the bay— he could just make out the forty-floor apartment building where his friends lived. And his wife, Wynter. He'd been absent from her only a few days, but it seemed like an eternity. He missed Chevy's Scriptural insights, Titus' witticisms, and Oleg's wisecracks about Titus' age, but without Wynter, he felt like part of his life was missing. Their whole future together was on hold—especially their trying to get pregnant—until he returned from this mission.

He missed the gentleness that Annette brought to the group as well. She had already established herself as a nurse and cook, tending to physical ailments and the hungry appetites of the others in the building. Wynter had a much more fiery disposition, which Wes most loved about her, but she laid it all down in the presence of Annette's softer temperament. If the two women hadn't become such good friends since the downfall of America, he and Titus would've had a challenge on their hands.

But Wes knew that after his departure, Wynter had been set to move upstairs to live on Annette's same floor. She wouldn't be alone. Casperteins naturally stuck together like that.

By now, Titus would've shared his ELM vision with the old COIL operatives. Wes had already ridden along on two Pacific States patrols, and each time he'd eagerly watched for signs of an elm tree painted around the city. He guessed that would be young Levi's good pleasure—to get word out to the city's inhabitants that ELM was a fixed presence for Jesus in San Diego—much to General Brogdon's chagrin.

"Trimble!" called someone from the hotel proper. It was an errand soldier whose duty was to watch over the hotel, which now served as the capitol building for the Pacific States. "Sergeant Lesage is waiting for you out front. He'll be leading the patrol today."

Wes waved his hand. He could see out front and the sergeant wasn't yet waiting with the vehicles, but Wes was used to the short treatment he received from most of the personnel. As an outsider, he was viewed with suspicion.

As a Christian, he was treated with disdain, especially by Sergeant Dom Lesage, the general's right hand. The night before at evening mess, Wes had silently bowed his head and thanked the Lord for His provisions. When he'd raised his head, every soldier at the table rose to their feet and relocated to another table. Lesage had smirked his approval from an officer's table nearby. So, Wes had contently eaten alone at the long table, but he was distinctly aware that he wasn't as under cover as he may have hoped.

Lesage did Brogdon's dirty work, Wes had deduced from the thirty-five-year-old's actions around the base. Twice, Wes had witnessed the sergeant mercilessly discipline soldiers for minor infractions, and other soldiers around the base told stories of how ruthlessly Sergeant Lesage treated civilians during patrols and property confiscations. The most recent rumor was that Lesage had drowned a young woman whom Brogdon didn't approve his son having on the base.

"Good thing I'm not here for too long," Wes mumbled and hopped off the gazebo railing. He reached through the rail and picked up his travel pack. Since Brogdon had assigned him as an intelligence observer, he hadn't been issued a rifle, but Wes carried two forty-five caliber handguns—one on his hip and the other under his arm. They were loaded with lethal bullets, as he'd carried during his Agency days. But ever since Titus had manufactured gel-tranqs for the nine-millimeter, Wes had kept a nine-millimeter in an ankle holster loaded with non-lethal rounds. The general knew he had all three, but didn't know about the tranqs.

He walked across the ungroomed grass of the hotel to the parking lot. Sergeant Lesage arrived with Kip Brogdon, the general's cocky son, as Wes arrived at the lead Humvee.

"You're in the last vehicle, Trimble," Lesage ordered.

Without answering, Wes obeyed and loaded his gear into the rear Humvee. He heard some of the troops sniggering, but he didn't mind. His passivity was only a temporary farce. In the few days he'd spent at the hotel, he'd seen all he needed to see—and said all he needed to say to General Brogdon. The troops on the island were quickly becoming like their leaders: brutal conquerors, ruthless but undisciplined in morals and character. Such disorganization at the fundamental level would hinder their effectiveness. As he and Titus had arranged, Wes had dropped the Maddix Striber name to the general, so the ELM movement was securely shrouded in inconsequential ambiguity. Thus, it was time to leave Coronado Island, but carefully if possible. Lesage was no fool, and a spy wouldn't be treated with kindness.

During his previous two patrols with common soldiers, Wes had ridden in the lead vehicle to survey strategic locations for the Pacific States military to set up defensive positions. Riverside Guard was rumored to be pushing south and the general wanted Wes to play a role in both defensive and offensive actions. As was asked of him by his temporary overlords, Wes had reviewed gathered intel on opposing armies to the north, and Brogdon's forces were far superior in both manpower and provisions. The northern forces were better equipped, but Wes knew wars were lost or won based on a military's ability to resupply. The PSDF's near and distant patrols had established themselves as able transporters, securing supply lines as far away as Laguna Beach—LA's backyard. Thus, Brogdon hoped to annihilate the Riverside Guard using his military's maneuverability.

Since Wes knew that the general's appreciation for his strategic skills hadn't translated into appreciation from the rest of the soldiers, it was just a matter of time before he was tested in some way. Maybe he would be required by Lesage to kill someone on behalf of the Pacific

States. This he wouldn't do. Compromise was no longer in his nature, even under cover.

The others loaded into Wes's Humvee and the three-vehicle convoy sped away from the hotel. They cruised down Orange Avenue, past the soldiers' family residences, and onto the Coronado Bay Bridge. Through the back window at his elbow, Wes gazed to the north, observing Seaport Village and the crumbling remnants of the Convention Center. He wondered what Titus had been doing since he'd left. No doubt, now that ELM was making excursions from the building, they were probably rapidly making an impression among the civilian population. The Casperteins had never been known to do anything in a small way.

During his first debriefing, Wes had been surprised at how much the general already knew about Titus Caspertein, but the general's intel was outdated. Brogdon saw everyone as an asset or an enemy. But where Titus was concerned, the general was split. He wanted to use Titus' influence and weapons for his own purposes, yet he was wary of Titus' obvious independence and religious fervor.

The convoy reached Chicano Park, the dump site for the island's residents. They plowed past civilians picking through the trash for anything edible or useful. The soldiers shouted and laughed at the starving people who leapt aside, then their vehicles swerved onto Interstate 5 to head north around the city.

Wes knew the military had been ordered to stay out of downtown since Titus had laid down his rule. Brogdon had said it was for the purpose of rebuilding that he no longer wanted traffic to enter between Chicano Park to Little Italy. But Wes had heard the whispers. The general didn't want to tangle with a local military presence that wasn't intent on anything but cleaning up the city streets. The Casperteins had spoken, and Wes realized Titus' word must've come with some heavenly dread since even

Sergeant Lesage hadn't violated city space since that arrangement.

They took Highway 94 east and careened past wrecked cars and trucks on either side—pushed aside in weeks past by a plow truck Coronado used strictly for clearing roads and highways.

On Highway 805, they turned south, and Wes realized this was no mere speedy patrol. No, intel must've come in. They were going after something specific. Wes had never been on patrol with Lesage, but he knew if the sergeant was present, some sort of enforcement was in the works. Someone had done something or possessed something, and now the Pacific States was responding with force.

The vehicles slowed, turned into a shopping center, and parked facing a monstrous department store. The soldiers piled out of the Humvees and readied their weapons. Wes was the last to climb out and study the storefront. Concrete barriers had been erected in front of the otherwise vulnerable entrance, and plywood had been placed where glass windows had once been. Narrow windows had been cut in the plywood, and Wes saw faces appear in those ragged holes. They were defensive firing positions, and the plywood was no doubt reinforced with tougher material behind it. The store had been turned into a fortress by someone familiar with repelling an aggressive force.

"Get the RPG," Sergeant Lesage ordered two of his men.

Wes stood idly next to his Humvee as the observer he was, but inside, his heart pounded. An RPG would turn the front of the store into kindling and kill anyone near the front. Lesage drew the shotgun from his back and used it as a baton to point out firing positions for his men. Two Humvees were parked farther away to flank any opposition.

Lesage still wore the black armband over his crimson jacket, but instead of being the only black band present, as Wes had seen a few nights earlier, two other men now wore the band. It seemed the sergeant was creating an elite savage force that answered only to him within the regular troops. Wes wore his own crimson jacket with anything but pride. As soon as God opened the door for him to make his exit, he was gone—eager to leave the shameful costume behind.

Where Lesage stood in front of the middle Humvee, he raised a bullhorn with his left hand while his right still wielded the shotgun.

"Citizens of Bonita!" The bullhorn squealed and Lesage slammed it against his thigh to silence the noise. "You have been found in violation of the hoarding laws of the Pacific States. No citizen or household shall possess more than is reasonably attained or held for consumption or used by said citizen or household. You are required to peacefully open your doors for inspection. Failure to comply will result in the enactment of Law Three. Justice will be swift against rebellious citizens. You have five minutes to comply."

Checking his watch, Wes didn't think five minutes or two seconds would matter. The people of Bonita existed off the provisions they'd gathered within the department store. To surrender what they had to the military would mean a slow death with no provisions. Rumor was in Coronado that Lesage left those who resisted with nothing—if he let them live at all.

"Four minutes!" Lesage shouted.

Wes surveyed the edges of the parking lot. Everyone was watching the department store. He could walk away right then—toward a fenced street of residential houses shadowed by trees. After walking for a couple of days, he could be back downtown, hopefully without running into the PSDF along the way!

But running away now wouldn't help the survivors of Bonita.

"Sergeant?" Wes joined Lesage's side. "Do you want a massacre or their provisions?"

"I don't mind the blood," Lesage sneered. "It sends a message."

"You could ruin a lot of gear in a drawn-out battle."

"That's what the RPG is for. It won't be drawn-out."

One of the men with a black arm band rested the grenade launcher tube and rocket on the dusty pavement.

"No doubt you have them outgunned. They see that. Let me go in and convince them to surrender."

"Three minutes!" Lesage yelled on his bullhorn, then to Wes, "Three minutes, Trimble. That's all you get. If you're not out by then, you join their fate."

Wes wanted to tell the officer he'd rather die with the lowly than reign with the proud, but he instead used those precious seconds to approach the building. There was a door fashioned in the plywood exterior with a window. He opened his jacket to show he was armed, but that his weapons weren't drawn.

Ten feet from the window, he stopped. A black-bearded Hispanic face filled the window.

"My name is Wes Trimble. I'm hoping to convince you to surrender so you can survive. Otherwise, Sergeant Lesage means to kill you all. He has priors."

Someone near the window spoke Spanish. The man responded then addressed Wes.

"You don't approve? Do something."

Tilting his head, Wes smiled. He looked back at Lesage standing without any cover fifty yards away.

"You know, my Bonita friends, I will do something, but it won't be the end. General Brogdon has five thousand soldiers eager to shed blood whenever they leave Coronado Island. You've been targeted. It won't end until they have everything you have."

"We won't be intimidated. What little we have is for our people."

"I know. But they don't care. They live by the law of greed. I suggest you leave with all you can before reinforcements arrive."

"And go where? We can withstand an attack. We're prepared for a siege."

"There won't be a siege," Wes said. "Ten minutes away, they have armored vehicles, tanks, and more RPGs. Or they'll just bulldoze your building down. If they can't take what you've got, they'll make sure you don't get to keep it, either."

"What're you gonna do?" asked the bearded man. "You said you'd do something."

"One minute!" Lesage shouted.

"When I get back over there," Wes said, "can you fire a few harmless rounds toward us?"

"Gladly, but I make no promises about them being harmless."

"Just try not to hit me."

"I can't promise that, either."

"In the confusion, I'll take them out." Wes shook his head. "But they'll blame you. And others will come."

"So you said. We'll make our stand here."

"Your women and children may not share your fatalistic approach. Go. Hide somewhere else."

Wes waited for him to respond, but the stubborn man was finished. He turned his back and walked back to Lesage.

"They want to make their stand here," Wes said. "I think they have steel plating behind that plywood. Small arms won't penetrate it."

"Maybe." Lesage glared at the store. "But a grenade will."

"Then you know what you're doing," Wes said. "Unless you want to give me a rifle, I'll just find some cover back here."

"Time's up!" Lesage announced, then turned to his grenade launcher. "Fire one right down their throat. See how they like shrapnel for lunch!"

At the front bumper of the middle Humvee, Wes knelt and drew his nine-millimeter and one extra magazine he carried of non-lethal gel-tranqs. He wasn't about to stand aside for a slaughter.

The black arm band with the RPG launcher raised the tube. A burst of gunfire spat from the storefront. Wes flinched as bullets peppered the pavement left and right of him, but his Bonita friends were either terrible marksmen or they missed him intentionally.

The troops opened fire with gusto, a steady stream of automatic gunfire. The RPG launcher hesitated after the first barrage, but Lesage urged him to fire.

Wes raised his sidearm and tranquilized the RPG carrier before he could fire. Then he gel-tranqed Lesage in the backside. None of the troops were experienced enough to recognize that the bodies falling among them were shot from behind them. They crumpled one after another as Wes stalked mere paces behind their line of soldiers.

He tranquilized eight men before the two men with each of the flanking Humvees turned their rifles on Wes. Wes rushed the Humvee on the right, welcoming more gunfire from the department store that kept the remaining soldiers pinned down yet exposed to him. The two went down. As he turned toward the last two men on the left flank, they seemed to count their chances and chose to flee. They climbed into their Humvee and sped away before Wes could tranq them.

The RPG shooter was unconscious from the gel-tranq, but the young soldier had also taken a round in the arm from the store. Wes took off the man's jacket and found his wound was a through-and-through. He dressed the wound by cutting up the jacket and tying it around the unconscious soldier's arm.

Another soldier to Lesage's left had been fatally shot, perhaps by accident or even by friendly fire, where he'd dropped unconscious from Wes's weapon. Wes felt for the man's pulse, then bowed his head in sadness for a moment. The consequences of violent living often returned upon the violent, though Wes had hoped to save lives, not waste them.

A dozen Hispanic men and women emerged from the store and cautiously approached Wes and the two remaining Humvees.

"You shot your own people," said the bearded leader. "I didn't believe you would."

"They're only tranquilized." Wes reloaded his sidearm. "They'll wake in an hour or less. Take what you want, but don't harm them, and leave me that Humvee. You can have the other one."

"They're only sleeping?" The man translated for his friends who were already stripping the soldiers of their weapons and gear.

Wes retrieved his field pack before it was taken, then watched the commotion of spoils being taken.

"You have made trouble for yourself," said the bearded man.

"Oh, you have no idea." Wes chuckled. "But it was worth it. Your lives matter. Every life matters to God."

"The one-eyed man has friends in Bonita." He offered his hand. "I am Miguel Garcia. Do you shake hands?"

"Friends are more important than fear." Wes smiled and shook the man's hand. "But caution for the virus is still wise."

"I agree!" Miguel laughed and joined his companions as they took away their trophies.

Lesage and his men were stripped of their weapons, gear, jackets, boots, and some even to their shorts. One of Miguel's women drove the Humvee away and Wes climbed into the other one. He waved as he drove out of the lot. The people had been warned of the wrath to come if they stuck around. The rest was in their hands.

Wes had his own safety to think about now. Of course, one perk for using non-lethal ammunition was that he couldn't be blamed for taking lives, so that wasn't on his conscience. As far as he knew, the Pacific States hadn't known of the gel-tranqs in ELM personnel use, but his actions that day would change all that. The relationship between the PSDF and ELM would now be strained. Titus had expected it to happen sooner or later—especially if Wes had to part ways under conflict, like what was happening that day.

The Humvee was his own spoil from a won battle, but Wes wasn't about to parade his trophy downtown. Nor did he want to enter the interstate and risk running into another patrol.

He reached the eastern side of National City and drove slowly along an industrial avenue until he saw a half-collapsed warehouse—its walls and roof of flimsy metal rather than steel. At medium speed, he drove the Humvee twenty feet into the side of the building, allowing the aluminum to collapse over him. Such was his hiding place for the vehicle that he could only exit using the passenger door. Then he crawled with his pack from under the metal sheeting until he reached the parking lot. Looking back, he couldn't see any sign of the vehicle, which had a half-tank of fuel and an extra gas container in the back. Nothing else of value had been left behind.

Shouldering his pack, Wes walked north. Though he was glad to be free from the Pacific States regime, he believed their fury would be long-lasting. However, he knew the Lord could use any situation for good in the long run. And it never hurt to have the Caspertein family in his corner.

Rather than walk along the bay, Wes chose to remain inland a good distance and followed the nearby interstate to the north on his trek back toward downtown. Evening was approaching, and though he figured he could reach his wife by walking through the night, he knew there were still roaming bandits who ruled the darkness. Since his number of gel-tranqs were getting low and he wasn't about to use lethal ammunition to defend himself, he kept his one good eye alert for shelter in the oncoming darkness.

On one cleared street between National City and Encanto, Wes noticed a school bus that might offer adequate cover through the night. The evenings had been temperate, so he guessed the Pacific States jacket he still wore would be enough in which to curl up on some bus bench or even on the floor. When traveling around the world for Pacific Rim Security during his Agency days, he'd slept in harsher environments.

The bus appeared to be in good condition except for the missing windows. He set a hand on one window sill to lift himself up and peek inside. Instead of examining the interior of the bus, he found himself looking down the barrel of a semi-automatic rifle.

He backed away slowly, his hands raised. People whooped and hollered as they materialized from the shop windows across the street and more emerged from within the bus. Wes was jostled by common citizens who shoved him into the middle of the street, surrounded him, and stripped him of his weapons, including his nine-millimeter in his ankle holster. His pack was taken, then his jacket was torn violently off his arms and handed to a middle-aged man in a polo shirt who may as well have been a suburban solar panel salesman by the look of him. His hair was trimmed and his face was clean-shaven, which was usually a sign of a source of hot water in those days.

"Is this your jacket?" The man turned and showed off the crimson jacket to thirty of the townspeople who each carried a firearm of some sort. His profile gave Wes a distinct view of the man's exceptionally large nose, narrow and pointed. "We've seen these jackets before, haven't we?"

"I'm not with the Pacific States Defense Forces," Wes said. "I was, but I left them."

"You did, huh?" The man lifted his head. "He says he left the military. How convenient. That couldn't have been too long ago. Your jacket is in good condition. Yeah, we've had your kind come through here before. We don't take too kindly to raiders and rapists. Understand?"

"Look, I'm just a traveler trying to get home to my wife." Wes slowly lowered his hands to his sides. "I made the mistake of keeping the jacket when I left my patrol unit."

"But how many people did you hurt while you were with your unit?"

The crowd shouted for him to be tortured, whipped, and starved among other things. The big-nosed man finally raised his hand and silenced the crowd.

"We're civilized here, mister. We have a city council and everything. Families, kids to raise, a retirement plan. Even started a school and a bakery. But the military keeps driving through here. They say they can take what we have and we don't have much. So, tell me, who cares about you? If you died, would anyone care at all?"

The people watched eagerly for his answer.

"Yeah, my wife. She'd care. I know good people, people who aren't in the military, who would like to see me returned unharmed. They'd be grateful to you."

"How grateful, huh?" the man asked and the people whispered and giggled at his connotation. "Would they be so grateful that they'd pay us? So grateful that they'd . . . feed us?"

"I don't know." Wes was starting to catch this man's intentions. "It's tough on everyone these days. We're all barely managing with basic necessities."

"You red jacket people seem to be doing pretty good. Maybe when they come looking for you, we cut a bargain for some food?"

"My people are kind-hearted," Wes said, "but they don't take kindly to threats. You don't need to threaten us to receive a helping hand if that's what you need. We fear God as followers of Jesus Christ. To us, every life matters."

A perceptible mumble swept through the crowd. Even the big-nosed leader suddenly seemed concerned.

"Why would you say that? Why would you say every life matters?"

"That's what we believe. Your life matters to God, so your life matters to those who worship God. We look out for our neighbors."

"You're one of them." The man backed away. "He's one of them, everyone! That's two of them in two days!"

"Two of who?"

"Every life matters. That's what the last guy said on the radio."

"What guy?"

"Levi Caspertein. He said he'd be back by now with food. We have his friend, Oleg."

"You have Oleg Saratov here?" Wes rested his hands on his hips. "You're holding him for food? I told you, my people would readily give you food or help you plant gardens. This isn't necessary! We're not your enemies. You have nothing to gain by crossing the Casperteins."

"Who is he, this Levi Caspertein? Will he return with food?"

"Levi?" Wes adjusted his eye patch. "You have to understand something about the Casperteins. They're reckless. They don't care about the odds against them. If you have Oleg, Levi will be back. The whole Caspertein family may show up. The Pacific States won't even tangle with the Casperteins."

"There's a lot of them? They're a big family?"

"It's not so much their number as it is their divine support. You never win taking on a Caspertein. You might want to rethink your whole strategy here. The virus is still circulating. The military is on the move. You need the Casperteins on your side, not as adversaries."

"What if we held both of you? Would the Casperteins pay us then?"

Wes shook his head. With everything going on and now this?

"What'd Levi tell you?"

"He said he'd be back here in a day or two with food. That was two days ago."

"Two days, huh?" Wes had been absent for about four days. Clearly, much had happened he didn't know about if Oleg and Levi were this far east of downtown. Titus had enough food in storage to feed these people, but not for long. Where else would Levi get enough food to pay a ransom for Oleg? "If Levi Caspertein told you he'd be back with food in two days, then he'll be back."

The crowd sighed, smiled, and visibly relaxed.

"Do you want to see Oleg?" asked the leader.

"Please!"

The leader's name was Reiser, he explained as he led Wes around the bus and into a building with apartments above. The people moved as one behind Wes, which Reiser said was okay because they did everything together in New Encanto. They were sixty souls total, half of them kids, and it took all of the adults to keep the street watched day and night for travelers to ambush. Only the military coming through had made them stand down—and twice the red jackets had stopped to search their buildings, taking everything of value, especially food.

Wes was brought to a back room where Oleg lay on a twin bed behind a washer and dryer covered with greasy engine parts. Two men with assault rifles sat in chairs nearby playing cards.

"Laying down on the job?" Wes asked as he stood over Oleg. When Oleg was slow to respond and Wes noticed his skin color seemed off, Wes quickly knelt and took his friend's hand. "You're wounded."

"Got me in the hip." Oleg was visibly weakened. "Lost some blood."

"It was a stray bullet," Reiser said. "A complete accident. We almost never shoot anyone. Travelers just give us their stuff. But he ran. And Levi Caspertein got away."

"You've got to get this man out of here," Wes said firmly to Reiser. "He should be on fluids and antibiotics. Reiser, no discussion! Look, keep me in his place until Levi shows up, but Oleg needs to get downtown to my people."

"The Casperteins?"

"Yes, Annette Caspertein knows all kinds of medicine. So does my wife, who is also a Caspertein."

"How would we move him?" Reiser shrugged. "We don't want him to die, but downtown may as well be fifty miles away."

Wes turned away. The Humvee was a risk, but he saw no way around it. Oleg needed to get home. The Pacific States might already be on the rampage, but Wes would have to worry about that later.

"I have a vehicle," he said to Reiser. "It's about a mile south. Give me one of your men and we'll go get it. Then I'm driving Oleg downtown. Don't argue with me! We'll sort out your food payment later. You have my word as a man of God, but we need to think of Oleg now."

"Okay. I'm trusting you. Go!"

# *Chapter Four*

Levi walked slowly beside Carla, both following the five thieves who'd tried to hijack the plane's contents. Carla placed her feet carefully on the packed sand, obviously concerned about tripping and hurting her shoulder more, but she wasn't the only reason their troupe moved so slowly.

"This is cruel and unusual punishment!" Dusty complained under the weight of three pallets of food. Levi had bundled each of the men's packs himself, making shoulder straps out of the blankets from the crew lounge. "You'll pay for this, Levi. I swear you'll pay for this!"

"You're right," Levi said. "I already told you I'm paying you for this. You carry this food for me and I'll give you some of it."

"I'm not even going to want to look at this food when I'm finished carrying it wherever we're taking it!" The second complainer trudged in front of Dusty. He was one of three men in Dusty's group of five who'd admitted to being released early from prison a few months earlier. "If I don't collapse dead first!"

Levi took Carla's good arm to steady her as they stepped over a drainage ditch, reaching the first paved but sand-covered street.

"Finally, out of the wilderness!" She looked back from where they'd come. "I'll almost miss it. *Almost.*"

"Can we take a break?" Dusty asked. "There's a container digging into my back."

"We just had a break five minutes ago," Levi said. "Remember our agreement when we started: we take water and bathroom breaks every thirty minutes. Keep going."

"How much farther?" whined another man of about thirty, prison tattoos covering one arm. "My legs are tired."

There was no need to respond, Levi figured. They'd gotten a late start since he'd needed to secure his porters one at a time from the plane's detainment area. He remembered Dusty's snide confidence that the five would overpower Levi, but Levi merely handed his pistol to Carla. After that, Levi duct-taped each of the men's left hand to the pallets of food they were to carry.

They couldn't free their hands without a knife to cut away the tape, and they couldn't run away or fight effectively with forty pounds of pallets secured firmly to their forearms. Each man carried three pallets. Though they were strong enough to carry more, Levi guessed they'd already be moving at a crawling pace as it was. He hadn't been wrong.

Carla was the only one who carried nothing. Levi had repacked a backpack of her possessions and hung it off his own pack, which contained extra water and food for the journey for all seven.

"I'm nervous." Carla held onto his right arm. Levi knew she didn't really need steadying on the pavement, but she was clinging to the only stable thing she knew, and that was him. "I haven't been around civilized people for so long."

"You never have to worry about being around my family. They accept and care for anyone who wants to be cared for."

"But I'm not a Christian."

"They'll still accept you even if they don't approve of your beliefs. Hey, guys, stay to the right up here. Avoid that pile of garbage."

"I don't have any beliefs."

"Yes, you do." Levi checked their surroundings. With six souls to think about, he wanted to spot a threat in advance. He sure never wanted to be ambushed again. "You may not yet believe in God, but you trust in something. That's your religion."

"I trust nobody but myself."

"So, you trust in your own thinking and ability as a human being?"

"No one else is going to look after me the way I look after myself."

"A minute ago, you said you're nervous. Do you know why you're nervous?"

"Like I said, I haven't been around people."

"I think you're nervous because of the unknown and you're out of control. A rejection of the God who created you leaves you grasping for things to replace Him. That's what my friend Chevy taught me. Nothing is out of God's control or knowledge, but you push Him away every time He touches your spirit, so you're nervous without Him when you think about what may happen next."

"You don't get nervous? You're never afraid?"

"When I am, I lean by faith on the Lord. Then I'm immediately set right. I'm not better than you, Carla. You and I were created the same by God. But we're choosing to rely on different things to fulfill us. The benefits we enjoy emotionally come directly from the stability of the things we believe in. What or who we rely on determines how we regard everything in life."

"There's no way you're only nineteen years old!" Carla cursed.

"You're only nineteen?" Dusty stopped and looked back. "No way is a teenager making me take another step. This is stupid! I would've never agreed to this if you didn't have those guns!"

The four others stopped as well. Levi walked to the side, knowing not to get too close.

"We all had guns yesterday," Levi said. "You had yours and I had mine. Since you had me outnumbered, you had the advantage. Where are your guns now?"

"I'm not playing this game with you anymore, Levi!" Dusty grunted in pain as he plopped down to sit on the street. He wrestled to take the pallet straps off his shoulders, but his left hand was still taped securely. "I'm finished."

"If you're finished, then you get no food. That was the deal, remember?" Levi drew his knife and clicked the lock-blade open with a snap of his wrist. "You want me to cut you free? I'll be leaving you here with no weapons. Look around. Those houses over there—who's to say there aren't cannibals living in them? People are starving."

"Cut us loose and I'm outta here," Dusty said.

"Oh, no. I'll be tranquilizing you again if I cut you loose."

"What?"

"Not us, Levi," pled one of the other four. "We never wanted Dusty with us in the first place. We'll carry the food. I just want this over with."

"Dusty, you'll be lying there all defenseless and sleeping right there in that filthy gutter. I'm not going to turn you loose so you can run back to the plane and get your guns and Carla's food."

"It's *our* food and you're taking it!" Dusty spat. "This isn't fair!"

"Carla's the last living occupant of the plane. You came and tried to steal the food. That doesn't make it yours. She's agreed to let me use the food to secure passage back to people waiting on me. Enough stalling. Are you going forward to receive food for your labor, or are you staying here with no food?"

"How long would I be asleep if you tranquilized me?"

"About an hour. By that time, I'll have reached New Encanto to tell them where they can find three more truckloads of food pallets. They're a town full of gun-toting people. You think you can beat them back to the plane with no boots?"

"No boots?"

"Well, I'm figuring whoever is in those windows over there watching us, once they see you napping against the curb, they'll come get your boots first, even if they're not cannibals."

Dusty hung his head and mumbled something.

"What's that?" Levi asked, stepping closer with his knife.

"I said, help me up. *Help me up, all right?*"

Levi closed his knife and lifted the man and his pallets back to his feet. Before letting go of Dusty's collar, he moved close enough for Dusty to take a swing with his free hand if he wanted to.

"I'm not giving you five the real punishment you really deserve. That's called mercy. You hurt Carla and tried to steal all that food. You're fortunate I showed up instead of someone else who believes in an eye for an eye. You'd be rotting in the wilderness right now instead of living a little longer to repent of your sins. Now march. We're nearly there."

The five picked up the pace ahead of Carla and Levi.

"Last night," Carla said, "when you claimed you would compel them, I doubted you."

"And now?"

"I'm learning not to doubt you."

Levi smiled, but wished her acceptance of his words extended to what he'd shared about God. She needed the Gospel, but she couldn't grasp the gift of eternal life until she understood her need of a Savior who would save her from the wrath of God. He prayed about this for another mile, which took twenty minutes to walk until the school bus came into sight.

As they drew near the site of the previous ambush, Levi was relieved to see the townspeople hesitantly emerging from their shops and the bus. They approached the five porters carrying the pallets, their faces full of disbelief at the amount of food before them.

"Who's Reiser? I'm Levi Caspertein," Levi called over their heads. Carla hid her face behind his right shoulder, gripping his ammo vest from behind. "Reiser, show yourself!"

"Yeah, I'm right here." The big-nosed leader pushed through the crowd. He held Oleg's comm in his hand. "It's almost sundown. I thought you'd be calling me on this by now."

"I had my radio off and my hands were full, as you can see." Levi pointed at a woman whose fingers reached out to touch a food pallet. "Stay away from them, ma'am. These men are criminals. Reiser, we had a deal. There's fifty times this amount of food a few hours away. It's yours. I'll draw you a map, but my man Oleg needs to be released."

"Oleg's already gone." Reiser looked away.

"He's dead? What happened? I thought he was only wounded."

"No, he's not dead, but he wasn't well. Your other friend, Wes Trimble, took him. He had a Humvee and they took Oleg downtown a couple hours ago for your people to treat him."

"Wes Trimble?" Levi studied Reiser's face. The leader couldn't possibly know the name unless he'd really met Wes himself. But for Wes to help Oleg by using a Humvee may have compromised himself with the Pacific States military. "Then we're done here. These men are now in your custody. They're thieves and probably killers, but I promised them food if they carried these pallets for me. Do I have your word they'll receive something from what they carried? The rest of the food is yours."

"What do we do with them?" Reiser asked with a critical eye on the five.

"Turn those four loose," Levi said, then took hold of Dusty's arm. "But after this one has had his final meal, I'd execute him. He's been nothing but trouble."

"*What?*" Dusty's eyes widened. "Levi, please! You're a Christian! I heard you talking. You can't kill me!"

"Your own men don't even want you with them. You'll be nothing but trouble wherever you go on your own. If they execute you tonight, they'll probably be saving someone's life by removing you from the Earth. I doubt you'll ever change."

"We don't mind, Levi," said Reiser. "We've had to execute a couple others already. They were thieves and killers, too."

"Levi, *no!*" Dusty gasped. "You can't let them kill me! I'll change. I promise! I take it all back. Carla, I'm sorry for hurting your arm. I just wanted—"

"Cut him free from the pallets of food," Levi commanded the men he understood were in Reiser's charge, "but keep him tied up until you execute him. Reiser, you have a pen and paper? I'll draw that map for you."

The five criminals were cut loose from their pallets. The four were each given a day's ration of food from the pallets, but Dusty was given nothing as his wrists were bound behind his back. One of Reiser's men pushed Dusty's face against the side of the bus and held him there.

The townspeople carried away the pallets of food to some communal pantry, and Levi was left on the street with Reiser and a few of his men and women. Carla remained close enough that he felt her against his shoulder.

"Levi," Carla said, "that's kind of cruel, don't you think? I mean, an execution for Dusty? What about the food you promised him?"

"They'll probably give him a last meal."

A woman gave Reiser a pencil and tablet who offered it to Levi. Taking off his pack, Levi sat on the curb in front of the bus to sketch a map to the plane.

"I'll spare his life," Levi said quietly to Carla, "but not until he sweats a little for it. People take for granted what they have until they realize it's all about to be lost."

"He's crying right now," Reiser observed, having heard Levi. "You Casperteins have strange methods, but they seem to work. I've never made a man cry about his wasted life before."

"Reiser, this is Carla." Levi didn't look up from his sketch. "I brought her back from the wilderness, too. The food pallets you're getting for your people were hers on the plane. The least you could do is offer her safe lodgings with your community here. She should know she has another option besides coming back to ELM where she'll be around us Christians."

"Levi!" Carla slapped his shoulder, then winced from the pain it caused her own shoulder. "I'm not staying here!"

"Well, you'd be welcome," Reiser said. "I suspect we're more capable than most neighborhoods nowadays. Except for when the Pacific States comes through, everyone else leaves us alone."

"But Levi, you said you were taking me to your home on the bay!"

"You agreed to that before you had anywhere else safe to go." Levi looked up from his sketch. "I don't want you to be uncomfortable. If you really don't like Christians that much, you'll definitely be uncomfortable, because that's all we are—a bunch of Christians."

"No, I thought—" Carla stuttered. "I don't understand you! But I don't trust anyone else. Unless you don't want me with you. I thought we, you know, we were getting along."

"We are, Carla. I just want you to be sure. Because us believers, we're not going back to thinking like the world thinks. We depend on God for our very life and future." Levi stood. "Here you go, Reiser. Right now, no one knows about that plane, but I wouldn't wait long. You need to go get those pallets and get them put somewhere safe immediately."

"There's really a lot, huh?" Reiser asked. "For all of us?"

"You'll see." Levi shook the man's hand. "Glad everything worked out between us, but I'll be needing that comm back—and anything else Oleg left behind."

"Wes Trimble took his gear with him. Except for the food in his pack, we returned it all." Reiser gave back the comm and transmitter. "For what it's worth, we're sorry about Oleg."

"God used a bad situation to bring people together." Levi gestured toward the bus. "I'd better see to Dusty, then get on our way."

He and Carla walked away from Reiser who was studying the map with several of his people.

"What are you going to do with him?" Carla asked. "I mean, if you're not going to have him executed, then what?"

"You think there's any hope for him?"

"I don't know. Maybe. I guess so. If he changes."

"So, what if what's best for him meant him coming with us downtown?" Levi watched her face. "Would you still want what's best for him then?"

"Coming with us?" Carla frowned. "I'm learning this is how you do things . . . If you think it's right, I guess so."

"Let me have him," Levi told the townsman who was keeping Dusty braced against the bus. The man left and Levi turned Dusty to face him. "What do you want, Dusty?"

Dusty's eyes went from Levi's face to Carla's and back again.

"Well, I . . . want to live."

"Okay. I'm not surprised. If you died today, you'd probably go to hell after the Judgement. Coming before God in humility for forgiveness is your only hope. It won't be easy moving forward."

"I've never done anything hard." Dusty swallowed. "I've always . . . taken the easy way."

"Yeah, I understand. And that's brought you here, to the point of execution. Not long ago you were cursing and threatening me. You and I are standing face to face now. Our meeting last night was no accident. I don't want our parting to be pointless. I'd sure like to see more of what God has in mind for you if you came to walk beside me. No games. No promises. I have hope that you'll find the path you can walk with your head held high, your conscience clear. Are you ready to see what the God of the Bible has to say about that?"

"With you?" Dusty glanced up the road. "No more carrying pallets?"

"And no more taking what isn't yours. God made you a man to live mightily, not like some weak predator in the dark. You willing to start fresh?" Levi offered his hand. "The past is forgiven in my eyes. Let's move forward. What do you say?"

"You're a strange one, Levi Caspertein." Dusty shook Levi's hand.

"That's what I'm always telling him." Carla smiled.

"Let's go home." Levi shrugged on his pack. "I don't know about you two, but I could sure use a hot shower."

"A shower?" Carla blinked. "I haven't had a hot shower in months!"

"There's hot running water back at ELM." Levi led the way up the street, away from the bus and New Encanto's ambush site. "Did I tell you about ELM, Dusty?"

"No." He walked on Levi's left while Carla stayed on his right, her good hand on his arm. "I'm still recovering from the news that I won't be executed."

"That's really what ELM is all about," Levi said. "ELM is a motto designed for everyone to realize their pardon from death. It was my dad's idea . . ."

On Levi's way out of New Encanto, he stopped at a construction site and searched several water pipes until he found Oleg's stashed rifle and ammo vest. He took a risk and handed them both to Dusty to carry.

✞

Titus stayed out of the way as Chevy and Wes moved heavy Oleg from a litter to his bed on the twenty-seventh floor. Annette and Wynter were already there. Wynter cut away Oleg's soiled bandages and clothing as Annette hung a bag for fluids and started an IV for direct antibiotics. If the others hadn't been there, Titus could've seen to Oleg himself. The two had traveled together for years and doctored each other's wounds after every serious mission. But Oleg was conscious and he would definitely prefer the softer touch of the women who were just as qualified to nurse the big Russian back to health.

Chevy hovered, perhaps more concerned than the others since Oleg was his roommate. Besides, Titus knew Chevy's heart was still carrying the fresh wounds of losing his four teammates in North Korea. Losing Oleg would add salt to those wounds. As Titus watched, Chevy bowed his head, his hand on Oleg's bare chest.

"We're gonna clean everything first," Annette said to Wynter. "Here, betadine and cotton. Go ahead."

Wes backed away from the bed and joined Titus against the wall where Oleg and Chevy had removed a huge flatscreen.

"It's not a fatal wound," Wes said, "as long as we keep infection at bay."

"Good thing you brought him back." Titus eyed Wes's red jacket. "I doubt the people he was with had the antibiotics we do. Unless you would've taken him back to Coronado Island with you."

"No, I've burned that proverbial bridge." Wes adjusted his eye patch, the strap on the back of his head having slipped during Oleg's transport. "I tranqed a whole PSDF unit that was about to massacre some civilians in Bonita."

"It ain't easy making your exit from wicked and unfriendly company."

"I got what we needed—and left what we wanted."

"Maddix Striber?"

"General Brogdon debriefed me himself—a whole day. It's just a matter of time before they start looking for the Chronicle."

"Levi will plant a vague seed here and there along those lines during his travels. We'll keep this between us three for the sake of the subterfuge."

"Noted." Wes slapped Chevy on the shoulder as he joined them. "He's in good hands."

"This was all some sort of accidental ambush he and Levi walked into?" Chevy asked. "Oleg said he left behind his rifle, but Levi knew where to look for it. Any word from your son?"

"I tried him a couple times." Titus shook his head. "No smoke signals. He's probably on his way back from the wilderness with the Sacred Cow survivor by now."

"Unless he runs into my mess with Sergeant Lesage," Wes said. "Two men with one Humvee got away from me. The locals took one vehicle and I took the other and made my getaway."

"We had a deal with Brogdon," Titus said. "Operational vehicles and fuel go to him. You've effectively departed their company. Now we need to keep to our word and return their Humvee."

"They aren't going to be happy," Chevy said. "How do we do this without inviting retribution?"

"Maybe you hang back and cover us, Wes," Titus said. "And get rid of that jacket."

"I'll put it in the closet. Might come in handy someday." Wes took off the jacket. "They'll be looking for me. I've endangered us all. We knew I'd be coming back, but not how. And it came as a surprise to them."

"Sergeant Lesage won't be the only one coming," Titus said. "Brogdon will probably take this personally as well."

"No doubt about it." Wes hid his grin unsuccessfully. "I tranqed his son Kip along with the others."

"This could blow up fast," Chevy said. "Options?"

"We act fast. Right now." Titus nodded. "Before God, we behaved in ways that preserve life, so our consciences should be clear on this. Let's not worry about the consequences of doing what's right. And we don't have to explain ourselves unnecessarily to the Pacific States. Tell them the truth: Wes, you stopped the slaughter of civilians and took your leave of the Pacific States. They don't need to know your departure was planned all along."

"After only four days?" Wes flinched. "It's a little suspicious, don't you think? They'll see through it, that I was gathering intel all along."

"I'm not worried about what they figure out after the fact," Titus said, "as long as we remain in the will of God. And none of this gives us an excuse to act unneighborly. Let's return the Humvee and come back here to wait for Levi. Wes, a drafted letter of resignation to Brogdon would be wise. We'll hand it over with the vehicle. Gear up. Ten minutes?"

The men agreed and went their separate ways to the different floors.

On the top floor, before Titus picked up his gear, he tried the radio again.

"ELM333, if you're listening, Cyclops stirred the island hornets. Be on your guard. We're praying for you. The Rus made it back to us. See you when you return. ELM777 out."

Downstairs, the three in full battle dress climbed into the Humvee and pulled onto Kettner Boulevard, then reached Harbor Drive. At the Hilton Bayfront, Wes climbed out. Titus and Chevy continued in the vehicle toward the bridge on-ramp.

"Wes will cover our retreat." Titus said as he drove through Chicano Park and the refuse that had piled up there. Civilians who picked through the dump hid themselves or kept their distance from the vehicle. "Once we pull onto that bridge, we're committed. It's a long swim back if this goes sideways."

"Are you saying I should've brought my arm floaties?" Chevy asked and chambered a round. "It's evening tide. Which way will we be swimming?"

"It ain't easy fighting ten problems at once, huh?" Titus chuckled. "Let's worry about that if we find ourselves in the bay."

Titus drove up the on-ramp to the bridge. The first checkpoint was positioned over the first concrete piling offshore; the water below was a choppy, dark blue. Two heavy machine guns, a wooden crossing arm, and a station house made up the checkpoint.

"I see only two men." Chevy studied the wide bridge. "Does that seem a little light for being ready for war?"

"There's a third guy in the house." Titus slowed in front of the crossing arm and stopped. He gave a friendly wave as the two guards outside raised their weapons at the strangers in the PSDF vehicle. "If they panic, I'll take these two. You take the one in the house."

"Copy," Chevy said.

"Get outta the vehicle!" One soldier aimed his rifle at Titus's head. The other covered Chevy. "Out slowly! Hands where I can see them."

"We're friends of General Brogdon." Titus climbed out, keeping his hands raised. "We're returning your vehicle. We're locals from downtown. I'm Titus Caspertein."

"Yeah, we heard all about you!" The soldier kept his rifle on Titus, but used only his right arm to cradle the weapon. With his left hand, he shoved Titus on the chest. "Turn around. Hands on the vehicle!"

When the soldier reached to shove Titus again, Titus dropped his hands. With his left, he pushed the rifle barrel aside as his right drew his nine-millimeter. He fired over the Humvee hood at the second soldier who was giving Chevy the same mistreatment. Then Titus put a round into the thigh of the first soldier.

Chevy's battle rifle thundered as he peppered the guard house window with gel-tranqs until the soldier inside slumped unconscious.

"Titus, you have incoming," warned Wes on the comm. "They're rolling in from the east. Five vehicles. Over."

"Oh, that's just perfect." Titus drew Wes's letter of resignation from his breast pocket and slipped it under the windshield wiper of the Humvee. "Chevy?"

"Ready."

"Stay on my left. I'll go right. Separate targets are harder to fight."

"I see 'em." Chevy moved into position against the left guardrail.

Five Humvees sped south on Interstate 5 toward the bridge.

"Wes," Titus said, "I'd say that's a rescue team bringing home your recently revived Sergeant Lesage. Over."

"Careful," Wes said. "I heard he's cranky after a nap. Over."

"This is just wrong." Chevy scoffed. "They're gonna kill us. We have no cover. We can't even jump off the bridge. Look, we're too close to the docks below!"

"It ain't easy being outnumbered." Titus gazed toward ELM, wishing he would've kissed Annette goodbye, but she'd been busy. "Wes, can you see me? If I scratch my brow, I want you to open fire first. Catch them in a crossfire between us and yourself. Over."

"Could get bloody," Wes said. "Maybe I should just tranq you and Chevy now. They'll take you prisoner, but at least you'll be alive. Over."

"And give them our weapons?" Titus asked. "Chevy? It's your call. Get tranqed to become prisoners or take a stand? Over."

"Becoming their prisoners would just mean our deaths in slow motion," Chevy said. "I'd rather stand than die in jail in the hands of Lesage. Over."

Titus' comm screeched with static.

"I'm getting some interference here, guys. Someone else might be on our frequency. Over."

"I don't hear anything," Wes said. "I'll cover you—as best as a one-eyed shooter can. Over."

The five vehicles slowed as they reached the bridge. Titus looked to Chevy and nodded. Chevy nodded back, his face resolute. If they died here together, it wouldn't be a bad death, but it would seem premature. Titus didn't like the idea of leaving Annette behind, especially with Oleg laid up. They'd have to leave the city. If Wes survived, he'd take them on the road, maybe north. And Levi wasn't even back yet from his first real mission.

Though Titus gripped his rifle with both hands, he didn't raise it as he planted his feet and waited against the south guardrail. The vehicles spread out, staggered, blocking the lanes to the mainland. He'd have to climb over at least one hood to get past, but they'd have to climb over to reach him as well! Their positioning gave Titus an idea. He touched his comm, not caring that the enemy could see him giving last instructions.

"Chevy, if there's gunfire, duck down against their own vehicles. Get behind a wheel well and let Wes mop them up. Over."

The men piled out of their vehicles and spread out to aim their rifles across hoods and over roofs. Five vehicles, twenty-two men. But not everyone had rifles! Titus smiled, amused, understanding that Wes or the locals must've disarmed the patrol when they were unconscious.

Sergeant Lesage ripped a rifle out of the hands of one of his soldiers and aimed it skyward, though his face of fury was aimed directly at Titus. Where Lesage stood behind one hood, Titus could see that the man would need to replace his Bowie knife and shotgun, which had also been stripped from his body.

"Where is he?" Lesage shouted. "Where is Trimble? You tell me now or I'll kill you where you stand! I'll throw your body into the bay, Caspertein!"

Titus studied all their faces, not only Lesage's. He and Chevy would find no mercy from these few. They were angry. Their egos were bruised. They wanted blood. He thought about scratching his brow right then and getting the show started. It would take about five giant steps to charge up and huddle against the vehicles for cover. The closer he could get to the enemy would be safer in this case. They wouldn't be able to shoot at him unless they shot underneath or climbed over the tops to reach him.

"Trimble returned in one of your vehicles," Titus said. "He's resigned from the PSDF. He left you a note on the windshield."

"I asked where he is!" Lesage snarled. "You have three seconds, Caspertein!"

"I'll tell you where he is. Wes Trimble is under the protection of ELM once again. And more importantly, he's in the palm of God's mighty hand. I'm not your enemy, Sergeant. Your general and I have an understanding, don't forget."

"Not anymore, not after you killed one of our men and took one of our trucks!"

"That's a lie!" Titus shouted back with more force, but not with contempt. "You know by now that we use only tranquilizers. If someone died, it was friendly fire by one of your own, or enemy fire, but it wasn't us. And the only vehicle Trimble took is right here. He used it to transport someone to receive medical care. No harm has been done to you by us except we used a little fuel. The general can tell me himself what price he'd like us to pay for the fuel, but this standoff isn't necessary, Sergeant. I'm not your enemy. Come back to ELM with me right now. We'll have a cup of coffee that I promised the general."

"No more of your tricks, Caspertein!" Lesage glanced at his men, perhaps ensuring their few weapons were ready, but only half had rifles. Their feet were visible under the chassis, some in only their stockings. "I'm ending your jurisdiction downtown right now!"

"Dad?" Titus' comm scratched, then cleared of static. "Dad, I'm not sure if you can hear me yet, but I heard you and Wes talking. I just ran up here. I'm south of you two hundred and fifty yards on the docks. I have elevated cover plus another shooter with me. Over."

*Levi was there!* But Titus couldn't visibly rejoice quite yet . . .

He raised his left hand to Lesage.

"Not yet!" Titus yelled. "You can't win, Lesage. I will decimate your troops again right here. I have shooters north and south of you. And the way you're parked, you can't even reach me without exposing yourselves. Don't do this!"

"Shut up, Caspertein!" Lesage swore. "You have no one out there. You weren't expecting me, but here I am."

"You're right. You caught me out here by surprise just now, but God has made arrangements on my behalf. My shooters are in place."

"Levi, this is Wes. I'm on the Hilton Bayfront to the north. If your dad scratches his brow, we open fire. Over."

"Copy that," Levi said.

Though Titus wanted to say something, to cheer, to pray and thank the Lord that his son had returned from Sacred Cow—he couldn't with almost a dozen rifles aimed at his chest.

"It doesn't matter!" Lesage fumed, then laughed with a deranged cackle. "Even if you did have more people within range, you shoot only tranquilizers, remember? You're no threat to me!"

"I'm warning you, Lesage!" Titus shook his head. "Don't do this. It'll be costly in other ways. Don't do it!"

Titus could read the sergeant's face. A few of the other soldiers didn't appear as committed—or armed—but they were forced to follow their commanding officer. An instant before Lesage braced to fire, Titus lifted his left hand and brushed his eyebrow.

Instead of waiting for Lesage to fire, Titus crouched and dove toward the nearest Humvee. Rifles blasted overhead. Rolling over twice, Titus came up against the front wheel of the vehicle. Now on his knees, he switched his rifle to fully automatic and laid down a spray of gel-tranqs underneath the vehicle. Men dropped to the pavement after gel-tranqs stung their feet, shins, and knees.

Farther away, three canons boomed. The .308 battle rifles had a distinct thundering sound that should've drawn the soldiers' attention, but the distant snipers were probably too far away to be spotted.

"Chevy!" Titus yelled over the gunfire so close. "Cover me!"

Now, Titus trained his rifle on the Humvee Chevy had found to hide against, and similarly, Chevy had a better line of sight on the vehicle that Titus was using for cover. Two men climbed onto the hood of Chevy's Humvee and Titus took them both down. Three seconds later, a soldier slid off the hood onto Titus. The man was unconscious from Chevy's targeting.

The two men remained vigilant for one another as the gunfighting raged on the other side of the vehicles—between the soldiers and the shooters to the north and south. Lesage's men finally realized that the shooters were a fact. And Titus figured his son must've recovered Oleg's rifle and given it to the rescued Sacred Cow woman.

It was over in sixty seconds. Titus leaped over the nearest hood to search the vehicles. They were clear.

"Wes and Levi," Titus said on the comm, "hold your positions until we're clear of the bridge. Chevy, collect weapons and ammo. We probably have two minutes before half of Coronado comes for us. Over."

Chevy jumped into action, collecting rifles and magazines. Titus remembered that Wes had stripped the men of their gear earlier, so he drew his knife to cut the laces of the boots of every man. Then he collected at least one boot from every man and tossed them over the railing to the docks and pier below. While his knife was out, he slashed the tires of all five vehicles, then changed to lethal .308 ammunition and fired a short burst into the engine of each Humvee.

"I told Lesage it would be costly in other ways if they fought us." Titus jogged away with Chevy, who'd dumped his collection of weapons over the side as well. "It ain't easy being soldierly without your boots and rifles, huh?"

"They'll probably declare war against us now."

"Maybe. Lesage will be asleep for a few more minutes. Hopefully, someone'll get Wes's note to the general. Brogdon may be a little tyrant, but he didn't become general by acting rashly. He's got bigger problems to think about than Lesage's ego. But if they come to us for a fight, we'll accommodate."

The two ran down the ramp to the north. When they reached the burned out Convention Center, they took positions on both sides of Harbor Drive.

"Levi, we'll cover you northbound on Harbor Drive. Come to us. Wes, peel off with Levi. Over."

When Levi came into sight, he was leading a blond with half her hair missing. She hustled with great difficulty, her arm in a sling. And another man was carrying Oleg's rifle, traipsing wearily a few paces behind Levi.

Wes emerged from the Bayfront and joined Levi's advance. The four reached Titus and Chevy's position.

"Slow down." Titus held up his hand. "We're clear. Chevy, take point. Wes, you have our six. Let's take India Street home."

Chevy jogged ahead as Wes stood his ground, gazing toward the bridge.

"Some homecoming, huh?" Titus laughed and threw his arm over Levi's shoulders for a few paces. "It ain't easy rescuing your old man."

"Something told me to return back on I-5." Levi's face was smudged with dirt, but he appeared refreshed—not at all like he'd just crisscrossed the county on foot in two days. "You always say God's timing is perfect."

"Whoa!" Titus moved to catch the injured woman as she stumbled and nearly fell. "Your passenger might need a break."

"I've got her." Levi unclipped his rifle and passed it to his father. "Carla, hold up. We have about seven blocks to go. Let me carry you."

"It was that running." She nearly collapsed, her face twisting in pain.

Levi picked her up in his arms, her braced arm out front. Titus now recognized her as someone well-known in the past, but he said nothing. Instead, as Levi walked stiffly forward, Titus fell in beside the stranger in his mid-thirties who was carrying Oleg's weapon.

"So, I'm guessing you have some story." Titus offered his hand. "I'm Titus Caspertein."

"Dusty. I mean Dustin Howard." He shook his hand. "Levi said I could come home with him."

"Sure. That's what we're here for. God is arranging all kinds of new things, isn't He?"

"I guess so. I was gonna be executed in New Encanto a few hours ago, but Levi decided to let me live. He said I'd go to hell anyway."

"Is that true?" Titus asked. "You're not at peace with God yet?"

"Guess not."

"We'll help you out with that. Stick close to Levi."

"I will."

"Did you do some shooting back there?"

"Yeah, but I don't think I hit anything." Dusty eyed the compact rifle in his arms. "I've never shot anything like this before. Just pistols."

"We've got a few blocks. Tell me your story, Mr. Howard."

Titus listened as Dusty started hesitantly, then warmed to sharing. He'd been raised in foster homes, ran away early and became a thug, drug addict, and street hustler. Pan-Day was a gift at first. He loved the chaos and carnage, but then the drugs dried up. He'd had to go straight if he wanted to live and not starve to death. For months, he'd drifted from neighborhood to neighborhood, stealing and looting. Then he saw the plane out in the wilderness. It'd taken him a day to round up a few local guys to take the plane and claim it. That's when they crossed Carla and Levi.

"Levi's the worst thing I've ever come across," Dusty said. "But he says God has a new path for me. I don't know. I'm no Christian. And I don't think I'll ever be one."

"Do you know anything about Jesus and why He died on the cross?"

"No, not really."

"Well, you should get informed before you draw too many conclusions about what you will or won't become. I've found that the older I get, the more I realize my first conclusions as a youth were pretty ignorant. Can you relate?"

"Yeah, I guess so."

"So, I grew up in Arkansas, then got into serious trouble with the law and went on the run overseas. They called me the Serval because I was known to live like a wild cat in the deserts of the Middle East and Africa. Probably like you, I thought I was in control and living the good life. A good man named Corban challenged everything I thought about myself. He gave it to me straight—what this life is about and what it means to be mighty. You'll need to wade through some important decisions real soon. Trust God, Dusty. I guarantee you'll come out of it with a peace that will preserve you through anything, even death."

"I'm surprised you guys would want anything to do with me. I've been to jail more times than I can remember."

"Jail?" Titus waved his hand dismissively. "Chevy up there on point did twenty years for murder. He got out last year and he's been living courageously ever since. He's now a good man of God. You should talk to Chevy about the miracle God can do inside you."

They reached ELM and Wynter opened the metal door downstairs. Levi set Carla down to walk on her own, but he didn't leave her side so she could lean on him. They took the dolly upstairs in stages. Titus, Wynter, and Wes were content to go last. Chevy got off to stay with Oleg at their apartment.

"You're letting Levi move awfully fast for such a youngster," Wynter said as Titus pulled on the cable. "Look how much went wrong for him on a two-day mission."

"He was ambushed by a whole town and he faced down five gunmen in a plane." Titus frowned. "Sis, how could I have handled that any better?"

"Well, he got Oleg shot."

"You know better than that."

"And you're letting him bring home these strays? That woman is our age, but she's hanging all over him."

"She's wounded and he just rescued her. And Dusty is ripe for the Gospel. Would you stop fretting?"

"I can't help it." She pouted. "None of you fret for yourselves."

"Your husband is back safely. Focus on that. You're not a widow."

"Until you send him away again."

"That's your call." He grinned. "It ain't easy telling your husband to stay home for you when everyone else is outside making an impact for Christ."

"Huh. I never could win arguments with you." She rolled her eyes. "And Rudy wouldn't even argue. He'd just shrug and do things his own way. You think Rudy is okay?"

"Meeker, Colorado, is pretty remote, but I'll keep trying to relay a message up there. I haven't found anyone with a radio around that area yet."

"Where's that Carla woman going to stay?"

"For now, I think in your old apartment next to us. You're moving back down to fifteen, right? You're back to stay, Wes?"

"Last I checked." He chuckled, obviously not interested in inserting himself between brother and sister.

"And what about Dusty?" Wynter asked. "Where's he going to live?"

"Ask Levi."

"You're just turning Levi loose, aren't you?"

"This is the world we live in now, sis. Levi's a man and a follower of Jesus. He's in better hands than mine, but I'm here for him, too."

"He's just like you were at that age."

"You didn't even know me at his age. I'd already run away. But Levi's more mature than I was."

"But just as reckless. I see it in his eyes. He's wild. He leaps without looking."

"As long as his leaps are leaps of faith for God, what does it matter?"

They reached the top floor where Levi and Annette were making arrangements with the newcomers.

"Thank you," Carla said after Annette's loving welcome and half-hug. "Everyone is so kind here. I don't know how long I'll stay since I need to find friends and family in the city, but I'm glad to be safe—thanks to Levi."

"I put your clothes in the room there." Levi pointed at apartment two, now her own. "Anything you need, Dusty and I will be in the next apartment, and Mom and Dad are over there."

"A hot shower and sleep are all I can think about." She looked them each in the face. "I'm very grateful for everything."

Annette returned to preparing meals for Oleg, and Levi took Dusty into their apartment to show him his private room that faced the bay. Titus followed Carla to the doorway of her apartment to speak to her privately.

"Keep the door locked when you're here alone," he said. "The condo is too big to know everything that's happening inside it. If someone gets into the stairwell somehow, we at least have door locks to secure us at night."

"But you all have those guns," Carla said. "And Levi's next door, so I should be safe."

"Probably nowhere safer, but only because we take precautions, right?"

"Okay. Thanks, uh, Mr. Caspertein." She started to close the door, but Titus hadn't moved. "Was there something else?"

"You didn't tell Levi who you are, did you?"

"It . . . didn't come up." She licked her lips nervously and looked toward Levi's apartment. "You recognized me—even like this?"

"Yeah. I've read your articles the last few years."

"Is that good or bad?"

"Let's just say it must be awkward for you to be with a bunch of Christians."

"I'll leave if you want me to. I mean, you must know my last name, too. And now you have trouble with the Pacific States. Levi told me."

"Carla, I have nothing against you or your father," Titus said. "Stay as long as you want. Annette's next door if you need any female advice."

"You know, speaking of recognizing people . . ." She wagged a finger at him. "Your wife . . . *Annette Sheffield?* I always wondered what'd happened to her."

"Still a beauty, isn't she?" Titus backed out of the doorway. "Have a good night, Carla."

She thanked him and closed the door. He remained in the hallway, considering the providence of God—and who Levi had brought home. *Carla Criswell!* The Lord certainly worked in mysterious ways!

General Galt Brogdon was in one of the first vehicles to arrive on the bridge. He ran from Humvee to Humvee, pushing aside his own soldiers, until he found Kip on the pavement. *His son was dead!* His only son. Holding him close, Galt cursed and wept as he knelt against the nearest vehicle.

The gun battle had been unmistakably clear from the island. Also unmistakable, at least to Galt's ears, had been the thundering rifles of an enemy—an enemy that had clearly decimated Sergeant Lesage's unit on the bridge—but had been too cowardly to approach the island itself.

"They're not dead!" announced one responder with a medical kit. "There's no blood!"

Galt clawed at his son's neck. *Kip had a pulse!*

"It's some sort of chemical attack!" warned another soldier. "They're all unconscious!"

Setting aside his son, Galt surveyed the scene, his mourning turned to curiosity. There were no rifles, most of the soldiers' boots had been taken, and the vehicles had been sabotaged. Tires had been slashed and bullets had riddled the engines. But none of the men had been killed?

More trucks arrived and a better perimeter was established farther up the bridge. The unconscious soldiers were tended to by medics, but there was confusion as to how to treat them. It wasn't a chemical or biological weapon that anyone had ever seen before. Bruises and developing welts were found on each solder. Inside the welts were tiny puncture holes where it seemed something had been injected into each soldier's bloodstream.

Rifle cartridges littered the pavement. But larger spent shells stood out from the .223 shells. Galt picked up one, sniffed it, and checked its markings. No markings. Who had custom ammunition in such quantity? It might've even been a .308 cartridge, but it was impossible to know for sure without finding a bullet—yet there were no bullet wounds to be found in any of the men. Maybe a bullet could be pried out of the ruined vehicles once they towed them back to the island.

The unconscious began to wake as the responding personnel continued to hypothesize about what it all meant.

Galt ignored his son, who remained unconscious, and knelt next to Sergeant Lesage who seemed to be the first to gain awareness.

"It was Caspertein." Lesage cursed and drank from someone's canteen. "Wes Trimble turned on us and tranquilized us across town at the hardware store. And then when the other patrol picked us up, we returned and found Caspertein here at the checkpoint. He'd already tranquilized the guards."

"*Tranquilized?*" Galt frowned. "But you had all these men. How did—?"

"Trimble took our boots and rifles back at the hardware store. Trimble did!"

"But there were over twenty of you." Galt scoffed. "Lesage, look around you. You guys put up a fight . . . against one man?"

"Two men. Caspertein and a smaller guy I remember seeing a few days ago at their building."

"Two men . . . did all this?"

"General!" A soldier squeezed between vehicles and waved a folded envelope. "A message for you, sir!"

"Not now!" Galt waved the man away. "Can't you see we're busy?"

"It's from Wes Trimble, sir. It was on that Humvee's windshield."

Galt eyed Lesage critically, then ripped the message from the runner's hand and read it aloud.

"General Brogdon,

I regretfully inform you that I could not continue with the PSDF after Sergeant Lesage attempted to slaughter women and children in the field. I temporarily incapacitated Lesage's unit and departed with one vehicle. Locals took another Humvee. Per Titus Caspertein's agreement to submit running vehicles to you, I return this Humvee to you in good running order. I trust my counsel was helpful for the short time I was with you. If you wish to further discuss anything with me, you will find me back with the Casperteins at the ELM building, for I have returned to live with them. May the peace of God rule your heart because of Jesus' sacrifice for you.

Respectfully, Wes Trimble"

"He's lying." Lesage spat "He planned this all along. Trimble was never one of us."

"So what?" Galt tucked the letter into his breast pocket. "He gave us more battle strategy in three days than any of our other intelligence advisors have offered in three months. Let me guess: Caspertein was returning the Humvee from Trimble when you found him here?"

"General, they attacked us without provocation!"

"Two men?" Galt held up a finger. "Watch your tone, Sergeant. This isn't the first time your anger has clouded your judgement. Lucky for you, Caspertein was using tranquilizers. But that doesn't explain how he and one other man took down all of you."

"You weren't here, sir." Lesage turned away. "I don't know how it all happened, but Caspertein wasn't fighting fairly."

"Sir?" called a medic. "Your son's awake, General."

Galt hurried around a vehicle bumper and embraced his son. Caspertein had shot his son. Wes Trimble had betrayed them. He would need to respond, but carefully. Obviously, Caspertein had tricks up his sleeves. If two of Caspertein's men could take out twenty soldiers, what would he need to bring down the whole family of Casperteins?

Worse yet, word of the failure on the bridge would spread through the ranks. Caspertein had beaten the military on their own turf, and Galt felt if he didn't respond, he would appear weak.

But there were multiple ways to respond. Maybe he couldn't fight Caspertein head-to-head, but perhaps a covert option was the answer? It would take time to bring down this man.

And Galt wondered what he could do with a unit of men armed with Caspertein's rifles . . .

# *Chapter Five*

Dustin Howard felt a hand on his shoulder and a voice calling his name, but just waking from his slumber, his mind needed a few seconds to catch up.

"Dusty?"

"Yeah? I'm awake. I think."

Levi stood over him, but the apartment was dark. He held a candle inside a glass lantern.

"Dad needs us," whispered the tall youth excitedly. "It's a mission!"

"Okay. I'm coming." Dusty sat up. "What time is it?"

"About four in the morning. Come on. We'll eat breakfast on the way."

Levi left with the lantern. Dusty's bedroom door remained open, so the lantern light from the living room helped him find his pants and shirt. *Four in the morning?* He hated to leave the clean sheets of the queen-sized bed, but he didn't want to miss a moment of this new life he'd found with the Casperteins.

As he laced up his boots, he reflected on the day before and how close he'd come to being left out of everything. If Levi wouldn't have taken him from the plane, if Levi wouldn't have pardoned him from execution, if Levi wouldn't have welcomed him to the ELM apartments . . .

Of course, Levi had said he trusted that he was obeying the will of God along the way, so Dusty had learned that Levi didn't absorb compliments, praise, or glory like most people.

Dusty rubbed his eyes as he emerged from the bedroom. He'd been up late with his new roommate being taught how to pack a proper field pack—clean socks, fire starter, rain poncho, one day of food and water, and a cooking tin. Besides an Army surplus backpack, Levi had given him an assortment of items to keep on his belt or in the pockets of his ammo vest—binoculars, a small flashlight, a compass, a knife, a water bottle, sunglasses, a lighter, and a mirror for signaling.

When Levi had offered him a thick pocket Bible, Dusty had accepted that as well. He'd initially accepted the book in an effort not to offend Levi, but Levi had immediately shown him where the Book of Proverbs was, and Dusty's curiosity was whetted.

"Read one of the chapters every day," Levi had told him. "You'll learn to discern life like God sees it. When you're ready, branch out to these other books to guide your life. God created us. No question about it. You'll want to read this whole book to learn *why* He created us."

So, this was why the Casperteins were so different! Different in a good way. Dusty had slipped the Bible into a chest pouch next to two .308 magazines.

Also the night before, Levi had explained ELM's philosophy about killing: they didn't harm their enemies in a lethal way. They showed grace and allowed God to deal retribution as only He could do so, justly and purely.

"We win people by showing them mercy and grace," Levi had said. "We aim for the best in people's lives. If they refuse it, that's on them. Our conscience is clear."

Dusty had fallen asleep after midnight with those words on his mind. A clear conscience? Mercy and grace? It all seemed so strange, yet Dusty couldn't argue with the results. He'd been pried from his past and drawn into the present so naturally that he wondered if this God of Levi's was actually looking out for him personally!

"Breakfast." With gloved hands, Levi handed Dusty a sandwich. "Ready?"

"I guess."

Sniffing the sandwich, Dusty followed Levi and the lantern to the door. *Fresh bread?* He took a giant bite— egg, cheese, and some sort of cream. Heavenly!

Levi similarly held his sandwich with one hand, fit his field pack over one shoulder, then picked up his rifle. Dusty's rifle was brand new—a battle rifle without any knicks or scratches like Oleg's rifle had. With the rifle had come four magazines of gel-tranqs and the explanation of how they worked.

The lantern was extinguished and left in the apartment. In the hall, Dusty found Titus had his own lantern, the glass much cleaner than Levi's.

"Be safe, boys," Annette called from her doorway. "I'm going back to bed. And I'd better not be woken up by gunfire!"

"Thanks for the sandwiches, Mom," Levi called.

"Yeah, thanks, Mrs. Caspertein," Dusty said past a full mouth. "It's good!"

"Bring 'em back in one piece, Titus." Annette closed her door.

Titus opened the elevator door.

"Levi, you got the cable?"

Stuffing the rest of his sandwich into his mouth, Levi accepted the duty of dolly operator for the three to descend.

"What time did you two get to bed last night?" Titus asked. "We heard you up late laughing."

"It feels like just a few minutes ago." Dusty shook his head as if to rattle himself loose from clinging slumber.

"We had to get his pack ready," Levi said.

"Good." Titus approved with a nod.

Dusty was learning that everyone at ELM operated under Titus' supervision. He was definitely the boss, probably because he was someone influential from the past.

Although Dusty desperately wanted to ask what their mission was, he resisted the urge. Whatever it was, he was glad to be with these warriors. Levi had been a ghost on the plane, taking down Dusty and his four pals. And the night before, Levi had fired up at the bridge and tranquilized maybe a dozen men on his own. This was no ordinary family.

On the second-floor balcony, Titus knelt and set down his lantern. Chevy and Wes knelt with them.

"Oleg?" Titus asked.

"Yeah, what's he doing?" Wes joked. "Taking the morning off again and sleeping in?"

"He's resting," Chevy said. "I didn't wake him. He's got his comm by his bedside if he needs anything."

"A new day before us, men." Titus looked them each in the face. "ELM needs to establish a defensive perimeter to keep aggressors with vehicles at bay. Foot traffic can come and go, but we need to stop patrols and convoys from charging through here at will. We're not going to block off the whole city, but I want a two-block perimeter around this building and the other five of these high-rise apartments. Wes?"

The one-eyed man unfolded a map of downtown. Dusty noticed his eye patch was a different color that day.

"The military has a plow truck they use for clearing streets of debris," Wes said. "We can't stop a plow truck, so all we're concerned with is stopping street vehicles. The patrols are off-limits from ELM. They'll get the message or we'll need to address their trespassing in firmer terms."

"Two-man teams," Titus said. "Wes and me, Levi and Dusty. Chevy, you're on overwatch."

Wes pointed out the intersections they hoped to clear by using vehicles to block streets leading to ELM.

"Put each vehicle in neutral," Wes said, "then push it and steer it to block the street perpendicularly. Leave room only for foot or bike traffic. Then slash the vehicle tires to plant the rims in place."

"It ain't easy playing bumper cars in the dark," Titus said, "but this is the job. If Brogdon or Lesage want to respond for yesterday, they'll be met by these barriers. Let's get it done before dawn if possible. Anything happens, we regroup here and hold the line. Chevy? We don't decide what to do and then cry to God for His blessing, do we?"

"No." Chevy's eyes were on the lantern. "I've learned we should determine what to do by knowing His will. The blessings of God are found only inside a life lived for Him. Let's pray . . ."

Dusty kept his head up as the four men bowed theirs. Chevy prayed, talking to God like He was really there, listening. When Chevy finished, Dusty joined in saying amen, but he was still figuring out this crew. Were they priests or warriors, or maybe warrior-priests? Levi was the youngest by far, but the others treated him as an equal. If anyone wasn't a warrior along with the others, it was Chevy, whose very physical slightness didn't compare to the others, yet Chevy was depended on for other important matters as an inside man.

The time for talking was over. On the ground floor, an older Hispanic man named Gustavo opened the door and closed it behind them as they left the building. The five marched as one to the west to build a barrier along the Pacific Highway first.

On his team, Levi was heavier than Dusty by at least thirty pounds, so Dusty was responsible for climbing into the cab of each vehicle, putting it into neutral, then steering it as Levi pushed from the front or back. Wes did the same as Titus pushed for that pair.

Vehicles weren't in short supply. At some intersections, there were too many vehicles to make a barrier right away. The traffic jams needed to be cleared first, then the streets were blocked with precision. Excess cars were left along the curbs instead of blocking the open streets any longer.

Once the first street was sufficiently blocked—four rows deep—they drew their knives and slashed at tires to sink the rims to the pavement. Wes had advised each row to be spaced from the next by about seven feet, so even an armored vehicle that climbed over the first row would find a gap before the next row. The gaps between the rows of cars were as important as the barriers themselves to trap invaders.

By the third street, they were functioning without yelling orders to one another. Dusty loved the teamwork—and the hard work! These were men who saw a job to be done and did it. Their stoicism helped Dusty. He hadn't complained or cursed all morning even though he'd never worked this hard his whole life!

As they completed blocking the sixth street, dawn lit the tops of the quiet apartment buildings above them. But they were only half finished.

"Do we stop?" Levi asked as they took a water break. "The island might see us."

"That's why we worked counterclockwise," Titus said. "The streets that Coronado can see best are already blocked. I vote we finish this morning. Wes?"

"Finish."

"A big brunch will taste that much better knowing we finished," Chevy said.

"Finish it," Levi said.

They looked at Dusty, the last to speak. *He had a vote?*

"Let's finish."

"It's unanimous." Titus slapped Wes on the shoulder as he started off. "It ain't easy keeping up with the young bucks, is it?"

"Are you calling me an old bull?" Wes grumbled in good humor.

The four laughed and went to the next street, now on the east side of ELM.

"Dead bodies." Dusty backed away from a van stuck in traffic. "What do we do?"

"Let it air out a few minutes." Levi opened the other doors. "Then we'll pull them out to bury them later. Chevy and I started a cemetery above Little Italy in the elm trees."

There were more dead as well, some on the streets killed as they'd fled or fought, and some in vehicles where it seemed they were still waiting for traffic to start moving again.

They finished mid-morning with Chevy calling out only one warning that a patrol of three Humvees was leaving the island for the mainland. But the vehicles continued east.

"You think they'll attack?" Chevy asked Titus.

But it was Wes who answered.

"The note I left for the general probably explained enough so they won't attack. A soldier died, but that was due to Lesage's tactics. Even the disaster they created on the bridge last night was their own fault, not ours. I'm hoping the general sees a path for peace."

"We don't want war with them," Titus said. "But we'll make it costly for them when their carelessness for human life seems to drive them."

They returned to the ELM building, their mission completed, and ascended to their respective floors.

As soon as they stepped off the dolly on the top floor, Carla was waiting for Levi, her apartment door open. Her injured arm was cradled by her other, the brace and sling straps hanging free. She'd showered and found new clothes. Except for her scars, Dusty thought the older woman appeared attractive, but he couldn't look at her without remembering that he was the one who'd injured her shoulder.

"Levi, can you tie this?" Carla asked. "Your mom wasn't sure how you designed it."

Titus went to his apartment, then returned to the hallway.

"Dusty, Levi," he called, "you guys want to have lunch over here? Annette has burritos ready."

"I'm in." Dusty left his rifle and gear with Levi at the door and walked into Titus' apartment. He sat at the dining table and plucked off his gloves. Everything seemed so . . . normal in here. Titus' wife was a true homemaker—cooking for them, nursing Oleg back to health, and the apartment was clean, like Pan-Day had never happened.

Titus said grace for the three, and this time Dusty bowed his head. Then Annette brought a plate of burritos from the kitchen to the table.

"Those are huge!" Dusty gasped, then checked himself. "Sorry. I'm just not used to real food these days."

"Annette keeps surprising all of us." Titus helped himself then passed the plate to Dusty. "It ain't easy working on an empty stomach, but she always has food ready when we return."

"I figure if the food is good," Annette said, "you won't wander too far away on some adventure."

"I'm not going anywhere without you, babe." Titus took a giant bite and kept talking. "I mean, what would I do on an adventure since I'm incapable of making my own food?"

"The way you cook, sweetie?" Annette blew him a kiss. "I wouldn't exactly call it food. Oleg has told me stories."

Dusty still hadn't taken a bite. He listened to the couple go back and forth. Her wisecracks seemed to land squarely on Titus' ego. And Titus seemed to respond with jokes that he knew would backfire, but he only laughed all the harder.

Muffled conversation came from the open door to the hallway where Levi was still helping Carla.

"Should we be worried about those two?" Annette asked. She was looking at Dusty. "Is there something going on with them? What happened at that plane out in the wilderness?"

"Uh, I don't . . ." Dusty glanced toward the door. Carla was in her forties and her face was all messed up. Levi was a nineteen-year-old with the wits and strength of an experienced soldier. "I think he's just helping her get her arm brace on."

"Titus?" Annette raised her eyebrows. "Your son?"

"I wouldn't worry." Titus shrugged and finished his first burrito. "He brought her home. She's his responsibility, as he sees it."

"Yeah." Annette leaned forward to speak more softly. "But does *she* know he's just looking after her? Why hasn't she tried to contact her people in the city yet? She said she knows people. I think she's staying here because of him."

"No, she doesn't like him like that." Dusty frowned. "She argued with him on the way here. She doesn't like Christians. She thinks you're holding humanity back by your traditions."

"I thought we were holding back sin," Titus said, "not humanity. What do you think, Dusty?"

"Well, I . . . never lived with anyone who wanted me around. Levi said God has something for me and I want to see what that is. I don't want to leave before finding out."

"Sounds like a good plan," Titus said. "It's hard to feel fulfilled in life when you don't even know why you're here on Earth."

Levi and Carla entered and sat down on the same side of the table. Carla's arm brace was tied the way Dusty had seen it before, holding her shoulders back. She waited as Levi served her a burrito and poured her water.

"I think Dusty and I will go on grave duty this afternoon," Levi said. "There's a woman Chevy and I met named Sunshine. She said there's some dead people who need to be buried. Unless you need us to do something else?"

Dusty looked to Titus who was halfway through his second burrito.

"But what about Lesage?" Annette asked. "I don't think any of us should be going anywhere. What if we're attacked?"

"If they were going to strike for yesterday," Levi said, "it probably would've been sometime this morning. Once it was daylight, they probably saw the new barricades on the street. And they probably won't attack if they know we expect them."

"That's a lot of probablies." Annette raised her eyebrows at Titus for a response.

"Well, Levi's probably right. Hey, you guys still have energy left after setting up that perimeter?" Titus studied Dusty's face closely. "Dusty, you good with that? Levi will go another day and night without stopping unless we humans slow him down."

"I'm good for anything now that I'm refueled." He smiled uncomfortably under the attention. "Honestly, I'm still running on adrenaline since getting here."

"Well, you're a hard worker." Titus nodded firmly. "We're glad to have you. The Lord will reveal to you the rest of what you're searching for. I've found that a place of duty is always a place of revelation."

"Then let me give you some revelation about your duty," Annette said. "One of the chickens on the roof was attacked by an eagle or hawk earlier. There's a mess of feathers. We need the rest of that chicken wire strung up."

"It ain't easy making egg omelets with no chickens." Titus winked at Annette. "I'll get on it after burrito madness here. How many you going for, Levi?"

"Is it a contest?" Levi's eyes narrowed. "If it's a contest, Mom might need to roll up a few more."

"*Mom* isn't rolling more burritos just so you boys can scarf them down." Annette ate her one burrito with a knife and fork. "Besides, we're having lasagna tonight and I'll make plenty."

"What can I do?" Carla looked from Annette to Titus and back again. "I have one good arm. I don't think I'd be any good at whatever grave duty is about. I don't even want to go outside again if I don't have to. But maybe there's something?"

"You could show her the gardens," Levi said. "On the balconies of the unused apartments, we have gardens. I know because I hauled up the soil myself. And all the extra clothes from old tenants need to be washed and sorted still. Someone will use that stuff someday, or we'll use it for bartering."

"Wynter and I were going to get to those clothes eventually." Annette cringed. "It's a lot of laundry, Carla. And I guess I thought I'd get to weeding those gardens, too."

"I can help with those things." Carla wiped her mouth after taking a small bite. "I want to do that—the weeding and the laundry sorting. It's perfect for me."

"Just don't let these guys talk you into doing their own laundry," Annette warned.

"Ah, you're no fun!" Titus threw his napkin on the table. "I can't be expected to hang chicken wire *and* wash my own knickers!"

"Uh, I'm pretty sure I'm not washing anyone's knickers." Carla chuckled nervously. "I'm not even sure what knickers are, but—"

"No knicker washing, Carla," Annette assured. "You can't give these boys an inch or they'll have you ironing and vacuuming in no time."

"I would kind of like my ammo vest pressed," Levi said.

"Oh, I'll press it for you." Annette pointed her knife at Levi. "With you in it!"

Dusty laughed so hard he almost choked. He could get used to these people. Even Carla seemed to be willing to stick around. And he began to notice what was concerning Annette, though he wasn't exactly sure why she was concerned. Carla was watching Levi as he ate and visited. There was something in her eyes, something more than gratitude. And Levi seemed oblivious.

Chevy was beginning to really appreciate grave duty, especially since Levi insisted on doing the digging. But this time, Dusty used the pick to dig with him.

Among the shadows of the elms where the first mound lay, they'd found fresh purple and white flowers spread around the deceased husband and wife's grave. Chevy was pretty sure he knew who had laid flowers there—Sunshine had returned to the new ELM cemetery.

"It's good for men to work hard," Levi said to Dusty between shovel loads, "even when we don't have to."

Standing with his back against the elm tree, Chevy kept watch as he listened to Levi repeat to Dusty what Titus had taught him. They were life lessons that shaped men to be masculine, faithful, and courageous, especially in the quiet moments. Chevy hoped Dusty was really hearing the principles that Levi was sharing with him. Even though Dusty was over a decade older than his younger friend, the newcomer seemed to have lived a rebellious life without moral or ethical standards whatsoever. Levi was taking the place of a father-figure in Dusty's life, much like Titus and even Chevy himself had done in the teen's life to teach him the wisdom of David, Solomon, Paul, Peter, Stephen, and others who'd received enlightenment and understanding from the Word of God.

Thunder rolled across the San Diego hillside overlooking the city. Chevy couldn't remember seeing any clouds before they'd entered the tree coverage. But Levi didn't seem concerned about the distant noise, so Chevy didn't say anything. It was far away, anyway.

The names of the two deceased they buried that afternoon were unknown. They were among those who'd died in their vehicles downtown—perhaps shot by looters, or from self-inflicted wounds, or from overdose. Their bodies were too decayed to know for certain. Chevy had written down the model of their car and the license plate in place of their name in his growing cemetery list. God knew who they were.

Levi and Dusty used their hands to pack down the new mound where the two were buried together. Chevy moved closer when Levi stood upright and folded his hands. Dusty did likewise.

"All of us are susceptible to dying," Levi said solemnly, "but death doesn't have to sting for believers in Jesus Christ. I like the way Dad said it: death for us is a graduation to the next life, not the next conscious death or suffering. Whoever these people were, their grave is a cautionary tale for those who refuse to prepare for the inevitable. Chevy?"

"Amen."

"Dusty?"

"Amen," said the newcomer.

Chevy smiled to himself as Levi and Dusty fetched their gear and rifles. Levi was involving Dusty in every gracious endeavor and Dusty hadn't yet resisted. It was the immersion technique of evangelism. Dusty still needed to trust in God personally, but Levi was exposing the man to everything Jesus intended for His followers. No doubt Levi intended the same for Carla, but since she was a woman, Chevy wondered if Annette and Wynter might become her greatest counselors.

Again, thunder drifted through the midafternoon air. This time, Levi stopped and turned his head.

"That sounded like gunshots."

"It came from up there." Dusty pointed north.

The three listened for more, but there was nothing to hear except birds in the trees.

"Probably just locals shooting a dog or something," Levi said. "I've seen it before. Hopefully, that's all it is. Let's go."

Levi led the way through the trees to the north where they'd agreed to try to find Sunshine. Chevy was comfortable with his station in life as a rear guard, so he came last, happy to explore an area he hadn't seen before except from the balconies of the ELM building. Balboa Zoo and the Air and Space Museum weren't far through the trees to the east, but they'd agreed to search out Sunshine before anything else. The little woman who hadn't known who she was had somehow survived out here.

They arrived at a residential street where elms and overgrown lawns bordered each upper-class property. The streets were littered with windblown trash and decaying leaves. Levi knelt next to two objects in the street where cars were still parked against curbs. Chevy drew close enough to see that Levi and Dusty were examining two bodies that were weeks dead. The outline of each figure was traced not by chalk but in flowers. Some flowers were dried and withered, and some had been arranged recently, replacing those that had blown away.

Dusty drew up the cart and positioned it beside the bodies. Levi handed Chevy their wallets and Chevy found their driver's licenses. Their names and photos seemed to indicate two men, maybe father and son. They'd lived at the same address up in Linda Vista, which wasn't far to the north across the interstate.

Carefully, Levi and Dusty loaded the two fragile bodies into the cart. They appeared as light as paper.

"Hey, Levi," Chevy called, then gestured to the right. "It's Sunshine. I'll go talk to her."

He approached the yard of a small mansion with an expansive addition that extended into the backyard. Sunshine wore the same smock and trousers as before, her white hair straight, perhaps brushed since it wasn't tangled with the twigs of a wild person.

As he'd done the first time, Chevy knelt in front of Sunshine where she stood in the mansion yard.

"Hello, Sunshine." When he offered his gloved hand, she didn't hesitate to give her hand to him. "The sunshine is nice out here."

"You're taking the people." She pointed with her free hand at the street. "I watched them until you came for them."

"I saw the flowers. That was very thoughtful of you. I've recorded their names in my Bible. Did you know them?"

"Um, I don't remember."

"That's okay. Do you live here?"

Before she could answer, she flinched from two distant gunshots. Her eyes widened in fear, then she withdrew her hand and darted to the side of the mansion where she disappeared into a shadowy grove.

"Either we're closer to them or they're getting closer to us." Levi gazed northeast. "That's probably not a local shooting of a dog like I thought. It's too many gunshots."

"While you two were digging, I heard another shooting," Chevy said. "We should get back to ELM."

Two more gunshots seemed to punctuate Chevy's words. Chevy carefully watched Levi, knowing the young man didn't want to return to ELM without identifying the threat, if it even was a threat. Oleg had shared his experience with Levi during the last mission, so Chevy knew Levi had his own way of responding to dangers. Like his father, he wasn't known to retreat.

"Someone might need our help," Levi said.

"We don't even know what's up there," Chevy countered.

"That's Hotel Circle." Levi checked his rifle.

"Levi?" Chevy called for his attention. The young man looked up. "There's just three of us, and Dusty's not ready to die."

"What?" Dusty scoffed. "And you guys are?"

The man in his thirties appeared ready to run away. His eyes looked wild.

"Yes, we are." Levi pointed at the mansion. "Dusty, hide in there with Sunshine until we return. It looks like there's a greenhouse out back. We'll retreat to you if necessary. Take the cart."

Chevy understood Levi's intentions. He buttoned the pocket that held his Bible and tightened his rifle sling as he'd done dozens of times before when preparing for battle.

Dusty pulled the cart into the grove without arguing at all with Levi who obviously intended to venture toward the unknown gunfire.

"What's your plan?" Chevy asked.

Levi knelt on the edge of the street and used his gloved finger to trace in the dust.

"Hotel Circle loops around like this alongside Interstate 8. Old Town San Diego is west. The stadium is east. The river and golf course are north. There's forest between these streets and the hotels. People are probably squatting in the hotels up there."

"How many hotels?" Chevy asked. "Sorry. I haven't studied the maps."

"Eight or ten. Big front lawns and large pools in the rear. I'll approach from the west, here, from Presidio Park. You come up here through the middle of the hotels. There should be lots of cover. But don't engage."

"Okay."

"Not unless you have to. If someone's to get blamed for starting something, it should be me. Let me talk to whoever is doing the shooting. Hopefully, it's nothing, maybe just target practice. You're my overwatch. Just move up to observe. Stay covered. Comm check."

"Check . . . check. We're good."

"Good call about Dusty." Levi offered his gloved fist. "We shouldn't knowingly risk his life if he's still dead in his sins."

"Copy that." Chevy bumped fists with Levi. "See you at Hotel Circle."

With that, Levi ran away. Chevy took a long look at the map in the dirt. The way the streets ran, he'd have to zigzag his way north, then hike through the forest to reach the hotel properties. Levi would be covering almost twice the distance to approach from the far side, but Chevy knew the young man was twice as fast and stronger than the average man.

He walked quickly on the sidewalk in front of shuttered houses where he guessed at least a few families still remained. They may have been observing him walking up the sidewalk, his rifle in his hands. Someday, he hoped to meet them.

There were two more rifle shots up the hill. Chevy didn't want Levi to be alone to confront an enemy, but he was right about checking it out first. Returning to ELM for reinforcements might take too long, and by then people's lives could be lost. They were well out of comm range of ELM now, too.

Chevy crossed the last neighborhood street then cut through someone's property to reach the forest behind. It felt like trespassing when he climbed the backyard fence, but Chevy knew few lived around there in those days. As long as no one shot at him, he'd assume people were just happy he was moving along.

The scattered gunshots northward guided him as he hustled through the forest. He needed to be in place long before Levi arrived at his spot.

The hotels in the clearing loomed ahead. He heard one gunshot directly north, and another to the right. Two shooters—maybe shooting at one another. It could be as simple as a neighborly property dispute, but he knew nothing was that simple any longer.

He paused at the edge of the tall grass and searched for cover that he might use between the hotel properties before him. There were a couple palm trees that might serve as good cover. Of course, anyone inside the hotel rooms behind dark glass might be looking out at him even then. But no, the gunshots sounded like they were outside.

"Levi, come in," he said quietly. "Over."

"Levi here. What's up?"

Though he was breathing hard from jogging, Levi's voice was strong.

"I count two different guns. One is mid-loop and the other is somewhere east-loop. No visual yet. Over."

"Okay, keep me posted. Over."

Chevy charged across the tall grass then tripped and fell a few feet later. He'd tripped over a dead body, months old. He checked his gear then his surroundings and climbed to his feet to pick his way forward more carefully. A large empty swimming pool reeked of death, so he avoided it altogether, not even wishing to glance into its deep end.

He reached a pair of palm trees between two hotels. Now he could see the interstate dissect Hotel Circle and the far side of the circle with its set of hotels to the north.

A gunshot! Chevy crouched low. That was close.

"Levi, that gunshot came from the front of the hotel to my left. I'm hiding behind two palms between the hotels. Over."

"Get closer. I'm on the street out front. You need a visual of me and them. Over."

"The other shooter is farther east," Chevy warned. "Be careful. Over."

*Careful?* Chevy forgot who he was talking to. Levi was like his father—recklessly willing to endanger himself to preserve the lives of others. It was their way of living out the Gospel message: making themselves vulnerable to danger to offer others safety.

Chevy edged up the hotel's outer wall until he could peer around the corner at the entrance. *There was movement.* Levi was walking up to the front of the hotel. He was completely exposed! Licking his lips, Chevy left his cover and aimed his rifle at the entrance as he advanced toward a row of artificial shrubs. He knew the shrubs were fake because every other piece of vegetation was overgrown and they weren't.

As he reached the artificial vegetation, he saw them—a half-dozen dead lay along the paved entrance to the hotel. The entrance roof was leaning, definitely from the car that had crashed into a supporting column. Chevy knew the dead were recently killed because he could smell the blood in the breeze.

Two figures emerged from the entrance. A woman whimpered as she was forced ahead of a masked gunman in a reddish-colored coat. *A coat in this heat and humidity?*

The woman fell to her knees.

"Please!" she begged her executioner who shouldered his rifle. "No!"

"Hey!" Levi called from mere yards away.

The killer lifted his head, then pivoted his rifle, but he was too slow. Levi fired once into the man's chest. As he fell, he fired his own rifle into the air.

Chevy turned and aimed to the east. The other shooter was out there. Levi's rifle gunshot had carried a much different, much lower, echo across the landscape. Any mediocre rifleman would've noted the difference in sounds.

Sure enough, a bullet zipped through the air between Levi and Chevy.

"Get back inside!" Levi ordered the weeping woman. He positioned his body between the shooter and the woman until she reached cover. "Chevy, where is he?"

"Don't know!" Chevy was emboldened by Levi's selflessness. Whoever they were up against was clearly cold-hearted to be executing civilians. He'd gladly risk his life for such a cause.

He advanced to the east, cut through the front property of the next hotel, and kept a wary eye down his rifle's quick-site. Levi caught up to him on his left by about twenty yards, keeping pace. They had no cover as the shooter fired again. Levi flinched but kept going, adjusting his muzzle toward the source.

"There he is!" Levi planted his feet and fired once, then again. Both misses.

Chevy saw the shooter. This one wore a red coat as well. He scrambled on all fours behind an elevated flower garden, but Chevy had a clear line of sight. One shot—and he dropped the man from behind.

Levi stood like a statue, his rifle still leveled.

"Shooter's down," Chevy said just loud enough for Levi.

"Just those two?" After a few seconds, Levi lowered his weapon. "I guess so. You good?"

"Yeah. I'm good. What's Pacific States doing out here killing people?"

"I have no idea." Levi approached the flower bed. "Keep your eyes open."

As Levi took the shooter's rifle and hovered over the unconscious man, Chevy eyed the other hotels.

"He's not Pacific States." Levi returned to Chevy's side where he disassembled the rifle but pocketed the ammunition. "Both guys are bearded. Brogdon's men are always clean-shaven. And these guys are wearing coats, not the light crimson jacket Brogdon gives his men."

"Imitators?" Chevy guessed. "They're trying to pass themselves for the Pacific States military?"

"Seems so. And shooting up civilians so close to the bay?" Levi shook his head. "Dad will know what this is about. So will Wes. Come on."

They returned to the first hotel and disarmed the first shooter. Chevy saw for himself that this one was indeed bearded. His clothing was filthy, his red coat torn and oil stained, and he smelled distinctly like smoke and the outdoors.

People slowly emerged from all the hotels around to see what had happened. Several fell weeping upon those already executed in the grass. Levi looked from Chevy to the people.

"What're you thinking?" Chevy asked.

"That these folks aren't safe here."

"They're not safe anywhere."

Chevy studied them—men, women, and children who were shielding their eyes as they stood in the sunshine, as if they'd spent weeks indoors. They were pale and lean, their clothes like rags on skeletons.

"I'm afraid to imagine what they've been eating since Pan-Day," Levi said.

"Insects, rats, and mushrooms." Chevy sighed. "What else is there?"

"This is no way to live."

"Any ideas?"

"Hmm, how about you go to that group over there?" Levi said, pointing to another hotel. "Tell them we leave for somewhere safer in ten minutes. If they want to join us, tell them we'll help them start over downtown."

"At ELM?" Chevy asked.

"No, there are other buildings in our perimeter we can set up with water tanks. We can help them. What do you think?"

"How will we feed them? We have provisions in the garage, but for this many?"

"Gardens. And I haven't seen anyone fishing out in the bay. Look at them. They won't last long like this even with no one trying to kill them."

Chevy left to share Levi's message. Each hotel had an average of fifteen people emerge. More may have remained inside, but the very air flowing from the hotel door forced Chevy back.

"What's happening?" A woman cried and clutched an infant that didn't appear to be alive. "Why hasn't help arrived?"

He stilled the group by raising his hands.

"Please, I know you have lots of questions, but we have to leave this place. It's not safe. You can call me Chevy. My friend over there is Levi. There are apartment buildings downtown that we can take you to. We'll help you get set up. Please be patient. It'll be safer than out here. If you want to go with us, we leave in ten minutes. Get your belongings and join Levi over there."

"How do we know you're any better than those killers?" asked a middle-aged man with glasses.

"I'm not a killer. This is how you know it."

Unclipping his magazine, Chevy plucked out a single gel-tranq and tossed it to the questioner.

"What's this?" The man held it up to the afternoon sun. "Some kind of bullet?"

"It's just a tranquilizer." Chevy pushed the magazine back into his rifle. "My people and I are Christians. As followers of Jesus Christ, we're committed not to taking but to saving lives. Your lives won't be perfect if you come with us, but we'll help you find housing, relative safety, enough food to stay alive, and maybe even jobs."

"Jobs?" asked a woman. "I was a nurse in San Bernadino. Is there work at a hospital around here?"

"All jobs are informal right now. We work to stay alive and barter for food. Come with us. We'll help you find your way and discover what God's will is in this fallen world."

Chevy gave a similar message at two more hotels. Some people hustled off to collect their belongings—or they remained where they stood, fretting about leaving.

"Is this everyone?" Levi asked him ten minutes later.

About fifty had gathered.

"The others are too afraid of change or they don't trust us." Chevy shook his head. "I can't force them at gunpoint to come, Levi."

"Everyone!" Levi called. He was tall enough to be seen by all. "I'll lead us south. Stay together. Help the person beside you. Chevy will bring up the rear. Chevy, we need a name for these people. Every exodus needs a name. It'll help us."

"Uh, isn't this place called Hotel Circle?" Chevy scratched his head. "Does it have any other name?"

"This is pretty much Hillcrest," said the middle-aged man with glasses. "That's what it's called."

"Okay, listen up!" Levi shouted. "You're now known as the Hillcrest Hopefuls. You've held out hope for a long time. Now, you'll hold out hope a little longer. The Hillcrest Hopefuls are seeking a better place, somewhere that God has prepared for you to go next, where your neighbors will be considerate and giving and friendly. And you'll be the same in return, even though we're all experiencing much loss. The Hillcrest Hopefuls are pulling out. Everyone ready?"

A few nodded, but no one seemed too enthusiastic.

"I thought it sounded good." Chevy chuckled. "Is it too late to change from ELM to be a Hillcrest Hopeful? I like the name."

"Maybe it'll mean something to them later." Levi shrugged. "Let's roll out before we have to deal with any more of those redcoats."

Levi led the way south between the two hotels with the two palms and across the tall grass clearing. Chevy walked slowly at the back of the procession. Everyone seemed to have someone to walk with except the woman with the dead baby. Her brunette hair hadn't been brushed in days and she carried no possessions.

Chevy took off his pack as he walked and drew out an energy bar, part of the standard ELM field pack rations. He opened the wrapper and offered it to her. She stopped and licked her lips.

"Ma'am," he said, "your . . . baby has passed away. You can't take it with you any farther."

He waited anxiously as she blinked down at the still infant.

"She wasn't my baby." She looked at Chevy.

"Whose was she?"

"One of the ladies those guys shot out front—she gave her to me."

"This baby's been dead for . . . a few days, I think." He moved up next to her. The odor was overbearing. "Take the energy bar and give me the baby. Now keep going after the others. Go on ahead."

She obeyed, chewing on her food.

Chevy neared the first tree of the forest. They had far to go, too far to carry the deceased in his arms. He lay her at the base of the tree and covered her with a few branches, sticks, and rocks. There were no words to speak, only a heavy heart to endure. Though Levi had saved fifty, there had still been painful loss.

Continuing to walk after the Hillcrest Hopefuls, he looked back after a distance at the tree where he'd placed the little one. He saw it was an elm tree.

✝

Levi rolled out of bed and grimaced at his clothes. Too exhausted the night before to undress, he'd slept in his filthy trousers after returning upstairs after midnight.

He showered, shaved, and ate a couple of sandwiches on the balcony with his Bible as he watched daylight spread across the bay. The evening before was still a blur, but he felt alive. This had to be what true living was all about: answering the call of God for others. There had been so many lives that needed saving, so many faces pleading for more, too many names to remember.

God had risen above the fray when he'd faced the gunman in Hillcrest, and he'd known he could prevail, overcome, and arrive home victorious. Nobody would think of him as a youngster if he continued to show his courage through fearsome moments as he'd been doing. His birthday was in two weeks. How he hoped he'd proven himself to no longer be treated as a mere teenager!

As he prayed for the day ahead, God touched his soul with gentle rebukes and reminders. His limitations, as well as his family's, needed to remain in perspective or he might stop relying on his Lord. He understood better now that it was okay to take risks for his Lord, but not for his own pleasure. No more zip line adventures!

The fifty Hillcrest Hopefuls needed to be established now that they'd been brought downtown, but he couldn't be their sole hope or helper. They'd need to be trained in how to survive. And if they were interested, they'd need to be taught about the God who still loved them and had died for them. The night before, and maybe through the morning, Chevy had already begun to distribute Bibles to those who wanted to know why Levi and Chevy had rescued them.

There was a knock on his door—his father's knock. Levi opened the door to find both his parents there. They appeared no less weary than he from the short night.

"This must be serious if you're both up this early." Levi moved aside to welcome them. "Dusty's still in bed, I think. Haven't seen him come out of his room yet. Want me to get him?"

"No, it's okay." Titus sat on the living room sofa and Annette sat on the sofa arm. "We came to talk to you. That was one busy night. Chevy just went to bed about an hour ago."

"He got the water working?" Levi asked.

"For now. The building next door wasn't prepped for habitation like this one, but with those people's help and patience, they'll make it work."

"Good." Levi nodded. "They were gonna starve up in Hillcrest, you guys. And with those gunmen slaughtering everyone . . ."

"That's why we're here, Levi. You told us so little last night. We were all busy moving those people in, so we couldn't talk. Even your mother was up half the night getting food to them."

"I didn't mind." Annette smiled sadly. "They're at least thankful. You're their hero, Levi."

"We have enough extra food in the garage?" Levi asked.

"Yes, we do, but they'll need to become self-sufficient within a matter of days. What we have needs to last so we can help others in the future. One thing for sure: those fifty will establish us as a city of refuge now. Chevy said you told them they can become fishermen in the bay. Things like that creates industry and industry helps a community's stability. God designed us to be fruitful workers and creative laborers. We'll help them enjoy that independence."

"I didn't think it all through." Levi sighed. "But I knew we had to get them down here, even if we have to send them somewhere else safer."

"Well, this has all forced us to take a few steps forward," Titus said. "ELM's influence and message will grow, and Christ's Gospel will be shared. This is what we're here for."

"Okay." Levi nodded. "Good. And?"

"The gunmen who were slaughtering the people . . ." Titus cringed. "Chevy offered very little last night when we asked him about it. He said you might understand more of what was happening. What's your take? I'll be talking to Wes and Oleg about this later this morning, but I need all the known facts."

"Well, you always taught me to hold off on drawing fast conclusions, so that's what I did. I only know what I saw. What it means is more in your and Wes's area of expertise."

"What did you see?"

"Two bearded gunmen in dirty red coats were shooting civilians who were too weak to defend themselves. None of them had weapons. You saw them arrive. Even Dusty carried that woman into the building next door. It looked like the gunmen were doing some sort of eradication, like the stories you've told me of warlords in Africa. They were killing off a whole group of people."

"You're sure they weren't Pacific States?" Annette asked.

"I didn't get a chance to talk to them, but they wore these bulky red coats, not the dark red jackets we know Brogdon gives all his soldiers. These guys were pretty sloppy looking, and they smelled like they'd come from the hills. You know, like a campfire."

"What do you think?" Annette asked Titus.

"Someone's going to a lot of trouble to make it look like the Pacific States is murdering people." Titus shook his head. "Well, Lesage does murder people sometimes as we've learned from Wes, but not to this degree. This is something else."

"So, what do you want me to do?" Levi asked. "I can scout around up north and track them to find where they came from."

"Let's push pause on that right now," Titus said. "You have a lot of people relying on you next door. We're all here for them, but it's your name they all wanted to celebrate last night. I think we'll need to respond to this threat up north sooner or later. Since we're not on talking terms with the Pacific States, we probably can't warn them very easily about a conflict on our doorstep. For all our sakes, I agree, we need to handle this swiftly, but only when we have proper intel."

"I'm ready for anything, Dad. You know that."

"Yeah, I know you are." Titus grinned, like he remembered the zip line test, then he stood and embraced his son. "It ain't easy being a shepherd, but you're doing what Casperteins have always done when they answer God's call. Let me talk to Oleg and Wes and I'll get back to you about a plan of action."

After they left, Levi returned to the balcony to apply his telescope to Coronado Island. He knew every inch of the island after watching it for three months. Now that he was free to explore the streets below and maybe the island someday, he wondered if he'd ever set down the telescope entirely. This had become a favored pastime—watching from afar, gathering intel, trusting God to guide him.

His parents had put on a brave face, but he could see through it. They were concerned. The Pacific States Defense Forces were exerting themselves more vigorously for control of local provisions. Meanwhile, other forces were vying for positions north and east. Maybe some enemies were even coming up from the south through Tijuana. Levi had seen caravans of people on the interstate in weeks past. They'd all been going north, never south. Mexico must've been impacted by the virus as well, but Pan-Day hadn't spared a single neighborhood in the U.S., either.

Levi returned to the kitchen and contemplated fixing more to eat and waking Dusty when a light knock on his door drew him. The Hillcrest Hopefuls probably needed his help in a thousand different ways.

"Good morning." Carla smiled up at him on his doorstep. Her platinum hair was washed and fashioned to cover part of her scarred face, and she'd found a new blouse in storage that matched her gray eyes.

"Oh, you look nice." He noticed how she held her injured arm. The sling was draped over her shoulder. "Come on in. Ready for your wing to be bound up for the day?"

"Yeah." She moved to the dining table where light poured in from the window. Levi lifted her up to sit on the tabletop where he arranged the sling straps to wrap her arm and shoulders. "It was a busy night, huh?"

"Yeah. I saw you helping Mom. I guess you know now about the garage full of provisions we put away before Pan-Day."

"I won't tell anyone."

"Thanks." Levi cradled her arm and tucked it gently into the sling. Her voice sounded different today. And she was watching his face in a way that made him self-conscious. Had she always looked at him like that? "You, uh, have plans for the day?"

"Laundry and gardening." She smiled. "Annette said she'd help me divide up potted plants on the balconies to take over to the Hopefuls. That was a good name you thought up for them. It's something they can rally behind. You're so much . . . wiser than your years."

"Just trying to live up to what's needed. Dad's the one who keeps everything running and coordinated."

He crossed a strap over her shoulder and diagonally across her back. If he wasn't mistaken, she was wearing lipstick. And she smelled like flowers.

"All these new people to take care of . . ." She cleared her throat. "You're not going to forget about me, are you?"

"Forget about you? How could I? I promised to take care of you."

"Yeah, but you have Dusty and all this stuff with the Hopefuls now."

"You'll gradually get more independent and you won't need me as much, right?" Levi said. "And you'll be looking for your friends or family soon. Did you talk to Dad? He has radio connections who can relay messages way beyond San Diego, at least when the frequencies aren't being jammed."

"I'm not sure I'm safe out there, not like I am here at ELM with you."

"There's got to be other safe places out there." He tied the two straps together over her right arm so she could easily undo it the next morning. "Your family is probably worried about you."

"The world's a tougher place for a woman now. Maybe it always was. Everything's so backwards. I just know I can't survive on my own. I don't know what I'd do without you, Levi."

"For sure, there are other good people out there." Levi shrugged. "Some, we just haven't found yet. You're gonna be okay."

"Do you think," she touched his arm, "you could ever fall for a girl like me? I mean, with the way my face is?"

"Your face?" Levi gulped and took her hand in his. "Carla, I don't care about what you look like. I'd count myself blessed to have a . . . woman like you. I mean, you're a little, uh, more mature than even my mom, but still, you're a looker."

"A looker?" She raised her eyebrows. "That's what I am? *A looker?*"

"Look, I'm only nineteen, Carla. I don't know how to talk to you like this. Dad and Corban and Nathan and Oleg and Wes—they trained me for survival and warfare and following Jesus. I have nothing else, no other interests and no other knowledge."

"Really? No other interests? I'm not asking for you to be more than you are, Levi." Her eyes brimmed. "I know you're young, but I don't care. Just tell me you want me. Tell me there's a place in your heart for me."

Levi stared into her eyes—and wished he were back in Hillcrest facing the gun barrels of killers instead. But he didn't draw away. He knew rejection could be more damaging to someone who craved affection, especially emotional or romantic attention.

"Listen very carefully." He took her free hand with both of his. "I'm your guy. You already know I'll cross a dangerous city and wilderness for you. But it wouldn't be fair for you to be with me. I'm always praying and reading my Bible and looking for God's way for myself. That would drive you crazy. I know you remember calling Christians weirdos and freaks at the plane. That's what I am. I'm never going to be anything different."

"But you can change!" She tugged her hand free and touched his cheek. "Don't you see that? I'll help you. You can be this amazing human being without all the superstitions. You're a hero, Levi. You don't need all that religious stuff. It's all in your mind. I've traveled the world. Everyone has a religion from the past. But I can help you move into the future. I can help you learn to love yourself without that Bible and embrace the you within that is a god. I would worship you, Levi. Don't you want that? I can see it. You could be a god in this new world. Let me be at your side. Trust me. Let me love you. I can help you so much!"

"Carla." He took her hand from his face and exhaled slowly, buying himself time as he prayed for the words. "God isn't in my head and there isn't a god within me. The things you like about me, that's all from the Creator. The best things about me I didn't have until I came to faith in my Savior just a couple of years ago. I can no easier give up my Lord for you than I could stop breathing air and start breathing water. You can't see it, but I'm not deluded. *You* are. God is real. He's the reason I care for you, not because we have an intimate connection. Love like that isn't even in my headlights right now."

She pulled back her hand.

"You're too brainwashed." She lowered her head. "I can see now that I can't get through to you."

"My faith in God will only grow stronger." Levi took a half-step back. "And my prayer for you will become more desperate. You can't get through to me because my heart is elsewhere. But I know God can touch your heart. Give it time, okay? If you want to stay here, I'll try to take care of you . . . like you're my aunt or something."

"Your *aunt?*" She scoffed and rolled her eyes. "You'll treat me like your Aunt Wynter? That's real comforting."

"Hey, you're the world traveler. What do I know about . . . smooth-talking a chick?"

"*Chick?*"

"Sorry." Levi chuckled breathlessly. "Look at it this way. You and I have something in common. You're closer to my biblical worldview than I am to whatever it is you believe in."

"Oh? Enlighten me."

"God's whole message is about forgiveness of our sins. Without His forgiveness, there can be no relationship with Him. And you know something about forgiveness. Your arm. Dusty broke your collarbone. He attacked you."

"He panicked. And it was dark."

"But he meant to harm you."

"Well, he didn't mean to. He just wanted the food in the plane. I see that now."

"Stop it. They would've left you for dead in the wilderness, and you know it. Yet, you've forgiven him, haven't you?"

"I understand he was just being selfish."

"You've forgiven him."

"Well, he's changed since then."

"Only because he knows he's been pardoned. That's how it works for us with God. Once we understand His forgiveness and trust in that, our lives change on the inside. You know about forgiveness. Now, you just need to believe you need it."

"I need forgiveness?" She guffawed and slid off the table to stand before him. "What've I ever done? I don't need anybody's forgiveness. God has no right to point out anything I've ever done, and you don't either."

"It ain't easy being perfect, huh?"

She slapped him on the cheek. It wasn't a hard slap and he'd seen it coming. But her face showed she was more surprised by the slap than he was.

"Don't call me perfect. I hate that more than you calling me *Lady!*" She collected herself and held her chin higher. "I shouldn't have slapped you. But you shouldn't have pushed me. Look at me—arguing with a teenager. Pitiful."

Levi stood with his thumbs hooked in his pockets a moment.

"So, are we good?" he asked.

"Are we good?" She wiped furiously at her eyes. "No, we're not good! I just . . . smacked you!"

"Oh, well, I'd tell you that you're forgiven, but I'm not trying to get smacked again. That really stung."

"Stop it."

"How about we shake on it?" He offered his hand.

"You're such a juvenile." She shook his hand.

"That's what I've been trying to tell you!" He moved into the kitchen. "Have you eaten yet? I've got fresh eggs from the roof. How about an egg salad sandwich?"

"Fine." She pulled out a chair and sat at the dining table, pouting. "Just don't call me Aunt Carla."

"How about Cousin Carla?" Levi asked from across the kitchen. "Prima Carlasita?"

Carla swore and shook her head.

"You've made your point. We're family. Can we just move on?"

"What's all the noise out here?" Dusty wandered out in the same clothes he'd worn the day before, his hair askew.

"Hey, I'm not the only one who slept in his clothes!" Levi laughed. "It ain't easy working night and day, huh, Dusty?"

Dusty slumped into a chair across from Carla and flopped his head on the table.

"It can't be morning already. I'm so sore!"

"Well, you carried that woman in your arms for a mile," Levi said. "Of course, you're sore! But that lady will never forget you. She would've been left behind to die without you."

"You carried me across half the wilderness." Carla frowned at Levi. "Were you sore?"

"Hey, I'm young, not stupid." He winked at her. "You were and always will be as light as a feather."

"Good answer." She scoffed.

"Do I have to carry anyone else today?" Dusty asked as he stretched. "When do we take a day off?"

"Who'd want a day off from all this fun?" Levi toasted bread for three sandwiches. "Dad's talking to Oleg and Wes right now. There's something going on with those redcoats we saw yesterday. If we go out, Dusty, you'll stay here to guard the perimeter."

"Who are they—these redcoats?" Carla asked. "Not Pacific States?"

"I'm just guessing, but I think they're invaders."

"Invaders?" Carla shook her head. "We're all Americans. We can't invade America."

"The PSDF has claimed territory and made laws. Others are doing the same. Los Angeles or Riverside probably recruited people from the mountains to put on red coats and come to kill and loot, pretending to be the PSDF. They're trying to cause confusion at a local level. It's an invasion before an invasion. Wes told me it happened during wars in the past."

"Can you imagine?" Carla hung her head. "On top of everything else happening, now there's going to be a civil war? Over what? Everything's collapsed!"

Levi brought their sandwiches and sat at the head of the table. Grilled and seasoned fries and a couple of dried peaches accompanied their sandwiches. As Dusty and Carla reached for their food, Levi bowed his head.

"Dear Father, we're just scraping by here on the Earth, but You continue to provide us with food, good friendships, and a promised future. Thank You. Amen."

Carla and Dusty remained frozen, glancing at one another.

"Can we eat now?" Carla asked. "Are you finished?"

"Sister," Levi picked up his sandwich, "I'm just getting started!"

✝

Sergeant Dom Lesage rode shotgun in the lead Humvee of three vehicles. This was no ordinary patrol. Nor was it a confiscation mission for provisions. General Brogdon wanted him to press farther north and east than they'd been before. Except by recon plane, Lesage hadn't been north of the I-8 in months. The assignment was so dangerous that Brogdon hadn't allowed his son to accompany Lesage, which was fine with Lesage. He hated the little whiner.

They drove slowly through the Balboa Park and Zoo buildings. Someone had loosed the wild animals—intentionally or not—and Lesage would've loved to pull over and hunt down a giant predator, but he had another hunt to undertake.

"Stay to the left up here." Lesage ordered his driver past a broken-down semitrailer. "Use Highway 163 to get to the I-8."

Though Lesage had planned their route for that day, the situation on the ground forced him in other directions. He'd seen from a distance that the I-8 was intact, but reaching it wasn't as easy as following the map. On and off-ramps were choked by vehicles sometimes twenty abreast, overflowing onto the grassy shoulder on both sides of access roads. Cars had been abandoned after an attempted rush to leave the city. Furniture, luggage, trash, and bodies choked intersections since the PSDF plow truck hadn't opened up lanes this far north.

Finally, they found an off-ramp they could take to reach the I-8 going against traffic, but no one was around to ticket the convoy. In fact, the lanes leading out of the city were bumper-to-bumper with frozen traffic, yet the incoming lanes were fairly clear.

"Slow down," Lesage said. Gazing north, he saw a caravan of people on foot, perhaps eighty people with backpacks, heading north on the 163. They were either Mexicans or locals leaving the city. Brogdon had given Lesage the standard instructions not to bother locals since the military would need them to rebuild some industrial framework eventually. But hoarders were fair game, civilian or not. "They've got nothing. Drive on."

The Humvee sped up to thirty miles an hour headed east. Lesage's window was down, his rifle muzzle on the sill. In the backseat sat a radio operator and a mortar specialist. If the patrol ran into any trouble, they were the two men Lesage wanted close by—one to call in reinforcements and another to repel the enemy.

The driver slowed as they approached the tangle of freeways south of the stadium. Abandoned cars spotted the lanes, but the convoy could still weave through them here.

"Unopened trailer!" The radio man leaned forward between the front seats and pointed at the westbound traffic. "The doors are still closed!"

"Impossible." Lesage gestured for his driver to pull up against the concrete median. "Keep your eyes open."

The radio man used a unit radio to inform the other two vehicles of why they'd stopped.

Lesage climbed out of the truck and straightened his black arm band on his left biceps. An experienced enemy combatant would know it represented something about his expertise more than his mere rank. The black bands were his idea and Brogdon had approved the move. The band created an elite Flash Troop within the PSDF, something the ordinary soldiers could aspire to join. Competition always aided in progress, especially in a military where Brogdon had simplified the ranks of his men with no rank higher than sergeant.

While Lesage studied the lanes of cars and trucks, he slid a new sawed-off shotgun into the scabbard on his back, then fit his rifle sling over his head and shoulder. He'd seen action in a half-dozen countries as a Canadian Special Forces officer. Urban warfare was his specialty, and he smelled an ambush. But an unopened semitrailer was too valuable to pass up. Nonperishable foods, camping gear, or clothing was every scavenger's dream. However, a trailer full of electronics would be a waste of time.

"Perimeter!" Lesage signaled the other Humvees.

Four men from each of the two rear vehicles scattered to establish a defensive perimeter all around. Lesage's driver, radio operator, and mortar specialist climbed out to stay near him, but each took up defensive positions against nearby vehicles.

Was it truly possible a trailer had been overlooked by scavengers? Vehicles nearby didn't seem as ransacked or burned as those downtown. Most fuel caps had been left open where others had siphoned the gas in weeks past, and some car doors remained open from looters searching for valuables or food. Lesage saw no dead here, either. The people had evidently just walked away with what they could carry.

"Tell command where we are," Lesage said to his radio man.

He hated to admit it, but getting tranqed twice by Caspertein's people had made him edgy. No longer was he as confident as he had been. Only by some strangers' "no killing" standards was he not dead already! It was just plain embarrassing—being humiliated by a few religious survivalist types, but he understood Brogdon's reasoning as well: tolerating the ELM people downtown would stabilize the whole city. Later, when the Casperteins revealed a vulnerability, he could punish them, but not before.

"No answer," reported the radio man. He was a youngster with freckles, but his discipline had earned him a place on this squad. "We're out of range, sir, or there's too much interference around us."

"Expected." Lesage cursed. General Brogdon was always complaining about their inadequate, short antenna tower. "Since it's useless, just leave the radio in the truck and go get the bolt cutters."

After climbing over the concrete median, Lesage crept cautiously toward the trailer. Three heavy padlocks secured the back door. That would certainly deter a common passerby, but not an equipped scavenger. How had they missed this trailer? Maybe it was too far out of town to be noticed, and those on foot hadn't bothered since they couldn't carry any more than they already carried.

The trailer had no markings on the outside. He couldn't tell by the tires if the trailer carried a heavy or empty load since most of the tires were already flat.

"What about our orders, Sarge?" asked the radio man.

Lesage understood the soldier's apprehension. Usually, provision gathering preceded all other priorities, but Brogdon desperately needed intel on enemy ground forces around El Capitan Lake. If the lake hadn't been taken yet, PSDF could move north and establish an outpost in the San Jacinto Mountains.

"Open it." Lesage aimed his rifle at the trailer. His men stood all around with leveled weapons. "Let's see what we get."

The radio man cut the first lock. Lesage imagined a trailer full of brand-new clothes for Coronado's population. Soldiers' families were always petitioning the president for more, which fell on the military to constantly bring in more provisions. Or maybe the trailer held a hardware store's inventory. He'd already brought back several loads of lumber and camping gear, making him the hero of the island. What he really craved now was something that might give him an edge over PSDF adversaries: military gear or even stores of food.

The second lock was cut. Lesage tilted his head. Had that been a noise from inside the trailer? Something had shifted against the wall inside. Someone was waiting!

He reached for the radio operator even as the third lock was cut. But nothing happened. His left hand rested on the shoulder of the freckle-faced young man.

"Wait, I thought I heard something." Lesage checked down the length of the trailer, then studied the nearby cars. A half-mile away, a lone deer grazed on tendrils of grass already growing from cracks in the pavement. "I don't like this."

"We've come this far, sir." The man reached for the sliding handle. "Should I open it?"

Lesage checked his team once more. They were spread out as he'd trained them. In the last three months, they'd been through thirty firefights. Though they still carried the bruises from the tranquilizer rounds, he'd count on them against any normal enemy. Again, he cursed Wes Trimble and the Casperteins for their part in cracking his confidence in the field.

"Do it."

As his man threw open the doors, he moved to the side of the trailer. Instead of looking inside himself, Lesage watched the face of the radio operator. The man blinked in his surprise.

"It's . . . *empty!*"

"Nobody locks up an empty—" Lesage's words were interrupted by a single gunshot.

His radio operator fell, then gunfire erupted all around and above Lesage. They were on the roof of the trailer! They must've been lying flat up there! But not only the roof—enemy fire teams materialized from the trunks of nearby cars. PSDF soldiers were caught in the crossfire between five or more shooters on the trailer roof and as many as fifteen shooters outside their perimeter.

From where he stood against the side of the trailer, Lesage couldn't fight. It was an ambush! His only chance was to escape and evade. He crawled under the trailer and eyed the side of the freeway. It was a forty-foot drop or more to the ground below, but he could fight down there if he survived the drop. Maybe he could even find cover and return to the island—if he could just get out of this jam!

His men screamed as they died. The enemy closed in and Lesage's window of opportunity to reach the side of the freeway diminished.

Bullets peppered the trailer over his head. *Someone had seen him!* He retreated from his plan and dove between vehicles closer to his Humvee. Maybe he could climb in and drive away!

More bullets chased him as he scrambled up the median, then he dove over the concrete divider. Finally, a little cover! The Humvee was only one car away. He crawled, tearing his trouser knees in the process. Cursing, he wished he'd worn his kneepads like he used to.

He reached the Humvee, crawled inside, and fumbled for the ignition. But no key. *The driver had taken the key!*

Rifle rounds slammed into the bulletproof glass and reinforced metal. Lesage climbed into the back seat. *The radio!* He slipped on the headset, turned on the transmit switch, then fell to the floor to hide.

Gasping for help on the radio, Lesage knew no one would hear. It was hopeless. Coronado Island was out of range. He gave the convoy's position as men screamed outside the Humvee. The gunfire was deafening even from inside.

A grenade hit the side of the Humvee and rocked the vehicle up onto two wheels for an instant. Lesage was shaken. Then the gunfire stopped. The radio headset was silent. Nobody was there.

Two bearded gunmen appeared outside the Humvee windows. Lesage looked down at his hands. Somewhere, he'd dropped or lost his rifle. His shotgun was still on his back digging into his spine and his Bowie was still strapped across his chest, but he couldn't fight from his back on the floor boards of the vehicle.

Then the radio crackled and a clear strong voice responded: "I hear you, PS2. If you can still hear me, I received your last transmission. We're coming to get you. Over."

Lesage knew that voice! It belonged to a man who'd humiliated him only days earlier. It belonged to a man the Pacific States allowed to live for social stability, but Lesage would kill him the minute Brogdon gave him the order.

However, the man's voice now gave Lesage hope. Slipping off the headset, he couldn't explain his relief that someone had heard his pleas. Even if it was *that man*, Lesage knew he wouldn't die anonymously with his unit on the interstate, duped by a triple-locked empty trailer.

He raised his hands to the enemy. The bearded soldiers opened the door at Lesage's feet.

"We've got a live one here!" yelled one of the combatants. "Come on out of there. Slowly!"

Sitting up, Lesage used the seat to climb to his feet. He allowed his fingers to glide over the radio's frequency dial to spin the knob one-third of the way around.

"I'm coming," Lesage said. "Don't shoot. I'm coming peacefully. I'm worth more alive."

"Ah, a real prize, huh? We'll decide that!"

Stripped of his weapons, Lesage was allowed to keep his crimson jacket and black arm band. Then he was hooded and handcuffed behind his back.

"Climb into their trucks!" ordered one man. "Beats walking back to the horses, huh?"

"Plenty of fuel here, Prosky!" announced a woman.

"Let's go!"

Lesage was stuffed into the back of one of the other Humvees. Under his hood, he tried to manage his breathing. His shoulders cramped and the cuffs bit into his wrists, but he was alive. *He had to survive!*

All his hope now rested on a man he'd hated since they'd met a week earlier—*Caspertein!*

# *Chapter Six*

Titus scribbled the location as fast as he heard the coordinates on the radio. The operator on the other end was begging for help, but no one responded. A patrol had come under fire. A man screamed in the background, mixed with gunfire. Then an explosion and all was quiet.

After months of listening to but never transmitting on PSDF frequencies, Titus pressed the transmit button and hovered over the mic.

"I hear you, PS2," Titus said. "If you can still hear me, I received your last transmission. We're coming to get you. Over." Titus released the button. He didn't want to say who he was in case an adversary was listening, but maybe he'd given the radio operator some hope.

Three days had passed since Levi had brought home the fifty Hopefuls. The redcoat infiltrators were still such an unknown that no one could decide a definite response, so they'd waited. And now this.

With the sounds of battle still ringing in his ears, Titus went to his wall map and tried to find the cross streets along I-8 that the radio operator had given. His map didn't have enough detail. Levi had taken all his best maps, Titus remembered with a smile. They were in good hands.

He left the radio room while still trying to still his heart. Annette was cooking and humming in the kitchen. The fifty Hillcrest Hopefuls Levi had brought in had placed untold strain on the ELM personnel, but no one had complained, not even Wynter. Everyone was rising to the challenge and stepping up to the strangers' needs. Wes and Levi had even dug into their basement provisions for fishing line and nets to begin teaching the new arrivals how to fish in the bay.

But there were other strangers who needed ELM now.

"I got a call on the radio." He kissed Annette on the cheek, then stood beside her against the counter. "I'll need to lead a rescue up into the hills past the zoo."

"You?" Annette stopped whisking. She had flour on her cheek and dried goat's milk on her apron front. "Well, I guess Oleg's not exactly up for the field trip."

"He would limp out there if we asked him to." He chuckled. "But no. I think Levi and I will take lead on this one together."

"Two Casperteins at once?" She clucked her tongue and continued to mix. "The world doesn't know what it's in for."

"I'll take Wes, but Chevy'll stay here since he's so busy getting things going for the Hopefuls. Dusty, too. Levi says Dusty is close to trusting in what they've talked about in Scripture, but I'm not sending anyone into a kill zone who isn't heaven-bound."

"No, you only send yourself and your son."

"Well, I'm glad you understand."

She set the whisk aside, wiped her hands on a towel, and faced him directly.

"How serious is this new thing? I mean, if you're going . . ."

"Some PSDF boys got ambushed."

"And?"

"And . . . they asked for help."

"They asked *you* for help?"

"Well, not by name." Titus grinned. "I may have volunteered."

"Brogdon and Lesage should clean up their own messes."

"That's the thing. I don't think Coronado got the transmission. Our range is much greater."

"So, tell Brogdon what happened."

"And miss an opportunity?" Titus winced. "We could mend this fence with an act of mercy. What's Chevy always teaching Levi? Grace breaks bondage."

"Rescuing your enemy when he doesn't deserve it?" Annette sighed and rested her arms over his shoulders. "Don't make me a widow already, Titus Caspertein. And don't take Levi from me. This world still needs the both of you. *I* still need the both of you."

He embraced her.

"You and Chevy can hold down the fort? It ain't easy leaving your side for even an hour."

She didn't answer for a moment as they held each other.

"Tell me where you need me," she said.

Twenty minutes later, Titus stood against the window sill in Oleg's apartment living room where Oleg's bed had been moved. Oleg was still recovering from his hip wound, but he'd remained alert enough to counsel Titus on ELM situations. Besides, Titus figured that in a matter of weeks, the aging Russian would be on his feet and active in the field again. He needed to keep his friend in the loop.

Wes and Wynter stood facing Titus, and Levi and Dusty leaned against a wall. Chevy sat on the foot of his roommate's bed, and Carla had posted herself just inside the doorway.

Titus offered a prayer for right hearts and godly motives, then studied the faces of his audience.

"It's been a good week," he began. "We've made new friends and settled them next door. Chevy even has more discipleship classes to host than he knows what to do with. But ELM offers more than just the amenities of a household. We're uniquely equipped to shut down aggressors. Three days ago, we didn't have enough intel to act on the redcoat threat up in Hillcrest. Now, I think we do."

He shared the details of the radio transmission he'd intercepted—and how he'd promised to respond. The redcoats were probably the antagonists.

"I thought we were staying neutral in the approaching war," Chevy said. "How are we staying neutral when we're taking the side of PSDF and attacking these redcoats or whoever these northerners are?"

"Good question," Oleg said. "I'd say we're responding to a distress call. It doesn't matter who sent it."

"The PSDF are our immediate neighbors," Titus said, "and if there is a government authority in this land, it's them, though they haven't fully figured out how to govern quite yet. I see this as an opportunity to heal some relationships, if possible. The radio operator's call sign was PS2."

"Pacific States, Unit Two," Wes said. "That's Sergeant Lesage's unit."

"Exactly." Titus watched everyone's faces. They all understood except Dusty and Carla. "We might—and I say again, *might*—be able to rescue PS2 and push some violent strangers back up north. Or we might meet some new people, open up a dialogue with them, and share the Gospel."

"General Brogdon will owe us," Levi said. "He'll trust us more as an asset instead of as a threat to President Criswell's new government if we do this."

"That's a possibility," Titus said. "But this mission of mercy could leave us vulnerable here on the home front. We'll need some of you to act as defenders. Chevy, you're in charge of ELM while Wes, Levi, and I hit the pavement. Everyone keep your radios handy."

"No problem." Chevy nodded sharply.

"Carla," Titus continued, "I'd like you up on the roof with binoculars and a radio for the first few hours. Annette will be in my radio room. You two can relay any activity to us that you see in the field."

"I can do that." Carla glanced at Levi, as if he'd made sure she was involved. "Thanks."

"Dusty and Wynter, I'd like you both armed and on the second-floor balcony in shifts until we get back. Relieve one another at irregular intervals."

"Someone should tell the Hopefuls to stay inside the perimeter while there might be a threat nearby," Chevy said. "I'll let them know."

"Should we say anything to Coronado?" Wes asked. "They'll be looking for their missing patrol real soon."

"Good question." Titus guessed the ex-agent already knew the answer, but he'd asked it for the benefit of the others. "Every life matters. Even the lives of the invaders matter. If we give Coronado the last known position of their patrol, they'll go in with guns blazing. People will die. But our way, no one dies. We can risk our own lives to save the lives of both sides—and possibly bring healing throughout. That means keeping General Brogdon in the dark—at least until we need a pickup. It ain't easy admitting my old legs will need a lift home."

"This doesn't sound like a quick in-and-out mission." Wynter moved closer to her one-eyed husband. "How long will you guys be gone?"

"We'll ration for two days." Titus nodded at Levi. "Two hard days."

Levi nodded back. Titus saw no fear in his son's eyes, only the prospect of honor and adventure and hardship. The young man would probably outdistance him and Wes if Titus let him, but learning patience and caution with older operatives would guide the youth for the future.

"It's only noon," Titus said. "I want to cover some distance before sundown. We leave in twenty minutes."

Since Titus was already packed, he was first to arrive on the ground floor after kissing Annette goodbye in the radio room.

"Headed to war?" Gustavo asked Titus. They stood on either side of the goat pen. "You look serious."

The old Hispanic man had already recruited people from the Hopefuls to gather brush and twigs whenever they found it around the city for the goats to eat.

"It's serious enough that I might give you my rifle and I'll stay home with the goats."

"Oh, no, Titus!" The man gasped in laughter. "I'd probably accidentally tranquilize myself in the foot before I even got to the door!"

Wes and Levi arrived. The one-eyed man's pack looked unnecessarily heavy and Levi's appeared too light. One was overprepared and the other perhaps kept light for mobility. Titus guessed his own pack held too much food and clothes as well—for PS2 survivors if they found any. He prayed they found some prisoners—and not just Riverside aggressors.

"Levi, lead us up to the ambush site on I-8." Titus turned the wheel lock. "We'll see if we can pick up the trail from there. Wes and I will keep a hundred-meter spread. I'll cover the rear."

Titus saw the pride in Levi's eyes that he'd been asked to lead. But Titus hadn't suggested his son take point just to honor the young man. Levi was a legitimate force to be reckoned with. His mission with Oleg and Oleg's own testimony were evidence that Levi was emerging from his training as Titus hoped he would. Of course, Levi's eyes and ears were clear and sharp since they hadn't been abused as much by hard living.

Marching away from ELM, Levi squeezed through the perimeter of vehicles as Titus and Wes walked side by side, still adjusting their packs for the trek ahead.

"The boy's not going to pace himself, is he?" Wes joked.

"Caspertein stamina!" Titus chuckled. "He knows only one pace. Oleg said he went like that for two days straight when fetching Carla."

"I guess I can't call him a boy any longer." Wes sighed and moved through the perimeter gap first. "He's mistaking me for a younger man with fit limbs and two eyes."

"It ain't easy having more scar tissue than skin." Titus tightened his rifle sling. "But it sure feels good to be out here, doesn't it?"

"Ask me tomorrow when my joints are screaming for a hot tub."

Once they reached the Air and Space Museum, Titus allowed Wes to walk ahead so all three shooters could cover one another. None of them could be attacked individually without inviting a response from the other two. Titus knew Wes was more proficient with sidearms than the battle rifle, but Wes's past target practice groupings had been accurate up to at least three hundred yards. That was half the distance Levi could steadily group his rounds, but the .308 in Wes's hands was still more effective than the common military rifle most soldiers carried.

Far ahead up the 163, Levi stopped and waited for the older men to catch up. Titus noticed that while Levi waited, he wasn't distracted by picking through nearby vehicles or opening a meal pouch for a snack. No, he remained vigilant as a good point man would. He stood atop a vehicle and used binoculars to look ahead and study the tree line nearby.

They reached the I-8 an hour before sundown. Titus felt like his body was just beginning to warm up to the march as they regrouped for a water break at the top of an on-ramp. Wes showed no sign of fatigue, regardless of his earlier comments of aging, and Levi appeared as fresh as a morning hiker.

"What're the chances of us running into the same ambush that the PS2 did?" Wes asked.

"I've been ambushed before," Levi said. "It was a place called New Encanto. I barely survived. That's where Oleg was shot. I'll watch out for something like that."

"The wisdom of life experience." Titus saluted both men with his water bottle. "If they sow the wind, they'll reap the whirlwind."

"Translation?" Wes said. "In what way?"

"We're not PS2. We won't easily be drawn into a trap."

Instead of walking up the relatively clear westbound lanes of the interstate, Levi picked his way through the vehicle-crowded lanes of the eastbound side. The going was slower, but Titus approved. Levi was searching out possible ambush perches before he walked into a trap. Every car or truck—lined as far as the eye could see—was a potential hiding place. Every trunk, back seat, or tool box needed to be considered. On occasion, Levi would lie flat on the pavement and scope ahead over entire lanes of traffic, checking under vehicles for sleepers.

"There's something up here," Levi announced. "The stadium is on the left. This is where it happened. Over."

Titus checked the sky. Their light was fading. He found a reefer truck and climbed onto its roof. After shedding his pack, he lay down flat and scoped the lanes ahead as Levi approached a large semitrailer, its rear doors wide open. If Titus wasn't mistaken, there were bodies in red jackets lying scattered across the lanes of traffic.

Wes joined Levi to inspect the ambush site, but Titus remained prepared on the reefer truck to offer cover fire just in case. He watched the other cars nearby, even farther away, for aggressors.

"Looks pretty clear, TC," Wes announced after several minutes. "You want to come up here? Over."

Titus made one last sweep of the lanes with his scope. No movement except a few crows circling.

"I'm coming. Over."

He slid off the front of the truck and walked cautiously up the lanes. There was something ominous about approaching a scene where many had died so violently less than twenty-four hours earlier. When he reached the site, Wes stood among the dead, but Levi had chosen an SUV to stand atop to keep lookout. So much death—it was a lot for a nineteen-year-old to witness.

"Looks like this was the bait." Wes traced his boot over steel padlocks on the pavement at the back of the trailer. "It was probably irresistible to a patrol always searching for loot."

"So far from Coronado and civilization." Titus shook his head at the bodies. "I count ten. What were they doing way out here?"

"There's an eleventh on the other side of the wall there." Wes gazed off the interstate at the trees and grass below. "They were probably doing recon on rumors of invaders, maybe the same things we've heard about. General Brogdon should've kept to aerial reconnaissance. He's too vulnerable out here to do guerrilla-style fighting like this—unless he's moving a hundred men at once. I told him that."

"Did you check the dead?" Titus asked. "If this was PS2 like the radio said . . ."

"Sergeant Lesage isn't here. This was probably a three-vehicle convoy. Four men per Humvee. Twelve men total."

"One unaccounted for." Titus turned east where he could see only a few hundred yards between vehicles. "So, we push on."

"We keep going?" Levi asked.

"Not tonight." Titus gestured up the freeway. "Let's go up a quarter mile. I saw an off ramp while it was light enough to see. I don't know about you two, but I'm not sleeping in the back seat of any of these cars."

They took the next off-ramp and left the pavement altogether for the trees and shrubs to the southeast. Titus gave Levi a spade head to dig himself a shallow burrow to sleep in against a fallen tree. Wes dug his at the other end of the tree and covered himself with his rain poncho, though the night was comfortable.

"Two and a half hour watches," Titus said. "Wes, you'll take second watch. Levi, he'll wake you for the last watch."

"I think Levi should keep watch all night," Wes said. "Maybe if he's a little drowsy tomorrow, he'll ease up on the pace."

"Or we could tranq Levi," Titus said, "but he'd still find a way to beat us to the next mile marker."

Titus knew Levi was listening in the dark. He smiled in his son's direction, wondering how he'd respond. In the building, he'd been the youngster among veterans, but he was no longer the unproven student. He'd rescued Carla from death, secured Oleg's survival, and brought Dusty to his knees. The fifty Hopefuls had a chance at living because of him. One mark of a man, as Titus had lived, was the ability to respond to a friend's banter in good humor.

A few seconds passed.

"It's nice that both of you act so old and crippled," Levi said softly, "so I feel more experienced and useful."

Wes did his best to muffle his laughter.

"He thinks I'm *acting* old and crippled? *Acting?*"

Titus settled into his own burrow, a smile on his face. The Lord was shaping Levi into the man Titus and Annette had prayed he'd become.

The next morning, they returned to the interstate and continued east, deducing that they were following the Humvees' route since the vehicles hadn't been left behind. Traffic choked most of the on- and off-ramps, so they agreed together two hours after sunrise that the vehicles had pulled off the freeway—down an on-ramp. Dust on the pavement showed three sets of tire tracks.

"It looks pretty rural." Titus observed a small town that lay in shambles before them. There were power poles down on its two streets, one gas station that was charred and ruined, and a derailed eight-car train at the nearest railroad crossing. "See anything?"

Using binoculars, Wes studied the background terrain that rose to steep hillsides with trees and shrubs. Levi used his rifle scope to watch their back trail.

"There's a draw at the foot of that nearest tall hill." Wes pointed north. "Good foliage for cover, but I don't see any campfire smoke. Looks pretty quiet."

"It's hard to say what we're walking into," Titus said, "but the tire tracks definitely lead off in that direction. Levi?"

Lowering his rifle, Levi eyed the town without his scope.

"If there's a military unit operating in this area, those people will know." He pointed at a two-story house with a one car garage. "We could ask them."

"That house?" Titus noted. "Did you see someone? I don't even see a clothesline. How do you know someone lives there?"

"You're testing me?" Levi smiled. "I'll go ask them."

Levi started down a grassy slope to reach the yard of the residence rimmed by leafy trees on the west and a fence and general store on the north.

"What do you guys see?" Wes sidled up to Titus. "Maybe it's just because of my one eye, but I see no sign of anyone living there. No animals, garbage, nothing. Right?"

"I don't know." Titus shrugged. "I'm not testing him. I really don't see anything, either."

They followed Levi down to the front yard and stood at the end of the driveway. Titus and Wes watched Levi knock on the door, though they did their best not to seem threatening. People who were hiding out in the small town probably didn't want to be bothered.

No one answered Levi's loud knocking.

"There's nobody here," Wes said to Titus, then nodded at the derailed train. "You think someone already searched those cars?"

"I'd guess someone derailed the train for the express purpose of searching the cars," Titus said. "Whatever those cars carried, even if it was full of clothes pins, there's probably nothing left to pick over."

"Listen," Levi said through the door, "I know you can hear me. The path on the side of the house is well-used, so I know you're in there. My name is Levi Caspertein. I'm here with my dad and our friend, Wes Trimble. We're not here to hurt you. And we don't want any of your food or supplies. If you need anything, you're welcome to what we have. A friend of ours has gone missing so we're tracking him down. Some sort of military unit took him prisoner. We'd just like to know who they are and if we're going in the right direction. Every life matters to us, so we're here to save our friend and talk things out with the military people."

"This isn't gonna work," Wes said to Titus. "People are too paranoid nowadays. We'd be better off following those tire tracks into the hills ourselves and hope we don't get ambushed."

Titus heard a thump from inside the house—perhaps a heavy brace was being laid aside from the door. Then a chain rattled and the door opened an inch.

"I don't believe this," Wes said. "Your son just—"

"Yeah, I know." Titus set a hand on Wes' shoulder. "He saw that path that we didn't notice, and now he's succeeding where you and I wouldn't have bothered. Listen."

But whatever was said, only Levi could hear. He conversed with the homeowner briefly, then the door closed and Levi walked across the yard to join Titus and Wes. Titus watched his face and read the worry in his eyes.

"They've got the virus," Levi said. "He had sores on his face. He and his wife are pretty sure they haven't transmitted it to their granddaughter, so they're sending her out in a minute."

"Why?" Wes asked. "Does she know about who we're tracking down?"

"Probably not. She's only eleven. I told them we'd keep her safe." Levi sighed. "But she's got Down syndrome, so she can't stay here."

"Well, uh . . ." Titus chuckled. "God is certainly keeping things interesting for us, huh, Wes?"

"We're taking on a passenger?" Wes asked, then answered. "Okay, we're taking on a passenger. What about Lesage?"

"The guy said they've been trading for food with some militia people up in the hills. They're usually on horseback, but yesterday they drove through town in three trucks and parked them behind the drive-thru of the burger joint at the other end of town. They have a compound about a mile northeast of here."

"Okay, and the mountain militia is now likely spreading the virus," Titus deduced. "That complicates things."

"Annette said the virus is probably only transmissible through sores and body fluids." Wes glanced toward the house. "What if this girl has it and doesn't know it? We've discussed the possibility of carriers before."

"Well, I guess you could tell the girl to keep her distance from you," Titus said, "but it's my experience that Down syndrome people are all about affection."

"We can't take the virus back into town," Wes said. "Titus, we have the Hillcrest Hopefuls to think about, not just us."

"I'll keep the girl with me," Titus said. "If she has it, she won't be contagious unless symptomatic. And we'll know within a few days if she's symptomatic. Otherwise, she should be in the clear."

"As soon as she's symptomatic," Wes said, "you'll get it if she's with you. Titus, this isn't safe."

"Sometimes doing the right thing isn't safe," said Titus. "We'll take precautions. I'll quarantine with Lesage and the girl when we get back to town. Beyond that, I believe we should stay the course. Don't you think?"

"Precautions." Wes nodded. "I guess that's the right balance between being careless and irrationally paranoid. Levi, you think these people are being honest?"

"Well, they're giving us their grandkid because they'll be dead in a week or less. They knew to keep the girl separate once they were symptomatic, so she hasn't been directly exposed. I'm not worried."

"What else do they know about the militia?" Titus asked. "Here she is. Levi, see what else you can find out."

A stocky child backed away from the front porch as she waved nonstop at a tearful woman in a mask and an aged man in overalls, a scarf around much of his face. Neither could stand unsupported. It seemed they were on death's door.

"God is full of surprises, huh?" Wes said to Titus as Levi returned to the front door. "You know, I'm not against helping this child."

"I know." Titus patted him on the shoulder. "You're just thinking of all the angles. That's what we all need to do."

"What're you gonna do with her?" Wes asked.

The girl was still backing toward them, still waving at her relatives. She wore a baseball cap, coat, and winter boots with laces dragging. A pink plastic backpack was fastened tightly to her back.

"Short or long-term?"

"Both."

"Short-term, we'll need to handle the militia boys with her at my side. And long-term, it looks like ELM just adopted a child."

Titus noticed Levi was keeping his distance from the grandparents as they conversed. The woman, emotional behind her mask, turned and went inside, but the man remained at the door to talk to Levi.

"Hi there." Titus approached the girl from the side. She had blond hair in a messy ponytail with bangs cut straight across under the faded Dodgers bill. "My name is Titus. What's your name?"

The girl stopped waving and smiled broadly. She offered words to Titus with great effort, but they were only a mixture of noises.

"Gabby Hillerman." Levi approached and handed Titus a plastic baton with pink and white tassels. "That's her name. But she doesn't really talk."

"She speaks in other important ways." Titus offered the girl the baton. "That smile speaks volumes, Little Lady. It's a pleasure to meet you, Gabby Hillerman."

Titus had planned on trying to keep his distance, but Gabby had other ideas. She accepted the baton and simultaneously wrapped her arms around Titus' midsection.

"It ain't easy pushing away an affectionate kid." Titus shrugged, knelt, and hugged the child back. "Anything else from the Hillermans?"

"They said her birthday is June first," Levi answered.

"I mean about the militia."

"They're about thirty-strong around here, but survivalist camps have popped up all over these hills. Sometimes they fight against one another and sometimes they band together to raid the suburbs to the east or south. These people were safe since they had nothing."

"This militia—are they the redcoats you crossed in Hillcrest?"

"When I asked if they wore red coats, Mr. Hillerman said no. But I think maybe they put on the red coats when they get closer to Pacific States territory."

"So," Titus said to Gabby as he tied her boot laces, "you're about to have a birthday. We have a lot of walking to do. You'll walk beside me, okay? If your backpack gets too heavy, I'll carry it for you. It feels pretty light. Probably mostly clothes. Maybe you can carry my pack when mine gets too heavy for me, huh?"

Gabby mumbled and slurred words incoherently while pulling on her backpack straps.

"Well, we'll work on understanding one another." Titus nodded. "You just tug on my arm if you need my attention, okay?"

She mumbled, smiled, and stepped back to twirl her baton around a couple times before she dropped it.

"The Caspertein family always needed a twirler, didn't we?" Titus asked Wes, and climbed back to his feet. "Yeah, Little Lady, you'll fit right in with us. Levi, lead us out—and cautiously. Let's look for those vehicles first. Wes, Gabby and I will bring up the rear."

"Someone could be watching us already," Wes warned Levi as they started toward the town's main street. "High alert, Levi."

"Copy that."

"Stay at my side, Gabby." Titus pointed to the ground beside him as he followed Wes. "We're going to see some unfriendly men about taking a friend of ours."

Gabby mumbled a response.

"It'll all work out." Titus readied his rifle. "It ain't easy adopting a new family, so you'll have to be patient with us. We'll trust God our Creator. He'll direct us through everything. You and I will have some good talks about Jesus along the way. Stay up with me here, Little Lady. That's it."

Sergeant Dom Lesage lay in a daze where his left ankle was chained to a horse corral post. The post was hard wood and thick, too thick to claw or cut through, even if he was left alone. There were fifteen horses in the corral. Their grain buckets had been filled that morning, but Dom's chain was only six feet long. He would've gladly eaten the horse feed if he could have—anything to fill his stomach.

"What plans do you have outside of San Diego?" asked a nearby young man who sat on a wooden rocking chair. He had shaggy, blond hair, and his facial hair was too light and patchy to be called a proper beard. "All of this can end the minute you start talking."

Dom's head rolled to the side away from Goran, his tormentor. They'd beaten him after his capture on the highway, but he hadn't been tortured in the traditional or expected sense. Mostly, they'd withheld food and sleep. His body shivered, exposed to the elements since they'd stripped him to the waist. Even if he were to get free from the iron shackle on his ankle, he had no boots, socks, or energy. His entire body ached.

"Where does Coronado Island get its fresh water?" Goran asked.

His questions continued as they had through the night. Or was it two nights? A half-eaten bowl of sweetened oatmeal sat on the dusty ground just out of reach. Dom could smell the molasses.

"Where does the PSDF store its food?" Goran pressed.

Turning his head, Dom eyed Goran hatefully. The young man couldn't have been older than twenty. The other man who was in charge had given Goran Dom's shotgun and Bowie knife. He was a double-chinned man whose name Dom struggled to recall through his exhaustion. Conrad Prosky. Yes, the bearded man with the double chin had introduced himself as the leader of the survivalist compound of about thirty men and a few women and children.

The compound was surrounded by steep, grassy hills. A single dirt road led out and down to the town from which Dom vaguely recalled being escorted. They'd left the bullet-riddled trucks in town and traveled about a mile. He'd been forced to walk while the others rode horses. Some of Prosky's men had assault rifles, but most had bolt action hunting rifles.

There'd been an armed lookout above the entrance to the small valley. Dom had expected to be blindfolded, but they hadn't bothered. With some anguish, Dom realized why: there was no escape from the valley and there would be no rescue. General Brogdon had no idea a fierce guerrilla fighting force was out there in the hills. These were men hardened from the adversity of America's collapse. The compound appeared to have been equipped in advance to endure any number of catastrophes. They had an underground source of water, and Dom had seen men come and go from a bunker or cellar dug into the hillside beyond the three-story house. Two Quonset huts—serving as the men's barracks—faced the big red barn where hay and more animals were kept.

"You can eat as soon as you answer my questions," Goran said. "Our porridge probably isn't as good as what you've got down on your island, but it'll stick to your ribs. Hey, wake up!"

Goran kicked the chain. The shackle bit into the raw flesh of Dom's ankle. He hadn't realized he'd nodded off.

Dom blinked through his thoughts of surrender, hoping he didn't speak of them aloud. He could survive without food for days longer, but not without sleep. They knew exactly how to wear a man down psychologically. With his last bit of awareness, he needed a coherent plan, even if it were to give in. But become a traitor to the Pacific States? It wasn't Dom's way, even if he wasn't from this country. The PSDF had given him purpose after being stranded in America from where he'd lived in eastern Canada. His loyalty wasn't for sale.

"Look, you don't owe them anything," Goran said as if Dom had spoken his last thoughts aloud. "They don't care about you. Nobody cares about you. It could be weeks before they even figure out you're missing."

"No." Dom tried to resist his growing sense of hopelessness. There had to be something to hold onto. *Anything!*

"Describe your island's southern defenses," Goran pushed. "What's your recon plane's normal flight path? What do you know about the Riverside Guard?"

Burying his face in his hands, Dom tried to shut out his tormentor's voice. There was something he'd remembered during the long hours of the night that had given him strength, but now it was gone. The radio? No, the radio was back in the Humvee. But there had been a voice on the radio! That's what he'd clung to! A promise. A man's voice telling him to wait or . . . hold on for . . . something.

Dom's mind cleared. The radio transmission hadn't reached Coronado, but it had reached someone . . . *Caspertein!*

"What're you smiling about?" Goran leaned down from his rocking chair. "I'm glad you think this is funny, because I'm loving this. We can do this night and day until you lose your mind. We've done it before. You won't last another night."

"Yeah." Dom took a deep breath. "Caspertein . . . is coming."

"Casper-*what?*" Goran scoffed. "No one's coming. Not for you. No one knows where you are. You're all alone."

"No." Dom lifted his eyes to the hills above. "He's too tricky. Even if he ruined me on the bridge. Trimble is coming, too. Embarrassed me . . ."

"Who ruined you?" Goran snapped his fingers in front of Dom's face. "What bridge?"

Dom blinked and focused with effort on Goran's face.

"You . . . don't have enough men." Dom chuckled. "I had men. They had guns. You don't have enough men. The elm tree is coming."

"What elm tree? You've already gone insane."

"I hate them," Dom said with a growl. "But they're coming."

A shadow passed over Dom. The double-chinned man was back—Conrad Prosky.

"He's talking?" Prosky always had two gunmen with him everywhere he went on the compound. "I told you to come get me when he started talking!"

"He just started, Mr. Prosky. It's just gibberish."

"What'd he say?"

"Someone is coming. Casper-something."

"Caspertein," Dom repeated. "Oh, they're tricky."

Prosky crouched next to Dom's head.

"Who is Caspertein, Lesage? He's one of your men?"

"My men? No!" Dom clenched his fist. "No, I hate him. But he's coming."

"See?" Goran said. "It's crazy talk. A minute ago, he said we don't have enough men, and the elm tree is coming."

"Did he say anything about Coronado Island? We need intel on the island, Goran! Vulnerabilities, resources, strengths."

"He's said nothing about that."

"Lesage?" Prosky used his hand to lift Dom's head from where he lay. "You're in bad shape. You won't last like this. You need to eat and sleep. We have a comfortable bed for you in the house. This Caspertein—is he on the island? Just tell me what we want to know and we'll get you inside."

"I'm going to be okay." Dom closed his eyes. "Caspertein is coming. Caspertein is coming. He said so."

Prosky let go of his head.

"This isn't working like it did with the others. He's holding out."

"So what?" Goran said. "I'll be here as long as it takes, Mr. Prosky."

"That's not what I'm worried about. Get him some food before he dies on us. Let him sleep out here. Get me

Lars and Isaiah. I want to talk to them again about what happened to them over at Hillcrest. Something else is going on out there.”

“Caspertein is coming,” Dom mumbled. “You don't have enough men . . .”

✝

Levi belly-crawled beside Wes up the hillside. This was the third time he'd climbed such a hill that afternoon—while checking all the angles on the survivalist ranch below. His elbows dug into the dry soil, giving him traction up the steep terrain. Behind and below, his father waited with Gabby Hillerman. They were about to move against a superior force. It would be dangerous for ten men to attempt, let alone three men and a mentally challenged child.

And that was the thrill! Levi could barely contain his excitement. Just like they'd prayed, God was showing them favor against the kidnappers of Sergeant Dom Lesage. It had been Levi who'd suspected a lookout on the dirt road from town. Sure enough, they'd circled to the north and carefully scoped the hills to find the lookout watching over the valley.

They reached the crest of the hill and eased up the last few inches. Levi again identified the lookout's location on the southern hilltop three hundred yards away, over-looking the road that dissected the two hills. The man was alone, seated on a block of wood. Then Levi raised his field glasses toward the ranch.

“This is where we need your dad,” Wes said. “It's the best angle. He can take out the lookout, then cover your approach and exit. The sun will be in their eyes and Gabby should be safe up here with him.”

“I agree.” Levi scoped the adjacent hillsides. “Where will you be?”

"Actually, I'd rather be the one going in, Levi. No offense, but I'm not sure they'll take you seriously. You're so young-looking."

"But it has to be me. We've been through this. You have a wife. Aunt Wynter needs you. Dad has Gabby. Besides, I can move faster down there if trouble starts."

"Not *if*," Wes said. *"When.* Those barracks buildings and the main house—twenty-five or thirty men, I'd guess. Maybe some women who'll raise a rifle as well."

"It's okay. I believe God wants us to help Lesage. I'll be fine."

"You have more faith than me." Wes clucked his tongue. "Me going into Coronado wasn't this crazy. I was undercover. You're walking into a stranger's hideout to bring someone out alive."

"Where will you be? Tell me so I can stay out of your line of sight."

Wes paused as he used his own scope.

"I'm not the sharpshooter your father is. I'll need to get closer to be of any use to you. How about on the north side where we saw that spring? There's cover up there. Even if I come down the hill a little, there's a ridge of a buried irrigation pipe for cover. It'll be a two-hundred-yard shot for me."

"No problem?"

"During a gunfight?" Wes sighed. "There'll be nothing but problems. But inside that distance, I can make a difference."

"I'll be drawing their fire," Levi said. "And once Dad opens fire, they'll be totally confused below."

"You'll have your hands full with Lesage. I don't think he's moving there next to the corral."

"There's just one guy with him now. I'll get him out."

"Do you know what you're gonna say?" Wes chuckled. "Never mind. I'm talking to a Caspertein."

"God'll give me the right words. Our mission is a holy one. Chevy always says there's comfort and confidence in that."

"Holiness isn't bulletproof," Wes said.

"Yeah, but I'll die pleasing God. And maybe Lesage will know he was cared for."

They backed away from the hilltop and returned to their packs where Titus was speaking quietly with Gabby over a handful of trail mix. Titus' palm was open with the mix as Gabby picked out the chocolate chips one by one. There seemed no concern for the virus in Titus' behavior, which Levi respected for Gabby's sake.

"That's definitely the spot for you," Wes said to Titus as he picked up his pack. "The sun's just about right. I'll get into place on the north side. Levi, tell him. I'll be praying."

Wes hustled to the northeast around the base of the hills.

Levi explained Wes's plan to use the mound of the buried irrigation pipe to get closer to the ranch structures.

"He's worried," Levi said as he hydrated and ate an energy bar.

"You're not?" Titus asked. "Wes has been around the world in a hundred situations. His worry has kept him alive."

"I can't think of my safety and Lesage's safety at the same time. One of us has to be a priority. You taught me that. And you've got my back. So, no, I'm not worried."

Gabby jabbered something and pointed at the blue sky.

"She's right," Titus said. "God's got all of us in His vision. Why don't you leave your pack by the road. I'll pick it up if you can't."

"Take the trucks back to town?"

"My legs are counting on it." Titus winked. "Let me know when you're in place. Once I take out that lookout, it'll be a hornets' nest down there."

"I'll be okay, Dad."

"Yeah, I hope so. I'm actually a little jealous. Moments like this—they're rare in life. Enjoy the opportunity to trust God when you're outnumbered and in the midst of danger, death on every side."

"It's just physical death." Levi shrugged and hoisted his pack. "I'll see you afterward. Bye Gabby."

"Bye Bee-bi!" Gabby grinned and waved enthusiastically.

"Hey!" Levi laughed. "I understood that!"

"I'm proud of you, Levi," Titus called as Levi backed away. "Stay sharp down there."

Levi waved back, then turned to walk away before his tears could be seen. Gabby and his father could be dead from the virus in a week or two, but all his dad was thinking about was the safety of others, even the enemy's. That's what Levi aspired to be more like!

A few minutes later, the dirt road came into sight, so he paused where he was still in the cover of the northern hill from the lookout. He readied his gear by unclipping his sidearm holster and tightening his battle rifle strap connected to his ammo vest. His stomach felt like he was riding a roller coaster, which he'd been on as a child. Helping Carla escape the plane and even facing Oleg's captors at New Encanto now seemed quite minor in comparison to this next endeavor. To his surprise, his father hadn't advised him on what to say to Lesage's captors. Instead, he was being trusted that he already knew what to say—or the Lord would give him the words in the moment.

"Lord, I need You," Levi prayed quietly as he tightened his fingerless gloves and checked his boot laces. "I've been learning about You for only a little while, but I believe You are bigger than anything I'm about to face. I sure don't want to let You down. And people are counting on me. Watch over Wes and Dad and Gabby. And Lesage. Oh, I can't wait to see his face, Lord!"

A moment later, he heard Wes's voice in his ear.

"I'm above the spring north of the valley," said the one-eyed man. "As soon as Levi gets their attention, I'll move lower and closer. Over."

"Okay. I'm in place," Levi said. "I'm ready, Dad. Do it. Over."

"It ain't easy firing the first shot," Titus said. "Let's do this. Over."

Levi smiled. His dad was the real hero—Oleg, too. Their missions into Syria, China, and North Korea to save hundreds or to save only one soul—would never be known to many in the world. But God knew. And Levi yearned to be such a warrior of righteousness, a hero within God's eternal purpose against dark forces.

The gunshot thundered overhead. The sound bounced off the walls of the hills around Levi. A full ten seconds passed before the afternoon air was still again.

"You're up, Levi," Titus said. "Give it to 'em straight, son. Over."

"Copy that."

Carrying his pack over to the road, Levi left it in plain sight. If worst came to worst, he could do without it. He had a water bottle on the back of his hip and a couple energy bars in his trouser pockets. But he expected his father to pick up the pack on his way back down the draw to the town and trucks. *The trucks!* There were three Humvees parked behind the drive-thru. He guessed he'd get to drive one back into the city after all this was finished.

He walked up the middle of the dirt road between the hills. The valley ahead slowly opened to him. Green grass, a few bushes and trees, and the ranch sat in the center. Wes was hiding several hundred yards straight ahead out of sight. Between Wes and his dad, every inch of the valley was covered and within their battle rifle range. And Levi wasn't deluding himself—no version of whatever happened ahead would end without gunfire. But when the noise ended, he prayed the enemy would be thankful they'd only been tranquilized and not killed. Their lives would be spared for them to contemplate their ways before death and the final Judgement.

"To say they're scrambling down there for an invasion would be an understatement," Wes said. "You definitely woke them up, TC. Over."

"It ain't easy," Titus said, "expecting an invasion but getting an intervention instead. Levi, switch your comm to voice-activated. We want to hear everything. Over."

Levi paused on the road and flipped the transmitter switch to voice activation so he wouldn't need to hold down the transmit button.

There was a tack shed forty yards away on the south side of the horse corral. Levi angled his approach toward that shed since it was the only cover across from the three-story house where gun barrels now appeared from every visible window. Four riflemen ran from the Quonset huts to the red barn on the northern corner of the corral. The horses pranced nervously in their pen, heads up and ears alert, obviously sensing the unrest.

Sergeant Lesage lay seemingly unconscious next to a corral post. Now, Levi could see him clearly. An empty rocking chair sat just out of Lesage's reach. The man was chained by the ankle on which a sore had festered. Flies were buzzing around it. The chain was padlocked, requiring a key or a carefully-placed copperhead bullet, but Levi had only gel-tranqs in his current magazine. Lesage had no shirt, shoes, or socks, and his naked torso was smeared with dried mud. Though his face wasn't entirely visible, Levi expected the sergeant had been somewhat abused, probably tortured for information.

Three men moved slowly from the main house toward Levi. Levi stopped next to the tack shed rather than continue forward to check on Lesage. The shed walls appeared to be mere plywood with a couple coats of lacquer painted on for weather-proofing. They wouldn't stop a rifle round, but maybe the shed was full of leather saddles and riding blankets, which might help stop a bullet.

"You're a little young to be playing soldier, aren't you?" The speaker, flanked by two larger men, was a bearded jowly man of about fifty. His eyes were small, his head bald, and his midsection revealed that these people weren't hurting for food. "Maybe you're lost. Is that it?"

The man's two bearded guards held assault rifles with semiautomatic pistols on their belts, but the speaker carried only a heavy revolver tucked into the front of his trousers. What Levi could see of their skin, they didn't appear to be symptomatic of the virus.

Lesage lay still—maybe he was dead already. The other riflemen around the ranch had found their cover and stopped moving. At least four were in the barn, a dozen or more in the main house, and three or four on the visible corners of both Quonset huts.

Studying the two guards, Levi saw one was Hispanic and the other a tan white man. He'd seen them before. In Hillcrest a few days earlier, they'd worn red coats. They casually aimed their rifles from their waists, but their staring eyes didn't betray that they recognized him. Sometimes the gel-tranq left people experiencing mild memory loss of the final seconds leading up to being tranquilized. He was thankful for those effects now.

"The elderly couple in the house by the highway," Levi said, "they have the virus. And it seems you've been spreading it."

"We know the rules and we already buried the two men who had it. Is that all you came for?"

Levi's eyes strayed again to the main house. *So many rifles aimed at him!*

"It ain't easy being hospitable nowadays, I guess, huh?" Levi asked.

"You're not a guest," said the man in the middle, "so you're trespassing."

"Then I guess we're both guilty." Levi watched their faces carefully. His right hand was resting on his rifle grip while his index finger traced the trigger guard around and around. The muzzle was aimed at the ground, but the compact weapon was designed to pivot and fire with little effort. "I'm trespassing and you're kidnapping. We've both crossed lines."

"What? *That?*" The man laughed and pointed at Lesage. "That's not kidnapping. He's my prisoner. We caught him trying to steal food out of the cellar."

"No." Levi shook his head slowly. "I saw the ambush site back on the freeway. This man's no angel, but I know he was only out on patrol, just looking around. And you killed his whole unit. You must have some pretty serious shooters out here to take out a whole military patrol."

"Yeah, we're serious shooters, every one of us." The man scoffed. "And you, Junior, just walked right in here in the middle of it."

Lesage sat up. *He was conscious!* But Levi didn't look directly at him.

"Sometimes hasty decisions are made." Levi measured his words carefully. "Sometimes survival and fear make us do things we wouldn't otherwise do. Right now, I'm not your enemy. I can overlook the past and leave with my friend there. He looks like you've gotten out of him all he was going to give you, anyway."

"And what if I say we *are* enemies?" The man scowled and pointed at the southern hilltop. "You shot my guy up there and you expect all to be forgiven? To just move on? No, Junior, we haven't gotten from Sergeant Lesage what we want, nothing except his name. Maybe we'll consider something if you answer me my questions. But it'll cost you—and whoever else you have out there watching your back. You killed my guy. I won't overlook that."

"You killed eleven of Lesage's unit. I'd say you're getting off easy. What's your question?"

*"Questions!* Yeah, that's right. I have a lot of questions I need answered. Like, what's the Pacific States' plans for the Riverside Guard? Is General Brogdon moving north or what? We've seen his recon plane."

"These boys are guerrillas for Riverside," Wes said in Levi's ear. "We suspected something like this. They're gathering intel for Riverside. Probably getting food and arms for intel and incursions against the PSDF to weaken or test for weakness. Over."

"Those aren't questions I can answer," Levi said. "You may be mistaking me for a Pacific States soldier, but I'm not."

"What?" The man laughed, then frowned. "Wait. Who are you?"

"He's not wearing a red jacket," said the one on his left.

"I'm just a citizen. A neighbor. Nobody special. I live down along the bay with my family. I'm Levi Caspertein."

All three men visibly stiffened. The middle one's small eyes darted toward the hilltops.

"Caspertein?" He licked his lips and glanced at Lesage. "I've heard the name."

"And you are?"

"Prosky. Conrad Prosky." The jowly man clenched and unclenched his fists. "Lesage mentioned you."

"Me?" Levi snorted. "I doubt that. I'm nobody."

"He said you were coming for him. Who is he to you?"

"Sergeant Lesage?" Levi smiled and finally looked Lesage in his bloodshot eyes. "My family and I have actually been at odds with the Pacific States lately. But we believe every life matters to God, so I'm here to take him home."

*"God?"* Prosky repeated, his eyebrows raised. "Did I hear you right? You're religious?"

"I'm a follower of Jesus Christ. I don't believe there's anyone else who can deliver us from sin and hell. Why don't I get Lesage cleaned up and we can sit on the porch and talk about it?"

Prosky looked at both of his guards, who stared with blank faces back at him.

"You, uh, have some nerve, Junior," he said. "Lesage has military value. The sergeant is a prisoner of war, or soon-to-be war. He's worth more to me as a pawn than he can act as a peace offering between you and the PSDF. And now I'm curious how you're still standing here if you've had some conflict with Brogdon. The word is that he's wiped out anyone who threatens his reign of terror around the city. Why didn't he just toss your bodies into the bay?"

"Careful, Levi," Titus said over the comm. "He's probing for intel about our own strength. Over."

"I think Brogdon realizes the value that good neighbors have for the city. But I believe our skirmishes of the past are finished."

"So, you're joining the PSDF?" asked Prosky.

"No, we're all about caring for our neighbors as Jesus would. We'll leave militaries and governing to others. The Caspertein family would like to know that Conrad Prosky is someone we might consider a neighbor as well."

Prosky grinned and again looked to his men for their reactions, which were still blank stares.

"You believe this kid? Shooting one of my men, then telling me about acting neighborly for Jesus? Junior, you've got something, but it ain't Jesus." His face darkened as he lowered his head. "Who's here with you? How many are out there? Come on. I know you're not here alone."

"It seems our friendly conversation has shifted." Levi's index finger slipped inside the trigger guard. "Your man on lookout isn't dead, no more than these two men after I tranquilized them a few days ago."

Their mouths fell open.

"*That was you?*" Prosky scoffed. "Lars here barely got out of there alive. And Isaiah—"

"Those people thrashed me so bad when I woke up," said the man on his right, "that I still have bruises!"

"No, you were executing unarmed civilians." Levi gave them his full glare. "Remember, I was there."

*"Tranquilizers!"* Prosky shook his head. "So, it's true. You shoot people with tranquilizers?"

"We won't intentionally take lives." Levi nodded toward the main house porch. "How about we explore this another time? Who has the key to Lesage's chain?"

"That's why Brogdon doesn't kill you." Prosky laughed and flapped his arms. "You're no threat at all!"

"None at all." Levi gestured with his left hand. "Lesage? How about it?"

"Enough of this." Prosky reached for his pistol in his waistband. A murderous look filled his eyes and his upper lip curled.

Levi was gripping his rifle with only one hand, but he was close enough to fire from where the weapon hung on its strap. He pulled the trigger as he lifted and pivoted the muzzle. The gun barked once, twice, three times diagonally, hitting Lars in the gut then Prosky in the neck. The third tranq was fired harmlessly into the sky, missing Isaiah altogether. An instant later, Levi turned and dove for safety behind the tack shed.

He rolled once and came up in a crouch, his back to the plywood. Panting wildly, he prayed for calm as .308 rifles boomed from the west and north. Levi turned off the comm's voice activation, then peered briefly around the corner.

Prosky and Lars were down. Isaiah was retreating to the main house when he went down, tumbled in the dust, then lay still. Levi ducked back as bullets kicked sand near his toe. The whole valley rocked with gunfire as Prosky's militants sprayed the hillsides and shed with bullets.

"Get Lesage, Levi!" Titus ordered, then his rifle barked. "Go! I'll cover you!"

Bullets peppered the shed, raking across the plywood, leaving holes above Levi's head. There was no way he could move into the open to reach Lesage. His father apparently couldn't see how many shooters were still out there!

Levi checked behind the shed. *The corral!* The horses were racing about the pen, but Levi hoped they wouldn't trample him against the fence in their frenzy. He climbed through four strands of barbed wire and went to his knees to crawl over dusty ground mixed with manure.

"Go, Levi!" Titus shouted. "Before they target him!"

Eight feet away, Lesage was already scrambling under the bottom wire of the fence. Levi lunged and landed on top of the sergeant as a bullet ricocheted nearby.

"Get behind me!" Levi ordered as he drew his knife.

Lesage managed to drag his shackle and chain around to position himself behind Levi, but shooters from the barn to the main house, and everywhere in between, were firing at them.

Levi stuck his double-edged blade under the fence staple that held the bottom barbed wire strand to the post and wrenched it free with one twist.

"Here they come!" Lesage pointed past Levi's head at a group of four riflemen approaching at a run toward the corral. *"Hurry up!"*

Dropping his knife, Levi raised his rifle to fire hastily into the group of men. Eight rounds later, and maybe with Wes or Titus' help, the men were put down not far from where Prosky lay.

A bullet smacked into the fence post inches from Levi's head, pelting his face with slivers of wood. Levi flinched sideways for a better firing position when searing heat surged up from his side. *That was no bullet!* He realized his mistake and rolled away enough to carefully draw his own blade out of his side. Two inches of steel came away bloody.

"Genius!" he scolded himself, then ignored the pain and blood to reach overhead to free another strand of wire. Two more to go.

"The barn!" Lesage slapped Levi's shoulder. *"The barn!"*

This time, Levi stabbed his blade into the ground for safekeeping, then raised his rifle to drop two men in the upper door of the red barn.

He took the knife again and rose to his knees to pull loose the next wire. Only one more. Reaching high, he torqued the knife too far up the blade and it snapped. Three inches of the blade flipped farther into the corral. But he still had enough length to try again, closer to the handle.

"Levi," Titus said in his ear, "exit north. I can't get the guys in the house. Exit north! Over."

"Copy," Levi said as he hugged the ground. "Exit north."

"Is your dad here?" Lesage asked. "Where is he?"

"Get ready to run." Levi pointed across the corral. *"Run!"*

"How?" Lesage shouted over the gunfire and shook his ankle chain. "I'm still chained!"

Levi grabbed the end of the chain and slid it up the post now free of wire. Once he cleared the top of the post, he threw the chain over his shoulder and lifted Lesage to his feet with one arm.

*"Now!"*

But Lesage was in no condition to run, besides having the shackle still attached to his ankle. Levi started to carry the sergeant across the corral when two horses brushed past them, sending Levi sprawling. He glimpsed a hoof overhead and twisted aside an instant before his skull was crushed. But the hoof grazed across his scalp with enough force to send him rolling against Lesage. Both were tangled in the chain as more panicked horses galloped around them.

Throwing off the chain length from his body, Levi sheathed what was left of his knife. Then he gathered Lesage in both his arms. The man was close to six feet tall, as well as a muscled combatant, so the strain on Levi's wounded side sent fire up his ribs from his hip to his shoulder.

"They have an antenna on that roof," Lesage warned as he gazed over Levi's shoulder. "It needs to be removed. You've got to tell your dad. They'll call in the Riverside Guard!"

"Give me a minute, would you?"

Levi walked stiffly with his burden to the far side of the corral, placing more horses between themselves and the shooters still in the house. He roughly set Lesage on the ground and pulled up the bottom fence wire for the man to scoot under. Then Levi ducked under the third strand and crouched low with Lesage. When blood trickled into his eye, he wiped at his scalp and his fingers came away with not only blood, but with what was left of the comm from his ear.

"They're coming around the barn." Lesage pointed down the fence line. "We need to move."

Squinting into the setting sun at the western hilltop, Levi also glanced at the radio antenna on the roof of the house. There was no way to communicate anything to his father, and from the sound of Wes's rifle, he had shifted to the eastern slope of the opposite hillside probably for better shooting. By now, both men would know his comm wasn't working.

"We're going through that gap." Levi nodded north where two hills intersected. He replaced a magazine and nodded to Lesage. "You ready? Can you walk a little?"

Lesage lifted the chain, his eyes desperate.

"I'm not sure how far I can go with this."

"Don't worry about it." Levi gave him his back. "Climb on. It'll be faster. Come on!"

The sergeant didn't argue. He climbed onto Levi's back and held the chain in one hand across the young man's chest.

Levi staggered to his feet and hefted Lesage's weight higher. He'd carried heavier loads up and down the stairs when setting up the dolly system with Chevy, and anchoring the zip line near the railroad tracks. Blood leaked down his right side, but he believed God would help him one way or another—at least until he could stem the flow himself.

The gap between the hills was two hundred yards away across an exposed slope. Levi carefully planted one foot at a time, climbing the most gradual line toward their destination. His exit north would put him adjacent to a highway headed north through the hills. The map was in his mind. Somehow, he'd need to get Lesage and himself back to I-8 and meet up with his father and Wes—before Prosky gained consciousness and regrouped.

Bullets whistled past his head. He dropped one of Lesage's knees to aim and fire several rounds at maybe only one sniper remaining near the barn. But at that distance from the ranch, the militants would be less accurate. Soon, he'd be out of their range altogether.

"I'm . . . slipping." Lesage gasped weakly as he slid down Levi's back. "I'm . . ."

Bending over more, Levi charged ahead to try to keep the man's weight higher. Lesage dropped the chain and his arm went limp.

Though the gap was close, Levi had to stop. Wes and Titus were still trading gunfire with Prosky's men, but the militants seemed to have lost interest in the two who were escaping northward. Levi slid Lesage to the ground and checked his pulse. He was still alive. Again, he lifted the heavy man into his arms and climbed the hill.

At the mouth of the gap, Levi turned and looked back. The sun was down now and the shadows were growing. Gunfire still popped from both sides. Levi knew his dad was ensuring his safe getaway. If he hadn't been so preoccupied with Lesage, Levi figured he could've opened the corral gate to free the horses. Prosky's men on horseback would have the advantage come morning.

Leaving the valley behind, Levi continued north. In the fading light, he noticed hills to his right that he'd need to skirt to circle around and head south.

The moon was already up, though only a sliver. It would be a long, dark night.

# *Chapter Seven*

Once more, Titus and Wes tranquilized all the downed men before they could rise to continue fighting. Then the last light was gone and the hilltop was painted in a blackness Titus hadn't expected. Gabby snuggled close to his side, trying to sleep now that the noise had ended. Below, only Wes skulked around the ranch to ensure no aggressors remained.

Thankfully, Titus had found a pair of earplugs for Gabby's ears in the bottom of his pack from a day of target practicing with Levi months earlier. Still, Gabby had covered her ears with her hands much of the last hour and a half.

A single candle was lit down by the main house, or maybe it was a flashlight. But Wes's rifle boomed and the light went out.

"Turn those horses loose," Titus said in his comm, "and let's R-V with Levi. Over."

"I don't know, TC," Wes said softly. "I sure wouldn't mind a juicy horse steak. Over."

"Always thinking with your stomach!" Titus kidded. "Careful down there. I can't see anything to cover you. Over."

Twenty quiet minutes later, Titus heard someone's labored breathing approach the hilltop.

"It's just me," Wes announced. "You there?"

"Over here."

Wes collapsed after tripping over Titus' right foot.

"Tranq me now," panted the one-eyed warrior. "That's more exercise than I've had for a few months."

They turned off their comms to conserve battery power.

"The night's not over." Titus stood and shouldered his pack. "Come on, Little Lady. A little more walking. Let's show Uncle Wes how real troopers don't rest until the job is done."

"Hey, who's been running all over the valley while you rested up here?" Wes sighed in the darkness. "I'd tell our wives on you if I thought I'd get any sympathy. Hold up, Titus. I'll take point."

Turning on a small flashlight, Wes shined it on the sloping ground to guide them down.

"One thing for sure," Titus said, "no one's moving too quickly in this darkness."

"We'll see anyone coming," Wes said. "Come dawn, it won't take them long to round up those horses and start looking for us."

"By dawn, we'll have Levi and be long gone." Titus held Gabby's hand and helped her down to the dirt road. "Careful, Little Lady. Uncle Wes didn't smooth out the ground here for us."

The walk down the dirt road to town was eerily quiet. They used headlamps freely to light their way since they guessed Prosky and his men were still a few minutes from waking from their last gel-tranq.

They finally reached the Humvees. Wes loaded his gear into one and Titus helped Gabby into another. But Titus didn't climb in right away. He turned off his headlamp and listened to the night. The small town off the freeway was so still, as if it had never existed. Gabby's grandparents were on the other end of town, suffering through their final days as their organs shut down. There was nothing that could be done for them. Levi had welcomed Gabby, and hopefully, the elderly couple's hearts were comforted by that. Knowing Levi, he'd shared the Gospel briefly with the couple when he'd been on their doorstep. The rest was in God's hands.

Wes stood in the door of his Humvee and shined his headlamp on Titus.

"You hear something?"

"No." Titus angled his ears in another direction. There wasn't even a breeze. "That's the problem. I was half-hoping to find Levi here already. He needs to take the third Humvee. I don't want to leave it for Prosky and whoever he's working with in Riverside."

"There's got to be a garage nearby." Wes climbed into the middle vehicle. "I'll park it somewhere else. Give me a few minutes."

Titus turned on his lamp again and shared a little food with Gabby. She wasn't too talkative since she was so tired, so Titus put her in the back seat where she could lay down and he covered her with his jacket.

He walked a few yards away from the drive-thru and Humvee and turned on his comm.

"Levi, come in. You there, son? Over."

Silence. Not surprising. Levi's comm had seemed to stop working in the middle of the gunfight. Or maybe he was still out of range. Lesage had appeared to be injured when Levi had helped him beyond the corral that evening, so maybe they were slowed in their rendezvous at the Humvees. No, Levi would assume his father had seen Lesage's condition, and exited north as Titus had told him. Levi would probably wait somewhere east on I-8 for a pick up.

Wes returned a few minutes later and climbed into his Humvee. Titus told him his estimation of Levi's actions. Both men rolled down their windows and Wes drove in front at a slow pace, watching and listening for sign of Levi. They reached the interstate and turned east into the spotted traffic frozen in the westbound lane.

Titus grew more concerned by every mile they crept. After fifteen minutes, he hailed Wes on the radio.

"This is too far east," Titus said. "There's a town up there. Levi would've cut south to reach the interstate before this. Over."

They turned around and started west, now slower. Titus turned off his headlights to watch for a signal light to the north that might indicate Levi's position, but he wasn't sure Levi even had a flashlight on his person. He should've already reached the freeway!

When they reached their starting point at the Hillerman's, Titus prepared to turn around and start back to the east.

"At some point, Titus," Wes said on the comm, "it becomes too dangerous for us to keep looking. Levi will know that. Anyone can see my headlights from miles away. We don't even know what this terrain looks like in the daylight, and we don't know who else could be out here taking notice. Prosky may have allies. Over."

"One more run," Titus insisted.

This time, he led the way at a crawling pace, stopping occasionally to listen to the night. But there was no sight or sound from Levi.

More than five miles east of Gabby's town, Titus suddenly applied his brakes and turned off his headlights. A stream of endless vehicle lights was approaching the interstate from the north and the town ahead!

"You seeing this?" Titus asked Wes.

"I see it. There's no way that's the PSDF. It's got to be Riverside. Prosky's people may have gotten word out somehow. They must be pretty tight with Riverside for them to send a whole battalion against us—so Lesage could remain detained. Over."

"Levi will see them, too," Titus said with a sigh. "He'll know we couldn't stick around. We didn't plan for another military joining the fray. Now with them here, we can't continue like this in the dark. I concede. Over."

"Levi's a Caspertein, TC. He'll find his way home. He has before. God is with him."

Titus nodded without responding. They drove west, away from the invading army, leaving behind Gabby's grandparents, praying Levi was safe with Sergeant Lesage in a land he didn't know.

General Brogdon woke on the island before dawn and met with his sleepy-eyed aids for an update. Sergeant Lesage was still missing and the recon plane the evening before had reported a major mobilization of troops from Riverside. Something had woken the serpent to the north. The island had been on alert for nine hours as war seemed inevitable. The only question was where the battle would be fought, and Galt didn't want it fought in San Diego. By some great fortune, Riverside hadn't progressed further south since the last reported sighting.

He woke President Criswell and waited ten minutes as the man washed up and donned a blue silk suit and a red and black beret. In the presidential suite, he listened quietly to Galt's thoughts before he responded. Galt didn't care about the politician's opinion, but every military command needed to present a diplomatic front at some point.

"Yes, I agree," Criswell finally said. His white beard hadn't been brushed regardless of his stylish, fitted suit. "It's unavoidable. Let's meet them in the field where we're stronger and they're weaker. We can throw twice the number of people at a conflict."

"We could lose half our forces," Galt warned.

"Losses don't matter. It'll be worth it in the end." Criswell nodded resolutely. "We need to unite all of California."

"I wanted Sergeant Lesage for this." Galt sighed. "I plan to use overwhelming force. He could've led this campaign. One battle. Total destruction. And push north all the way to Riverside, maybe even Sacramento."

"Think of the resources we could gain!" Criswell smiled. "The loss of life will be forgotten once we claim the fleet of vehicles and other equipment up there."

"Tanks, too."

"Do it." Criswell folded his hands. "We can't move forward until these skirmishes with challengers are squashed. There can be only one government. My cabinet is ready to extend a welcoming hand to territories north of us. We are the Pacific States. Anyone west of the Rockies who doesn't want to unify with this new world, they'll meet you on the battlefield. What are your greatest concerns?"

"Resupplying in the field." Galt shook his head. "But that's not a problem, as long as everyone does as they've been trained to do. The rest is just the process. We'll engage the enemy and take losses, but we'll overwhelm them by outlasting them."

"A decisive victory now will win the hearts of the people we don't yet rule." Criswell smiled. "Crush them, Galt."

"I plan to, but I need to stop and see the Casperteins on my way out of town."

"Those people?" Criswell scoffed, stood, and poured himself a coffee, offering nothing to Galt. "I thought they were do-gooders who weren't a threat."

"Oh, I'm not stopping there to fight with them. They're not a threat to the Pacific States, but they do carry influence. We know they're stronger than they appear. They may have a network that extends beyond San Diego. Trimble mentioned someone named Striber Maddix. I just need to know if they know anything about Lesage or Riverside that might be helpful. Then I'll be on my way."

"How soon?"

"Everyone's already on alert. Vehicles are fueled. I'll lead a mobile forward command ahead of the column which'll split north of the city. Then we'll intercept and flank the Riverside Guard. My plans are to leave in an hour."

Rallying his other sergeants and commanders, Galt gave them their orders. He wasn't a motivational speaker, so he didn't offer them further inspiration. It was an age of winning or dying. Without the Pacific States, their comfortable way of life would end. They had to annihilate or be annihilated. Absolute control in the midst of chaos was the only way to continue as a society.

From all over Coronado Island, armored vehicles and personnel transports lined up at the head of the bridge. Since Galt didn't have the heart to deny his son the opportunity to see real conflict, he told the fifteen-year-old he had to ride with Forward Command or not go at all. The young man submitted and climbed into Galt's Humvee.

"You have your orders," Galt said on the PSDF frequency to his commanders. "Don't stop until we reach Riverside. Let's roll out!"

Galt's driver followed a pair of Humvees that displayed a forty-caliber gun mounted in each turret. One armored truck followed Galt's vehicle, which carried ten men including a mortar squad and an anti-tank unit. Farther back rolled two hundred vehicles with twelve hundred fighting men. Some vehicles were mere SUVs confiscated from the mainland. The rest of Coronado was held in reserve for resupplying and reinforcing. Messenger Jeeps were deployed for recon and to maintain contact between units where radio range was hindered. The recon plane took off with orders to radio Forward Command troop movements, breakdown, and unforeseen challenges. This was war!

The four vehicles that made up the general's Forward Command turned onto Harbor Drive, and a few blocks later they ran into the two-block perimeter that Galt had heard the Casperteins had placed around their main building.

"Give me twenty minutes," Galt told his drivers. "I'll expect an update from you when I get back. Stay on the radio."

He took only Kip who was already armed for battle, and walked through the perimeter vehicles to approach the ELM building from the south.

"How do you want to play this?" Kip asked as he chambered a round in his rifle. "You want me to shoot a few warning shots when we first see them?"

"Put that thing away!" Galt slapped his son's hand on his rifle stock. "We're just talking to them."

"But they already shot us up a bunch, Dad. They shot Sergeant Lesage. They shot me!"

"It's complicated, Kip. Just keep your mouth shut and learn something. The Casperteins aren't pushed around too easily. If you fire a warning shot, they'll respond with overwhelming gunfire. We've already seen that. Learn from your mistakes, son."

"They only have tranquilizers."

"And do you want to be tranquilized again?" Galt scowled. "The Casperteins aren't our enemies, not overtly anyway. We're riding into battle. I'm not trying to get tranquilized in the first ten minutes of our campaign, so restrain yourself until we see Riverside's troops."

Arriving at the north side of the building, Galt looked up at a giant elm tree painted in white over the ground floor encased in metal shielding.

"What's that mean?" Kip asked. "They're sure not very good artists."

"Quiet, Kip."

On the second floor, a middle-aged man with salt and pepper hair leaned a rifle over the balcony. Galt saw that the Casperteins weren't people who could be easily surprised. They must've kept a lookout day and night. Only a military mind could keep them so vigilant.

"I need to speak to Titus Caspertein," Galt called up to the man with the short rifle. It was one of the .308s he'd coveted since seeing them almost two weeks earlier. "We're pulling out and I'd like a word with him."

"He's not here," the man said. "I'll gladly give him a message when he returns."

Galt swore.

"Well, how about you? What's your name?"

"My friends call me Chevy, so you may call me Chevy, General."

Galt didn't know whether to scoff or smile. How could anyone be that friendly?

"Okay, Chevy, do you know anything about my sergeant's disappearance? Sergeant Lesage. You guys have crossed him twice now. If anyone has reason to make him go away, it would be your people."

"We're not fighting for the same things, General," Chevy said, "which is why we have no problem submitting to you. We haven't moved against you. Quite the opposite. When we heard Sergeant Lesage was in trouble, Titus took a small force out to attempt a rescue."

"Well, why wasn't I told?" Galt growled under his breath. "Attempt a rescue? How long ago was this?"

Chevy held up a finger for Galt to wait a moment. *How dare he!* No one told him to wait a minute! Galt stammered for a response, aware that this was happening in front of his son. He wanted to draw his sidearm and shoot off Chevy's raised finger. But then he realized the man wore a headset and he was receiving a communication right then.

A moment later, Chevy pointed with the same finger at a street to the east.

"There he is!"

Galt heard a vehicle engine that very instant. In the company of anyone else, especially in that disastrous city, Galt would've drawn his weapon and ordered his son to take up a defensive position behind cover. But there inside the ELM perimeter of vehicles, with at least one of those battle rifles in the hands of a Caspertein man, he knew there was no danger for himself or for his son.

Two Humvees parked on the far side of the four rows of vehicles. One-eyed Wes Trimble emerged from one vehicle. Galt recognized the battle-weary appearance of a man who'd fought hard and had returned home exhausted. Wes shouldered one strap of his backpack and weaved through the vehicles. Anyone else who'd left his command after only a few days, Galt would've had them executed. But Trimble wasn't his enemy, even if the man disagreed with PSDF methods.

"Hey, General!" Wes's face lit up. "Fancy meeting you here. I thought you'd be leading the charge. We saw the column heading out."

"I am leading it." Galt gazed past Wes. "Is that Titus? Did you guys find Sergeant Lesage?"

"We found him." Wes stopped beside Galt and looked back at Titus. "Last I saw him, he was with Levi Caspertein."

"So, he's alive? I mean, he's in good hands if he's with a Caspertein, right?"

"I see you're catching on." Wes chuckled. "Titus can fill you in. Kip, good to see you, young man. You're looking sharp."

Kip scowled at the man until Galt backhanded his son's shoulder.

"Yes, sir." Kip lifted his head. "You as well."

Wes continued to the ELM building.

"You can hate your enemy, Kip," Galt said quietly, "but you retain power over them if they don't know you hate them."

"He tranquilized me, Dad!"

"Now learn from someone who bested you. We might need to destroy these people one day, but it won't be because they're our enemy."

"Then why?"

"Because they have what we want."

"Their rifles?"

"Shush." Galt lifted a hand toward Titus. "You made it home safely, I see."

Titus stopped twenty paces away. His empty left hand rested on the shoulder of a Down syndrome girl who smiled and waved nonstop at Kip.

"General, I'd shake your hand, but my friend and I might've had some exposure to Meridia."

*"The virus!"* Galt checked the distance between them both. "Why did you bring it back here?"

"I'll lay low for a few days." He gestured at the building. "What brings you to ELM?"

"Sergeant Lesage. Trimble says he's with your son?"

"Yeah, they're still out there somewhere." Titus sighed, obviously burdened with more than mere weariness. "We got separated after a firefight and Levi's comm stopped working. I would've kept searching, but Riverside was on their way south."

"How many vehicles?"

"Headlights in the early morning darkness stretched as far as I could see."

"But Lesage will be safe with your son, right?"

"Nothing like safety is guaranteed in this life, General. Only hardship and eventual death are sure things. But God tells us His answer to man's sinfulness is forgiveness. Levi is probably talking to Lesage about that very thing right now."

Galt bit his tongue. The freedom in which Christianity boasted always conflicted with the control his military mind needed to hold over everyone around him. His command and the Christian God were mutually exclusive.

"You recovered our vehicles? What of the others in Lesage's patrol?"

"All dead. Ambushed on the I-8 headed east."

"Riverside did it?"

"No. A character named Conrad Prosky has a ranch a mile north of I-8. Sounded like he's been doing recon for

Riverside. He even pulled some guerrilla tactics by putting on red coats, impersonating the PSDF, and executing civilians."

"So, you talked to this Prosky?"

"Levi did when he went into their compound and got Lesage out. Lesage looked like they'd been interrogating him pretty harshly for a couple days. He must not have talked because he was still chained up when Levi lit out of there with him."

"Good." Galt nodded. "What possessed you to intercede for him? We haven't been, uh, exactly on speaking terms since the bridge incident."

"God's compassion isn't limited only to friends, General. Jesus died for me when I was His enemy. He has enough love for all people. Every life matters. That's God's policy, so it can be ours as well."

"But your son is out there." Galt frowned. "You know he could die trying to show this compassion you think everybody needs."

"Levi's a big boy." Titus smiled. "And he wouldn't mind dying for something so important as reconciliation between us and you."

"I sure don't understand your kind." Galt scoffed. "But I can't argue with the results. Anything else I need to know about Riverside incoming?"

"Just some advice for you."

"What is that?"

"You want to disarm your enemy? Show them a little mercy when you're justified in showing them wrath. Watch what happens."

"They'll get no mercy from me, Titus." Galt glanced at his son. "Good luck with that virus."

"You too. It's going around up there."

"Let's go." Galt gestured to Kip and they started toward their convoy. He yelled back at Titus: "Tell Lesage to catch up with us if you see him before I do. And he'd better be the same Lesage I've relied on for months. Don't try to change him!"

"No promises, General."

Titus' laughter followed Galt as he reached the opposite perimeter. It would be just like a Caspertein to ruin his most ruthless sergeant with the compassion and mercy of Jesus. They were soldiers. There was no room for compassion on the battlefield!

✝

Sergeant Dom Lesage sat up in a dimly-lit room and reached for his sore ankle. The shackle and chain were still attached. The skin had been filleted to the bone in places and a smelly reddish ointment had been applied to the wound.

He glanced around at a machine shop. No, it was an auto garage with two bays. Most of the tools from two huge tool boxes lay scattered across the floor. His memory of the night before was spotty at best. That boy had helped him escape the ranch, but then what? Waking in the garage was a surprise. At least he was indoors!

When he shifted to look around more, the cushions under him tipped unevenly. He lay on an oily car seat that had been placed on the concrete floor, and someone had spread a large flannel shirt over his naked torso. Boots that appeared to be his size sat next to the car seat, socks with them. It wasn't his shirt and they weren't his boots, but anything was better than being chained half-naked to the horse corral post.

And he'd gotten sleep! He actually felt rested—rested enough to worry about the shackle still on his ankle.

The lighting in the garage changed. Dom's eyes squinted at the sunlight coming through a dusty window. Levi Caspertein sat in a chair with his shirt off. With needle and thread, the young man was sewing up a bleeding cut over his ribs.

"You're wounded." Dom touched his neck and cleared his throat. He was parched. "I didn't know you were shot."

"I wasn't." Levi's hand was steady as he finished a crooked stitch. "Crazy, but I fell on my knife. All those bullets and I almost killed myself on my own blade! Must've barely missed my lung. There's food and water there for you. That's all we've got, so go slow with it."

Dom's hand trembled as he reached for a plastic bag of edibles that lay on top of a backpack. He took a couple swallows from a water bottle, then tore off a bite from an energy bar. *Delicious!*

Moving from the window, Levi donned a t-shirt, then a flannel of his own.

"It's almost noon. How do you feel?"

"Better now." Dom spoke with a full mouth. "My ankle's been better. *Whoa!* Your face . . ."

Kneeling next to the car seat, Levi examined Dom's ankle.

"Yeah. I took some splinters off a fence post. And a horse mistook my skull for cobblestone. But I'd say God was looking out for us. I could've lost an eye and you could've been shot while I hauled you away from that corral."

"You couldn't find any tools to get this thing off?" Dom frowned at his ankle. "I think I could walk a little without it."

Levi reached behind the seat and produced a mallet and an iron wedge.

"I found the tools, but we're sort of pinned down in here." Levi pointed with the mallet handle. "About two blocks that way, Riverside Guard decided to set up camp. Striking that shackle is going to be loud unless we work together."

"Riverside is here?" Dom gazed in the direction Levi had pointed. "Why isn't Brogdon pushing them out of the city? I don't hear any artillery."

"Um, that might have something to do with us not being in the city." Levi folded an oily rag over the head of the wedge. "I got turned around in the darkness. The hills were like a maze. We ended up in a small town about six miles east of the Prosky ranch. Wes Trimble and my dad probably saw Riverside's troops and pulled back."

"How many troops?"

"About a thousand, I think. They took over a school gym, parking lot, post office, and athletic club. But I only scoped them from a distance. I didn't want to leave you unguarded for long. They might send out a scavenger unit or a recon patrol any minute to search these buildings."

"And I have no weapons." Dom touched his chest where he'd kept his knife. "They got my Bowie—the one I replaced after Trimble made me lose my last one. I'll kill that Conrad Prosky. Oh, I'll make them all pay!"

"Well, I can't imagine Prosky's ranch will be a priority for the PSDF now that Riverside is on their way."

"Why aren't they advancing?" Dom frowned. "And why are they stopped here, so close to moving into San Diego? There can't be many resources here. They'd have the elevation advantage for their artillery if they pushed south."

"I don't know what they're doing." Levi held up the mallet. "You ready to try this?"

Dom accepted the iron wedge with the rag to muffle the sound, and rolled from the car seat to the concrete floor.

"If you miss, I'll lose my foot." Dom placed the wedge edge against the shackle's locking joint. "Don't miss."

"Look at it this way . . ." Levi raised the mallet high, "whether I strike true or miss and you lose your foot—you won't have to worry about the chain any longer."

"Just do it."

Though Dom saw Levi hesitate, he wasn't worried. He'd seen something of the young man's skills the evening before. When he'd been captured after the ambush, Dom had counted on Titus Caspertein coming to his rescue. But he'd realized in the corral that the son had the skills and courage of the father—and apparently the same dry sense of humor.

Levi swung and struck the wedge so squarely that the head didn't even slip sideways.

"Don't move," Levi said and struck again.

The shackle tumbled loose from Dom's ankle. He reached to rub the limb, but decided not to touch the ointment Levi had applied to the broken skin.

"That was still pretty loud." Levi took his rifle and went to the window. "Someone patrolling nearby might've heard it."

Dom stuck his toe in the sock, and with care, unrolled the sock up his shin to cover the wound and ointment. He tugged on the hiking boots and laced them loosely, then stood and limped around slowly.

"I can walk with this," Dom said. "How far would you say we need to go?"

"It's five or six miles just to get back to the Prosky exit. We'll have to get creative to transport you or you'll rub that wound inside the boot worse than it already is."

"You're doing a lot for someone who hasn't been, uh, neighborly, as your dad might say," Dom said as he watched Levi use binoculars to gaze out the window.

"Oh, I'm not taking the past too personally." Levi fit on his ammo jacket and strapped on a small caliber handgun under his arm. "You belong to the military. I know you have to think of your own people. What you've done has been for your military standing, so I get it."

"Yeah." Dom winced. "But I hated Trimble for shooting me across town. I had to crawl back to Coronado with no boots, only to be tranqed by your dad on the bridge. Twice in one day? I was fit to kill all of you! It wasn't about the military to me. Your dad made it personal."

"Dad didn't tranq you, I did. I was at the bridge trying to get everyone out of there alive."

"*You?*" Dom swore. "Figures."

"Sometimes pride blinds us from seeing our greatest assets." Levi drew his sidearm. "ELM is definitely an asset for any society, if society is what you guys want for the Pacific States. Dad knows how to build people up so they're independent in their own way. I would think people are a good investment for a local government."

"Since Pan-Day, I haven't seen anyone on the mainland as an asset." Dom took another bite of food. "That's what Trimble called it—*Pan-Day*. I just wanted what people had and took it for myself."

"Well, that's in the past now." Levi moved to the side door with his pack tied tight. "I've shed blood for you in a battle zone so I don't think you'll look at the Casperteins in the same way. Come on. Let's scout around a little."

"What do you hope to find?" Dom walked gingerly to the door in his new boots. "I thought it was swarming with Riverside troops out there."

"That's just the thing—it's not. It's like they set up camp here last night and still haven't gotten out of their sleeping bags. We might find a vehicle or even a radio. My comm was busted when that horse trampled me."

"This is insane." Dom reached the door and leaned against a cabinet. "Even if I'm not exactly mobile, we should get started south. Brogdon will be out looking for me. I know where our patrols will be since I made the search grids myself."

"Brogdon's probably not out searching for you." Levi opened the door and checked the alley. "With Riverside on the move, the general has bigger concerns. Trimble says that's the problem with any government. They're too busy trying to control the people that they don't care for the individual. It looks clear. Put your hand on my left shoulder so I know you're with me."

Raising his silenced pistol, Levi eased into the alley. His perfect shooting posture would've shamed most of the soldiers Dom himself had trained on Coronado Island.

"Listen, I'm only going to slow you down," Dom whispered. "You should go ahead and look for transportation. Then come back for me."

"I'm not leaving you behind. We'll be okay if we take it slow. Together."

Levi stalked cautiously to the end of the alley and peered around the corner.

"No movement," he reported. "This is so weird. Have you ever heard of a military abandoning the fight before the battle even starts?"

"Maybe they pulled out in the night and you didn't hear them?"

"That couldn't be—I was awake all night. Besides, I'm looking at a whole line of vehicles two blocks away. Fuel trucks, Humvees, transports, and at least two armored trucks."

"It could be a trap," said Dom. "Or a decoy for Brogdon to attack. Maybe the Riverside infantry is lying in wait somewhere nearby."

"If that's the case, they won't mind a couple of bums poking around. Neither of us has any Pacific States emblems visible, right?"

"The only military issue I have left are my trousers, but they're unrecognizable."

They started up the street toward the post office with an empty flag pole outside. Dom eyed the first vehicle, a fuel truck, as they reached where it had been parked in front of an elementary school gym.

Levi led him between the vehicles and found the sidewalk to continue forward. Tents had been erected on the grass in front of the gym, but no voices could be heard and the tent canvas moved only from the midday breeze.

Suddenly, a Jeep tore through the next intersection. It passed so quickly that Dom noticed only that it carried four men in uniform—*the Riverside Guard!*

"Where is everyone?" Dom asked.

"Let me check something. Wait here." Dom watched as Levi vaulted over the six-foot-high school fence like it was half that height. He approached the nearest tent with his pistol leveled. Crouching, he lifted a tent flap to peer inside. A few seconds later, Levi returned. "Now we know."

Dom saw the concern on Levi's face and he then understood.

"Meridia? Here?"

"Yeah." Levi licked his lips. "That's my guess. A tent full of sleeping men, but not just sleeping. There was some quiet moaning, too. Prosky said he'd buried a couple men from the virus recently. Riverside's probably been sharing it with everyone lately while getting ready for this invasion."

"But it hit them so quickly!" Dom lifted his shirt to cover his nose and mouth. "Brogdon has talked about weaponizing the virus, but that's not what this is. They've spread this themselves. We need to get outta here!"

"My mom says it's transmitted mostly by body fluids, like someone coughing in your face or talking too close. It's a droplet virus, not aerosol or airborne. All these people were probably fine two days ago. The symptoms were light yesterday as they started out from Riverside. No one said anything, then it hit them last night. Regardless, you were around Prosky's men and I've been around you. We'll need to avoid people when we get back downtown."

"How long? Does your mom know that?"

"A few days to be safe—to make sure no symptoms pop up. Right now, I say we pick a vehicle for ourselves and hit the interstate."

Suddenly, four figures in full green hazmat suits stepped onto the sidewalk in the direction of the post office. They froze for an instant, and Levi lifted his pistol. He fired rapidly and dropped three of the men, but the fourth dove back between the trucks. There was yelling, and then through a windshield, Dom saw the suited man running clumsily away.

"He's getting help!" Dom said. "Hurry, we need to—"

"No, he's radioing for help! We've been made. The fuel truck might work, huh?" Levi opened the passenger door and boosted Dom into the high seat. "You're driving. I don't really have any experience with anything this big."

Dom scooted into the driver's side. The keys were in it! The engine rumbled to life and backfired. Far up the street, a dozen men ran their way—with no hazmat suits but plenty of rifles.

"Back up! Back up!" Levi rolled down the passenger window and readied his rifle.

Reversing the laboring truck, Dom smashed over a fence as he attempted to turn around. Levi leaned out the window and fired several rounds at the soldiers.

Once Dom straightened out the truck, he checked the side mirror and found their pursuers had scattered.

"We have one of their fuel trucks," Dom said. "They'll definitely be coming after us. Everyone in the country will be after us!"

Levi flipped the switches and turned the knobs of a CB radio.

"ELM, are you there?" He tried channel after channel. "This is a Caspertein mayday. Come in, ELM."

The truck tore down the street, crashed through an intersection choked by cars, then careened over a curb. The front bumper of the truck dragged on the pavement from where it hung off one side, casting sparks along the side of the truck.

"There's the interstate!" Dom checked the mirrors. "We've got company—two Hummers with thirty-caliber guns!"

"We'll never outrun them in this." Levi pointed ahead. "Take the on-ramp! Halfway up the ramp, park sideways. Block the whole road to the interstate."

"And go on foot?"

"Better than a fireball if they open fire."

"Next time, I pick our transportation!"

Levi laughed like he was having the time of his young life. He opened the door and jumped out as Dom slowed to park sideways across the on-ramp, from metal guard to concrete guardrail.

"Get free of the truck!" Levi yelled from the pavement. "Take my pack!"

Dom shut off the engine and tossed the keys out the window. He heard Levi's rifle boom as wheels screeched.

With Levi's pack in hand, Dom half fell out of the cab to the pavement. He crawled under the truck to reach the far side, then he continued up the on-ramp with a skipping run to favor his leg.

The gun battle behind him was brief. It was over by the time Dom reached the interstate. Instead of joining him, Levi went to the two Humvees where he'd tranquilized four men as they'd tried to emerge and fight them. Far away, another vehicle was racing to join the fight.

"Levi!" Dom shouted. "Incoming!"

Disappearing inside one Humvee, Levi emerged with a duffel bag. He hustled up the on-ramp, climbed under the fuel truck, and rose to the far side. Once more, Levi paused and dug into a breast pocket.

"What're you doing?" yelled Dom. "Get outta there!"

When Levi turned, he was running. Dom swore, realizing what Levi had done.

The fuel truck burst into flames. Black smoke billowed into the sky. Levi reached Dom and dropped the duffel bag at Dom's feet.

"Someone must've opened the fuel valve," Levi said as they watched the on-ramp become engulfed in flames. "Oh, yeah. *I* opened the fuel valve!"

"You Casperteins are crazy."

"But effective, yeah?" Levi grinned.

Dom rolled his eyes and knelt to open the duffel bag, which held some soldier's personal clothing. Together, they grabbed what they thought might be useful, stuffed a few items into Levi's pack, then walked away. As Dom hobbled along, he fit a wool sweater over his flannel shirt. The weather was temperate so far, but he knew if they slept outside, they'd need the layers—and Dom was finished sleeping outside with no shirt.

Levi offered his left arm to aid Dom's gait up the interstate, but Dom couldn't continue like this. Soon, once safely away from what was left of the Riverside column, he would have to admit to the younger man that he needed to stop or he'd lose the foot to irritation and infection. Besides, it hurt too much to walk for long. Prosky hadn't been kind with that shackle, maybe crippling him for life.

"It's too exposed up here." Levi stopped and checked east and west. "Anyone could come upon us. Or pick us off from below. Prosky's property is a few miles ahead on the right. With his horses, he could range this far east, maybe even to meet up with Riverside. We don't want to run into them again."

"No argument from me." Dom reached the guardrail facing south. "I've been ambushed one too many times up here already. It's only about ten feet down to the grass right here. I see some houses a couple miles away through those trees."

After climbing over the guardrail, Levi hung, then dropped down to the grass. Setting aside his pack and rifle, he reached up to receive Dom. Dom thought it strange that he didn't feel inferior around the young man, even with his injury. And Levi didn't treat him as an invalid. There seemed to be an unspoken agreement that this was best for both of them, though Dom knew Levi would've been more mobile and safer without catering to a wounded soldier.

Dom let go of the rail and dropped a few feet to Levi's arms. Both men grunted and collapsed to the ground.

"Next time, you catch me!" Levi joked.

They laughed as they recovered to their feet. Dom didn't remember a single instance when he'd laughed so freely with anyone on Coronado Island. Every moment since Pan-Day at the base or headquarters had been spent drilling the men or proving his own fortitude before zealous soldiers seeking a black armband.

"This'll take us longer to get back to the city," Dom said as they continued south with Levi's arm around him.

"Yeah, but it'll be safer. Bad things happen when we rush."

"Another lesson from your God?"

"He's your God, too. But no, just common-sense wisdom from my dad."

"General Brogdon said Titus Caspertein was a legend in his prime. I guess he still is."

"My dad was a thief and an arms smuggler most of his adult life," Levi said. "He's told me a little about it. And Oleg Saratov shared some of it, too. Oleg went undercover to try to stop Dad from selling a chemical weapon to the Palestinians. He used to be Interpol, but Oleg's at ELM now."

"ELM is full of misfits, huh?"

"Misfits who know their place before God. I'm not even twenty years old but I've learned I'd rather be outnumbered on the right side with God than with the majority who're following a bad leader."

"Brogdon's not a bad leader. He's a visionary. He understands how to rebuild this country by discipline and rules."

"And we counter that with faith and love."

"Yeah, I know." Dom stopped to catch his breath in the light cover of a sparse forest. He looked up at Levi's face. "A week ago, I would've mocked you for saying something soft like that, but I've seen how you do it. There's nothing soft about you Casperteins. Maybe you're a little unbalanced, but not soft."

"It ain't easy admitting those crazy Christians are onto something, huh?" Levi grinned.

"Shut up, Caspertein, and help me." Dom shook his head as he leaned on Levi. "You have a plan for dinner or should we begin gnawing on tree bark along the way?"

"The Lord seems to provide in these situations." Levi helped him over a fallen log. "It's kind of exciting, isn't it?"

"What?"

"To be living by faith. We're in a desperate situation. Meridia Virus behind us and miles of dangerous suburbs in front of us."

"And we have no food," Dom added.

"I guess it'll be exciting to see how we make it back home."

"We have very different ideas about what is and what isn't exciting. Expecting your God to drop manna from heaven is just pure delusional."

"Oh, I don't think it'll be manna." Levi chuckled. "But it'll be interesting to see, nonetheless. I'm glad you at least know the stories of God's provision from the Bible. Now you just need to wait on Him."

Dom swore under his breath. Of all the people who'd come to his aid, it had to be this young man! Of course, if he brought it up to Levi, he'd just say that God planned it this way. So, he kept his mouth shut and hobbled along beside him.

✝

Carla Criswell quickly walked the fifty yards between the ELM building and the Hillcrest Hopeful's building.

Chevy emerged from the front entrance before she reached it.

"Thanks so much." He held the door open with one foot as he accepted her armful of potted tomato plants. "Did you want to come upstairs and hand these out with me?"

She'd accompanied Annette and Chevy into Hillcrest in previous days to offer provisions that ELM had in abundance.

"No, not today," Carla said. "Annette has me running errands." She gestured to the vinyl lunchbox and strap over her shoulder. "Sorry. We're all shorthanded."

"Pun intended?" He nodded at her injured shoulder and arm still in the sling.

"Oh, yeah." She forced a smile, still adjusting to the sense of humor of these people. "Annette says I have to keep it on for a few more weeks. She helped me put it on this morning since Levi isn't here."

He cocked his head.

"The youngster sort of grew on you, huh?"

"Yeah." She felt her neck redden, hoping Levi hadn't told anyone of her romantic notions toward him a few days earlier. "I'm a little confused why we're all continuing like business as usual with him out there maybe needing help."

"No one knows what Levi needs more than Titus, and Titus returned home." Chevy shook his head. "There's no reason to believe Levi is in trouble out there. We could find our own pile of trouble by running all over the countryside looking for him. You've seen Levi in action. So have I. He may be short on life experience, but we both know he has the Lord's favor."

"Do you mean like, luck?"

"God's supporting hand on His servants' lives isn't luck. His favor is His faithful response toward those whose loyalty has been tested and proven."

"But Annette acts like she's not even worried."

"That's because she's not." Chevy shifted the plants in his arms. "Annette's faith was borne in the midst of adversity. Her trust in God's provision is the source of her composure, but she's still Levi's mother. Her concern is rational, so you don't see it so much outwardly. You should ask her about it."

"I already did." Carla scoffed. "Basically, she said the same thing. Then she said she wasn't worried as much for Levi as she was for whoever crossed him. She said it as a joke, but I don't get it. You guys really think you're invincible? Oleg is still healing and Titus might have Meridia."

"Oh, I think you misunderstand why we think lightly of safety and danger. It's not that we think we're always physically protected as God's people, Carla. It's that we're spiritually enlightened to the truth that our physical protection isn't a priority. Personal safety isn't driving our decisions. Oleg may never get out of bed, Titus may die of Meridia, and Levi may never return."

Her heart sunk at the prospect of never seeing him again.

"Don't say that, Chevy."

"But that's my point. I'd miss any one of them, but the Bible promises believers their *spiritual* protection. I'll see them in glory. We don't cling too tightly to this life because it's so fleeting. Our hearts and minds are already functioning like we're in heaven where there is no death. These are all things you can learn about if you'd begin to read the Bible."

"I'm not ready yet." She looked away. "All I know is that you Christians aren't anything like what I thought you were before Pan-Day."

"Well, I can tell you're curious." Chevy used his foot to open the door wider. "I'll pray your curiosity becomes a desire. Once you realize your need for a Savior, that'll be the end for you in one way and the beginning for you in another way."

"That makes no sense." She laughed. "I'd better get this to Titus."

"Thanks for the tomatoes."

Waving goodbye, she continued on her way to a third apartment building they'd only recently opened—for quarantine purposes. Annette had insisted that Titus, Gabby, and two new Hispanic arrivals quarantine in a building completely separate from ELMs ventilation system. For the next few days, Titus was shut away—to restore the new quarantine living quarters. Carla had already taken him tools, blankets, and buckets to make a few of the lower floor apartments livable. But the building really needed Chevy's engineering expertise to get a dolly-elevator system operating and the electrical and water flowing.

So far, the most Titus had done was cover the first-floor windows with boards or metal—whatever he could find to temporarily enclose and secure himself inside the building.

Carla banged on the metal door that hung on a slide rather than on hinges. After setting the vinyl lunchbox on the concrete in front of the door, she backed up about twenty feet.

The door opened a moment later. Titus appeared with a wrench in one hand, and mopping his sweaty brow with a handkerchief in his other. For an instant, Carla saw Levi's young face in the older version before her. He certainly didn't appear to have any Meridia symptoms, nor did his energy seem hindered by whatever exposure he'd had.

"It ain't easy working in this sweatbox with no A/C." He noticed the lunchbox. "Dinner?"

"Potato, carrot, and onion soup, with fresh bread. I'll bring you more milk later. Gustavo said he wants to chill it for you first."

"Wow, I should get Meridia more often for this kind of room service!" He winked. "No, I'm kidding, Carla. I don't think I have it."

"What about the little girl?" Carla peered past him into the darkness behind him. "Is she okay? No symptoms yet?"

"She's helping me gather linens that people left behind. Plenty of laundry for you later. But no, she's showing no symptoms, either."

"Okay, good." She hesitated to leave. As casually as possible, she scanned the ELM balconies next door. Wes, Wynter, and Dusty were inside somewhere. No one else was listening. "Have you said anything to anyone about, you know, who I am?"

"Nope." Titus took the sealed containers of soup and bread and left the vinyl lunchbox on the stoop. "Your family name is your own business. Oh, this soup is still hot!"

"If they knew I was here with you, it might help you people with the Pacific States. My dad would intercede for you with the general."

"That's not the way followers of Jesus live, Carla. We wouldn't want anyone to take credit themselves for what God Himself already provides."

"Well, that's just stupid. I mean, there doesn't need to be bad blood between you and Brogdon."

"Christians don't rely on the world for what Jesus has offered Himself to be. Peace is only genuine if there's reconciliation God's way. That's why we went to rescue Sergeant Lesage."

"But you didn't rescue him. You lost Levi!"

"Not knowing where Levi is and losing him are two different things, Carla. Some of the finest men and women I've ever known have trained Levi. Even if he and Lesage perish, things are already better between us and Brogdon just by him knowing we tried to assist his first officer. I don't need to manipulate your father by using you to force peace here. That's healing that the Lord brings between parties when believers are Christ-like."

"At Levi's expense?"

"Peace is never free, Carla. Peace is costly. Someone always pays to ruin the divide between two peoples. Jesus did that—He brought peace between us and God. It was costly so it could be freely offered to those of us who know we're weak and sinful and undeserving."

Carla stared at the leaves and trash scattered across the concrete. More blew in from all over the city every morning when the land breeze drew it toward the sea.

These people were so weird, but they spoke as if what they believed and lived was totally natural.

"I don't understand how you people lived like this before Pan-Day without anyone knowing."

"Lived like this?" Titus waved his hand at the disaster around them. "Lived like what? I've never lived like this before."

"Oh, I mean, you lived your lives for others. You risked everything to help people all over the world. Annette told me. I've never read anything in the press about what you guys have done for years for others."

"We weren't trying to get publicity or even to make Jesus famous in the world. That's why you've never read about God's people in the secular press. The world hates Jesus Christ, so it hates those of us who follow Him. And we're not trying to bridge that gap that should never be joined. Instead, we live quietly but boldly, sharing the truth with people so they can join the side of life. We're all facing eternity, so that's on all of our minds."

"Well, no one really knows what happens when we die."

"Just because you believe that lie, Carla, doesn't mean it's true. People who reject the truth will always try to undermine God's Word. The Bible contains very clear explanations about heaven, hell, the different judgements, and the eternal kingdom."

"I don't believe you could really know that stuff."

"Why? Because they didn't teach it to you in your university?" Titus smiled sadly. "You're going to trust what an atheist says about God's promises? An atheist spends all his energies trying unsuccessfully to prove that complicated systems evolved without an Intelligent Designer behind it all."

"It could happen."

"Sure. Given enough time, dust blowing in the wind could form a complex biological species. You don't need faith to believe in that, only delusion. I remember the articles you wrote about God's people, Carla. In your arrogance, you thought you were enlightened, but you proved otherwise by helping no one discover the truth. It's time for you to admit your worldview has been wrong all along. No one cares about your pronouns and politically correct obsessions anymore. Though you intimidated people to adopt your thinking, all your efforts meant nothing. My past before Christ came into my life was the same—empty pursuits and self-delusions. Don't wait until it's too late to take hold of God's promises meant for you personally."

Carla walked away from the quarantine building. She wasn't sure if she was angry or hurt by Titus' words. Levi had spoken just as directly to her. Annette was gentler, showing her tips about living. Chevy had his own style, too—allowing her to accompany him upstairs to disperse food, bedding, and hygiene items to strangers. But their message was the same: love others based on the love their God had shown them.

Two figures emerged suddenly from the Hillcrest Hopefuls building. She veered away before she realized they were two women, one middle-aged and the other young. They wore their hair back in ponytails and on their feet were new tennis shoes—thanks to the ELM stores.

Mostly, the fifty Hopefuls had remained indoors, slowly making homes for themselves in the long-abandoned apartments of deceased tenants. But occasionally, Carla had seen from a balcony of ELM that they came outside to walk around the courtyard. Or when there'd been little danger, they ventured beyond the perimeter to collect feed for the goats. Everyone knew the value of having milk in their diets.

"Excuse me," said the older woman. "You're one of the ELM ladies, aren't you? You were helping Chevy and Levi the first couple of days, right? With Annette?"

"Yes." Carla smiled, happy to be recognized for doing something helpful after she'd felt so useless with her one arm. "I do what I can. Do you need something?"

"Oh, yes!" The woman stepped close enough to grasp Carla's hand. "My daughter and I—we're so scared! We were hoping you'd pray for us. We know you're Christians and we heard Chevy, Wes, and Annette praying for some of the others. You're all so strong. We don't want to die like this. We have no one. We have nothing. We don't know what to do now. The world is so frightening and confusing. The future is unknown and we can't imagine anything good happening tomorrow. Please, please, pray for us!"

Carla stared wide-eyed, then tugged her hand away as she backed toward the ELM entrance.

"I'm . . . sorry." Her chin trembled. "I'm sorry."

She turned and fled to the front door of ELM and knocked loudly on the metal. A moment later, Gustavo, the unofficial doorkeeper, slid the door wide. Without greeting him, she darted inside, pushed off the goat pen fencing, and dashed for the stairs.

Alone in the dolly, she pulled on gloves and tugged on the cable, ascending the platform far slower than she wished. She wanted to disappear. The world was so cruel. God didn't seem to be real, so how could she possibly talk to Him for two women who asked her for prayer? Their fears were *her* fears! If not for Levi and his family, she would've gone on to Coronado Island to join her father—

but for what? Politics didn't hold her interest any longer, and she wasn't a soldier. ELM seemed to fit since she was safe here and felt useful. Until now.

At the dolly stop on the twenty-sixth floor, she climbed the stairs to the next stage, but stopped on the twenty-seventh-floor landing. Chevy was in the Hopefuls' building, so Oleg was alone. The others spoke of Oleg with reverence, but Carla hadn't spoken to him alone before.

Knocking on his apartment door, she found it unlocked, and eased herself inside.

"Hello?" she called.

"Yes, I'm here," he responded in his slight Russian accent. "Come in."

Carla found him in the living room where Chevy or someone had positioned his bed next to the living room window looking east. Pillows propped up his head and he was working on a radio transmitter disassembled across his lap. Binoculars sat on the window sill within reach and his battle rifle leaned against the bedside table.

"Uh, Carla." He frowned. "I wasn't expecting you this afternoon. I would've cleaned up if I'd known I was having company."

"Oh, it's fine." She walked closer. The place was a little messy and he hadn't shaved in days.

"I was kidding." He set the radio components on the table. "Anyone who knows me knows I don't clean up, and even when I try, it doesn't seem to fit me."

"It's okay." She smiled, actually feeling at ease. "Can I sit with you?"

He gestured to a chair with clothes on it. She set the clothes on the sofa and moved the chair closer to sit down facing the window.

"You've been crying?" he asked. "Sorry. Your eyes are red."

"Oh, I just . . ." She sighed and gazed out the window at the distant green hills where Levi was possibly traveling. Her tears ran afresh and she wiped at them without much care that Oleg saw her. "I don't know what I'm doing here."

She scoffed at herself, glancing at Oleg to see his reaction, then returned her eyes to the window. He wasn't a handsome man. His features were rugged and bold, but his eyes were gentle. Or sad.

"Here on Earth, or here in a crippled man's apartment?"

"Here . . . at ELM."

"Oh."

Carla licked her lips, waiting for him to speak. The Casperteins and Chevy always had something to say. Oleg must've had something helpful for her.

His Bible sat on the bedside table amongst the clutter. Its black cover was weathered. The edges of some pages were stained red. It didn't seem odd at all to wonder if the stains were blood. Of course, it was blood. That was just who these people were.

"A couple of women downstairs asked me to pray for them."

"Oh." Oleg nodded.

"It freaked me out."

"I see."

"They thought I was one of you people."

"Oh. I'm so sorry. That's terrible."

She frowned and cast him a quick look, but realized he was smiling.

"No, I didn't mean it like that," she said.

"Okay."

"I mean, you people have your way, but it's just not me."

"It's not my way, either," Oleg said. "Or, it wasn't."

"But I thought you were a Christian."

"Oh, I am now. But it's not the way I chose for myself. Not at first."

"You worked for Interpol, Levi said. I've known people at Interpol."

"For most of my life, I drank too much. But I gave myself to law and order and catching criminals. The last criminal I tried to catch was Titus. He made me look like a fool. Then I lost my job. I was a disgrace."

"Um, I didn't know it happened like that."

"My way was to drink myself to death on the cold streets of Moscow. One night I was getting mugged. I was too wasted to fight them off. Then Titus showed up."

"Titus saved you?"

"The first of many times."

"He says you're the one who always sacrifices yourself for him."

"Yeah, I try." He waved his hand. "Usually, he just ends up rescuing me again. I'm no hero. What I'm saying is that my way wasn't following Jesus, not at first. Titus believed in Jesus and came and found me—the Interpol agent who'd failed to arrest him. But Titus showed me the right way—an ex-criminal showed a failed police agent the way of Jesus. We all need someone to show us the right way from the way we've made for ourselves."

"I don't understand what's so wrong with my way."

"What did your way have for the women downstairs who asked you for prayer?"

Carla didn't want to answer, so she kept silent. And Oleg wasn't the type to hurry anyone. She saw that now. The Casperteins were leaders. Oleg was a follower, but no less strong or intelligent. Now she wished she'd talked to him days ago.

"I made a fool of myself with Levi."

"Oh?"

"He didn't tell anyone. I guess I panicked or something. I told him I'd be a good match for him. I just didn't want to be alone in this world. I mean, with a Caspertein at my side, even just a kid like him, I'd be all right, right?"

"What'd Levi say?"

"Oh, he let me down easy. I was so embarrassed, but he didn't rub it in. A nineteen-year-old turning me down. I'm such an idiot."

"You're trying to find traction in life. That doesn't make you an idiot."

"I don't know . . ."

"Just make sure you find your traction," he said. "Eventually. Look in the right place."

"Is this where you talk to me about God as well?"

"It sounds like others already have."

Carla sat back in the chair and watched the sky above the building next door. She didn't want to face the Hopefuls again, but Annette had set out more items to be delivered—towels and toilet paper for the dozens who had little.

But for now, she enjoyed the silence with Oleg. She needed this—to sit and gather her thoughts, even to share her blunders. And ironically, he was a Russian—someone she would've despised prior to Pan-Day just for being Russian. Maybe God was trying to tell her something about her past. It certainly hadn't helped her the last few months. All her opinions and judgements seemed so pointless now, just like Titus had said downstairs.

"You know what I've been thinking about?" Oleg asked. "We should have another system to make deliveries to the other building. Maybe hook up a rope system with them. It'll save us from going downstairs all the time."

"How would we get a line over there? It's too far to throw something, isn't it?"

"Do it like they still build bridges anywhere around the world—with a crossbow."

"We have a crossbow?"

"I have one in my bedroom. Put a line on a bolt and shoot it across. You could use the balcony next door."

"Yeah?" She stood. "*I* could do that?"

"Of course, you could. And I'll come with you. Just so I keep pressure off this hip for a while still. You find the crossbow. It's in my closet. We'll also need a light line, and some heavy nylon. I'll cock and shoot the crossbow. Then you can run over to the other building and pull the line in and anchor it, maybe in an apartment nobody's using. Yeah, everyone will love this!"

Carla went into his room—a bigger mess than the living room—and sorted through his closet full of gear she'd expect to find in the hands of a Special Forces operative. She found the crossbow and held it in her hands. Her heart was so light and full, she almost told God she was thankful. *Almost.*

# *Chapter Eight*

Conrad Prosky felt numb as he turned off his HAM radio. He'd gambled and chosen Riverside Guard over the PSDF—the wrong choice. Now, he had nothing. His contact in the Riverside invasion convoy had told him the news: Meridia had taken out half his troops. The other half had returned to Riverside, abandoning much of their equipment just five miles east of Conrad's ranch.

There would be no war. Conrad would see no spoils.

And he wasn't at all surprised that the virus was still impacting fighting efforts to such a devastating degree. His physical contact with Riverside a couple weeks earlier had transmitted it to two of his own men, who'd given it during trade to the elderly couple down by the interstate. It had taken a few days, but now all of his men and their few women and children were showing sudden and severe symptoms. No one had been spared. Except him.

He walked from the bedroom to the front porch where he'd set up the radio months earlier. Just twenty-four hours earlier, the ranch had been the scene of one of the fiercest gun battles Conrad had ever imagined—and he'd been unconscious through most of it. The Casperteins had been a formidable bunch, maybe fifteen or twenty out there in the hills firing weapons with a longer range than any of his men had. At least that was the claim of those who'd been conscious during at least some of the battle.

Someone coughed from one of the barracks buildings. The Quonset door was open, but Conrad wasn't going near to close it. He'd never heard of anyone surviving Meridia. All who showed symptoms died from the inside out within a few days. The ranch was finished. The whole place was diseased.

One of his riding horses whinnied at him from the door of the barn as if to remind him the quarter horse was still free. Most of the horses from the corral had returned to the trough for water and to the barn for hay. They apparently preferred the hay over grazing on the grassy hillsides.

It was time to leave and start over. Now, Conrad wished he'd chosen to side with the Pacific States, but Riverside had been first to offer him lucrative food supplies and the promise of spoils once San Diego was taken from Coronado. But Riverside's food bribes had been short the last few weeks, and he admitted to himself there would be no spoils in taking San Diego. The city and suburbs were disaster zones where bands of looters still roamed and neighbors shot neighbors over a single can of soup.

Conrad went back into the house and started packing. He couldn't go north if Riverside was having an outbreak. Besides, Los Angeles was dealing with her own problems after a series of earthquakes. Going east—he wasn't interested in braving the wilderness to reach the central United States. That left south—Mexico. If he stayed along the coast, maybe he'd find an occasional water source for his horses by way of streams and rivers. A small Mexican town would suit him just fine, somewhere he could hire out his gun to the locals and live in peace. Somehow, he'd escaped Meridia. He wasn't willing to stick around and test his luck further!

Out in the barn, he saddled a horse, tied on a rifle scabbard, then caught two more horses for his pack animals. He gathered twenty assault rifles and ammunition to trade along the way, and packed enough food on the second horse to feed a family for a month. If he left now, he could travel through most of dangerous San Diego under cover of darkness and reach Mexico by dawn. Skirting Tijuana would require some creativity, maybe swinging farther to the east. Yes, he'd need more water jugs. The natural well on his property—oh, he'd miss that!

Mounting his horse, he felt the pain from the three welts he'd received from the Caspertein tranquilizers. *Tranquilizers!* Evidently, they'd been a family of sharpshooters to obliterate his thirty-man army. There were no buzzards circling over the nearby hills, so Conrad guessed no Casperteins had been shot and left behind. They'd simply disappeared into the night—taking Sergeant Lesage with them. Unbelievable.

As Conrad rode past the main house, he tossed a flare through one window. He'd leave it to no one, but the barn he'd leave standing for the remaining horses. They'd go wild or be caught someday by passersby. The ranch that'd been in his family for three generations was no longer his home.

He rode in front, leading his two pack horses down the dirt road toward town. His sidearm holster remained unbuckled. The route south would be unpredictable—as unpredictable as a tall blond youth and his family invading his ranch for a man they didn't even like. That puzzled Conrad all day. Lesage didn't know how lucky he was since Conrad had meant to execute him rather than keep him alive after he'd spilled what intel he had. Of course, it would've all been pointless. Riverside had been decimated. There was no one to share his intel with even if he'd gotten anything useful out of the sergeant.

Not surprisingly, Conrad found the space behind the drive-thru empty. The Casperteins had been thorough and taken the Humvees that Conrad had stolen during the interstate ambush.

A few minutes later, he reached the other end of the small community town and rode past the Hillerman residence. He'd known them since he was a child. Mrs. Hillerman had given him cookies as a boy on more than one occasion, and Mr. Hillerman had once given Conrad a ride home from school in his truck when his bike chain had broken. But now the residence was dark. They'd taken in a relative, a mentally challenged child, not long ago. Conrad guessed the child would be lost now as well.

Rather than travel east or west on the interstate, Conrad crossed the lonely lanes and continued south. He'd lived on the ranch his whole life, so he knew the surrounding neighborhoods to the south—Lemon Grove and Spring Valley. Many weeks earlier, a few of his men had ranged south along the wilderness edge and witnessed a jet airliner go down, but they hadn't made the effort to investigate for fear of bandits drawn to the crash site. At least with the horses he could choose a route without roads and hope to avoid most civilians. The adventure ahead rather appealed to him—alone, free, heavily armed, and the future unknown. If someone along the way had something he wanted, he'd kill them and take it. Life now was simple like that.

South of the interstate, he rode through a low pass between two bald hills and came upon the first San Diego suburb of middle-class residences. Most had red roofs, white walls, backyard pools, and two-car garages. They all looked alike. Conrad turned in his saddle to study the houses as he kept his distance by trotting along the edges of back yards.

The sun was setting. Another community stretched far to the east. He could spend two hours going around the area or just charge through to the south. By dawn, he wanted to be beyond the border.

Nudging his horse forward, the street seemed eerily quiet. Trash and cell phones littered the asphalt. Portable basketball hoops lay toppled from some past windstorm. Garbage bins spilled onto every street. The bags had been torn open and sorted through by people or predators. Some houses were even burned down, maybe in an effort to leave their lives behind as he had done—or to burn away the disease of the deceased.

Conrad was thinking how lucky he was that he'd survived everything—when his horse stumbled and fell under him. As he leapt free and rolled across the pavement, he wondered if his mount had fallen into a sinkhole. But then the report of a gun echoed. *It was an attack!*

The two pack horses spooked and trotted away. Conrad scrambled to his now dead horse and tried to pry his rifle free, but the animal had fallen on its right side, pinning the rifle under it.

Using his elbows, Conrad slithered through paper litter around his horse to use it for cover. Against the belly of the animal, he drew his revolver. There were no other shots and no one showed themselves. The two houses nearby still had their windows, and their doors remained closed rather than ajar.

His pack horses stopped one hundred yards up the street. Given time, he could've gotten the saddle off his dead horse and put it on another, but not under fire. At this point, he could still walk to Mexico by leading his horses along.

He supposed the people were just hungry. That's why they'd shot his horse and not him.

Then Conrad saw them as they showed themselves. They were standing on the roofs of the houses before and behind him! There was no hope to win by shooting his way out of the community. He dropped his pistol as he stood and raised his hands. Two defeats in two days. *How humiliating!*

"It's all right," he shouted and walked sideways toward his pack animals. "I'll just move on."

Licking his lips, he hoped they let him go. His other horses had plenty of guns, food, and ammo. They couldn't see it, but he'd come south with quite a bit of excess.

The next shot came from behind him. It spun him sideways on one heel like a top, then he fell on his back in the street. Panting and staring at the sky, he lay frozen and tried to assess his injuries. *How unlucky!* Maybe this was what he deserved after he'd sent his men to the city to impersonate the PSDF and execute civilians. Or maybe this was for the way he'd treated captured prisoners like Lesage, torturing them for days for information.

The world as he knew it was cruel, but Conrad had always expected to be at the top of the food chain. His family had been wealthy. They'd enjoyed the rural western life of rowdy rodeos and loud concerts, burning whisky and loose women. This cruelty now, to die as a middle-aged man, was inconsistent with his past. He wanted to live!

They picked over his body like he was already dead. His boots were removed first, then they stripped him of his shirt, belt holster, and pants. When they were gone, his head rolled to the side. Now they were taking his pack horses.

It was miles back to the ranch. And wounded? He couldn't muster the strength to sit up. Lying flat on his back seemed best. Just sleep. Rest, yes, that's what he needed. Everything would be better after a good night of sleep.

His luck would be better tomorrow, too. No more virus. No more shooting. And no more Casperteins.

✝

Levi watched the red-roofed houses for five minutes before he approached the carcass of the butchered horse. He kept his battle rifle against his shoulder. The odor of death was overpowering. Whoever had gutted the animal had made a mess, even puncturing the intestines. Amateurs. Desperate. Blood still ran toward a clogged rain gutter. This was fresh.

A saddle lay near a residential driveway. This had definitely been an ambush. No one killed a horse someone was riding unless they were just after the meat and cared nothing for the rider's life.

Sure enough, a few yards away, a smaller pool of drying blood marked the place where someone had been wounded. If the person had died, Levi guessed these were the kind of people who would leave the dead to rot since they already had the horse. But still, the person had lost a lot of blood. He was dragged or he'd crawled south.

"What a mess!" Winded, Lesage arrived behind Levi. He used a makeshift crutch from a metal shop to aid his walking. "The vultures haven't even gotten here yet. This is real recent."

They'd covered only a few miles since leaving the interstate, but Levi wasn't in a hurry to get home just to quarantine. Lesage had agreed that he too would rather spend his quarantine days out there than on the island under the disdain of the other soldiers.

"There's probably more horses." Levi pointed out horse manure down the street. "Maybe the rider put up a fight."

"Could be those horses from Prosky's place," said Lesage. "Maybe your dad turned them loose after we left. How far away do you think we are from the ranch?"

"Four or five miles." Levi's eyes narrowed. "We need to find somewhere for the night. If these people are shooting travelers, you and I are a little too exposed out here."

"Levi, look!"

Following Lesage's gaze to the southwest, Levi saw grayish smoke drifting into the air.

"You thinking what I'm thinking?" Levi asked. "Horse barbeque?"

"They have to cook the meat somewhere."

"Everyone in the area is going to see that." Levi used his rifle scope to search the sky east and south. "You feel like crashing a barbeque?"

"I feel like going way around this whole place, but my armpit is screaming from this crutch. So, you're really aching for horse meat, huh?"

"We don't have much of anything on us to steal." Levi tugged at his pack straps. "My pack is mostly empty. They'll see that. We need the food. Maybe they'll share."

"Don't think I'd count on it." Lesage snorted. "They'll be too afraid of you—a mercenary with his finger on the trigger."

"A mercenary with cuts and scrapes all over his face. Is it that bad?"

"Not unless you're looking for a girlfriend at the barbeque."

"It ain't easy using a fencepost to scare potential brides away." Levi grinned. "It stings a little, but it's effective."

"You Casperteins are crazy. Look, if you think you can get a bite of meat for us, I'm game. I haven't been too impressed with your ability to feed us today."

"Dad said the best way to fit in is to act like you belong. We could try to blend in."

"Look at us." Lesage held up his crutch. "Do we look like we belong anywhere?"

"Put this under your shirt." Levi drew his twenty-two-caliber handgun. "They'll see you're wounded and won't suspect that you're armed. It's me they'll be watching."

"You have a plan?"

"I have an idea."

"Care to share—since it could get us both killed?"

"Offer hope to hopeless people."

"How will you do that? These people are already probably used to shooting strangers who happen through here."

"Well, I don't know. God's giving me direction one step at a time."

"You and your God . . ." Lesage shook his head. "Okay, lead out."

"Actually, I think it's your turn to take point. I want their first impression of us to be you."

"Great. Shoot the cripple first." Lesage feigned annoyance and hobbled east on a driveway that led out of the neighborhood. "Just when I was beginning to admire your courage."

Chuckling, Levi followed a few yards behind. Except for the sergeant's pain, Levi thought they'd been enjoying their time together. The slow pace had allowed Levi to stop and study the terrain and the layout of each community. Such knowledge would be valuable in the future if he were ever this far east again.

As they walked, Levi also talked to God about his family. He knew ELM would be concerned about him and Lesage, especially with the Riverside military and Meridia Virus pressing in, but he'd seen no sign that his father was out searching. A column of black smoke sometime that day would've been an indication of something, but he knew his dad wouldn't want to draw aggressors to them by way of smoke signals. Everyone would just need to wait until he and Lesage made it home.

A block from the gray smoke, Levi smelled the meat. He'd eaten well the last three months from their stores in the parking garage, but this aroma of fresh meat was something so savory that he prayed right then that God somehow opened the hearts of the locals to share. His hunger overrode the uncomfortable thought of eating a large domesticated animal.

Levi followed Lesage around a street corner where restaurants, a fast-food drive-thru, and a car dealership lined four empty lanes. Midway down the block on the right side, a small block party had spilled onto the street.

Except for the smell of meat, it wasn't a party Levi would've attended under different circumstances.

The pavement itself was covered in packed sand. Trampled and tracked in the sand were millions of shards of glass that sparkled like diamonds as the sun arced toward the west. Trash lay strewn everywhere, whether dropped or windblown.

The people reflected their environment. Lesage continued to approach the scene without anyone stopping him. A few late arrivals to the party carried handguns, but Levi saw only two rifles, one of them an old assault rifle. No one appeared to have access to running water. Their long greasy hair on both men and women clung to their scalps. Unwashed faces revealed blotches and sores. Their clothing was faded, loosely hanging on skeletal frames that had suffered more days unfed than fed.

The restaurant that drew the crowd of about thirty adults had no front wall or windows. The roof was on the verge of collapse as if a car or truck had driven through the supporting wall. The clutter of dining tables and chairs didn't seem to bother those standing idly, staring at the rear kitchen from where the smoke billowed from a serving window.

"No one's even paying attention to us," said Lesage as Levi came to stand next to him, his eyes wary. "Look. People are still arriving. It seems pretty calm. Maybe whoever has meat does this all the time—they share what they kill."

"I don't think so." Levi saw the look on some of their faces. "Do these people look like anyone takes care of them? They haven't eaten in days. We're not going to see a single steak, Sergeant. Look back there."

Sure enough, at the swinging door to the kitchen, an armed man with a shotgun stood guard. More people were milling around in the kitchen, visible through the serving window.

"You know what I think?" Levi surveyed the area more carefully. "I think these people saw the smoke same as us and came to the smell of grilled meat, but they came for nothing. The people who hijacked that horse and rider are back there grilling the meat for themselves. They have the guns and the food, and I don't see them sharing their kill with these people, let alone us."

"They won't give us any?" asked a woman nearby as she clutched her midsection. Her cheeks were sunken. "Why won't they give us any?"

Levi held Lesage's gaze.

"I don't like it either," said Lesage, "but this is survival, Levi. Let's push on. Let them fight over their own kill. They can eat each other for all I care."

Nodding sadly, Levi sensed God's heart for the forgotten souls around him.

"Where would you be if someone had left you to survive on your own?" Levi turned to the hungry woman. "You'll eat, ma'am. I'll feed you myself or die trying. Lesage, post up by that other swinging door to the kitchen. If anyone comes out with a weapon, tranq them."

Lesage growled under his breath but obeyed.

"It's gonna be okay," Levi assured a slender man and woman who clung to one another lest they fall over. "Let me see what the holdup is on dinner."

Levi worked his way through the people to the back of the dining area. The man with the shotgun wore a threatening scowl for the people, but his expression changed when he saw tall, blond Levi approaching him with his ammo vest and black battle rifle.

"How's it going?" Levi nodded and turned to stand beside him as if to guard the kitchen entrance with him.

"Pretty good."

"The meat must be about ready, huh?"

"Uh . . ." He eyed Levi.

"You're not going to bring the meat out this way, are you? You'll take it out the back, right?"

Ejecting one gel-tranq round from this rifle, Levi fumbled with it in his left hand.

"Yeah." The man's eyes twitched to Lesage and back to Levi. "You're not with Dooley."

"Is Dooley back there?"

"Yeah. He's packing up the meat they're cooking. You're not from around here. I'd remember you."

"I think what's more important is that we remember these people out here."

"There's not enough for everyone."

"You and Dooley's people can eat for a week on hijacked horse meat, or you can share it with all these people for a day. What's your conscience telling you is the right thing to do with meat that isn't even yours?"

"Eat for a week?"

"Wrong answer."

Levi slammed the gel-tranq into the man's chest muscle. With his other hand, he forced the shotgun muzzle to the ceiling, but the guardian of the swinging door slumped unconsciously without firing a shot.

The wonderful juicy smell from the kitchen was almost overwhelming. Heat wafted from the serving window. But the people in the restaurant area fell back rather than surge forward after seeing Levi put the guard out of commission.

"Go in!" Levi mouthed and gestured to Lesage at the other swinging door. "Go in!"

"No!" Lesage mouthed back and held up his crutch. "I can't fight!"

"One, two, three," Levi counted with his fingers, then yelled, "Go!"

Levi pushed through the door. On the left, two men were packing cooked meat into a pair of grocery carts. Two women were wrapping the meat as it was cooked, and two more men stood with tongs at a huge oven where steaks were sizzling. A couple of the men wore sidearms, but the rest of the weapons were rifles—leaning together against the walk-in freezer wall.

Lesage barged through his own door an instant later, but much less gracefully. The swinging door flapped back and hit him on the arm. The pistol he tried to level fired an accidental shot. Though silenced, the clicking sound from the weapon was loud enough for everyone in the kitchen to hear over the sizzling sound.

One of the women wrapping the meat collapsed, unconscious. Lesage knew he was the cause and cringed with an apologetic look at Levi.

"No one move." Levi saw their eyes take in the size of his rifle barrel. "The lady was just tranquilized. She'll wake up in an hour. Who else wants to get shot? You? You? Okay, who's Dooley?"

"I'm Dooley." A sandy-haired young man at the grill raised his tongs. "What's this about?"

"You shot a horse." Levi let his muzzle drift across the other five who all looked to Dooley for guidance. "That's common enough, but now you're keeping all the meat to yourself. There are people out front who haven't eaten in days. I have a proposal for you."

"What's your proposal?" Dooley's eyes strayed to the rifles against the wall. "You have our attention."

"Take the meat you already packaged in the first cart. That's yours." Levi pointed to the serving window. "The rest—you start serving to them out there."

"That's more than half." Dooley's head lowered. "It's our meat!"

"No, it isn't. You shot the horse out from under some rider, so don't act innocent. You want to argue? I'll take it all and give it all away."

"There's not enough for everyone," Dooley said.

"Well, there's enough for everyone for today. Think about it. You can be the hero of the neighborhood. Why don't you feed a bunch of starving people and show how every life matters?"

Dooley glanced at the others in his group. A couple men shrugged while the others seemed concerned about the unconscious woman or their rifles out of reach.

"You can serve them if you want to." Dooley tossed the tongs onto the grill and backed away, his hands raised. "So, you want to be the big hero? See what happens when you give all your food away."

The other cook set down his tongs as well.

"Take your lady friend there." Levi watched them closely, especially the two with sidearms. "She'll be fine. And leave the rifles. You've lost your shooting privileges for the day."

Hesitating, Dooley's eyes were on the rifles. But then he seemed to notice Levi's barrel was aimed directly at him, and he pushed the grocery cart toward the back door.

"You'll pay for this," Dooley said, "whoever you are. I'll find you someday. I promise."

"I'm with Maddix Striber," Levi offered, remembering his father's strategic words. "If you want me, you come looking for Maddix Striber."

The five opened the back door and carried their unconscious friend out along with their grocery cart of packaged meat.

"That's not the first time I've heard the name Maddix Striber." Lesage frowned at Levi. "Trimble mentioned him to Brogdon. Who is he?"

"Forget it. He's a nobody," Levi said truthfully and locked the back door. "Get on that grill. These portions are too large for the people out front. Their stomachs can't handle too much. Let's cut the steaks in half. You done shooting people?"

"Sorry." Lesage stuck the handgun into his waistband and picked up the nearest tongs. "I didn't mean to. But I wouldn't have let them leave with anything."

"I don't know what happened with the horse and rider and neither do you, so I won't judge them further. All I know is hungry people are out front and we can make sure they're fed something."

"You're not worried about that man's threat?" Lesage began flipping steaks. "We have maybe two days left on the road at my pace."

"Dad taught me not to worry about things that haven't happened. I heard Dooley's threat. If he wants to carry it out, that's up to him. These first steaks are done. Let me get some help."

Levi emerged from the kitchen to find that no one out front had moved since before he'd passed through the swinging door.

"Hello there!" Levi waved at a broad-shouldered black man, his muscled arm around a woman in a bulky sweatshirt. He appeared no less eager to feed his wife and himself than the others, but Levi recognized a calm clarity in his eyes for the task ahead. "I'm Levi Caspertein. Can you two help pass out the meat?"

"Me?" He looked into his wife's eyes. She appeared to have been crying recently. "Where do you want us?"

The man's name was Jovon. He'd been an out-of-work contractor before Pan-Day. His wife didn't seem as capable once Levi brought them both back to the kitchen, so he gave her a small piece of cooked horse meat to eat as Jovon wrapped and prepared to pass through the window what Lesage was finishing on the grill. A pile of cuts a foot high were placed on the counter, so Levi told Lesage to grill a few pieces well-done for the two of them to take with them.

Leaving his pack in the kitchen, Levi returned to the front to stand next to the serving window.

"Listen up, people!" He raised both arms for their attention, allowing his rifle to hang free off the chest strap. "We have fresh meat for you, but hear me on this: I know some of you haven't eaten recently. Don't eat too quickly. Each of you take one portion, then come back through the line for more to take home. Be sure to eat it within a couple of days before it spoils. That's it. Make a line here. Come past the window. Jovon is inside doing the serving. Thanks to God Almighty, we have a little unexpected food for the day!"

The people were fed and starting through the line again before Levi realized his own stomach was growling. The people passed him, their mouths full and smiles dripping with meat juice, and Levi's heart broke for them. This was their food for today, maybe for two more days, but then what? Perhaps unable to leave the city and too unskilled to provide for themselves, they would turn against one another or die of starvation in the weeks ahead. He had to do more!

Other locals arrived at a run and passed through the line until Jovon had no more to pass out through the serving window. The people sat along the curb in front of the establishment, a remarkable lightness to their mood. Some righted old dining chairs and visited as they ate. Others ran aside and vomited, having eaten too much too quickly.

Lesage, Jovon, and his wife emerged from the kitchen.

"Two days' worth in here." Lesage gave Levi his pack, then offered him a wrapped steak to eat right then. "Well done?"

"As long as it's edible, I'll eat it." Levi tore open the wrapper and took a bite. "Tastes kinda like deer meat."

"With the right spices," Jovon said, "I can slow grill meat that'll make your toes curl."

The four sat on the curb, though not too close, and savored their meal. Levi told Jovon about the virus north of the interstate and their exposure.

"You have no symptoms," the man said, "so you can't transmit. We know how it works."

Jovon shared that they'd buried their teenage daughter the day before from suicide. The harshness of living day to day, the prospect of eating rodents, insects, and roots had become too much for the young lady.

"A number of small hidden gardens could solve the hunger problem around here," Levi said. "My family has seeds. We can help you get started."

"The PSDF will gladly deal with the Dooley problem," Lesage mumbled, then lifted his head with concern. "I mean, I'm sure the president's new government will look out for the citizens out here eventually."

"Yeah." Levi smiled at Lesage who was obviously intent on remaining under cover yet relevant at the same time. Lesage was the very man who General Brogdon would send to address civil unrest like the Dooley group. "Grow enough crops out here, and you could set up some trade with us on the bay or Coronado Island. Everyone could benefit."

They made more concrete plans and Levi gave the couple directions to ELM. The more they talked, the more Jovon seemed to be lifted from the melancholy of his loss. Levi asked if he could pray for them all, and Jovon welcomed him. Lesage didn't participate in the prayer, but Levi was glad the sergeant didn't openly object or interfere.

Afterward, when Levi lifted his head, he noticed a half-naked man crawling west on the sidewalk across the street in front of the car dealership.

"That poor guy!" Levi stood. "Look at him. There's glass all over the place!"

Jogging across the littered street, Levi spotted dried blood on the man's chest and scalp. As Levi reached him, the man stopped crawling and lay on his side with his eyes closed. He was balding and bearded and there was spittle and debris from the street that speckled his facial hair. His palms and exposed knees were scraped and bloodied from crawling through the broken glass.

"Hey, buddy?" Levi rested a hand on his shoulder and rolled him over to see his face better. He seemed to have been assaulted beyond his self-inflicted injuries. "Why don't we get you cleaned up, huh?"

The man rolled onto his back. Anguish showed on his face as he held up his damaged hands and fingers. A deep gash had split his head open so that it was swollen beyond the shape of a normal skull. But he wasn't so deformed that Levi didn't recognize him.

"Lesage!" Levi called. "Get that other shirt from my pack!"

Levi trickled water from his bottle to wash dried blood from the injured man's eyes and cheeks. Lesage arrived at a hobbling skip and knelt next to him.

"What happened to him?" Lesage shook out a flannel shirt. "This guy needs some pants, too. Whoa! Levi, look who it is!"

"Yeah, I see who it is." Levi peeled off his ammo vest and used his knife to cut off a patch from his own shirt. He used it as a cloth to clean more of the man's wounds. "Here, hold him upright."

"I'm not touching him." Lesage threw the extra shirt onto Levi's lap. "He tortured me and almost killed me!"

"That was two days ago. Hold him up. Come on."

"He did this to my leg. And he tried to kill you, too!"

Levi let Conrad Prosky lay where he was and stood to look Lesage in the face. Lesage was a muscled older man, but Levi had learned from his father how to use his own size to make a necessary point. He rested his hands on his hips like he'd seen Wes Trimble do.

"Every life matters," Levi stated softly.

"That's your motto, not mine."

"When you're with me, it's your motto, too."

"Well, I'm not touching him unless it's to put him out of his misery. Give me that broken knife of yours and that's just what I'll do. The world will be better off without Conrad Prosky."

"Yeah, that may be, but he's better off with us. This is a crossroads for you, Sergeant. You don't hold even a bad man down if you can help him become something better."

"That's not me you're talking about."

"You and I make a strange pair, Lesage. Though you don't follow Jesus, you've felt His mercy. Prosky's head is pretty bad. He probably won't survive a brain injury like this. A little mercy doesn't change what he's done or who you are."

Clenching his teeth, Lesage eyed Prosky with disdain.

"What's he doing out here anyway?"

"Who knows?" Levi knelt again and continued to clean his wounds. "But you and I just ate his horse. He had to be the one who was riding when Dooley ambushed him. This is a fresh bullet wound on his head."

Lesage crouched beside Levi.

"All right, what do you want me to do?" he asked in resignation.

"Help me sit him up to get this shirt on him, then try to find him some pants."

Together, they wrestled Prosky's arms into the sleeves and Levi buttoned up the front.

"Something's wrong with him," Lesage said. "His mouth—he's drooling all over himself. He's not gonna make it, Levi. This is pointless. I've seen head injuries before. He doesn't even look like he understands us."

"Maybe not, but he's not dying today just because we neglected him."

Levi picked Prosky up in his arms and carried him across the street to lay him where they'd eaten horse meat just minutes earlier. Jovon's wife said they had some old shoes that would fit him and Jovon jogged away to the house they'd claimed recently to find a pair of pants.

"You knew him?" Jovon's wife asked Levi as she took over the washing of dried blood. Her name was Wanda, her curly hair reduced mostly to unwashed waves since water was so scarce.

"He did us harm recently." Levi watched Lesage. "Actually, he's done a lot of people harm recently."

"There's a lot of that these days." Wanda touched Prosky like she might touch a child. "The world is so cold now."

"That's true." Levi sighed. "But the world doesn't determine how we're going to respond. A little compassion can change everything."

Lesage swore and crutched away. Wanda looked after him.

"Your friend doesn't see the world as you seem to. Most young people don't speak like you do, Levi."

"I've been brought up by Christians. Since I don't know much else, they and God get the credit for whatever good I've become."

Jovon returned with tennis shoes and pants that he helped Levi put on the man. He'd also brought back a sheet they tore in strips to bandage Prosky's head and hands.

"You'll stay with us tonight," Jovon said. "If this man dies in the night, we'll bury him where we buried our daughter."

Prosky was able to stand and walk with assistance, but he was unresponsive when spoken to.

"Come on, Lesage!" Levi called "We'll be staying at their place tonight."

The two men supported Prosky, and Wanda carried Levi's pack. Lesage followed close behind, mumbling complaints just loud enough that Levi heard and continued to pray for the military man.

☦

Titus held up his long field knife high above his head. On the first floor of the quarantine building, he stood before chairs he'd piled into an altar. A bundled blanket lay on top of the chairs.

"And then Abraham raised his knife like this," he said as his audience of three watched with gaping mouths. "But right before Abraham plunged the knife, God stopped him and provided a ram to be sacrificed instead. There was a ram, a big ol' sheep, nearby and Abraham was told to kill it instead. This is the story of how God tested Abraham's love for Him against the love he had for his son, Isaac. Some test, huh?"

His audience applauded—a husband and wife from Mexico and Gabby Hillerman. Titus rescued the bundled blanket off the alter and set the chairs in order, then sat on one.

"I believe this story is a picture of Jesus dying for us. We are like Isaac, and God provided a ram—Jesus—to die in Isaac's place. But it's also a lesson about prioritizing our love for God. No one should come between us and our love for God."

Gabby blurted something in her incoherent speech and gestured with her hands.

"Oh, don't worry," Titus said. "We have another day or two of quarantine. I have a lot more stories to tell you."

"Titus!" Annette called from the courtyard. She banged on the door outside. "Are you there?"

He crossed the floor and slid open the door. Annette had taken a few steps back, but not as far as she or Carla had stood in days past.

"What's the problem?" he asked.

"Are you showing any symptoms yet? Any of you?"

Gabby squeezed her smiling face and arm past Titus and the doorframe to wave at Annette.

"Nope, we're all still clear. What's happening? Is it Levi?"

"No, nothing from Levi yet. There were two ladies from the Hopefuls who didn't come back last night. They were over late with Gustavo and the goats. But they headed back in the dark, Gustavo says, and no one's seen them since."

"What does Chevy think happened? Maybe they just left to stay with friends in the city or somewhere else?"

"No, he checked their apartment. All their stuff's still there, even the toothbrushes we gave them. He and Wes agree with me—strangers came into our perimeter last night."

"There'll be tracks, if that's true." Titus licked his lips. "What do you want from me?"

"Your quarantine is over. Maybe it's unreasonable to quarantine, anyway, when you guys are showing no symptoms. Wes is waiting for you on the eastern perimeter."

"Okay, but what about these three?" Titus referred to Gabby and the couple with him.

"I figure you want Gabby at ELM, so I'll watch her for symptoms for a couple more days. The other two can join the Hopefuls. Come here, Gabby. Let me get a proper hug from you."

Gabby pushed past Titus for an embrace from Annette. Titus went up two floors to fetch his gear. Finally, something to do outside! But he'd made good use of the last couple days with Gabby, teaching her about Jesus and other characters from the Bible. There was also the weight of Levi's absence on his heart, and he hadn't been able to get to his radio to eavesdrop on PSDF transmissions for updates on whatever battles were raging to the northeast. Annette was willing to check the radio periodically, but she had her own responsibilities and couldn't be expected to sit in the radio room as he'd done over the weeks.

He emerged from the building with his ammo jacket, rifle, and day pack, ready for war. After a kiss from Annette, he hustled to the eastern perimeter. Wes was kneeling on the street where the gap between vehicles had been left for pedestrians to pass through.

"What have you got?" Titus was careful not to trample the sign in the dust. "Looks like four men, huh?"

"You're the Serval." Wes scoffed with a smile. "I can't tell one from the other."

"That pair is small, narrow, almost like a child's prints." He pointed out the tracks. "See the scuffs? They were putting up a fight, not walking willingly. Definitely a kidnapping. And you've got four different men here. Tennis shoe, tennis shoe, and another in a different size. And this is boot tread here—wide, long soles that make a deep print. Four men."

"So, what color hair do they have?" Wes joked.

"I'll tell you when I have them in my scope. Come on."

With his rifle held in both hands and ready to fire, Titus led out at a jog. The trail turned south after one block, then east again beyond Broadway Circle. Then the tracks led up a walkway into a dark office building.

"Let me take the side," Wes volunteered and darted to the right to enter from another door.

Titus approached the building's double doors, now open and barely hanging on their hinges. Most of the windows above had been shot out or smashed, leaving glass everywhere. It looked like that had been done the first weeks after Pan-Day. The city had gone crazy. Great effort had been spent to destroy as much as possible. Maybe more people would be alive, Titus thought, if that same energy had been spent preparing during the weeks leading up to Pan-Day.

Using his flashlight, Titus followed the tracks down a corridor to the left and found their footprints exiting the building on another route—but only the men had made their exit.

"Wes, over here," Titus called. He glanced into a conference room as Wes joined him. "They're dead."

"Oh, no." Wes moved past Titus and took discarded clothing to cover the two bodies of the women. Then he returned to the corridor where Titus was waiting. "Well, we found them. What do you want to do about it?"

"We're not policemen," Titus said somberly, "but we told Brogdon the city is where we'll make our home and keep the peace. Those four will just come back again unless we make it clear this absolutely won't be allowed."

"I'm not sure what our objective is by going after them," Wes said. "As believers, we're more inclined to forgive, not exact vengeance."

"God's forgiveness is wide open even to murderers. We'll offer that to them. And we'll offer fatherly discipline as well. Discipline isn't vengeance. We can pray they take heed. ELM won't ignore sin in the city."

"Okay." Wes nodded, his one eye showing he understood. "Let's not spare the rod."

The tracks of the four led south from the building, then east again. Titus moved like he was twenty-five years old again, hopping over debris in the street and crouching between vehicles to study sign. He was back in the Libyan desert, stalking an enemy across sand and stone.

The clang of metal a block ahead drew Titus and Wes up behind an overturned patrol car. Both men scoped the intersection. Glass broke. Men hollered and laughed.

"They're in that huge warehouse with the high windows," Wes said. "I see a garage door. There are probably other doors on the ends."

"I'll take this garage door. That's my entry."

"But it's exposed." Wes checked the sun. "There's no cover in this daylight."

"It ain't easy facing evildoers head-on." Titus glanced at Wes. "See if you can find one of those other entrances. If you can't, come in behind me. Comms on."

Wes patted Titus on the shoulder and dashed left to circle to the north side of the building. It lay against the railroad tracks where all sorts of merchandise had once been transported, so Titus hoped it contained gear that might be useful for citizens in the city.

"There's another open garage door on the north end," Wes said on his comm. "I hear more men, too. Over."

"Copy. I'm going in. Over."

Titus unclipped his shoulder holstered nine-millimeter and tested the sling on his rifle.

"Calm, Lord," he prayed for himself. "Your way or no way."

He knew he was rushing, but he hadn't packed for a lengthy mission in the field. Like an amateur, he admitted now, he'd brought no water or food, so waiting to see how many men he'd be facing wasn't an option.

Down the center of the street, he walked with alert eyes on the visible garage door. Since the day was bright, he couldn't see into the darker interior of the warehouse. The men inside were making a ruckus, breaking glass, laughing, and hollering.

"They're living here, Titus," Wes said. "I've got mattresses on the floor and looted merchandise all over the place. Over."

"Copy. I'm at the garage door and going in. Find your way to me. Over."

Walking through the door, Titus let his eyes adjust to the dimmer room, but high windows offered plenty of light once inside.

Wooden crates and torn cardboard boxes lay scattered around a variety of consumer items meant for shipping. The most obvious and largest product was a piano, its crate frame partially broken open. Bicycles, pallets of condiments, lumber, cookware, even a collection of baseball caps lay strewn across the concrete floor. Farther back, thousands of smaller packages sat on rows of metal shelves that reached to the ceiling. It was a shipping hub of some sort, or maybe even a customs storage facility.

There were no footprints to follow in the warehouse, but the men were noisy enough to find. And smell. Titus noticed freshly spilled booze splashed onto the floor. He let his rifle hang off his vest and drew his silenced pistol.

Leveled, he aimed straight ahead and moved in a crouch down an aisle.

A man with a baseball bat walked into the aisle and swung at a box on a shelf. Titus tranqed him in the chest, stepped over his body, and turned up another aisle. Two men kneeling over a box of magazines looked up. They appeared to be about Levi's age. Their clothes were filthy, their faces scruffy with patchy beards. He shot them both and swerved into another aisle for the fourth.

The last man of the four was standing on a stepladder, reaching with one hand to a shelf overhead while holding a bottle of alcohol in his other hand. When Titus shot him, the young man dropped his bottle, which shattered on the concrete an instant before he crumbled on the stepladder and rolled to lie in his alcohol.

Titus listened to the warehouse for further noise but heard none. It took only a few seconds to check the four men in the three aisles and their footwear. These were the four who'd prowled into the ELM perimeter—the four who'd taken and murdered the two women from the Hopefuls. He hadn't known the women, but Chevy had been working in each apartment to set up water and plumbing and even limited power. And Annette had already become friends with several of the ladies.

"I got them," Titus said in his comm. "Wes, I'm in the main warehouse space. In the metal shelf section. Come on over to me. Over."

There was no response from Wes.

Dragging each of the four men away from the shelves, Titus left them in a heap next to the piano and its smashed crate. He checked his watch. It would still be about fifty minutes before the four woke—just enough time to slow down and pray for God's words to speak to the killers. Before he sat down on the piano bench to wait, he selected a thick four-foot board from the ruined crate. Their whipping would accompany his message of repentance and redemption. Maybe their blistered hides would soften their hearts since the city in chaos had clearly not brought them to their knees.

"Uh, Titus?" Wes called from behind him.

He turned to find six young men, one of which held a pocketknife to Wes's throat. Wes's rifle was cradled in the hands of a stringy-haired thug with multiple piercings on his face.

"Not so fast, big guy," said the one who held the knife to Wes's throat. This one had been sleeved in tattoos up both arms. "Drop your guns or I cut your buddy up."

Wes's head twitched as if to say no, but the knife pressed harder, drawing blood above his collar. His face was full of apology. He was a veteran operator who'd been taken captive, so he was embarrassed above anything else.

"We're only here for these four." Titus used his board to point to the murderers. "They killed some friends of ours. Let us leave and this won't extend to you all."

"We've all killed someone. There's six of us and one of you. Do the math and do what I tell you to do!"

Titus wasn't about to bend his knee to these anarchists. By the determined look in Wes's eyes, he felt the same. Wickedness couldn't be given free reign.

"It's been a while since I've had a good rumble." Titus leaned his board against the piano bench. The six didn't seem to have firearms except for Wes's rifle. "How about no guns and we have at it?"

The knife man cursed and swore what vulgar things he'd do to Titus during a fight.

"Come on." Titus unclipped his rifle and set it atop the piano. "It ain't easy getting whipped by an old man."

Making a show of it, Titus carefully drew the pistol from his shoulder holster. As he lowered it to lay beside his rifle, he pulled the trigger. The silenced round smacked the chest of the one who held Wes's rifle. The young man fell backwards and lay still.

"You did that on purpose!" shouted Knife Man.

"Of course, I did." Titus tightened the wrist strap on his shooting gloves. "Just making the odds a bit more even. Wes, it's just a knife."

Wes took the cue and used his fingerless gloved left hand to grip the knife blade itself. He twisted it down and away from his neck, then elbowed Knife Man in the gut. Stumbling forward, Wes sprawled onto the floor in front of Titus.

"Get behind me, Wes!" Titus told his partner.

Lunging back to his feet, Wes held his bleeding fingers. Titus could see that Wes's hand was probably cut badly, but it was better than his throat.

"Well?" Titus picked up his board and hefted its weight in one hand. "God hasn't gotten your attention so far. Maybe this will wake you boys up."

He waded into their midst while they were still looking to their leader for direction. Perhaps they expected Titus to batter them on their heads and shoulders, but Titus had faced many contrary characters over the years. An immobilized enemy ceased to be a threat.

With cracking, sword-like accuracy, he swung at their knees.

Knife Man was first to go down. Titus didn't want to feel that man's blade in his gut. One of the five ran away while the others jumped at Titus together. They may have expected him to fall under their weight with fists clobbering his head and back, but he elbowed and swung until he'd thrown them all off and gained some breathing room. His superior height hindered their blows, but he felt blood trickling down his face regardless.

Wes was beside him then, his hand sufficiently wrapped in a handkerchief, and his fists raised.

"Let's go, boys," Wes invited. "Now it's a little more balanced."

They closed on the two men who fought close enough so no one could get between them. But during a lull, Titus lifted his head to find the one who'd run from the fight had returned with nine more! This time, they were all carrying clubs and knives.

Titus licked his bleeding lip and felt the developing bruises from a half-dozen punches. The prospect of disciplining the four murderers seemed unlikely now.

"Retreat?" Wes asked.

"No need to retreat," a louder voice said as a shadow filled the garage door. Eyes shifted to take in the new arrival. Levi fired a deafening rifle round into the ceiling, and two more men joined his side—one with a single crutch and another bearded man who wore a blank look on his face. "It's really not in our nature to retreat."

Chuckling, Titus lowered his fists. The man with the crutch—Titus recognized Sergeant Lesage, who now held Levi's silenced pistol. He couldn't wait to hear Levi's tale of their adventure for nearly four days absent! And they'd picked up . . . *Prosky?* The bearded jowly man didn't appear to be himself at all. Levi had certainly been busy!

"Weapons down." Levi stalked slowly in front of the warehouse dwellers, challenging them one at a time under his gaze. As they dropped their tools of violence, he kicked the weapons across the floor to the nearest shelf. "Now, sit down, everyone. *Sit. Down!*"

Picking up Wes's rifle, Titus returned it to him, then reclaimed his own weapons from the piano, but he kept his wooden board. Levi nodded at his father and backed off to stand watch over the rabble. Lesage was accompanied by Prosky to the piano bench where they sat. There would be time for greeting, but for now, Titus sat on the floor as well, facing the young men.

"We will sit here in silence." Titus checked his watch. "We'll sit here in silence for thirty-five minutes. My son Levi here will shoot anyone who speaks or tries to get up. Levi?"

"I'm ready." Levi made a show of readying his rifle. "Thirty-five minutes. Check."

"Think about the punishment you deserve for your many evils before God," Titus said softly. "All sin must be punished. Wes, watch those four as they wake up."

"They aren't dead?" asked Knife Man as he held one knee.

"*Quiet!*" Titus shouted. "I'll speak when it's time. Now, we reflect on our lives in silence and stillness, praying for God's mercy for the way we've mistreated our neighbors."

The warehouse dwellers lowered their heads and snuck worried looks at one another. Titus was elated to see his son safe, though his clothing was torn and bloodied, and his face showed the marks of healing scratches or cuts. But the bodies of the two young women still burdened Titus' soul, so his mind was on a necessary response in that troubled time.

He watched the faces of the men, some of them only teens. They were slender and filthy, maybe starving or dying from disease. It was likely they'd found each other in their shared acts of anarchy and destruction over the last few months.

After ten minutes, one man scoffed and shifted to his knees to climb to his feet.

"Forget this!" he said. "You're not going to shoot me for—"

Levi fired. The man clutched his stomach and fell flat.

Titus didn't move. And the others definitely didn't move—except their eyes were busy, perhaps trying to make sense of his intentions, or the intentions of the one-eyed man behind him, or the purpose of the two odd men at the piano.

The four unconscious woke slowly. As they gained their senses, Wes ordered them to sit still where they were. Finally, all four were aware and blinking. Their faces showed their befuddlement as to how their comrades had joined their sad state of capture.

"I am Titus Caspertein." He shifted so he could see the four as well as the others that Levi had brought into submission. "I am your friend, but I'm not approving of your behavior. I'm speaking specifically of your treatment of the people of this ruined city. Some of that ruin is not your fault, but some of it is. These four here . . . they are guilty of kidnapping, raping, and murdering two of our women. We live in the ELM complex where the giant elm tree is painted on the north side of the main building. Today, these four men will bear the punishment for their behavior, though they, like us all, deserve much worse than what they'll be getting."

With pity, Titus looked at the four whose eyes were wide and shifted between defiance and outright fright.

"ELM stands for *every life matters*," Titus continued. "Your lives matter. Each of you matters to God. Even these four rapists are loved by God, but He doesn't love your sin. All of you, living to do violence and evil to your neighbor—you're on the path to hell. God will judge you justly when you die, and you'll spend eternity in regret and in a burning reality. It will be horrible, but it will be just what you have chosen and what you deserve.

"Before these four are punished, you must hear a message of hope. God offers His compassion to you the same as He offered it to me. Once, I was a criminal. But a kind man told me the truth. Unless I trusted God for His mercy, I would die in my sins. You may know the history—that Jesus, the Son of God, came to Earth and died for the sins of all people. By accepting in confidence His gift of life, you receive forgiveness of your sins and God makes you right before Him. Only in a state of forgiveness will you escape hellfire. God welcomes you, but He doesn't welcome your sin. Turn from your unbelief and submit in faith to Jesus your Savior. Anything short of your repentance ends in misery forever."

Titus eyed the four guilty men. At least they were listening.

"Every life matters. You matter to me. That's why I'm available to you. This is Levi Caspertein, my son, and this one-eyed man here is Wes Trimble. We are willing to help you live obedient lives in the footsteps of Jesus. But you must come with empty hands. Whoever mistreats the people of this city—and if I hear of it—you will meet my paddle."

Suddenly, Titus slapped the board on his palm. The loud noise widened the eyes of his audience.

"Or, you may face the justice that the Pacific States Defense Forces offers you on Coronado Island. Sergeant Lesage, what happens under General Brogdon to rapists and murderers?"

"If I find them," Lesage said, "I kill them. We usually shoot them dead in the street."

"You four?" Titus stood tall and looked down at the men who seemed so meek and small now. "I followed you from the ELM perimeter. Wes and I found the two bodies of the ladies you kidnapped, raped, and killed. I don't care if you leave this city or stay here, but right now, you'll feel the pain of punishment that uniquely fits this terrible day. You'll choose between seven swats of the paddle or the punishment for murder on Coronado Island. You first. What'll it be? The paddle or death?"

It was the man with the boots, the prints that Titus sadly knew very well. The criminal swallowed hard and looked into the faces of his companions—who avoided his eyes altogether since they could offer no assistance. Alone in his decision, he mumbled his response.

"Speak up!" Titus yelled. "Let everyone hear your choice under guilt."

"The paddle. I said the paddle."

"Fine. Stand up. Don't be a coward now. You weren't a coward when you snuck up to my building last night. Bend over the piano there. Reach out. Lesage, hold onto his wrists."

The man nervously leaned over the top of the piano, and Lesage took hold of his wrists and braced for resistance.

"I take no joy in the pain this will bring you, young man, but I hope that by this method you'll find a new path before God. Sometimes, physical pain has a way of teaching us when no other method will do."

Titus set his rifle on the piano, then stood beside the man's backside. He felt the weight of the four-foot paddle, then swung with one arm. *Thwack!* The man leaped and screamed.

Six more paddles followed, then Lesage let go of his wrists. The man would've slid off to the floor if Titus hadn't caught him by the collar and laid him moaning on the floor.

"You're next." Titus pointed with his paddle. "You were there as well. Step up, son, and choose your method. The paddle from me or death on Coronado Island?"

He chose the paddle, as did the last two. In the end, all four lay writhing and weeping side by side.

Setting down his paddle, Titus walked to Knife Man. Before this man, Titus knelt on the floor.

"How're your knees?" he asked. "Can you stand and walk? I hit you pretty hard."

"Yeah." He seemed suspicious of Titus' concern. "I'm okay. Just bruised."

"Hey, me, too!" Titus smiled and rubbed his jaw. "You guys landed some good ones on me. How about we don't make this a regular occurrence, huh? ELM is offering good jobs for food and provisions. We're looking for neighbors, not villains. That's what's best for everyone. How does that sound? Does that make sense?"

"Yeah." He shrugged. "Makes sense."

"So, I'm Titus Caspertein." He offered his hand. "You're welcome to ask for me. Okay?"

"Okay." He furtively shook Titus' hand.

"You look after the interests of the citizens here, and you'll be looked after." Titus browsed their faces. "Act against these people, and we'll track you down. And you better hope it's me who finds you and not the Pacific States. I've got a paddle. The PDSF has a bullet for you. Okay?"

"Okay."

"Look after those four. They'll be sore for a few days, but maybe they'll think twice next time. All right. We're leaving." Titus stood. "Levi, you've got our six."

"Copy that."

Titus gathered his people and led them to the garage door. Lesage hobbled along on his crutch, and Prosky huddled against Lesage's left arm, like a chick seeking protection from its mother hen. Wes took point and Levi hung back a few seconds to leave the warehouse without further incident.

"The paddle or the bullet, huh?" Levi asked his father as they walked away. "Creative."

"Hopefully, effective. We want good neighbors, not a penal colony. It ain't easy showing tough love." He nudged his son's shoulder. "Where've you been, anyway? Your mother and I have been wearing our knees out in prayer."

"My radio got busted. We figured we'd take our time."

"See the sights, huh?"

"We found Prosky about two day's slow walk east of here. His horse had been shot out from under him and he suffered a brain injury we think."

"How's Lesage taking it?" Titus asked. "Prosky was his captor."

"You can see them. Prosky won't leave his side."

"Interesting how God works, isn't it?"

"I'd say so. I can't count how many enemies we had a few weeks ago. Now I see nothing but reconciliation happening."

They walked straight back to ELM, but it took thirty minutes since Lesage was slow and needed to rest often.

When they reached the perimeter, they found General Brogdon and a small contingent of soldiers among four vehicles. Titus shook the general's hand and presented Lesage as he hobbled up.

"It took some time," Titus said, chuckling, "but the long-lost soldier has returned."

"You all look like you've been to war and back!" Brodgon nodded at Levi. "And you make your family proud, Young Caspertein. Never thought I'd see you two again."

"We just needed a little bonding time." Levi patted Lesage's bald head as he crutched away to the nearest Humvee. "Don't forget to write, Sergeant."

"Just let me know when the next barbeque is." Lesage grunted at the general's confused look. "It's a long story."

Prosky went to the side of the Humvee with Lesage, but Levi took the poor man by the arm and led him back.

"No, Conrad. You're with me. We'll see the sarge again soon. He'll come visit."

"I actually came to tell you about Riverside Guard," Brogdon said to Titus. "We came across them way up on I-8. They've all but pulled back. Left half their army dying of Meridia this side of Santee. Doesn't look like there'll be a big fight after all. As soon as Meridia calms down in a few days, we should be able to go up there and wipe out the whole army."

"You know, General," Titus stepped closer, "you have an opportunity here. I know you're a soldier, but would you rather slaughter your enemy or gain their strength? Fact is, you may not need to fire a single shot to win everything—equipment, territory, and citizen support."

"What are you proposing?" The general frowned. "I like the no-shot-fired prospect."

"Okay, you, me, and these four vehicles." Titus nodded. "Yeah, that should do it. And a white flag. We'll talk some reason into them. What's left of Riverside will join the Pacific States. Let's keep the peace if we can. When are you headed back up?"

"About three days, I'd say."

"Come by and pick me up. I'll be ready."

"Well, I don't know about a white flag . . ." Brogdon scratched his chin. "You Casperteins have some strange ways."

"And I'll go, too," Lesage said from the Humvee's open window. "I've seen how Levi does it. It'll work. We'll take a white flag so they're not on the defensive, then we'll show them mercy. They'll know it. Then we'll gain our enemies as our friends."

"You taught him that?" Titus asked Levi.

"I didn't know he was even paying attention." Levi grinned.

The small convoy drove off and the travelers walked through the ELM perimeter. Prosky huddled close to Levi's side as they returned home.

"We have two bodies to collect and a funeral to plan," Titus said to Wes. "I'll tell Chevy the bad news."

# *Conclusion*

Levi lay on his belly gazing through his telescope at Coronado Island. A week had passed since he'd returned home. His body had healed and he'd been working with Chevy to set up more utilities in the Hopefuls' building.

The funeral for the two women had been a sad occasion. It was a reminder that evil could find them even there where ELM offered a little security. None of them would be safe in this world, Chevy had eulogized, until they were home in glory with the Savior.

At the funeral in the woods, Carla had stood next to Levi and wept. He thought she hadn't known the Hopefuls too well. When he'd asked her if she'd known them, she'd said one of them had asked her for prayer the day before they died. She seemed too pained to explain further.

Conrad Prosky had found a new friend in Gabby Hillerman, who seemed to order him around in her unintelligible speech. As he'd once padded alongside Lesage, now he plodded after Gabby wherever she ventured, even standing beside her at the funeral. Gabby especially liked the flowers that Sunshine placed around the grave mound when the elderly woman arrived toward the end of the funeral service.

Across the bay, a single man in Levi's telescope limped away from the buildings on Coronado Island and stood below several palm trees above the shoreline. The man raised binoculars to his eyes. Levi smiled. It was Sergeant Dom Lesage. Maybe he was just studying the city or looking for threats. But Levi hoped the man's heart had softened. They'd spent four days and nights together.

More than once, Levi had saved his life. He liked to think that the sergeant was looking across the bay, maybe hoping for a glimpse of his new friend—the friend who'd carried him from harm in his arms and walked him home through the violent streets. And who'd taught him about mercy enough for Lesage to counsel the general to absorb Riverside into the PSDF.

It was hard to say what tomorrow held for the people of ELM. Levi knew their adventure in San Diego wasn't over, not if they truly lived and loved like every life mattered.

But today was Levi's birthday. And no one had thrown him a party. No one had made him a cake or asked him to blow out candles. Finally, no one had treated him like a child. He was twenty years old.

I pray you were blessed by reading Book One of *The ELM Series, EVE of CHAOS!* If you enjoyed it, please leave a review wherever you bought this book. It would help me to know if I hit the mark with this new series. Thanks so much! *—David Telbat*

## *WHAT'S NEXT?*

Book Two of *The ELM Series* is coming next! Go to the next page to read Chapter One of *EVE of DESPAIR.*

# *EVE of DESPAIR*

## Book Two of *The ELM Series*
## Chapter One

It was evening. Oliver Gleason stood on the street in front of his house and watched the orange glow of flames reflect off low, dark clouds. Either someone's cook fire had gotten away from them or anarchists were starting fires. It wouldn't be the first time. The blaze was creeping closer to where Oliver had barely provided for his girlfriend and son the past six months.

He glanced toward the front door. Milli Lusis, his sweetheart since junior high, had crawled through the hole in the otherwise barricaded door and now stood gazing up at the evening sky as well. The smoke was heavy in the air. There was no hiding from her this potential danger. Her fragile soul needed constant attention and reassurance. Sometimes, he kept the truth from her entirely—when their water was low or when he'd found that yet another neighbor had been killed.

Six months had passed since Pan-Day—the collapse of American society, including the electrical grid. The Meridia Virus had sparked quarantines across entire cities. Oliver had fortunately listened to his parents who'd helped him stock up on food and water for his small family in the middle-class suburb of San Diego. But the food had run out. The twenty-five-year-old had plucked a rifle off a dead body and learned to load and shoot it accurately. His family had lasted this long on the meat of stray dogs and bartering for vegetables with a tiny community network.

But the approaching flames threatened everything. They had nowhere to go.

"Why would they be burning?" Milli asked as she joined his side. Her unwashed red hair was tucked under a ratty blanket she used as a shawl over her shoulders. "What is it, Oliver?"

Shifting his bolt action rifle to his left hand, he took her hand in his. Smiling, he lied to her as he had a hundred times before.

"I'm sure it's nothing." He cleared his throat against the heavy smoke drifting like swamp fog. "See the breeze? It's blowing toward the desert. Go ahead to bed. I'll keep an eye on it."

She watched the darkening sky another moment.

"If you're sure." She kissed his bearded cheek. "I'll take in your jeans tomorrow, okay?"

"Okay." He grimaced at her reminder that they were still losing weight. It was shameful that he wasn't a better provider. But he'd only been a minimum wage construction laborer straight out of high school with no vision for the future. Like most people his age, he'd been too wrapped up in social media and material possessions to build necessary skills for Pan-Day's aftermath. "I'll come inside in a little while."

Milli left and ducked through the hole in the door. Their son, Rory, was probably still awake in his room. Oliver had taught the six-year-old to be sure to blow out his candle when he was done playing. The youngster had become obsessed with the game of chess since Oliver had taught him a few months earlier how the pieces moved. Keeping the child well-supplied with homemade candles for his mock-chess games where he played both sides was a minor inconvenience for Oliver. The well-mannered boy kept himself entertained, and that allowed Oliver to scavenge for food and supplies, or to comfort Milli through her spells of despair.

Night fell on the neighborhood, but the stars couldn't be seen through the smoke above. Oliver's eyes stung and his lungs burned. He tried to tell himself that the glowing night sky northward was moving east or that it only seemed brighter since the sky was now darker. But, no. The fire was drawing nearer. And the building noise was unmistakable, like a commercial jet engine upon takeoff.

Oliver turned from the orange sky and faced west. He'd scouted around the area only a few hundred yards, searching abandoned houses for forgotten supplies. It gave him a chill to think of the horrors that lay beyond the areas he'd explored. There had to be more survivors out there, like the couple of families he'd found two blocks south. They'd taught him how to butcher a dog for meat and how to plant sweet potatoes in the spring and to harvest them in the fall. They were probably watching the looming disaster approach them as well.

It was unlikely that Oliver would've met his neighbors or learned from them if he hadn't first been approached by Levi Caspertein, the blond, lone traveler who'd spoken volumes in just a few minutes of interaction three months earlier. Levi had changed his life, given him hope, and equipped him with bits of truth that had given Oliver the ability to endure. And it was Levi who Oliver now considered going to find. If this fire really was approaching as he feared . . .

The Casperteins lived downtown. A couple others in Oliver's small network had heard rumors of the heavily armed and self-sufficient family who kept the peace around Seaport Village and provided safe refuge for the needy who came to them. Oliver hadn't even given his name to Levi that fateful day, but he'd sensed the stranger's genuine offer of hospitality. However, Seaport Village was all the way downtown—several miles of the unknown stretched between downtown and where Oliver lived. And Oliver had Milli and young Rory to think about.

From his back pocket, Oliver drew a rolled-up book, its cover wrapped entirely in duct tape. One of the pieces of advice Oliver remembered from Levi was that Oliver should find a Bible. After searching for three nights, he'd found one in a house office one lane to the west. He'd even begun reading it when he knew Milli was sleeping, busy with chores, or playing chess with Rory. The Bible didn't make much sense to Oliver, but he didn't doubt that Levi Caspertein could help him understand its promises and message of compassion. However, Milli had always sworn there was no God. To avoid upsetting her further, he'd kept his Bible reading quiet, even plastering the cover with duct tape so it looked like a self-help manual or something a plumber might carry in his back pocket.

Flames over the house tops to the north licked at the sky. Oliver flinched at the sound of a gunshot from far away, then another closer. This wasn't an accidental fire. Something terrible was happening. Destruction approached, though it was unthinkable there could be a more destructive force than the isolation and starvation already plaguing the land.

Far, far up the dark street to the east, a handheld torch seemed to float across an intersection. Oliver crouched low, realizing the torch wasn't floating—someone was carrying it. Then two more torches followed the first. As he watched in disbelief, flames grew in the wake of the torch bearers. He heard shouting, then a gunshot.

They were burning the houses! Oliver didn't know who they were or why they were doing it, but they were coming his way!

He rushed back to the door and leaned his rifle against the outside of the house. After kneeling, he crawled through the door, his mind burdened with thoughts of personal inadequacy to flee with his family. His survival thus far could be traced back to his familiar environment and the kindness of strangers he'd met since

Pan-Day. How could he survive with Milli and Rory if he led them into unfamiliar neighborhoods where unkind survivors hoarded and defended what little they had?

"Milli, get up!" The roar of the approaching flames was loud even inside the house. "Get Rory ready. Hurry! I'll grab our stuff!"

Regardless of her fragile spirit, she leapt from the mattress that lay on the floor and drew on trousers. Months ago, they'd burned the wooden bed frame, and the rest of the room consisted only of piles of clothes and a large cooler they used as a pantry. The pantry was usually empty.

A candle still burned in the living room where Oliver's eyes darted over the heaps of gear he'd scavenged and collected. What to take now? He tugged an empty backpack from a hook on the wall and began shoving items inside—dome tent, two water bottles, a bag of lighters, water purification tablets, an extra knife. After stuffing in a few more necessities, the backpack was too full to zip closed, but he hung it over one shoulder, anyway. They were leaving so much behind!

"Oliver, what do we do?" Milli held Rory by the shoulders. The boy carried only his travel chess set, hugging the box against his chest like a life preserver. "Is that the fire? I thought it was burning toward the desert!"

"Get your coat!" Oliver snatched up a tarp and an assortment of clothing. "Get outside! We have to get clear of the house. Now!"

Milli found her coat, then she hustled Rory to the hole in the door. She crawled through first, then drew Rory after her. Oliver thrust his armful of gear through the hole, then pushed the backpack into Milli's hands. For a moment, he surveyed the interior of the house. The candle in the living room was still burning. It hurt him deep inside to leave the home in which he'd raised Rory, where they'd found refuge during the long months of danger and hardship. The blankets were still nailed over the windows and a hose he'd attached to the rain gutter outside was still taped to an empty water jug. All his projects and safekeeping—now abandoned.

In front of the house, Rory was the one weeping instead of Milli for a change. The firelight flickered on her face, revealing sheer terror.

After giving Milli the overflowing backpack, Oliver took up his rifle, tarp, and sleeping bag. The clothes he'd haphazardly gathered were left behind as he led the way to the street.

"Back! Back!" He ordered their retreat back to the house as he noticed the men with torches were only one house away. The street was lit up like apocalyptic daylight. "Over the back fence!"

"Oliver!" Milli cried in panic as she obeyed, dragging Rory with her.

"Shhh!" he hissed, worried they might be heard over the roaring noise. "No talking!"

The chain link fence at the back of the property was only five feet high, but Rory wasn't very coordinated at only six years old. The youngster had spent more time playing on his phone when the power had been on than running around the neighborhood as boys should.

Quickly, Oliver helped Milli over the fence, letting her tumble onto the dead grass. Then, as fast as he could, Oliver tossed their few belongings over the fence, some of it landing on Milli's head and shoulders.

The men with torches were at their house!

He lifted Rory over the fence. As soon as Milli reached for her son, Oliver let him go. Mother and child collapsed together on the dry ground. Galvanized steel gouged and tore at Oliver's forearm as he climbed over and gathered his family.

"Over here, quickly!" He didn't give them time to find their feet or gather their things. He tugged them in the flickering light to the edge of a backyard pool. "Milli, go first!"

The waterless pool was anything but empty. It had become a garbage dump and septic tank for the neighbors before they'd died of the Meridia Virus. Whatever disease might've hidden in the smelly refuse, it was now their only refuge.

Milli dropped into the deep end of the pool and into several inches of muck. Oliver lowered Rory to her uplifted arms, then he dropped into the concrete pit with her. Somewhere above, he'd lost everything he'd brought from the house, even the rifle!

Men whooped and hollered at each other, then they moved on as the flames grew and rose and the heat radiated closer to the family. Oliver held Milli who held Rory against the side of the pool. Embers floated on the night breeze and caught fire briefly on the piles of debris.

The smoke was suffocating. Oliver tore off his t-shirt to cover Rory's face, then he gave his thermal to Milli to breathe through. He buried his own face in Milli's red hair and mentally willed his lungs to function through the ash and black smoke and choking odors of superheated toxins all around them going up in flames.

Minutes passed and their situation worsened as the neighbor's house that bordered the pool was also set afire. But then the night breeze shifted and the smoke lifted to float more southward. Rory and Milli coughed aloud, and Oliver let them. The evildoers rampaging through the neighborhood seemed to be gone, but the heat from the structures was still too intense to climb out of the pool.

Thirty minutes passed. Oliver gathered a few pieces of cardboard nearby for his family to kneel on instead of standing as they waited out the fires. A distant scream and gunshot reminded Oliver that even while the fire danger was past, the violent danger would still persist.

Finally, Oliver climbed his way to the shallow end of the pool and ascended to level ground. The flames were low. His house had been reduced to rubble no taller than his shoulder height. Neighboring houses fared no better.

Smoldering or burning structures haunted the landscape in every direction. Everywhere Oliver gazed, the world seemed remarkably flat and empty, unrecognizable.

He lifted Rory out of the pool, then Milli. She was first to begin gathering items they'd dropped after climbing back over the fence.

"What do we do?" Milli asked him softly, clearly guarding her voice from Rory. "Where will we go now?"

"I don't know yet." He drew on his long sleeved thermal again and unrolled the sleeping bag. Whatever items couldn't fit inside the backpack, he stuffed into the sleeping bag. "Milli, you carry the backpack. Rory, you okay, son?"

"Yeah." The boy examined his bare arm. He'd pulled on jeans only after he'd been hauled from his bedroom, and he wore only a thin t-shirt. "I got burned from a spark."

"Can you make do?" Oliver still choked from the smoke in the air, his voice raspy. "We can put a bandage on it when we get out of this mess."

"I'm okay." Rory held his chess set closer. "Now it's cold."

Oliver fit his own t-shirt over the boy's head for an added layer, then he picked up the sleeping bag of gear. He hefted the items over his shoulder and Milli handed his rifle to him for the other shoulder.

"Let's see if Bruce and his family made it." Oliver faced southeast. "Let's go this way. Stay together. And no talking."

Bruce Ramis had taught Oliver how to field dress a dog for meat. Oliver had proven himself as a marksman, so the Ramis family had traded vegetables from their garden with Oliver and he shared his meat with them. Their relationship was strained since they competed for what seemed to be a dwindling food supply, but Oliver didn't know anyone else who might give him advice or help.

The Ramis family lived only two blocks away, but it took Oliver twenty minutes to lead Milli and Rory over and around the blackened and smoldering structures. Oliver had never shot at a man before, and he wasn't sure he could, so he preferred to move cautiously along the way rather than keep his rifle ready to fire.

The swath of fire destruction spanned several blocks wide and continued southwesterly toward the ocean. Bruce's house was one of the buildings that'd been lit on fire along the eastern side of the turmoil. Oddly, the houses farther on remained dark and untouched.

When Oliver walked up, Bruce was stumbling through the ashes of his residence.

"Stay here," Oliver told Milli, dropping the sleeping bag, and proceeding alone. In the last three months, he'd not exposed Milli or Rory to outsiders. No one could be absolutely trusted. "I'll talk to him."

Stepping into the ashes, he reached Bruce, who didn't seem to be his normal alert self. Bruce was a survivalist, the one from whom Oliver had learned how to collect rainwater and plant a garden. Now the man sobbed openly and carried no rifle.

"Bruce?" Touching the man's arm, Oliver turned him. "Where's—?"

He didn't want to say Bruce's wife's name, or his son's name. The answer seemed obvious.

"Come over here, Bruce." He led the distraught man to sit on a metal water tank that had weathered the flames inside what had been the garage. "Take a swallow."

The man accepted the water bottle from Oliver, took a gulp, then passed it back.

"It's all gone." Bruce's face was blackened except where tears had left streaks. "*They're* both gone."

Oliver glanced back at Milli were she stood watching from the edge of the charred property. He didn't want to be insensitive toward Bruce, but he needed to get his family out of there.

"Who was it, Bruce?" Oliver coughed up ash from his lungs, then wiped his mouth. "Why'd they do this?"

"They surprised us." Bruce shook his head. "We were all sleeping. Now, look . . ."

Where was the tough survivalist he'd once known? Oliver hadn't come here to comfort Bruce but to be guided by him. Levi Caspertein had encouraged them to work together to endure, but Bruce had always been the one Oliver had relied on, until now.

"Do you have any gear stashed someplace?" Oliver asked. "You can't stay here. They could come back."

"It was that Dooley Gang." Bruce suddenly looked up. "He's insane. He shot my boy right out front there, on the porch. He asked only one question."

"What question?" Oliver wasn't sure Bruce was thinking straight. The man had never before mentioned anyone named Dooley. "What did he say?"

"He asked for someone named Maddix Striber, then when Bruce Junior didn't answer, Dooley shot him then and there, on the porch. Nothing left. Nothing . . ."

Indeed, Oliver studied the front door area of the ruins, but saw no body—of the son or the wife.

"Who's Maddix Striber?" Oliver leaned forward. "Bruce?"

"How do I know?" Bruce stood and wrung his hands with a fresh bout of sobs. "It makes no sense, burning us all out just because he's looking for someone."

"Bruce, we need to get outta here. What do you think about going to the bay? Maybe find Levi Caspertein. Remember him? There's gotta be something to the rumors about them, right? We'll be safe there."

"Nobody's safe from Dooley. He's insane." Bruce suddenly spun on Oliver and clutched his arm. "Don't go, Oliver. You'll never make it. It's too dangerous. Think of the distance. The cutthroats are everywhere. Better to go back home. Home . . ."

"Hey, Bruce, I have no home left, either. Come on. Why don't you come with us?"

"No home." Bruce wandered away. "No home . . ."

Oliver watched the man fall to his knees in the ashes. He hadn't explained who the Dooley Gang was, but now Oliver understood they'd caused this carnage in their search for someone. Unfortunately, Oliver couldn't take care of both his family and Bruce at the same time.

Returning to Milli, he rested his hand on Rory's shoulder. The fires dwindled in the distance, but the barren landscape was still visible.

"What'd he say?" Milli asked.

"We're on our own." Oliver knelt and drew his son closer into one arm. "Remember the young man I told you I met a few months ago? Levi Caspertein? His family lives on the bay, down by the shorefront. They're good people."

"How do you know they're still there?" Milli hugged her midsection. "There are no good people left, Oliver."

He felt the bulge of the duct-taped Bible in his back pocket, but he didn't want to tell Milli he'd begun searching out God on Levi Caspertein's advice.

"It's not safe anywhere around here." Oliver sighed. "I'm sure we can find our way to the ocean, and maybe find the Casperteins. We have to try. There's nowhere else. And we have no supplies . . . or food. We'll need to work together. Be strong together. Like we have been."

"Are we gonna die, Dad?" Rory asked.

Though Oliver was inclined to recall something hopeful he'd read in the Bible about God, Milli was watching him closely and she didn't believe God was real. He didn't want to upset her further.

"We'll be okay, son," Oliver said instead, "if we can find the Casperteins."

The End<br>
*EVE of DESPAIR*, Chapter One

# *Character Sketch*

**Galt Brogdon** – This self-appointed general of the newly-formed Pacific States reigns with a heavy hand from Coronado Island in San Diego. His son is teenager Kip Brogdon.

**Kip Brogdon** – As General Galt Brogdon's son, this fifteen-year-old reveals his entitled expectations as he takes what he wants and uses his father's rank to go where he wants.

**Annette Caspertein** – As the wife of Titus Caspertein, this ex-model and UN activist has quickly established herself as the matriarch within ELM.

**Levi Caspertein** – At only nineteen, he's eager to prove himself as a man in the shadow of his renowned father, Titus.

**Titus Caspertein** – After years of traveling the world, this resourceful and witty special agent has established ELM in downtown San Diego where he leads his family and surviving friends against the wickedness of the day.

**Wynter Caspertein** – The younger sister of Titus Caspertein, this fussy woman finds her meaningful place next to Annette Caspertein and her brother. Her husband is Wes Trimble.

**Arthur Criswell** – Once a senator in California, this aging socialist has become the political leader of the PSDF. His daughter is Carla Criswell.

**Carla Criswell** – From the prestige of the president's press corps, this woman approaching middle age finds herself dependent upon people she once despised.

**Neil Dooley** – Strangers and friends alike are potential targets for this gun-wielding bandit leader who ambushes and rules the suburbs of San Diego.

**Gustavo Hernandez** – Though aging, this light-hearted believer is content to serve within ELM beside his rowdy milk goats.

**Avery "Chevy" Hewitt** – Once a member of the Kindred of Nails special operators to North Korea, this ex-convict now applies his engineering and mechanic skills to the furtherance of the Gospel's outreach within ELM.

**Gabby Hillerman** – She is an affectionate youngster with Down syndrome adopted by the Casperteins after her grandparents are found dying of the Meridia Virus.

**Dusty Howard** – Raised on the troubled streets of San Diego, he finds his criminal career meets a sudden stop when his life is checked by Levi Caspertein.

**Dom Lesage** – Once a Canadian Special Forces soldier, this sergeant is known for his ruthlessness under General Brogdon within the PSDF.

**Conrad Prosky** – As a rancher in the hills outside San Diego, this gunman hires out his gun and small army to the Riverside Guard.

**Oleg Saratov** – Once an Interpol agent, now this aging Russian ex-spy offers his dependability to Titus Caspertein.

**Wes Trimble** – Recently married to Wynter Caspertein, this one-eyed ex-CIA agent applies his strategic mind and field skills to assist ELM in the cause of Christ.

# *Glossary*

**BBG** – Acronym for <u>Bondage Breaking Grace</u>

**ELM** – Established by Titus Caspertein, **<u>Every Life Matters</u>** becomes his family's motto for representing the Gospel of Jesus Christ across San Diego.

**Hillcrest Hopefuls** – This label is given to about fifty refugees by Levi Caspertein after he rescues them from gunmen and welcomes them into ELM's protection.

**Pan-Day** – This term refers to when American citizens reacted to the fear of the Meridia Virus pandemic and the panic and rioting that followed. The world changed; cities were quarantined, the electrical grid collapsed, and people starved.

**PSDF** – The <u>Pacific States Defense Forces</u> is head-quartered on Coronado Island where General Brogdon leads a force of five thousand.

**Riverside Guard** – This aggressive and violent military is composed of Los Angeles and Riverside personnel intent on invading Pacific States territory by any means necessary.

# *Acknowledgements*

This new series has had the benefit of relying on faithful Beta Readers who have proven themselves with my past books by advising, editing, and reviewing. I'm happy to be working with my assistant, Dee, and the rest of my team, to make this next series the best yet. Special thanks to Sharon L. for her honest critiques and meaningful input. Also, my special thanks go to the following two people for their feedback and counsel. In the research phase for this book, I interviewed Gail O., who offered her experience with Toggenburg goats, which will be special guests in this whole series. And Jon L. shared his forestry knowledge about elm trees, of which I'm excited to sprinkle throughout the coming novels. If these books were automobiles, then these several individuals would be the mechanics that keep the cars running as intended. I'm grateful to be working with you all!

## *About the Author*

D.I. (David) Telbat is a Christian author best known for his **clean, Suspenseful Fiction with a Faith Focus**. This includes his bestselling and award-winning *COIL Series, Steadfast Series, Last Dawn Series, Hidden Humanity, Called To Gobi*, and other Christian suspense and End Times novels. He wrote his first book at age 14, and he hasn't stopped since!

David studied writing in school and worked for a time in the newspaper field. Getting into serious trouble with the law as a young man became a turning point in his life. The Lord used that experience to draw David into a personal relationship with Him. Re-focusing his life for Christ, he now seeks to honor God with his life and writing by doing what he loves most—writing and Christian ministry.

Subscribe to receive David Telbat's FREE, bi-weekly **D.I. Telbat Newsletter** with one of his Christian short stories, or an Author Reflection, or his Novel News Update. Also receive **exclusive subscriber gifts**, such as his ***Three For Free—three-novels-in-one eBook!*** Come join the adventure, discover D.I. Telbat books, and subscribe to his newsletter through his ditelbat.com site or his author pages at books2read.com/ditelbat/.